An Island
Promise

ABOUT THE AUTHOR

Patricia Wilson was born in Liverpool. She retired early to Greece, where she now lives in the village of Paradissi in Rhodes. She was first inspired to write when she unearthed a rusted machine gun in her garden – one used in the events that unfolded during World War II on the island of Crete.

www.pmwilson.net
🐦 @pmwilson_author
📷 @patriciawilson.author

Also by Patricia Wilson:
Island of Secrets
Villa of Secrets
Secrets of Santorini
Greek Island Escape
Summer in Greece
The Summer of Secrets

Patricia Wilson

An Island Promise

ZAFFRE

First published in the UK in 2023 by
ZAFFRE
An imprint of Bonnier Books UK
4th Floor, Victoria House, Bloomsbury Square,
London, England, WC1B 4DA
Owned by Bonnier Books
Sveavägen 56, Stockholm, Sweden

A CIP catalogue record for this book is
available from the British Library.

ISBN: 978-1-80418-124-9

Also available as an ebook and an audiobook

1 3 5 7 9 10 8 6 4 2

Typeset by IDSUK (Data Connection) Ltd
Printed and bound in Great Britain by Clays Ltd, Elcograf S.p.A.

Zaffre is an imprint of Bonnier Books UK
www.bonnierbooks.co.uk

For Michelle and Peter, with all my love.

'And thus, the heart will break, yet brokenly live on.'

Lord Byron

THE ARTIST

A rainbow of every shade and hue,
Silver-green olive trees all in flower.
The artist stares out from the Isle of Corfu,
Sea and sky make a plumbago bower.
With the lick of the brush, a white sail is flew
Fully blown though sea breezes do cower.
She thinks of the princess her grandmother drew,
Powerful, yet devoid of all power.

A heart that stayed strong in a breast that stayed true,
Saving fellows in their darkest hour.
Yet they didn't acknowledge, pay homages due,
Or place her in an ivory tower.
Still, the woman in grey, on her knees, in a pew
Prayed for those whose love had gone sour.
And she helped all who asked, with no further ado.
She had wisdom, and strength, and willpower.

Then by God or good luck, her justice came through.
Now her portrait will always empower.
Her bones laid to rest, under skies of deep blue,
On her stone, a dear prince placed a flower.
In an ebony sky, her star shines for you,
Nebulae of the love we endow her,
And never forgotten, by Gentile or Jew,
She's held dear in our hearts now forever.

Patricia Wilson

PROLOGUE

Corfu, Greece, 1967.

ELEGANT TREES STRETCHED TO THE sky around the grand villa of Mon Repos, shading an elderly nun from the sun's fierce heat. On a manicured scrap of lawn, hidden behind a glut of ancient woodland, Reverend Mother fell to her knees. She embraced the cool ground against her tired shins and enjoyed the sweet, earthy scent of spring that rose from the grass. Birds trilled their joyful songs, welcoming this season of growth and colour and new life. Insects hummed a contented melody from honeysuckle vines that tangled lazily through a gnarled acacia. With hands clasped in prayer against her dull-grey habit, Reverend Mother Superior, Alice, abbess of Saint Mary and Martha convent, gazed to the heavens where cotton-wool clouds hung lazily in a dazzling sky.

'Look at that, blue as the stripes on a new Greek flag. How can anyone doubt there's a God on such a glorious day, Maria?'

She doubled over and buried her forehead in the short pasture. The early April sun sliced through tall cypress trees, sending long shadows – like prison bars – over the area, lashing the reverend mother's shoulders. A peacock released its plaintive cry.

Spooked by the eerie sound, young novice Maria crossed herself and cast a nervous glance around the deserted area.

Meanwhile, Mother Superior reprimanded her God.

'Holy Father, of all things, have you forgotten the line, "Give us this day our daily bread"? The little nippers down here are starving. I know you've a lot on your plate, if you'll excuse my turn of phrase, but these innocents have nothing to eat! Please remember the poor, the weak and the starving children of Greece, and particularly those in troubled Athens, where things are really terrible right now.'

She considered the past twenty years. Greece had endured a second world war, a civil war, and now martial law. In terrible prison camps, Greeks tortured their fellow countrymen to death. Would this land Alice loved so much ever be free of troubles? The sun rose above the conifers and elms, banishing shadows and bathing the devout woman in a pool of shimmering light.

'And if you can, spare a little holy oil for my knee joints, dear Jesus,' she begged, unable to get up. 'Maria, give me a hand!'

The young novice jumped out of her daydream, watchful of the angular seventy-one-year-old.

'Yes, Holy Mother.' Unsure of herself, Maria wanted to please the abbess, especially after the dramatic and heartbreaking stories she'd heard.

The old woman smiled kindly. 'Just "Mother", if you please, Sister.'

Maria, a homely girl from a poor background, had gasped in awe when she learned her superior's long royal title. She had told her own mother, '. . . they say she's not just the abbess, but a real princess and a living saint.'

Mother Alice's legendary bravery, and loyalty to the poor, had stirred the heart of every Christian in the convent and beyond. Rumour said she had founded the Greek Orthodox convent, in a hamlet outside Athens, in memory of her Russian aunt. The Grand Duchess Elizabeth Feodorovna, who also devoted herself to the starving, had been most horribly murdered by her fellow countrymen.

'Help me to the bench and light me a cigarette, child,' the abbess ordered, tugging a flattened pack of Karelia and a box of Swan Vestas from her habit pocket. She gazed out from the grounds of Mon Repos, across the Corfu strait where the sea shimmered turquoise near the shore, darkening through aquamarine and eventually reflecting the cobalt sky. A glorious postcard-picturesque view, divided on the horizon by the majestic Albanian mountains. Chiselled peaks pierced the heavens, and valleys melted into a pale sea mist.

'Who can doubt the existence of God when they embrace such a panorama?' the older woman preached.

'It's beautiful, so very peaceful,' Maria admitted, turning so the abbess could read her lips.

Tears teetered on Alice's lashes, then overflowed, sliding like slippery serpents down the crags of her face. She ignored them, tilted her head back, and blew a column of cigarette smoke towards God, then stared intently as if waiting for Him to take shape in the plume. Her face broke into a mischievous smile.

'Sister Maria, you'll be pleased to know that when this portrait's finished, you'll be rid of me. I'm going to stay with my blessed son.' She took another deep drag on the cigarette. 'He's worried about the political situation, and that I might get myself thrown into prison again.'

Startled, Maria turned towards the abbess, taking in her high cheekbones, narrow nose and wide mouth.

'You went to prison, Mother?' She crossed herself. 'God, have mercy on us!'

The abbess concentrated on Maria's mouth, her eyes narrowing before she nodded.

'Yes, when I tried to sell the last of our family jewels,' she said. 'Needed a few essentials for the convent and an outfit for Philip's

3

wedding. I called my darling son. Thankfully, he pulled some strings and got me out of trouble. Now, he insists that I live with him and his wife in London.'

'Your son lives in London?' Maria blinked at the mottled skin and lined face, and wondered what suffering this bone-thin woman had endured. 'I didn't know you had a son, Mother.'

'Yes, I have. And we must thank God that I was lucky enough to give birth to him before that mad doctor, Freud, fried my insides. He is married to the Queen of England – my son, I mean.' The enormous eyes in her lean face moved slowly round to gaze, unblinking, at Mon Repos mansion. 'I gave birth to him on the grand dining room table in the big house.'

She stuck out her chin, pointed to the imposing residence, then manipulated her mouth to blow a slowly expanding smoke ring which hovered overhead like a devilish halo.

Maria's eyebrows rose. *Married to the Queen of England indeed . . . What next?* She used a hand to stifle her giggle.

'We'd better get back inside, Mother. They're eager to finish your portrait.'

1

FLORA

England, present day

I FLUNG OPEN THE KITCHEN window of our beautiful semi in Crosby, outside Liverpool. The April sunshine poured in, bringing the scent of fresh-cut grass from my neighbour's pristine lawn. Clumps of daffodils nodded blessings from my border, and fully blown roses burst with life. Nature glittered, showing off her spring dress after a light shower.

Mark Champion was missing it all.

How dare he leave me alone like this?

I sensed his spirit in the mauve and white crocuses that ran riot across my lawn, and remembered how we laughed when he threw bulbs into the air and planted them where they landed. There was an urgency to our actions in those final days. So much to do – so little time.

Images of happier occasions morphed into a Polaroid scene swimming with tears. A pair of blue tits flicked their wings while feasting on a fat-ball that hung from the magnolia tree. He had loved nature and taught me so much about wildlife.

We'd wanted to start a family ... Now my insides ached, empty as a derelict building. Clutching my stomach, I snarled at the injustice of it all.

Oh, Mark!

Unable to anchor or focus, I closed the window and turned away. Sometimes, I longed to join my darling husband in death, but then I took a breath and shook myself. My duty to Mark was to live for us both in my empty world . . . and I will, but confusion and loss still overwhelmed me.

I don't know how to deal with grief. Unable to work, I wasted endless days on self-imposed compassionate leave. I padded over to the kitchen table. Our 'new' kitchen was two years old. He had loved it. The flat-pack units had come with a book of instructions and a special spanner. We'd put it together, a team. Sometimes, I still glimpsed him sitting opposite me, sleep-tousled, toast in hand, too much butter and a slick of Marmite; his wide smile beaming right at me.

If only life came flat-packed with a book of instructions and a special spanner. I blinked. He'd gone.

I sorted through the morning post: bills – mostly final warnings sent by snail mail because my phone and internet were already disconnected. A fat tear dropped onto the top envelope. What was I going to do? A handwritten letter stuck out from the pile and aroused my curiosity. Maybe condolences for Mark's death. Then I noticed the Greek stamp – my grandmother, Daphne. Mark and I had booked and paid for our holiday before the chaos of Covid, three years ago. Every spring, we went to see Granny in Corfu. The holiday, postponed again and again, became available just after New Year, last year, but Mark felt a little unwell . . .

Now I was alone. In my late thirties, I was embarking on my first ever solo holiday and I can tell you, it was a little scary. I read through the brief letter, checking Daphne hadn't asked me to bring something specific. Her favourite treats were already in my case: Bird's Custard Powder, Johnson's Baby Powder, Tesco's ginger biscuits, or dunkers, as she called them. With the letter stuffed into the back pocket of my jeans, I completed my holiday to-do list: case packed; Barkley, my cockapoo, to the kennels; central heating off; fridge-freezer turned down; windows locked; hall light on for safety; shed padlocked; boarding pass downloaded; phone in handbag; Kindle in pocket; chargers and adapters in suitcase.

Everything was done, except for that one last thing.

* * *

I laid daffodils from the petrol station on Mark's grave. Every day, I walked to the cemetery, talked to him, plucked out the occasional weed, and polished bird droppings off the black marble. Ours had been the perfect love story . . . well, until he caught me deceiving him, of course. The ache for my husband became so unbearable, a sob shuddered through my lonely body.

I'm going to Corfu to see Granny Daphne, darling. I need to get away – though I can't bear to leave you behind.

My throat was stiff and I bit my lip to hold back tears. Could he see me?

I miss you, Mark, but I'm managing. This holiday proves I can do things for myself. I look forward to seeing dear Daphne. Give me a push in the right direction if you catch me wandering off on a tangent, darling.

* * *

In the departure lounge, I tried to block the echoing airport noise and faint smell of bleach. I held my hand a little way from my side and imagined it was in Mark's grasp, but then I felt my emotions welling up and let go. On a seat at a wine bar, I ordered a glass of Prosecco to take the edge off – then I remembered the letter and pulled it out of my back pocket.

Dearest Flora,

It's almost time for me to head for that great Greek island in the sky, but before I go, I have a task for you. Sorry about this, agápi mou, but I need to see you soon. Dare I say 'very soon'? I have something important to tell you. You sent me a letter saying you were coming over at last, but I've lost it and can't remember the date of your impending arrival. Come to Corfu now. Mon Repos Cottage. I'm waiting for you.

All my love and kisses,

Your Grandma Daphne XXX

I smiled, *agápi mou* – my love, in Greek. I tried to learn a few new words each time I visited, and to help me, she used those words as often as she could. Granny's hope was to reach 100 and get a telegram from the King. With only six months left to reach her ambition, she stood a fair chance. However, Daphne was neither a British subject, nor in the UK. My challenge was to get her the royal congratulations – although I might have to fake it. I knew a man in St John's Market who sold trophies and certificates.

'Will Mrs Flora Champion, the last passenger for Corfu flight EJ4538, proceed to Gate 26? The plane is ready to depart.'

Holy God!

My heart thumped and my cabin bag snapped at the backs of my ankles and passing children. Muttering 'Sorry! Sorry!', I raced under the arrows on signs above my head, knowing I would develop a crick in my neck.

Gate 26 was a mile away!

* * *

Inside the full plane, I crab-walked up the narrow aisle, avoiding black looks from passengers already strapped in. The overhead lockers were stuffed, every cubic centimetre crammed full. My face burned with embarrassment. The flight attendant strode towards me.

'Let me take care of your bag, madam,' she said. Her chilling look spoke for all the passengers, and was accentuated by her perfectly tattooed eyebrows and chemically enhanced, frown-free forehead.

To reach my window seat, two irritated, overweight male passengers had to unbelt and shift out. They tutted, sighed and squeezed into the gangway. I shuffled, sighed even louder, and plopped into my seat just in time to see the cabin staff throw my case into an overhead locker in business class, then draw the curtain that separated us from the elite. Through the window I had a view of the wing, which I stared at, instructing my bladder to hang on for the flight duration.

* * *

Last off the plane, I found my cabin bag all alone up front, then my matching electric blue suitcase tumbled onto the carousel right after the priority luggage. As I waited for a taxi, I noticed a woman sitting on a blanket surrounded by hand-painted pebbles. The colourful beach scenes pleased me, so I bought one for Granny. A short taxi ride hurtled me to my beautiful beachfront all-inclusive – our home for a honeymoon week after Mark and I married, and our destination for a spring break every year since. Granny Daphne's ramshackle cottage, in the grounds of Mon Repos, was ten minutes away.

'I'm here, Granny. See you right after breakfast tomorrow morning. Love you!'

I put down the phone, and for the first time in months, began to relax.

My grandmother lived with her carer in a cottage on the mansion's parkland estate, which used to be a royal residence. Granny had never spoken about her past, but I had a strong feeling she wanted to on this trip.

* * *

The next morning, I stepped onto the balcony with my coffee and the ghost of my husband. In lingering silence, we shared the dazzling second-floor view. Panic rose in my chest. How could I live the rest of my life without him? What was the point? With the calming scent of stephanotis and thyme, which drifted up from the luscious hotel gardens, my shoulders relaxed and my heartbeat slowed. The buzz of honeybees and the trill of a songbird made me realise I wouldn't ... He'd always be with me.

At the balcony railing, I took pictures on my phone. Lost in the beauty of it all, I turned to comment on the utter peace – then realised I was alone. My jaw stiffened. Glancing at the magnificent sky, I felt the cool, scented breeze caress my skin.

This is heaven, and I'll enjoy it for both of us, darling.

Beyond the pool lay an empty beach supporting rows of sunbeds and beach umbrellas, their early morning shadows reaching towards the edge of the sea. The hotel was in a small bay. On either side of the sandy shoreline, a promontory of sculpted red rocks promised good snorkelling and adequate shelter from any strong winds.

I anticipated spending part of every day with Granny, glad to have my mind taken away from art restoration and my recent exam results. The assignments were taxing, but I imagined all those damaged masterpieces lying in dank museum basements waiting to see the light of day – El Greco, Tintoretto, and of course, the master, Michelangelo.

My newly acquired pay-as-you-go phone showed no results yet. I glanced at my cabin bag, which remained closed on the spare bed – Mark's bed. The white sheet and the perfectly plump pillow, undisturbed. For a moment, I imagined him lying there.

'Don't leave me,' I whispered. 'I'm not ready to be alone.'

I closed my eyes against the exhausting grief and returned my thoughts to our first kiss.

* * *

Mark had cornered me in the student pub we frequented every Friday night, me out with the girls, him with his mates.

'Want to come see Gormley's new installation tomorrow?'

'If you like,' I said, hoping I wouldn't blush.

We had been out together on assignments before, but always in the company of others. The Saturday of our date it poured with rain. I had a little folding brolly that blew inside out. He brought an enormous, brightly coloured golfing umbrella under which we entwined arms and braved the drenching downpour. A mile along the deserted beach, our shoes squelched and salty gusts stung my cheeks. Then, horrified, we realised the tide was coming in! We hurried back between the solid iron men, our strides urgent, our breath billowing. I imagined clinging on to a barnacled effigy of the artist as the sea rushed over our heads.

The rain eased; late afternoon sun lit rolling clouds with all the drama of a Rembrandt sunset. Fingers of orange light fanned down to the turbulent sea, illuminating ships that headed for the port of Liverpool. Laughing, we both reached for our phones. In the distance, container ships slid out of the Mersey estuary, and into the Irish Sea. Beyond these juggernauts, the elegant blades of an endless wind farm turned, startling white against the angry sky. Watching the iron men become submerged felt quite surreal and very dramatic, even though it happened twice a day. We tramped back to the shuttered ice cream van at the end of Crosby prom, drenched to the skin but unaware of the cold.

'That was amazing, thanks for coming,' he said, then in one magical moment, he hugged me against his chest. 'Are you cold?'

I shook my head, so filled with emotion I couldn't speak.

His kiss was like no other. His lips touched mine, softly at first. Even now, I blush to think of it . . . of my response, of the incredible heat that coursed through me. We held each other, sodden and steaming and leaning against that garish vehicle with a giant ice cream cone on its roof. I wished the moment would last forever. When his mouth released mine, I felt limp and helpless against him, and totally in love.

'You just made it the best afternoon ever,' he muttered, rain dripping off his hair and down my neck; and we laughed and laughed.

So, our love affair started until, three years later, we married without fuss in St George's Hall and had a buffet wedding breakfast in a Crosby pub. Sweet, sparkling cider for the toast, and proper wedding cake from Marks and Spencer.

* * *

I woke to find the room flooded with light. I'd fallen asleep again. The night before, I'd unpacked clothes and toiletries from my big case, and now my new, three-year-old sundresses had dropped their creases. After tugging on the stubborn zip of my cabin bag, I threw back the lid.

'Shit!'

The contents of my new, unmistakable luggage glared back at me. Boxer shorts, an electric razor, shirt, T-shirt, jeans, trainers, a top-of-the-range Apple Mac and a beige folder marked: URGENT – Agenda & Schedule.

It was not my case.

2

DAPHNE

Corfu, present day

DAPHNE SAT BACK IN THE wheelchair and, as always, turned her face to greet the morning sun. She appreciated her surroundings and all the precious memories connected to the parkland. A breeze rustled through the treetops, catching her attention and causing branches to touch and sway, as if dancing around her in a childish game. Her scant eyesight presented her with a shadow theatre that brought back memories of her adorable little sister Elizabeth. She would be ninety-five now. Could she still be alive? Why hadn't she kept in touch? Still, it was enough to know they had escaped the Nazis, and she imagined Australia was heaven. She touched the locket around her neck. No point in opening it. She wouldn't be able to see the miniature family portrait inside.

Life was full of regrets, but also full of the greatest joy, and she appreciated all she had, especially darling Flora and, of course, Yánna, who took such good care of her. The ash, spruce and eucalyptus, four-hundred-year-old sentinels, had watched over her since the day she arrived on Corfu as a frightened young woman with a tiny baby. Daphne knuckled her eyes, clearing her vision for a few seconds. A couple of blue and yellow butterflies rose from the grass at her feet, spiralling upwards in a mating dance, or a territorial fight. Who could tell? Although they didn't see much, she closed her eyes. An uprush of joy surprised her and made her smile.

Flora is coming today.

The poor girl would still grieve, of course. To lose the one you love at any age is a tragedy, but especially painful when they're taken in their prime. Daphne knew better than most. She hoped this holiday might help Flora accept her man's death; Daphne recalled the terrible pain. She had received steady support from Kyría Alice – princess, nun, dearest friend. The time had come to repay all those blessings. Everything she had would go to Flora and Yánna when she died. Her heart squeezed for Flora. The poor girl had no other family.

'Is it today?' she called to Yánna. Her high-pitched voice squeaked with age and excitement. Was her carer in the vicinity? 'Flora's interested in art, you know, like me and Aristotle,' she said, hearing Yánna's heavy breathing. 'She paints, and works for . . . I forget who, but she has a very important job.'

Even raising her voice was an effort these days. Time had become a burden, always confusing. What with her mid-morning nap, afternoon siesta and regular bedtime, she didn't know if it was day or night. It wouldn't be long before she'd lay her head on the white satin pillow of eternal rest. She wasn't afraid to meet death – so long as it wasn't this week.

A sharp pain stabbed in her chest. She clutched the front of her blouse and whimpered.

Is this it . . . ? No, please, not yet. Dear God, give me a chance to tell my granddaughter everything, then I'll come without a struggle. What about the treasures? I have to put things right!

Daphne's story had begun in a different time, but the remnants hung in galleries worldwide, for all to see.

'Yes, Daphne, it's today.' Yánna's voice came from behind her. 'About ten o'clock this morning.'

'Listen, Yánna, I'm going to tell Flora everything. How do you feel about that?'

Yánna eased Daphne forward, plumped her pillow, then nudged her back.

'It's your call. If you feel strong enough and that's what you want, then do it.'

'You don't mind? I mean, you know about . . . Well . . .' She swallowed hard, saw a dark shadow pass the pale screen that was all her sight amounted to at that moment.

'You mean about what happened to my family, and how you . . .' She sighed. 'Yes, I know, Daphne. I don't remember, of course, but I know. And it's fine by me if you tell Flora.'

Daphne smiled. 'You were a wonderful child, Yánna. You were the sunshine in my life, especially when things got difficult. Hard to believe you were only fifteen years old when you started caring for me.'

'And only sixteen when I married that pig of a husband.'

'We all make mistakes. Do you know, I've forgotten what happened to him.'

'That leggy bus driver left him six months later. *Poutána!* Whore! Best thing I did was move back in here. Shall I order fresh croissants to go with the coffee?' Yánna pulled a mobile from her pinny pocket. 'There's no signal again. I'll have to use the house phone.'

'Yes, do. I'm quite excited.' Her gaze lowered, sadness falling over her face. 'People say she looks like me at her age. They claim her flaming tresses come from me, having the thick dark hair of the Papadopoulos family – and her Austrian grandfather's fine, fair hair. Dear Aristotle . . . Wasn't he handsome, Yánna?' The lie came without a thought. She had told it so often. 'Don't let me nod off, will you?'

She had lost direction on Yánna and wondered where the woman was.

'No, of course I won't. I'm just going inside for a quick dust around.'

When Daphne felt the pen-shaped alarm pushed against her palm, her fingers curled around it.

'You just press that button if you need me, all right?'

'You're an angel. I'll be fine.'

Today would be a good day; Daphne felt it in her rickety bones. Secrets kept too long and promises made many decades ago needed to be set free. She'd locked them away in her heart, and at the same time, they'd imprisoned her. The people involved were all dead now . . . apart from her and Yánna, so what did it matter if she released herself from this burden.

A pain exploded in her heart. She whimpered again. She shouldn't get upset. Must stay calm.

Would Flora understand when she knew everything? Daphne had broken Aristotle, shattered him like a dropped mirror. He had never mended, never recovered. How could he? Anyone would think the opposite: that the German would break the Jew. Daphne Abrams, aka Papadopoulos, had destroyed so much. Did she say 'German'? She must remember to say 'Austrian'. How could she ever forgive herself? But would her granddaughter condemn her?

This story of hers must be accurate, of course. The details were clear in her mind and without confusion. Names and facts were precise, and in chronological order. Kyría Alice, clever and funny, humble and devout – she had forgiven Daphne. That woman hadn't had a dishonest bone in her body. Against all odds, the princess had founded the convent – a nursing order of Greek Orthodox nuns: formally, the Christian Sisterhood of Martha and Mary. This was in memory of her beloved aunt, Grand Duchess Elizabeth Feodorovna, who was doing the same until they captured her and her family, bound them all, and threw them down a mine shaft, followed by several hand grenades. Daphne shuddered. The poor children. The poor parents, too. How cruel men could be.

Without help from the Greek princess, it would have been ashes to ashes for the Abrams family in 1943. She must tell Flora about the starving Athenians saved by the kindness of Kyría Alice, and the Jews saved from the Nazi gas chambers by her unselfish bravery.

The press should be ashamed, clinging on to a few months of her friend's mental breakdown. Mixing facts with religion and sensationalising the details. Where was the doctor–patient confidentiality? Terrible things had happened to poor dear Alice when she could not defend herself. The press could be such vultures. Never a mention of the dear woman's bravery, her selflessness, her love of her fellow man. How many children did she save from starvation?

Exhausted by her own anger, Daphne closed her eyes and recalled the grounds of Mon Repos all those years ago. She saw the ghost of her darling Aristotle. He appeared from nowhere, drifting towards her, a silhouette backlit by the sea. His athletic body was old before its time, marred by the lopsided limp and a lame arm that had improved little since his stroke. She ached for him, her heart hammering too fast for comfort. Had he come for her? Dropping back against her cushions, she took a deep breath, telling herself to calm down. She needed to be strong and alert when Flora arrived. Her quivering moments of hesitation fell away. Flora would learn the whole truth. It was no good trying to hide unsavoury events; she would just confuse herself. Daphne cradled her arms and rocked her imaginary infant. Tears broke free and ran down the crags of her gentle face.

'Why did it happen, Aristotle?' she whispered as her bony chest jerked with a sob.

'Don't get yourself upset, Daphne. She'll be here any minute.' Yánna's shadow blocked the light for a moment as she dabbed her face. 'Let's dry those tears before she sees you snivelling, old girl. There, try to think of joyful things.'

'If I tell her everything, do you think she'll ever forgive me?'

'Give her credit, Daphne. There's nothing to forgive, you silly old fool. She loves you, as I do. She'll understand.'

Daphne's thoughts went to her husband's portraits. She had painted the one on the wall in the cottage, though she hadn't signed it. People supposed it was a self-portrait by Aristotle, and offered big money for it. Would Flora reveal her grandmother's big secret once she knew it?

Memoirs written in an old diary were somewhere safe. They contained impressive names: important people, royalty, the SS, Hitler . . .

She rested against the plumped cushion and, like a sunflower, turned her face towards the light and heat, feeling herself energised. She must put her thoughts in order. Mustn't sound like a rambling old fool once she started.

When did it all start? Ah, yes: World War II.

* * *

Daphne's thoughts drifted back to Thessaloníki, where her family had been part of an enormous Jewish community. How she had cried to leave her school friends when her father had moved them all to Athens in January 1939. His promotion to the government's financial department was cause for many congratulations, but Daphne dreamed of going back to her old school and greatest friends. Her parents, understanding her unhappiness, had tried to pacify her.

'Miss Daphne, show me top marks in your German language lesson, and I'll allow you to take another art lesson with von Stroop this week,' her father said, believing Germany and Greece were about to unite. He was determined that all his children would learn to speak German fluently. 'To mark your seventeenth birthday, I'll book you in for a full year of tutoring with Aristotle von Stroop. What do you say to that, miss?'

'Oh, Babá, you're the most perfect father in all of Athens.'

She flung her arms around his neck and kissed his cheeks.

How wrong they had all been, believing nothing would happen to them because her father worked for the government. In the late summer of 1940, on her seventeenth birthday, she wore her first grown-up frock – pale blue cotton dotted with white daisies. The tight bodice showed off her blossoming figure; elbow-length puffed sleeves made her swelling breasts appear glorious and full. The circular skirt flounced around her calves, and when she twirled before her bedroom mirror, she glimpsed her pale thighs and thrilled at her own sexuality. She wore black patent shoes with a small heel and a buttoned strap, with the whitest ankle socks. After rubbing a little olive oil into her scalp, she brushed her long, dark hair until it shone, then clipped it up and back over her ears.

Her oldest brother, Noah, thrust a small box into her hands.

'Happy birthday, princess.' He kissed her cheek.

She unwrapped the package and, to her delight, discovered a dainty oval locket, which opened to reveal a miniature family photograph. A copy of the grand portrait that hung on their dining room wall.

'Oh, Noah, it's the most beautiful thing I've ever owned!' she whispered as he fastened the silver chain around her neck.

'I have something for you, too.' Isaac, only two years older than her, blushed, then grinned with mischief. 'It's nothing, really. Just to remind you that we should always have crazy days, even when we're all grown up.'

He put his fist over her palm and pretended to give her something. When she opened her hand, she found a tiny curled feather and remembered the pillow fight that got them both into trouble with her mother. She turned her head towards the ceiling and recalled the white duck-down snowing over them when the kapok pillowcase burst. How they had laughed.

'It's perfect. I love you.' She kissed him and placed the feather in her locket.

Feeling determined, she clutched her art portfolio and marched to her lesson with the divine Aristotle von Stroop. Her heart raced as she hurried to the studio.

Von Stroop, tall with light brown hair and pale grey eyes, was a handsome twenty-five-year-old Greek of Austrian descent. He made a stiff bow as she entered the studio.

'Welcome, Miss Daphne.' His observant eyes came up to meet her face, even before he straightened. Eyes that made her blush with joy. 'You look very different today.'

'It's my seventeenth birthday.'

'So, what can I do to make the day special?'

Kiss me.

As if reading her thoughts, he collected her hand and kissed the back of it.

'Will you help me practise my German, conjugating verbs, while I paint, sir?'

'Now you're seventeen, Daphne, you may call me Aristotle when we're alone.'

She thought she might float right off the floor with pure happiness.

* * *

'Mama!'

Daphne jumped, snapped out of her memories. Knuckles to her mouth and eyes flying open, she recognised the housekeeper's shape looming over her.

'Sorry, dear. Did I startle you?' Yánna asked. 'You'd nodded off. Coffee's ready, and your granddaughter's here. Shall I bring her out, or would you rather come inside? Are you all right?'

'Of course I'm all right. Why wouldn't I be?' Daphne snapped, her heart crashing under her ribs. 'Let's have our coffee out here. I'm sure Flora will enjoy that. Bring a table and another chair on to the lawn – and my big-brimmed hat. I don't want to ruin my skin, do I?'

She fumbled for her glasses, delving among the folds of skirt fabric in her lap. Her fingers traced the shape, opened them, and slipped them on. Now she could see a little more clearly.

'Granny, how wonderful to see you!'

Flora approached from the left, stooped, and kissed her cheeks, lingering for a joyous moment with their faces pressed fondly together.

'Flora, you lovely darling girl, thank you for coming,' she said, switching to English for her granddaughter's sake.

'You look really well, Granny. It's been so long! I've left your biscuits and stuff on the table, and I brought you this. It's just a silly thing, but I thought you'd like it.'

22

Daphne felt the cool, smooth pebble placed in her hand. 'Thank you. Give this old lady another hug, will you? I've waited three long years.'

'I wished to come sooner, of course I did, but with Covid, and then Mark's . . . you know.' She sighed and sniffed and, after a second, continued. 'Also, I had exams, Granny. I'm trying to get a promotion, but it means increasing my qualifications. I had to take an Open University course. Anyway, I've brought some pictures on my laptop of the Tate gallery, in Liverpool, where I work. You can see some of the pictures. I've made a video for you, too, which I thought was rather ambitious. It shows you where I live outside the city. It's beautiful there, in Crosby. Also, dear Granny, I wondered . . .' She hesitated, swallowed hard, and continued. 'Do you think I could paint your portrait while I'm here?'

'Oh!'

*　*　*

Events from a lifetime ago came rushing back to Daphne with shattering clarity. Sudden heartache made her press a trembling hand against her bosom. She remembered the summer of 1940, when she sat at her easel. Aristotle's breath caressed her neck as he spoke over her shoulder. Her toes curled as the thrill of his nearness rushed down her spine.

'Daphne, do you think I could paint you? I can't pay the full fee, but I'll give you something, and waive your lesson fee. Of course, I'd be the perfect gentleman in every respect.'

'You mean in the . . .' She blushed, stared at the floor, unable to say the word 'nude' when referring to herself.

He cleared his throat and nodded.

'I . . . Well, I'm not sure . . .' She felt the heat rise in her cheeks. 'Sorry, I mean—' She gulped, glanced at his face, saw concern.

He looked away, busied himself with washing brushes.

'No need to apologise, young lady. I understand. Really, I shouldn't have asked and now I've embarrassed you. Please forgive me?'

She couldn't speak and sat there blinking, afraid she might cry. Thankfully, he continued speaking. She couldn't have coped with silence.

'Now, next week we're going to start work on the human form,' he said. 'We'll begin by sketching a young male in pencil. The model is arriving at five o'clock, so please don't be late.'

3

FLORA

Corfu, present day

I HAD APOLOGISED TO GRANNY for being late and told her what had happened with my case, starting with my phone call to the airport.

'Hello, Corfu Airport? Look, there's been a mistake. I have somebody else's suitcase.'

After I'd been passed around like baggage on the carousel, a fresh voice said, 'Yes, madam. The owner called us yesterday. He's desperate for his luggage and wants to collect it himself. Will you agree?'

'Absolutely!'

'Can you call him with your location? He left his phone number with us.'

Forty-five minutes after my airport phone call, Spyridon Faliraki strode into the hotel lobby with my unmistakable electric-blue cabin bag. Wearing a deep frown, eighteen hours of stubble, and a crumpled cream linen suit, he stared around the foyer. He saw his luggage before he noticed me, then did a double take on my flaming red hair.

I sensed his agitation. Reluctant to shake hands but well-mannered enough to realise he should. He placed my case next to his, and we stood, facing each other like villains, except one case was not full of money and the other wasn't bursting with bags of white powder.

He introduced himself in English, as most Greeks do in the face of a foreigner. 'Spyridon Faliraki. May I ask what delayed you?'

'Flora Champion,' I replied. 'Pleased to meet you. To be honest, I was so exhausted last night, I didn't open the case until this morning. Who'd guess something like this would happen?'

'I had to cancel two days of meetings,' he grumbled. 'Still, at least you had the honesty to inform the airport.'

'And why wouldn't I?' I said, pulling my chin in with indignation.

'Well, the laptop alone is top spec, and the content value is even higher.' He glared right into my eyes and pathetically, just for a second, I floundered for words.

Anger burned into my cheeks and I feared he'd think it was a blush of embarrassment, damn him!

'What are you suggesting? I'd steal your belongings, or that I'd hack into your laptop?' How dare he be annoyed with me! 'I'll remind you whose fault this is. You took my bag. I was last off the plane. You'd already left with my luggage. It never occurred to you that my vital medication might be in your possession. Or that the consequences of your carelessness might threaten my life. No, you are only worried about your laptop!'

He ran perfectly manicured fingers through a mop of thick, dark hair. His white gold cufflinked shirtsleeve slid back to reveal the most expensive looking watch I'd ever seen. A Rolex, perhaps.

'Sorry, I apologise. Are you all right?' he asked brusquely. I nodded. 'Are you sure?' His eyes lightened. 'Let me get you a coffee.' He raised a hand towards the hotel's alfresco cafe in an open courtyard, near reception.

After ordering, we sat in awkward silence, then both spoke at once. I shook my head and indicated for him to go ahead.

'I wondered if you were on holiday . . . with using a schedule flight and not a tour company?'

'Good thinking. No, I'm here to visit my grandmother. She's almost a hundred years old.'

His phone pinged. He frowned, took it from his pocket, glanced at the screen, then laid it on the table.

'Clearly, you're here to work,' I said. The phone pinged again. His face darkened. 'Look, it's OK, answer it. Here's the coffee.'

'Thank you.' His voice softened and the corners of his mouth curled into the beginnings of a smile. 'Excuse me for one moment.'

Before he picked up, Spyridon unzipped the front pocket of his case and checked the laptop and file were there, then spoke English into his phone.

'Yes, Jack? OK, pass on my apology to everyone and reschedule for twelve o'clock today, this evening, and tomorrow morning, all right? Yes, everything's in order. Yes, yes, all right. I'll meet you and the building manager at the property. Sure, noon it is.'

He ended the call and turned to me. 'He's English, my assistant. Here on student exchange. Clever boy, in his final year.'

There was something appealing about his mouth, and his eyes were kind when he wasn't frowning.

He glanced at my bag. 'Shouldn't you be taking your life-saving medication with the coffee?'

'Ah, no, that was an example, Spyridon. I'm not exactly ill at all.' I studied the tabletop, testing myself with painful words. Could I say them without breaking down? 'It's . . . Well . . . I'm having a difficult time right now. My husband died three weeks ago. This is my first time abroad, on my own.' There, I'd said it without too much of a tremor in my voice, even if he was only a stranger. 'We had this trip booked three years ago. Covid, you know, messed up our plans, then he got sick, died . . . My husband.'

27

'I see. I'm sorry. You're very brave. Please, call me Spiro.' The smile threatened to break again. 'I wondered how a bottle of multivitamins for the over-thirties could save your life.'

My turn to quip, but as I opened my mouth to make a smart remark, a tear slid down my cheek. Damn. I swiped it away and forced a smile.

'All right, I apologise, too. If I hadn't been last boarding, my case wouldn't have gone into the business class locker. Let's forget it, shall we?'

* * *

Delighted that Granny would sit for me, I hurried into town to buy a few things. An hour later, I returned to Mon Repos cottage with a 50 × 40 stretched and primed canvas under my arm.

'She's gone for her nap,' Yánna said. 'Usually takes an hour or two.'

'That's fine. Can I leave my painting stuff here?' She nodded and indicated the solid wooden dining table. 'I'm looking forward to a stroll around Mon Repos. They've restored it since I was here last, am I right?'

'Yes, is a museum now, many people visit. You can see plenty of nice things inside, Flora. Very beautiful. They have a guide if you want. I think a painting from your grandfather is on the wall, too.'

'Really? Amazing! I'll see you shortly.'

I strolled along a path fringed with trees and caught sight of the sea on my left. A simple bench drew me. I sat for a while, enjoying the peace and the greenery of this sun-drenched island. Something white caught my eye in the deep shade of a holm oak. A clump of wild cyclamen, delicate petals turned up like white candle flames in the vegetation. Across the lawn, a tree-lined driveway led to a turning circle. Beyond stood the mansion of Mon Repos. Painted in peach, cream and faded burgundy, the magnificent building wore the dusty hues and faded rouge of Pompadour grandeur. Intricately detailed marble griffons supported the entrance columns on their backs. I imagined the wide forecourt would accommodate two gilded carriages drawn by plumed and polished, high-stepping horses.

The nineteenth-century neoclassical architecture had pillars and porticos a plenty. I took pictures from every angle. A grand stone staircase led to higher ground around the back, from where I hoped for a breathtaking view down to the sea. Before I reached the top of the wide steps, I noticed three men studying a set of plans. I recognised Spyridon Faliraki, who pointed a pencil at Mon Repos, then at the plans. I stepped out of sight and listened.

'It has to come down. Let's build something modern and earthquake-proof, right? Are we all agreed?' There was a pause before he continued. 'Jack, my secretary will help you to source the contractors. Manno, I suspect there are pockets to line, which will push the price up. I'll leave all that in your hands. Let's get it demolished quickly, before some conservationists complain. Over the weekend is best.' The tone of Spyridon's voice made it clear he wasn't to be argued with. 'Try to stick to the programme. We've had enough trouble, and I don't want anyone else getting hurt.'

What?

I couldn't breathe for the fire that raged in my chest.

They can't knock down the beautiful old mansion!

I went up a step, and saw the plans rolled and slipped into a tube. The men turned. I ducked and hurried around to the front of the building. A sign pointed the way into the Museum of Corfu, otherwise known as Mon Repos. The three men were right behind me. I dived behind a postcard stand, which saved me from recognition. The three men disappeared through a heavy oak door that said DIRECTOR on a brass plaque.

*   *   *

Granny Daphne and Yánna sat at a round table on the neat lawn in front of the cottage. Yánna waved, then said something to Granny, who also waved. I suspected Granny's eyesight was worse than she had let on.

'Come and have tea with us. Your *yiayá*'s been waiting. She's too excited.'

I smiled to hear the Greek word for 'grandmother' – the word Mark had always used.

I kissed Granny's cheek, glad to see her radiant smile. It's wonderful to be loved so unconditionally.

'Did you sleep well?' I asked.

'Yes, I did sleep, Flora. I dreamed of the old days, of Grandad Aristotle and the princess. How was the museum? Quite grand, I imagine.'

Her short, shaggy hairstyle suited her rebellious attitude to life. Daphne had the sweetest face; I suspected she had been a great beauty in her time.

'Grandad and the princess? Sounds like an intriguing memoir. What's that all about?'

'I'll tell you later. Now come on, I want to hear about the old house. Did you peer into the dome with all the little windows? Did you enter the room where my dear friend Alice gave birth to your beloved Prince Philip on the dining table? Did you see the sumptuous bedrooms with their heavy taffeta and brocade

30

curtains?' She giggled. 'I can tell you a story or two about those curtains . . . Oh my!'

I reminded myself that this little old woman was an ardent royalist and I was determined to get her a birthday telegram from the King.

'Did you know there's a beautiful plaque on the front gates stating it's the birthplace of Prince Philip, Granny?'

She crossed herself. 'May God rest his soul. I believe he was a wonderful man. Very loyal to Her Majesty Queen Elizabeth. May they both rest in peace. I never met him personally, but his mother was my dearest friend.'

I stared at her, my little Greek grandmother in her wheelchair.

'You met Prince Philip's mother . . . the queen's mother-in-law?'

'Yes, we were good friends. She saved my family, you know. She lived here for a time, in the mansion, or the museum . . . whatever they choose to call the big house.' She stared into the distance. 'I'll tell you this story right now, because I may never remember it again. My friend Alice had a fault – she gave everything she had to the needy, to the poor, to the starving and the homeless. When she got a telegram to say her son was going to marry the love of his life, Elizabeth, Alice gave him her own royal wedding tiara to be made into the engagement ring. However, she had to arrange travel to the wedding and had no money left for a suitable outfit.' Daphne giggled.

'She's off,' Yánna said, placing our coffee on the table. Ice cubes tinkled against the glass jug as she poured glasses of cold water. The coffee was strong and sweet and the aroma filled my head.

'So she couldn't attend the wedding?' I asked.

'Ha – twaddle and bunkum! Nothing was going to keep Alice from seeing her Fílippos happily married. She adored the boy, but missed such a big part of his growing up.'

31

'How come?'

'Because they'd locked her in an asylum.'

'What? That's shocking! How did she get a wedding outfit that was appropriate for such a grand occasion?'

Daphne paused for effect, waiting for me to put my coffee down.

'I heard, and I believe it's true, that she took down a long green velvet curtain and made her outfit from it.'

'You're kidding me!'

'I've got a photo of it somewhere. She seems to be wearing velvet, and it might be green, so who knows?'

'And the other story? You said you had two stories about the Mon Repos curtains.'

'Yes, we'll get to that later. Alice risked her life to save my family, and one can only guess how many other Jews and starving children.'

I blinked at her. 'Jews? But you're Greek, Granny. My stepmother told me your maiden name was Papadopoulos and my grandfather was also born in Greece, though he came from Austrian blood – von Stroop . . .'

She replied with a nod, followed by a gentle shake of her head.

'Yes, we were born in Greece, and our ancestors, too, but our religion? Well, Abrams was my family name. Like many Sephardic Jews, my distant family came from Spain in 1492 and settled here in Greece.'

'Then, how come . . . ?' I could hardly grasp what she was telling me.

Daphne patted my thigh. 'We changed our names, though it didn't save us all.' She clutched the gold locket on a chain around her neck, sadness dragging at her jaw. 'But I'll tell you everything soon enough, so go on, describe the mansion.'

I struggled to get back on track. Daphne was Jewish and survived the Holocaust?

'Flora! The mansion? Pay attention, child.'

'Sorry, Granny, it's quite a lot to take in. Right, Mon Repos, completely renovated on the inside, though it needs a lick of paint outside. All very lovely and quite regal, with lots of beautiful furniture and pictures – both portraits and landscapes. The staff are nice people, too, helpful, informative. I guess you've been inside since it reopened?'

'Dear child, my eyes aren't working too well these days, especially indoors. No point in staring at paintings I can't see.'

'What's the problem, Granny?' I asked, gently taking her hand.

'Besides cataracts? Something with a fancy name . . . macular degeneration. Inoperable, and not going to get better.'

'When did you last have an examination?'

'Three years ago. I flew to Athens, but the travelling is all a bit much, so I've decided to let things take their course.'

'Can't the optician come here?'

'He needs his high-tech equipment. Anyway, I've given up on it.'

How awful to lose your sight!

'Will you allow me to research a little and speak to the doctor?'

'If it makes you feel useful, but trust me, you're wasting your time, darling Flora.'

'Is this why you've invited me over – because you're losing your eyesight?'

Daphne nodded. 'I wanted to see you.' She squeezed my hand with her long, slender fingers. 'You're all I have left, Flora, the last living person that has my blood. You are part of me. Also . . .' With a frown, she compressed her lips, then sighed.

33

'There's something I must tell you.' After a moment's silence, she continued. 'I've kept a secret for too long. It's like a pain in my heart.' She nodded again. 'If that modern phone of yours makes a video, you must record what I'm about to tell you.'

I blinked in disbelief. 'But why? I don't understand. What's going on, Granny?'

'Because people will call you a liar.' She closed her eyes. 'And there's the art. Decisions must be made. I'm not up to long stretches of anything these days, and I'm likely to get emotional, so we'll have to do this in brief sessions. Is that all right with you?'

'Yes, of course, but I need to check my phone for messages before we start.'

'Is it so important, dear girl?' she said with tired resignation.

'Sorry, I know it's rude of me, but I'm waiting for exam results.'

'You'll be lucky if you get a signal, child.'

'You're right – only one bar. I hope to have upped my restoration game to cover sixteenth-century art.' I took a breath and told her the whole story. 'It was all a distraction, you see. Mark insisted. He said I should do the course for him. Something to concentrate on through the worst moments of the past year, when life was so unbearable. If I couldn't focus on my studies, he would get angry and say I should forget everything and concentrate on the work . . . He said that if I promised to do my best, my utmost, and not give up on the course, no matter what was going on, then he would do the same. He swore to try to stay strong, to keep going until the very last second, hoping for a bone marrow match.'

Suddenly, I realised I was crying.

'Oh, Granny! Why did it happen to us? I loved him so much.'

The floodgates opened; everything I'd held on to for so long came out in one great deluge.

34

'Poor girl. It's not your fault, none of it. You must forgive him for leaving you. Stop being so angry.'

I sniffed hard, my body vibrating from the sobs, and stared at her. How could she understand how I felt?

'You forget, I lost the man I loved more than my own life,' she said, answering my question.

'You did?' I tried to make sense of her words.

'Yes, and I was much younger than you, too. I'll tell you everything, but first, you tell me about this exam. Was it difficult?'

'Mm, a little. You remember I'm a freelance art restorer for the galleries and museums in the UK?'

Daphne's jaw dropped. 'You mean you bring old paintings back to their former glory? Yes, of course you do. Oh, my!' She gasped, her mouth hanging open a little longer that one would expect. 'How could I forget such a thing? I put it down to my age. Restoration, eh? I've heard that people in your line of work make excellent . . . hmm . . . What's the word . . .? Counterfeiters.'

Daphne had a delightful vocabulary. She loved speaking English and always challenged herself to use the longest words she could. I brushed the tears from my face.

'Granny, I'm shocked! You're not suggesting I would . . . Well . . .' I started laughing. 'I'm not a forger!'

'No, no, of course not, but you never know when such a skill might come in handy. In fact, I'd like to commission you to copy that portrait of Aristotle in the house. Could you do that for me?'

I realised my mouth was hanging open and snapped it shut.

'Granny, what exactly are you asking?'

She turned her head and stared into the space between us.

'Well, can you do it or not? Paint in oils, with a lead primer, and fake the craquelure varnish?' She seemed to get quite excited, breathing rapidly, eyes sparkling. 'I can tell you how it's done if you don't have the skills already.'

I couldn't think of a thing to say. Was my grandmother a forger?

'I can do it, though I might require your help to fake the age,' I said. 'And I'd need a lot of time – perhaps a year, if you want it in oils.'

'That's total bunkum. I haven't got a year. I'll be dead.'

She didn't mince words.

'Then it has to be acrylics,' I said. 'Just a week to paint, and it will look the same, craquelure varnish and everything, but it wouldn't pass the test of being an original.'

'Marvellous, I'll consider it.' She always seemed to know what I was thinking. 'Yes, I've done several forgeries in my time,' she admitted. 'Right now, some of my best counterfeiting hangs in very prodigious galleries. Others are in private collections.'

Speechless, I shook my head in disbelief.

'Portrait painting can be very rewarding work.' She chuckled. 'Perhaps rewarding is an understatement.'

I muttered, for want of something to say, 'I'll just check my phone again, then set my easel up to start on your picture.'

'You're wasting your time. We only have a Wi-Fi signal when a low-flying plane comes over.'

'What? You're kidding?'

'Yes.' Her eyes sparkled and her shoulders jigged. 'It's so lovely to have you here.'

'It's wonderful for me, too, Granny. But you can be such an imp!'

'Imp, imp?' She frowned. 'Ah, mischievous you mean? Yes, well I do my best, and why use three letters when you can use eleven. I love your language, Flora – it keeps my old brain working. Some forms of art are more satisfying than others, don't you think? To be immortalised by a great artist is an amazing experience.' She had such a joyful grin it lifted my heart; then she straightened her face and lifted her chin in a quarter pose.

My curiosity was piqued. I was beginning to see a whole new side to my grandmother.

'Is your recorder turned on? Shall I start my memoirs?'

'I'm ready, crack on, Granny.'

* * *

'My name is Daphne von Stroop. I was born in Thessaloníki in 1923, to Elijah and Lotte Abrams. My father, Elijah, worked for the government. In 1939, they transferred him to the capital, so we took up residence in the centre of Athens. I had two older brothers, Noah and Isaac, and one younger sister, Elizabeth. We were a happy family, quite wealthy and very well educated. Life changed little for us at the start of the war.' Daphne chuckled with a swooping uplift of spirits. 'I hope I've made the right decision to divulge my life story. It's rather exciting for me, but also a little frightening. I fear you may be shocked by my revelations.'

4

DAPHNE

Athens, 1941

'GOOD EVENING, MISS DAPHNE. Please remove your coat and make yourself comfortable. I've placed an easel near the window for you, and a chaise lounge for our models. They'll be here any minute.'

'Models? Plural?' Her heart pattered. She was seventeen now, practically a woman, yet her pulse raced the moment she discovered herself in an adult situation.

Pull yourself together, Daphne!

She glanced around, searching for an escape, then scolded herself. How would she become a great artist if she couldn't study the human form?

Her tutor draped a swag of blue velvet over the sofa.

'Excuse me, Aristotle, can I ask you something?' She hoped he wouldn't notice the tremor in her voice. He turned and nodded, peering into her face. 'I'm feeling flustered, perhaps overexcited, or afraid of failing, I don't know. I mean I've never . . . Well . . .' She tutted and tried again. 'Is it normal for the artist to have a bout of nerves on these occasions? It's where to look, you see. I'm a little embarrassed to be on such an intimate standing, with all that . . . flesh exposed and so much expected of me.' Her words tumbled out, leaving her blinking and breathless.

Aristotle von Stroop peered into her face, as if studying her features again. A smile broke through his seriousness, white, even teeth flashing and beautiful grey eyes sparkling as the corners of his mouth turned up. In her agitated state, Daphne trembled under his gaze.

'Everyone's nervous the first time, don't worry. It's your job to relax the model. Go about the task as if painting a vase of flowers. Your brushwork won't flow unless you lose some of this tension.' He massaged her shoulders, but that only heightened her agitation. 'Take deep breaths, let them out slowly. I'll set my easel beside yours. If you get stuck, you can copy what I'm doing.'

The door knocker rattled.

'Ah, here they are.'

He hurried towards the door. She realised they were talking in the hall before he returned alone.

'I know it's unnecessary in this case, Daphne, but I've found that in order to save any embarrassment, it's better for the model to pose while not under the scrutiny of the artist. Therefore, I'm going to ask you to sit on the other side of the screen while the models prepare. Come out and start sketching when I call you, all right?'

Daphne's mouth dried. She nodded, scooted behind the folding bamboo panels and waited. In the cramped corner, she sat on a wooden stool and faced the wall, fists clenched, knees pressed together. There was no escape now . . .

Oh, what a dreadful situation!

'We're ready,' Aristotle called. 'Daphne, your models are waiting.'

She kept her eyes glued to the floor, made her way to the easel and took a soft graphite pencil in hand. With a deep breath, she peered from behind her canvas.

'Oh, not what I foresaw,' she whispered to herself, then caught the twinkle in her tutor's eye. 'I suspect you deliberately misled me, sir.'

39

She gazed at the beautiful composition. The woman wore an old-fashioned blue gown unbuttoned to the waist – a delightful baby boy was naked at her breast.

* * *

That evening, every member of the Abrams family looked up when the front door slammed. Noah came crashing into the drawing room.

'This is war! We're not simply overrun by Italians, now we have a swastika flying over the Acropolis!' he shouted, hardly making sense to me. 'Nazi troops, Hitler's mob! War has reached us, as I told you it would. The Germans have invaded Greece and Yugoslavia. Right at this moment, many more troops are marching on Athens! We must leave immediately. Pack up and get the next ship to Haifa.'

'Lower your voice, young man!' Babá said. 'There're ladies present. Show some respect.'

Daphne sat on the low windowsill of the big bay window, her bare feet on the piano stool and a sketchpad resting against her thighs.

'Daphne, that's not a very ladylike way to sit,' Mamá said, dragging her eyes away from Noah.

'Sorry, Mamá. I'm trying to capture our family life, and hoped nobody would notice me sketching. It's my homework.' She draped the end of the curtain over her exposed shins.

Babá lowered his newspaper, glared at Daphne's twenty-year-old brother, then stood.

'Twaddle! Where did you pick up such nonsense? There've been absurd rumours all year, but nobody comes up with proof, do they?'

'Everybody's talking about it, Babá. You'd think the Axis would have learned a lesson from the way we knocked Mussolini's lot back last year, but apparently not. There's unrest throughout the country – even the politicians are fidgety. The Germans aren't hiding the fact that they blame the Jews for their economic down-turn. All the Jews in Holland, Belgium and France have to wear a yellow star on their clothes. If they refuse, they're shot! They claim it will happen here in Greece, too.'

Babá glared at him, taking in the information.

Daphne's pencil flew across the paper. Caught in the moment's drama, she tried to catch expressions and body language. She recalled Aristotle's instructions: 'Don't worry about likeness, or proportion, just capture the mood, the passion. Show me if blurred fingers wave dismissively, or in greeting? Is a fist clenched in anger, or tenderly encapsulating a butterfly?'

Daphne strived to impress Aristotle. If her sketches were respectable enough, she would show him the following day.

Her father turned at the window, the light bouncing off his forehead, darkening the furrows of his brow. She snatched a 9B pencil, soft and dense, then flicked back to an earlier sketch and squiggled thick ruts across his temple. Satisfied, she reached for a 4H, its fine, sharp lines capturing the apprehension around his mouth.

Noah, assistant photographer for the Athens press, was passionate about the news and longed to be a reporter himself.

'We've just received word from our correspondent in Berlin – Hitler's given the German Jews permission to flee the country and return to the land of their forefathers. But – and it's a big *but* ...' He paused while his parent took in this information.

'Get on with it!' Babá roared.

'They can only take two suitcases each, and they must abandon their property, businesses and bank accounts.'

'He can't do that! Who does he think he is?' Babá bellowed, stuffing his hands into his trouser pockets and pacing the room. 'Seriously? Nobody's going to leave their homes and businesses – the very things they've worked for all their lives!'

'Depends on what you place the most value on, Babá. They say Hitler's government plans to rid Europe of its "imperfect people".' Noah turned to Daphne, horrified to think she might have been listening. 'Not a single syllable of this conversation to anyone, Daphne. Understand? Especially not that German art teacher of yours.'

'He's not German. He's Austrian, Noah.'

'Don't be naive. Hitler's Austrian, and Austria's part of Germany now. They're all the same. Where do you think the Austrian Jews have gone? They're certainly not in Austria.'

Daphne's heart pattered. 'What? You're saying my teacher's a bad person because of where his grandfather was born?' Anger rose in her chest.

How dare Noah make such an assumption? He doesn't even know Aristotle.

She kept her mouth shut. It would do no good to argue with him.

'They're all the same, the Aryan race. Promise me you won't repeat anything I've said, Daphne. It could put all our lives in jeopardy.'

Before she protested again, her father cut in.

'This is an absurdity put about to sell more newspapers. They'll hold your editor to account for printing such rubbish. To start with, where would the Nazis hold every Jew in Europe?'

42

'Hate to contradict you, Babá, but the paper's not allowed to reveal these matters. Don't underestimate Hitler. Our man in Berlin says the Germans are building massive prisons in Germany and Poland. They'll house thousands, and although Hitler calls them work camps, there are whispers of far more terrible things. It's not safe to be a Jew in Europe. We must leave, at least until this war is over.'

'I work for the government – we will not run, Noah. I'd never get such a well-paid job anywhere else. Now stop this foolishness – you're frightening the women.'

'No disrespect, sir, but the Germans have already occupied Thessaloníki.' He softened his voice. 'They arrested the Jewish leadership in the city yesterday morning. The Rosenberg Task-force is confiscating manuscripts, property deeds, works of art, even our holy books. We know because one of our reporters sent a telegram telling us to get out of Athens immediately. Some Greeks back the Nazis and hope for some kind of alliance. Who are we supposed to trust?' Noah's voice had climbed until he was almost shouting again.

'Don't raise your voice to me. I am still your father!'

'Sorry, Babá, but I'm nervous. What will we do?' He glanced around the room, his eyes lingering on Mamá, and then Daphne. 'There are other things that have grabbed our editor's attention.'

'Well, come on, spit it out. We'll all probably see it in tomorrow's paper, anyway. What's happening that calls for all this drama?'

Daphne saw her brother's frustration. Her father just wasn't getting it. Noah stared at the carpet for a moment, then at Mamá.

'Listen, Babá, I can promise you won't read this in the paper. Yesterday, they rounded up all the Jews of Thessaloníki. Thousands upon thousands. They claimed it was to prepare

43

for transport to a labour camp. The community gave over two billion drachmas for their release, which the Nazis accepted, but still took the Jews away. Nobody knows where they've gone. All we know is they're on cattle trains heading north. There are whispers . . . If they were going to work camps, why would they take the grandmothers and babies?'

5

FLORA

Corfu, present day

'HOW MUCH DO YOU KNOW about Mon Repos, Flora?'

I shook my head. 'Not a lot, Granny. I can do some research online this evening, if it will make your task easier.'

She smiled and nodded. 'Forgive me, but sometimes I get muddled. You are Rachelle's girl, yes?'

'Yes, Granny. I'm Flora, Rachelle's daughter. She died of breast cancer when I was pretty young. Zoe and Bob, who worked at the British embassy in Athens, raised me. We went to England, where I attended school and then university in Liverpool.'

Granny patted my hand. 'Of course, it's all coming back. It's my age, you understand.' She took a breath and said, 'Now, where shall I start? Let's see . . . 1940, because that was when everything changed. I can see the day so clearly. Mamá wore her sewing glasses and sat with her embroidery hoop, working the vibrant colours of a peacock butterfly. Babá had his head in a newspaper, as usual, and another tabloid cluttered the dining table, but I can't remember why he was home on a weekday afternoon.'

I tried to imagine the family scene.

'I sat in the window, sketching, when Elizabeth burst into the room, wailing her head off. She flung herself into Mama's lap and sobbed onto her shoulder.' Daphne shook her head and stared ahead. 'My little sister was only thirteen years old, but on that day, her dream of becoming a doctor ended.'

I poured Daphne a glass of water and, after a few sips, she continued.

'They'd sent her home from school with a note for my father, you see. She continued to cry, her chest jerking with sobs. Babá opened the letter; Mamá was at his side before he reached the end. With each line, his face darkened, and I expected an outburst of anger, but he simply murmured, "They've expelled you." Elizabeth wailed, "Babá, I did nothing wrong. It must be a mistake." She fell into my mother's arms again. "I've tried really hard and had wonderful marks in everything this month." Babá looked at her sadly. "It's not your fault, little sparrow – you're expelled because you're Jewish," he said. "Jews can't go to the city school."

'So perhaps Noah was right, I thought. Discrimination is a terrible thing, Flora. We were all shocked that it should happen to us. We were what you call "well to do".'

I tossed and turned in bed that night. How strange, to suddenly discover my ancestors were Jewish.

* * *

Woken by the sound of birdsong and morning light, which filtered through my muslin curtains, I found myself eager for the day. After coffee on the balcony, my swim, and breakfast, I took the bus into town. While we could have hired a car, Mark and I had always opted for the local bus. Perhaps I should do things differently now, but I find comfort in routine and there is no better way to watch the world go by, or to understand the locals, than a bus ride. Two stops later, prepubescent schoolchildren boarded the crowded vehicle. Their bad-mannered racket and uncivilised screeching shocked the foreign passengers, yet the locals nodded and grinned, clearly delighted to see their children so happy. The moment I stepped onto the pavement, Corfu wove its magic around me. Architecture hinted at its glorious past. I walked into the Old Town, admiring the multifaceted buildings. Shafts of spring sunlight illuminated Renaissance, Baroque, and classical styles left behind by the Venetians. Lines of colourful washing spanned narrow alleyways. Smiling Corfiots sipped their morning coffee in secluded squares packed with little tables.

Enchanted, I strolled through a complex of narrow cobbled streets with marble stairways and vaulted passages. Jewellery shops and quality gift emporiums lined the streets, and I found myself tempted by hand-painted silk scarves and unique silver rings depicting dolphins and starfish. Before long, I wound my way to the National Gallery of Corfu in one of the oldest streets. When Mark and I visited the gallery together, we stood side by side, silent, enjoying the paintings. It is difficult to explain our shared love of art, a joy that happened on a telepathic level, with seldom a need for words. The sun sliced between the stonework wherever it could, blinding me for a second. The gallery promoted Greek art by hosting artists from Corfu and across Greece. I spotted the establishment's pride and joy, an El Greco, but I could see it was a print on canvas.

A beautiful portrait caught my eye, then I realised it was part of a triptych by the same artist. A brass information plaque titled the work: *For the Love of Laurel*. The artist appeared to have studied the same woman over several decades, perhaps executing the works in her teens, twenties, and maturity, so she was older in each painting. *Laurel in Spring* showed a beautiful reclining nude in the first flush of womanhood. The model was relaxed under a young tree bearing small, spear-shaped leaves

47

and white, star-like flowers. The second portrait, *Laurel in Summer*, depicted a voluptuous woman wearing an open diaphanous gown. Her back was against the tree, which bore small black berries. She held a baby boy to her breast and gazed at the infant. In the final painting, the model was alone. Her greying hair, piled on her head, also spilled over one shoulder. She reclined on a blanket of leaves under a bare tree. The mountains in the background were snow-capped. I found myself lost in this painting, *Laurel in Autumn*.

A man's voice broke my concentration.

'Do you think the artist loved her?'

I turned to see a handsome, clean-shaven male a little older than myself, dressed to impress in a pale grey linen suit, with Aviator sunglasses sticking out of his top pocket. He oozed quality. Our eyes met and a little thrum of excitement stirred in the pit of my stomach. It took a moment before I recognised him – the architect.

'Oh, hello, we meet again,' I said, remembering his plan to destroy Mon Repos. 'Yes, I suspect he loved her. So, you're interested in art?'

'If you understand the market, it's a brilliant investment. Besides, the architecture of these old buildings is art, too. It's my job to house our treasures in safe, dry, and hopefully ancient buildings. Much of Corfu's heritage is lost already, and many old properties are in a dire state right now. If we don't attract some serious money, Flora, I'm afraid several important examples of these old constructions are doomed.'

I was impressed by his speech, and that he remembered my name.

'That's awful, to lose historical buildings. Sorry, I've forgotten your name.'

'Spyridon Faliraki. Spiros. Yes, it's very bad. I'd like to show you around the gallery, if I may . . . I'm an incorrigible show-off, and very proud of what we have here in Corfu.'

With a hesitant smile, the corners of his mouth curled in the charming way I had seen when he returned my case. I was surprised for a second and blinked at him. His smile expanded, and I realised he thought I was batting my eyelashes at him.

My tension lifted. He was easy to be with, like an old friend from long ago, though I hardly knew him.

'In that case, go ahead,' I said, drawn to the three paintings again. 'But in this set, I feel the artist is telling us something. In the first, she's a young girl, a virgin, which is suggested by the white flowers on the tree.'

'Laurel,' he said. 'It's a laurel tree.'

'Ah, my mistake. I thought that was the girl's name.'

There was mischief in his smile and a roguish twinkle in his eye, which I ignored and carried on with my appraisal of the paintings. 'Next, the laurel has borne fruit, and the woman as well. We see a baby, the fruit of her womb. Then, in the third work, the tree is mature, limbs bent with age, foliage thinned out, and no blooms or berries to be seen. What's the artist telling us?'

Spiros smiled. 'I sense it, too. It's a riddle. I feel it's as if he knew, when he painted this, that one day we would be here standing before his work, trying to understand his message.'

I gasped. This Spiros character reminded me of Mark in the way he talked about art and architecture. I blinked at him, not sure if the similarity was a good thing for the tender state of my emotions.

I turned my attention back to the triptych. 'If there's one thing I know, it's that we can learn through art and nature things that can't be taught with words. We must open ourselves to the

49

suggestions presented on the canvas. I stepped forward to study the small brass nameplate below the pictures. 'Avon Stroop? We have Stroops in our family. My grandmother's surname was Stroop after she married.'

Spiros turned from the painting, to me, then nodded at the plaque. 'It seems Stroop disappeared. He was a man of exceptional talent and painted some amazing masterpieces. His greatest works took place here, on Corfu. Some say he married a beautiful Jewish woman who was deported . . . They say he would not leave her side, and so he perished with her in Auschwitz.' He studied the three portraits. 'It might just be gossip, but if we're talking about the same Stroop, this would be the woman he died for.'

'What a romantic, tragic notion. I'll ask my grandmother what she knows. She's always refused to talk about her past, but suddenly Granny Daphne wants to tell me everything.'

'Daphne? You say her name's Daphne?' His smile widened.

'Yes, why do you ask?'

'You don't speak Greek, do you?' I shook my head. He gave a sharp nod. 'I guessed not. If you did, you'd realise that "Daphne" is Greek for laurel.' His eyes slid back to the painting.

My jaw dropped. What did all this mean? Until now, Granny had refused to discuss my family tree. Once I learned to write, my adopted mum had encouraged me to send letters to Daphne, my grandmother in Greece. Taking my envelope to the postbox became a Saturday ritual. All I knew about my real mum and dad was that my English father had perished in an accident at an olive factory and my Greek mother had died from cancer. Zoe and Bob from the British embassy became my foster-parents. They adopted me before we left for England, where they looked after me until I moved into student accommodation.

Spiros lifted his hand towards the three paintings. 'You're right about the artist. He loved her. Even in the first painting, she is thin, yet he paints her with voluptuousness. The way light falls on her body seems to soften every angle, and she glows. Look into her eyes – she's connecting with him.'

He sighed, silent for a while, and in that pause, I could see he was right.

'How wonderfully romantic,' I whispered to myself. 'You realise when he painted that first painting, he had already planned to spend the rest of his life with her?'

Spiros turned to stare at me. 'How can you know that?'

'He's made a strong play on light, from the left in the first picture, full frontal on the centre one, then the light comes from the right in the third. Also, the seasons – spring, summer, autumn. The triptych was planned from the outset.'

'Aristotle von Stroop came from a dogmatic German family that supported the Nazi regime. His cousin, Jürgen Stroop, was a general for the Reichsführer-SS, Heinrich Himmler. The model . . .' He nodded at the nude. 'They say she was a beautiful, aristocratic Jew.'

Not the Jewish thing again. I wasn't ready for this.

'Then it must be coincidence. My grandmother is Greek – Papadopoulos was the family name, before she married.'

Even as I stared at the young woman in the painting, I wondered if it could be Daphne.

Spiros continued. 'Theirs was a most unfortunate love affair, doomed from the start—'

'Stop! Don't tell me anything more.' A sour feeling built in the pit of my stomach as thoughts raced through my head.

'Are you all right? You've gone quite pale.'

'I'm a little dizzy. Can we sit for a moment?'

He took my elbow in an old-fashioned way and steered me to a bench in the centre of the gallery.

'I didn't even know my grandfather, but if he had been this great portrait painter, wouldn't there be some works of art in the cottage?'

'Are you telling me perhaps your grandfather was Aristotle von Stroop?'

His voice trembled, eyes sparkling with excitement. He was so like Mark in his enthusiasm for art. Once again, my thoughts returned to the Gormley installation on Crosby shore. How thrilled Mark had been to stand next to one of the iron figures with his arm over its shoulder, as if they were old friends.

'Take a picture of us,' he'd said, his rain-drenched hair plastered to his forehead. 'Because neither of us will ever be exactly as we are now, at this second.'

I still have the photo. Mark was so very young, and the effigy of Antony Gormley seemed bigger, and almost rust-free. I felt an urge to write to the artist and explain how much pleasure Mark and I'd had from his work over the years. I closed my eyes and sighed, suddenly wishing I was there, among all those solid men looking towards the future, with the sound of gulls overhead and the wind in my hair.

'Sorry, I didn't mean to pry,' he said, misinterpreting the moment.

I shook my head. 'It's fine, just my husband . . . Well, it's all so fresh, so painful, you understand? Memories.' I took a breath and swallowed hard. 'Do you know Antony Gormley?' He made a tut and lifted his chin, the Greek 'No'. 'He has an art installation just outside Liverpool, on the beach. A hundred life size men look out to sea. They're solid, strong, permanent. *Another*

Place, it's called. It gives me so much peace to stand among them. I wish I was there right now.'

'Are you getting enough sleep?'

I nodded, shrugged, peered at my feet and changed the subject. 'About this Avon Stroop. If he was my grandfather, wouldn't my grandmother have mentioned his fame to me? Anyway, my grandparents were Athenians, actually.'

Surprise, or perhaps shock, flashed across his face. 'Both von Stroop and his model came here from Athens, and they both loved art, but that's where their similarities ended. It's a little-known fact that Athens was a divided city at the start of the war.' He stared at the floor, then apparently decided to drop the subject. 'Anyway, von Stroop called himself Austrian, like many Germans who were uncomfortable with the situation in their homeland.'

'What did you think happened to him?'

'It seems he disappeared after 1945, although over the decades, several of his paintings did come to light. There were lots of rumours. Some said they murdered him for helping Jews escape from Corfu. Others claimed Hitler commissioned von Stroop for a portrait, then shot him when the Führer wasn't impressed. Another story says he was involved in the plot to assassinate Hitler, and they executed him. We can presume, as he was an artist, von Stroop's distaste for the Nazi regime would have been apparent in his image of its leader. However, several portraits of important dignitaries, and even royalty, appeared after his disappearance.'

'Being commissioned to paint people he disliked would have put him in a difficult position.'

Spiros nodded. 'Others claimed he left for Austria after they deported his greatest love to Auschwitz, and then he died of a broken heart, though I'm not sure I believe that. I mean, we have this third portrait, which suggests he stayed with her, if that is indeed his wife or lover, and he must have been middle-aged when he painted it.'

'Unless it's futuristic and he produced it from his imagination. But the spilled brushes suggest it was his last work.'

Spiros sighed. 'After the war, they discovered stolen artworks from Greece and the rest of Europe in Hitler's vaults, and in the salt mines where he stored many treasures. They catalogued the artworks and returned them to their rightful owners. Some of von Stroop's earlier portraits came to light. Apparently, he continued to paint at least until the 1960s. These works are prized by collectors and there's always hope that more paintings will appear.'

If they had deported Granny to Auschwitz, and she'd survived, wouldn't she have a tattoo on her arm?

6

DAPHNE

Athens, 1943

WHISPERS HAD FILTERED THROUGH TO Noah's office about terrifying camps in Poland that held the fifty thousand Jews from Thessaloníki who had been rounded up and transported out of Greece in old cattle trucks. He feared the same thing would happen to the Jews of Athens: valuables and artwork removed from their homes, schools, and synagogues; Jewish public property levelled to the ground; the city's Jewish cemetery flattened. As for the Jewish community? After entering Poland, they had simply evaporated.

Daphne heard Noah trying to enlighten her father.

'Vanished, I'm telling you. How can fifty thousand people from Thessaloníki disappear, Babá? Where are your family   my aunts, uncles and cousins? Why haven't you heard from them?'

Babá found the facts his son put forward impossible to believe. He paced the floor.

'It doesn't bear thinking about, Noah, but if what you say is true, I agree, we should prepare.' He peered through the window at the busy thoroughfare below. 'The rules of surviving a war are unchanged. Stock up with food, then find a secure place outside Athens to keep the women safe.'

'Babá, there's nothing to eat in the shops. The city's starving. We have to leave Greece, and to do that, we need documents stating we're Orthodox Christians.'

'What? Never! I will not betray my religion!' he yelled. 'Not for some arrogant Nazi! And if you're any kind of man, neither will you.'

'With respect, sir, it depends on what's more important to you – your religious beliefs, or the lives of your wife and family. They have rights, too – we shouldn't be so quick to condemn anyone for the sake of their race or religion. After all, isn't that what's happening to us?'

'How dare you tell me what I should do, Noah? What is this – mutiny? Haven't I always kept you safe, given you a good life? We should pray for guidance and stability in this time of war.'

* * *

There was so much Noah wanted to say, but his father would shout him down. Noah had to persuade him they were doing the honourable thing, not betraying themselves by saving the family.

'We have the power to protect those we love by disguising ourselves as Orthodox Greeks. I believe we'd be wrong to turn our backs on this solution.

Babá's moustache bristled as he chewed his lip.

'All right,' he said. 'Let's take advantage of the opportunity. Can you manage it, son?'

Relief rushed through Noah. He fell into his chair with a sigh.

'Yes, Babá. The bishop's issuing baptismal certificates to say the owner is a member of the Orthodox Church. Also, our editor whispered that the chief of police is arranging Greek identity papers for all the Jews.'

Babá raised a halting hand. 'You don't mean Angelos Evert? He's even grown a Hitler moustache to show his devotion to the Nazis!'

Noah nodded. 'I appreciate your opinion that he's a *mafiosa* racketeer taking protection money wherever he can. But I understand that, along with the archbishop, he's organising Christian identity cards for everyone who asks. Many Athenians are on our side. After all, we are also Greek. With the help of our fellow countrymen, we might get out of the city before the Nazis erect more roadblocks. The whisper is that they plan to relocate us all – women and children, too – to enforced labour camps in Germany and Poland. We already know about the fifty thousand or more Jews forced on to trains and railroaded out of Thessaloníki, so we must presume they mean business.'

'I still think this is hysterical gossip, Noah.' Babá sounded calmer now. 'Would the world watch such things happen and do nothing? I don't think so.'

Noah was quick to respond. 'You didn't see the declaration in today's *Gazette*, Babá?'

His father scanned the tabloids on the dining table and shook his head. 'When I arrived at the kiosk, there were no *Gazettes* left.'

Noah pulled a folded newspaper from his back pocket and read aloud:

'"According to the authority I exercise in the name of our Führer and the Supreme Commander of the German Armed Forces, I order the following: Article 1, all Greek residents aged between 16 and 45 years old are bound to perform any work or services the German Army shall demand."

'Archbishop Damaskinos has already exchanged bitter words against the Act. They can't conscript us! Anyway, Damaskinos won. Wing Commander Speidel has retracted the conscription order.'

Babá's jaw dropped. For a few seconds, he struggled to speak. 'You mean Damaskinos stood up to the Nazis?'

Elizabeth rushed into the room and peered at her older brother, curious to know what was causing the loud voices. Mamá, white-faced, flung her arms around the girl's shoulders and pulled her close.

Babá stared at his family, then addressed his son.

'How can we trust a man who supports anyone who'll give him a kickback, from casino racketeers to collaborationist spies?'

'I don't know about the gossip, Babá, but it's a fact about the documents. We need photographs for new ID cards right away.'

Babá glowered, his body stiff and hunched over.

'Can't you take the pictures?'

Noah shook his head. 'Special paper.'

'Then organise it for everyone. Tomorrow morning for the women, and after work for us.' He slumped into a chair and rubbed his eyes.

Daphne heard Noah's sigh of relief. 'Good. It's better done in a studio. I'll telephone my editor and organise it immediately.'

* * *

'No more art lessons with the German, Daphne.' Her father's voice was so harsh, the family flinched at the start of each sentence.

'But, Babá, I keep telling everyone, he's not a Nazi, he's not even German. Aristotle was born here in Greece, and his family is Austrian. He's a perfect gentleman, and the best teacher in the city.'

'Aristotle now, is it? Hitler is Austrian! No more art lessons, and that's final. Attend your lesson tomorrow, straight after having your photograph taken. You tell him you won't be coming back, and don't argue with me, young lady!'

'But it's not fair—'

58

'Don't answer me back. Go to your room!'

Filled with anger and dismay, Daphne snatched up her sketching things and flounced out. She left the door ajar for fear of slamming it. In her bedroom, she kneeled on the ottoman under the window and stared over the city. Everything looked normal. She could see the Acropolis silhouetted against a navy sky. The quarter moon was a sharp smile, and pinprick stars twinkled merrily. The men in her family were becoming agitated about silly rumours. How could she survive without Aristotle and her art?

* * *

Elijah Abrams strode through Athens, clutching his polished black briefcase stuffed with drachmas. Angelos Evert was in his office with Archbishop Damaskinos.

'You know what I've come for,' Elijah said. 'I don't care what it costs.' He placed his briefcase on the police chief's desk.

Evert, in full uniform, squinted through thick glasses. He had the drooping eyes of a man who hadn't slept for a long time. His face, pale and drawn, seemed emotionless.

'Photographs?' he said.

Elijah nodded. 'In the bag. Just tell me the price and when I can collect them.'

'I'm overrun here. They'll go to my associate, Tsitos. With luck, we'll have them ready in twenty-four hours.'

'And the cost?'

'Whatever the lives of the recipients are worth to you.'

After a moment, Elijah passed the briefcase over. 'I'll return tomorrow evening. I'd like the bag back – it was my father's.'

* * *

The chief of police and the archbishop spent the night working in the newspaper office. They fed pale, thin card into the printing press. The two men battled against the clock, hearts pounding, sweat dripping from their tired faces. They printed false baptismal records and fake ID cards for the Jews of Athens, Piraeus, and some who had escaped from Thessaloníki. With every haste, they worked through the night, fearing the Germans would search the building at daybreak. If they did, it would be impossible to continue.

Further complications went unresolved. They needed to remove the heavy machinery and all the accompanying paraphernalia while the hours of curfew were still in force.

* * *

Noah ducked in and out of alleyways to get to the newspaper office with his offer of help. A special knock on the back door got him inside.

'How's it going?' he asked, peering into Evert's bloodshot eyes.

The chief of police nodded, chewing his lip – an action that made his neat moustache bristle. Noah had been right. The whiskers suggested his allegiance to the Führer, as did the swastika flag draped on his office wall – all part of Evert's deception.

'I have news!' Noah kept his voice low. His chest expanded with pleasure that he could offer real help. 'I discovered there's an underground fortification in Kolonaki, under Lycabettus, built by Metaxas in '39. The resistance hid the entrance, but it's accessible.'

Evert frowned, too tired to experience any elation.

'What're you suggesting, young man?'

'We should dismantle the smaller printing press, take it down into the bunker and reassemble it there. Problem solved!'

Evert thought for a moment, then nodded.

'If you're right, we could set up the photography there, too. Good work. What's your name again?'

*   *   *

Three days later, the members of the Abrams household were quarrelsome.

'Mamá, I'm sure we don't have to wear the yellow star,' Daphne said, pulling on her coat, feeling shocked and victimised to be labelled in this way. 'Babá works for the government. You'd think that he, and us – his family – would be exempt.'

Mamá stopped sewing and looked up from the pile of clothes next to her chair. Daphne wondered how she could accomplish any needlework with such swollen, red-rimmed eyes.

'Nobody's exempt, child, and your father no longer works for the ministry. He's employed in the canteen, peeling potatoes.'

'*What?*'

'Don't say *what* to me!'

Daphne stared around the room, searching for clarity. 'Why? None of this makes sense. Anyway, who would know we're Jewish?'

'Our name tells the world, and there's a *J* stamped on our ID card. They can stop us in the street at any moment, or barge into our home. If a soldier sees by our identity card that we're Jews, and there's no yellow star on our clothes, it's instant execution.'

'What are you saying? That we'll be shot? That can't be right, Mamá. You've misunderstood.'

61

Daphne's eyes widened. A shudder of fright ran through her. Suddenly cold, she rubbed her arms and stared about her, feeling unbalanced and lost.

Her father had his back to the room and appeared to be staring out of the window. His shoulders juddered as if he was gasping for breath. Daphne went to approach him, but Mamá, anticipating her move, placed a hand on her arm and shook her head.

Without turning around, Babá added, 'The cloth ones are only temporary. I've ordered Bakelite yellow stars you can simply pin on your lapel. Uncle Emmanuel, with the enamel factory in Warsaw, is manufacturing a deluxe badge for six zlotys each. He's going to send me some. If we've got to wear them, then we'll wear them with pride. After all, it's the Star of David, our national insignia. Also, we must be home by seven o'clock. Take note, Daphne – no exceptions, no excuses. It's a new law for Jews.'

'Why? What difference does it make?'

'Don't keep asking questions! Just be quiet and obey the rules, all right?' he said bitterly. 'And never, ever, forget to wear the yellow star, or we may never see you again.'

* * *

When Aristotle opened the studio door, he glanced at the badge on Daphne's coat and muttered, 'Dear God!' Then he bundled her inside.

She worked extra hard during her lesson, desperate to do well, and then found herself blushing when his praises came at the end of the session.

'You've made substantial progress, Daphne,' he said. 'So much that I've decided on a treat for tomorrow. I'm going to take you to the national art gallery, where we'll study and discuss the works of Picasso, El Greco and Caravaggio.'

She gasped, unable to speak, her eyes wide with pleasure. Without a thought, she stood on tiptoe and kissed his cheek, then felt her neck burn with a rising blush.

He laughed. 'You're pleased, then? We'll also see works by prominent Greek artists, both old and modern. So don't be late.'

'I won't, I promise.'

She recalled her father's words the evening before: 'At the end of your lesson, you give this letter to von Stroop, do you hear me, Daphne?'

After a night of little sleep, she had continued to rack her brains. There must be a solution. At all costs, she had to avoid handing over the envelope, yet she'd never disobeyed her father before. Could she forget to hand it over? Yes, that was an excellent excuse; it would simply slip her mind.

She couldn't allow the precious afternoon with Aristotle to be spoiled by her parents.

✣   ✣   ✣

Keeping close to the buildings, so as not to draw attention to herself, she hurried towards the studio. Someone reached from the recess of a doorway and caught her arm, gripping the fabric of her blue worsted coat. She spun around and faced the thinnest woman she had ever seen. White, tissue-thin skin was stretched over the bones of her face. Gaunt sunken eyes, wide with distress, peered at her. The woman let go of Daphne's sleeve and swayed as if she had spent more energy than she possessed. She placed both hands against her cheeks, her mouth hanging open as if her head were spinning. Daphne recalled a painting by Edvard Munch.

'Forgive me!' the woman begged. 'My baby's dying of hunger. Please . . . Please help her!'

At that moment, Daphne noticed a small bale of rags at her feet. The woman stooped, and with great tenderness, lifted a tattered bundle.

'Here, take her. I can't bear to have her die in my arms.' She sobbed, thrusting the infant at Daphne.

'Oh! No, no, what can I do?' Daphne protested.

'Give her some milk, I beg you.'

Daphne eased the ragged blanket away from the infant's scrawny face and gasped.

7

FLORA

Corfu, present day

SPIROS GLANCED MY WAY, SMILING. 'You enjoy studying the portraits, don't you?'

'Of course. Paintings are my job, my livelihood – my life.'

He shook his head. 'Sorry, I don't understand.'

'I restore seventeenth- to nineteenth-century artworks for the galleries and museums. It's my job . . . what I do best, how I earn a living.'

'That's interesting.' Our eyes met, and I was taken aback by his amazing lashes. It was difficult not to stare.

'Yes,' I said with a smile, returning my attention to the portraits. He glanced at his watch, then at me, and hesitated on the verge of speaking.

'Look, I . . . My meeting starts in five minutes, but I'd like to continue our conversation. Can I take you for lunch?'

'That's kind of you, but my grandmother's expecting me.'

'I see.' He pulled out his wallet and handed me a card. 'Tomorrow, perhaps? Call me when it suits you.' He studied his Rolex again. 'Sorry, I must go.'

* * *

'A head and shoulders, darling Granny,' I said, setting my easel in the shade of the enormous pine tree. 'Unless you'd like something else? It's not too late to change the composition.'

'It's too chilly out here for a reclining nude, don't you think, dear?' She cupped her breasts and gave them a little up-push, her bony shoulders jigging as she giggled.

'Don't encourage her – she gives me enough trouble,' Yánna called from the door.

'You're so naughty, Granny!' I smiled, loving her all the more. 'The light's perfect now.' I glanced at my watch: 4.30, the hour when a warm luminescence flatters even the sallowest skin tone.

'You didn't have to buy a canvas,' she said. 'I've plenty in the cellar left from when we had the studio.'

'Is that so? I didn't realise the cottage had a cellar, or that you had a studio.'

She held her pose, silent for a moment, yet her gaze darted about while I guessed she struggled to sort matters out in her mind.

'No, you're right, of course. I get confused. They're in the basement of the big house.' Her eyes swivelled towards Mon Repos.

I worked in silence, using a graphite pencil to sketch the contours of her profile, then I started on her eyes. Daphne's focus settled on distant trees.

'But it's no good. You'd never find them. We cemented over the trapdoor. You can't even tell it's there now.'

'Why did you bother to hide a few canvases, *Yiayá*?' I liked to use the Greek words I knew and found the one meaning 'grandmother' pleased her.

She smiled, then frowned. 'I'm not sure. I've forgotten. We hid my husband's paintings down there, too, and my own – wrapped in oilcloth and tied with string. We'd heard the Nazis loved art and stripped the walls of galleries and homes all over Greece.'

'I didn't realise you painted.'

'Of course I did, Aristotle taught me. Weren't you listening?'

'Sorry, Granny, of course, it's just that sometimes . . . Well, it's Mark. He just turns up and distracts me from everything. Then he takes over my heart and mind, as if the real world has melted away. It's really like he's with me . . . standing next to me. Then, I've no clue what's going on, and yes, I realise that sounds bonkers—'

'What does "bonkers" mean?'

'Mad – or at least, a little crazy. Did you feel like this after my grandfather died? Sometimes I think I'm going mad from the loneliness.'

I tried to concentrate on the canvas. I'd become an expert at distracting myself from the grief that waited to pounce if I let my guard down. Daphne had the most wonderful eyes: pale, pale blue from cataracts, yet so open and honest, accentuated by arched brows. I sketched the shape on to the white canvas, allowing my love for her to control my fingers. To my utter dismay, when I looked up to study those eyes again, I caught the tracks of her tears glinting in the sunlight.

'Oh, *Yiayá*! Please don't cry.'

She blinked. Her eyelids, putty-like, almost translucent, pushed plump tears over her lashes and down the valleys and canyons of her angelic face.

'No, it's not you, my darling,' she whispered, her voice thick with sadness. 'It's the memories of what happened. I try to forget – not them, of course – not my family.' Her hand went to the locket. 'Not Isaac or Noah or Aris, but what happened. You see, I did something terrible.'

I shook my head, unable to believe my grandmother could do anything unforgivable, but then I wondered: who was Aris?

Daphne took a deep breath before she continued. 'When I realised what I'd done, well . . . you can't imagine the pain. The

67

glorious thing about my death is that I'll be able to let go of all my sins, at last.' She sniffed hard. 'It will be such a relief. Will you remember that, Flora? You'll be sad, of course, but remember my words. I'll be free of the guilt that's robbed me of sleep and given me so much pain all these years. Best of all, I'll lie in the arms of my dearest Aristotle once more.'

I'd lost the thread of her story. What had she done?

'Sorry, Granny, are you talking about your family?'

'Try to pay attention, Flora.'

'Yes, sorry again.'

I speculated: what if her artworks really were in the cellar of Mon Repos? But, more likely, she was muddled. Before I could ask, she went on.

'I stopped painting after my darling Aristotle passed on. The muse that had supported me since I was a young girl flew to Heaven with him and never returned.' She remained silent for a minute. 'The colour had gone out of my world. Everything was monochrome. I was holding him when he died. Your grandfather, I mean.' She placed the back of her hand against her palm and lifted her arms into a vacant hug. 'Over the years, four people died in my arms – all wonderful – or on the brink of a remarkable life.'

I reached for another tissue and dabbed her eyes.

'Do you want to talk about what took place? Sometimes, it helps to share these things, lightens the load, so to speak.'

She closed her eyes. 'No, I don't. The world is such a beautiful place, it's not good to dwell on the darker things that have happened in it. I mean, look around, Flora. Tell me what you see and describe them to me.'

She made me smile, and as I glanced around, a dark cloud seemed to lift.

'All the surrounding trees are very old, but regal and in robust health. Apart from the earthen paths, the ground is grass-green, and the sky, cerulean blue. Your cottage needs a lick of paint, and next time I come, I'll buy a roller and a can of white emulsion and do it myself.'

She chuckled and muttered, 'Crazy woman!'

'Whoop! There's a swallow, the first I've seen this year, skimming the ground, then soaring upwards. A real acrobat, looping the loop. I see a clump of little iris-type flowers, bursting through the leaf mould under the trees. Also, the chinaberry tree is covered in dainty mauve flowers. Beautiful – there'll be lots of yellow berries hanging off her later. In contrast, the japonica, across the path, is laden with big orange plums.'

'Not plums – *mousmoula*,' Daphne said. 'Loquats, simply delicious.'

'Whatever. I'll pick a dish for you later. I love the leaves, big and bumpy and covered in that fine silver down. The fallen fruit has made a colourful puddle around its trunk and is attracting the bees and butterflies. There's a pair of clouded yellows, flitting up and down, either fighting or mating – it's difficult to tell – and a beautiful red admiral sucking up the fruit juice through his long tongue.'

'Listen, that beautiful song, it's a Sardinian warbler. Can you see him, Flora? Black head, white bib, and a red ring around his eye.' Her excited voice had risen an octave.

I peered at the lower branches of the trees, towards the trilling.

'Sorry to disappoint you, but I'm not great at spotting birds, Granny.' A memory of our Saturday afternoons' birdwatching came back to me and my heart squeezed. 'Mark was the expert on our feathered friends.'

She turned her head and raised her chin. A regal expression with an air of stubbornness – or was it strength? I decided to paint her in the soft colours of spring, and daubed a selection of acrylics onto my palette. Then I began mixing for the background. When I looked up again, she was sleeping with a soft smile on her lips.

8

DAPHNE

Athens, 1943

DAPHNE PEERED AT THE SCRAWNY baby, her heart thudding with equal measures of love and loathing. So shocked by the little skeleton that blinked at her, life hanging by a thread that could snap at any second, she couldn't stop a sob. Yet, at the same time, she wished to push it back into its mother's arms. Lifting her gaze to speak to the woman, Daphne found she had fled, running impossibly fast for a woman so thin.

'Wait! Wait for your baby!' Daphne shouted, alarming the infant.

Riddled with guilt, she remembered her mother's warning of TB and lice and smallpox caught from beggars. She rushed towards the studio and rang the first-floor bell. A window opened above her head.

'I'll be down just now!' Aristotle called.

'No! I must come up. Let me in!' she replied, hardly able to get the words out.

'What's going on?' he asked, opening the street door. 'What have you there?'

The sympathy in Aristotle's voice broke her resolve to be strong.

'It's a little baby. It's dying, Aristotle, dying!' Aware of her tears collecting, she swallowed hard and continued. 'Please, do you have some milk? I feel responsible for her and can't bear the thought of losing her.'

'Yes, of course. Come on up.'

They hurried to the studio where Aristotle inspected the tiny child.

'She's cold. Wrap this around her.' He pulled at a muslin cloth that covered a painting, and Daphne caught it as it slid from the canvas.

'Oh, how exquisite,' she muttered, after gasping at the painting of a shapely, and obviously wealthy, aristocratic woman.

Depicted in rich creamy skin tones, her ochre hair, amber jewellery, and the deep burgundy of a swirling velvet cloak complemented one another perfectly. Backing this opulence, a clear, billowing blue and white sky blazed from the canvas and seemed to stress the unfair situation at hand: the haves and have-nots. She returned her attention to the grey baby's bony face, which seemed even paler now.

The child must live!

'How can we feed her? I don't have a bottle.'

'Like a bird. Look, I have some cotton gloves for charcoal work. Put one on, then dip your finger into the milk and let her suck it.'

Daphne followed his instruction. The infant sucked three times, then went limp. Its eyes relaxed, peaceful, almost smiling, but then glazed.

'No! No, you must suckle,' she implored. 'Come on now, be a good girl. Your mamá will miss you.'

Gently, she tapped her finger against the baby's lips, but the baby's mouth fell open in a lifeless gape. All the futility of war and persecution rose up inside Daphne.

'Aristotle, help me, please. Make her feed. The baby's my responsibility. What am I doing wrong?' She gasped, refusing to accept that the baby's life was over.

He reached for the tiny child.

'She's gone to God, Daphne. There's nothing we can do.'

He lifted the baby from her arms and laid it on the armchair.

Daphne stared at her cradling arms, cupped before her but empty now

'Oh, I feel so sad, Aristotle. The poor little mite. She hadn't a chance – look how thin she is.'

'I'll take her to the church. They'll give her a Christian burial. You stay here and wait for my return.'

Overwhelmed by sadness, Daphne collapsed against Aristotle's chest.

'Why couldn't I save her? I failed so badly, but I didn't know what to do.'

'Don't criticise yourself. The poor baby was beyond help, Daphne. Even though the mother knew she was about to die of hunger, she couldn't save her own infant. What chance did we have?' Aristotle spoke gently as he bundled the infant up. 'I'll be back soon. Don't answer the door to anybody. Will you be all right?'

Despite her breaking heart, she nodded, unable to speak for the pain in her throat. How tragic to have a child and fail to keep it alive. Her spirit wilted under the enormity of it. A little baby who didn't even have a name that she knew of, had died in her arms. Tears rolled down her cheeks.

Aristotle put the infant down and opened his arms to Daphne again. She melted into the comfort of his embrace until her sobs quietened. He rubbed her back.

'She's at peace, dear Daphne. Please don't cry. I can't stand to see you upset like this.' He kissed her cheeks, then her tear-stained eyes.

Daphne pressed her body against his and tilted her face upwards, longing to feel his lips on hers, and when she did, her legs almost collapsed beneath her. Knowing she would never feel exactly like that again, so lost in love, her heart beat like fury. The moment of her first kiss would stay locked inside her, and she knew she would recall every sensation whenever her spirit needed lifting – to the end of her days.

'Oh, dear. I'm so sorry, Daphne. Please forgive me. That was most improper – I apologise.' He eased away from her.

'It was wonderful,' she whispered.

His eyes widened. 'Please, forget it happened. I must take the baby to church. Make yourself at home and I'll return as soon as possible.'

He seemed flustered, angry with himself. She noticed a tremble in his voice. Her fingers flew to her lips.

He kissed me!

Daphne's heart raced, and then plummeted with thoughts of the poor dead infant. Her insides shook, tumbling like a clockwork clown.

Aristotle returned in less than half an hour.

'The priest will take care of everything. It's been an upsetting morning, but I think we must still go to the gallery, Daphne. The trip will take your mind away from all this.'

They set off at a brisk pace. When he saw a German patrol at the end of the street, Aristotle nudged her into an alley.

'It's forbidden, Daphne. We can't be seen together. I'll meet you inside the building. Do you have your papers with you?' Daphne nodded. 'Good, give me a minute, then follow me.'

He stepped out of the alley and headed towards the art gallery.

Now she was alone, Daphne's legs trembled. The baby's death had made her weak, disconnected from the real world. She

74

glanced around in search of somewhere to sit and noticed some steps in a nearby doorway, a little deeper into the alley. However, an intolerable stench assaulted her senses – the disgusting odour made her belly heave. Her head spun so violently, she almost lost her balance. She staggered back to the open street and leaned against the corner stones, gulping deep breaths of fresh air. Relieved, she saw the soldiers had turned down another road, so she rushed towards the gallery. Almost there, she recognised two school friends standing outside.

'*Yiasou*, Drosoula and Maria, what's happening? Are you coming into the gallery?'

Delighted that they would see Aristotle at her side, her nerves and nausea settled down.

They shook their heads. 'There's a sign – No Jews! We can't go in.'

A German soldier strode towards them.

'What is happening here?' he demanded.

'We want to visit the museum,' Daphne said. 'But they won't let us in.'

He stared at the yellow badges on each of their coats.

'Split up. Three or more people together are a gang, and against the law. If you don't want to get shot, go home!' He stood with his feet apart, shoulders square, and his hand on the black leather pistol holder at his waist.

'Shot!' Drosoula trembled. 'We're schoolgirls . . . You wouldn't shoot us, would you?'

They huddled together, arms around one another's shoulders.

His eyes narrowed. 'Don't be difficult! Just split up and leave!' Another two soldiers marched towards them. 'Run, now!' the first soldier said. 'Or they *will* shoot you!'

The three girls raced away, Drosoula and Maria in one direction and Daphne back the way she had come. Halfway along the street, she saw a distant platoon heading her way. Dramatic events from the morning filled her with fear and confusion. Panic welled inside her as she stepped back against the building. She wanted to melt into the architecture.

What will they do if they get hold of me?

Trembling, she dived into the same alley that had repulsed her earlier, then hurried along towards the stepped doorway. Until the coast was clear, she would hide there. Pulling a sleeve over her mouth to filter out the worst of the stench, she pressed herself into the door's alcove, waiting until the soldiers had passed, and praying they hadn't seen her.

The sound of stamping boots drew nearer. Her heart pounded. The stink became so overpowering that she held her breath until her lungs were bursting and her head buzzed on the verge of a faint. Turning, she leaped up the three stone steps, flattened herself against a door, and kept her sleeve pressed against her mouth. The stench, now horrific, swirled about her; then a thick cloud of flies appeared, buzzing and bumping into one another close to her face. She felt creepy tickles on her legs and inner thighs, and then one on her face. She almost cried out; fear of the insects clamped her mouth closed. Forced to breathe through her nose, she inhaled the awful stink of death, then saw the cause. A body, filthy and in rags, was huddled in the dark corner of the doorway, appearing to be nothing but a pile of rubbish. As she stared at it, a bluebottle crawled out of its nose and buzzed towards her. Daphne's stomach heaved.

German soldiers turned into the passage. The sound of their marching boots on cobbles drew nearer. Trapped, she thumped on the door – there was no escape! The stamping boots came closer and closer, and just as they were almost upon her, the door opened.

Daphne didn't know if she was in the territory of friend or foe as she fell onto the parquet floor inside. She scrambled to her feet and, without even glancing at the person who closed the door again, raced straight through the corridor towards a heavy oak door ahead.

Sobbing and desperate, she threw the bolts and tugged desperately at the locked door before everything rushed away and she was falling, falling, sinking into a dark abys.

* * *

'There, there, you're safe, don't worry.' A woman's voice drifted down into Daphne's semi-conscious mind. Light filtered under her lashes, but she lay still. 'Everything's all right. You just fainted, but you're in safe hands,' the woman's voice continued.

Daphne felt a cold, wet cloth press against her forehead.

A young man's voice said, 'She's coming round. She'll be all right. It must have been a terrible scare, to see old Mavro in that state.'

'They're coming to take him away, poor soul,' the woman said. 'He's been there over the weekend, judging by the state of him.'

Daphne opened her eyes. 'Where am I?' she whispered, staring up, then squinting against the light from a bare bulb in the beamed ceiling. You're in the soup kitchen. I'm Kyría Alice.' The thin, middle-aged woman wore a simple grey dress with a starched white collar and flat lace-up shoes. Her dark hair, pulled back into a tight bun, had released a few strands that hung around her face in spiralling tendrils, softening her appearance.

'What's your name, korítsi?'

'I'm Daphne Abrams. I wanted to go to the museum. I was supposed to meet my art tutor, Aristotle von Stroop.'

Kyría Alice tugged the arm of a youth standing near the door.

'Hurry down to the museum, find von Stroop and tell him what's happened, but be quiet about it. Quickly now!'

Minutes later, Daphne was sipping herbal tea with Kyría Alice.

'We do our best to help the needy here,' she said, 'in particular the hungry, but we've struggled for money since the beginning. My aunt was a saint in the last war, and I owe most of my expertise in running the soup kitchen to her. Now, I'm almost out of cash, food and ideas.'

'Can't your aunt come and help you?' Daphne asked, turning to stare at the door and the thud of passing soldiers' boots.

The kindly woman cupped Daphne's chin and turned her head so they were face-to-face. 'I'm deaf – I need to see your mouth when you speak, to lip-read. Say that again.'

'Can't your aunt come and help you?' Then, feeling stupid, she realised she had over pronounced the words.

Kyría Alice smiled forgivingly. 'She would if she could, *korítsi*. The Bolsheviks murdered her and her family after the revolution. My aunt was the Grand Duchess Elizabeth Feodorovna of Russia.'

Daphne gasped. She'd heard that name in school. So who exactly was this woman? 'What, murdered? Why would anyone do such a terrible thing? Weren't you afraid for yourself?'

She smiled. 'The British government spirited my husband and children to safety. I'll always be grateful.'

Daphne wondered what this gentle woman was doing working in a soup kitchen if she had a husband and children and was protected by the British government.

'What will you do?' she asked, eyes swivelling to stare at the front door, afraid soldiers might barge in at any moment.

Kyría Alice stared at her mouth, then followed her gaze.

'I put my life in God's hands.' She turned her large blue eyes upwards and crossed herself. 'We need money for food, and more help, so that we can stay open around the clock and seven days a week. If we'd been open over the weekend, I doubt old Mavro would have died. The poor man has six children, and every drachma he earned went towards buying them food.'

'This is too awful,' Daphne said once she had recovered, and looked around the sparse room. 'I had no idea this was here.'

She suspected the building had once belonged to a rich sea captain or a noble merchant. Now the room lay stripped of its magnificent furniture and carpets. All that remained of the great gilt-framed paintings were pale squares of clean plaster on the tobacco-stained walls. The only fixtures to be seen were shelves stacked with an odd assortment of bowls, and simple trestle tables on the bare boards. Kyría Alice, with dark circles under her eyes and a grey pallor to her skin, seemed exhausted.

'If my father will allow it, I'd like to offer my help,' Daphne said, when she learned that they fed the starving children of Athens in the building, twice a day.

Kyría Alice glanced at the star on her coat and lowered her eyes. 'I'm n-not sure . . .' she stammered.

'They might forbid me from helping you because I'm Jewish?'

'These are difficult times. We don't know from one minute to the next what's allowed. I'll have to check, but I appreciate your offer.'

The door opened and Aristotle hurried inside.

'Here you are! What happened, Daphne?'

She told him everything while Alice made tea for them all.

'I despair at what the world is turning into,' Aristotle said to Kyría Alice. 'I've heard of the good things you're doing here. Thank you for helping my student.' He glanced at the door. 'The soldiers must not see us together, Daphne, but I'll follow you to make sure you reach home.'

This was a good time to give him the letter from her father, yet she hesitated. Instead, she peered at Kyría Alice, then Aristotle.

'How long will this war last?' she asked.

Aristotle put down his cup. 'That's a big question. I guess the war will end when the strongest side wins.'

'Yes, but how long, do you think?' she pushed him.

'It could be months, but it could just as easily be years.'

'Years? Oh no . . .'

She sighed, wondering once again if she should hand over the letter, when someone started banging on the front door. She caught Kyría Alice's attention. 'Someone is knocking,' she said, making sure the woman could see her lips.

'Who is it?' Daphne called, opening the door a crack and peering out.

'Please, miss, we need help,' a young boy answered.

Kyría Alice peeked out, crossed herself and said, 'It's all right.'

She opened the door and saw two dirty barefoot children in rags. The older one, a skinny boy of about ten years old, held the hand of a little curly-haired girl of around four, whose body shook with silent sobs.

'Please, miss, do you have a little bread for my sister?' the boy said. 'She hasn't eaten for two days.'

'Where are your parents?' Kyría Alice asked, reading his lips.

'Papa left for America six months ago,' he said boldly. 'He promised to make a better place for us, but we haven't heard from him since Mamá died.' The dark fear in his eyes betrayed his devastation.

'I'm sorry, child. How did your mother die?'

'She was having a baby, miss. The baby died, too.'

'God have mercy on us,' Kyría Alice said, crossing herself. 'Come in, quickly now!'

* * *

Grateful for the kindness of Kyría Alice, Daphne shook her head in despair.

'I'll try to send you food. When's the best time to bring it?'

'We live in dangerous times. I'd suggest in the morning, right after curfew, at six o'clock. The streets are so busy then it's easier to go unnoticed. Leave it against the back door, where we found you. Knock once, then go. We'll appreciate every scrap you can bring – crusts, rice, plate scrapings, potato peelings, bones . . . everything. Even a piece of mouldy cheese will allow a child to live another day.'

That night, Daphne could not relax. The starving children and dying babies of Athens haunted her. In the end, she pulled her sketchbook and charcoals from her bag, sat on her bed, and drew all the scenes that had disturbed her. Dawn light seeped under her curtains when, exhausted, she fell asleep. Sunlight blazed through her bedroom window when her mother pulled the curtains back.

Mamá placed a hand on her daughter's forehead.

'You're ailing with something,' she said. 'We couldn't wake you this morning. Come down, breakfast is ready.'

Horrified, Daphne dressed and raced downstairs.

'Mamá! I have to take food to the soup kitchen. There are starving children. I promised Kyría Alice.'

'The soup kitchen? No, no, no! I've heard of these places. The dregs of the city go there to eat. I heard from Cook that one of them used a knife to kill a man, all for a piece of bread, only last week. It's not the establishment for a nice young lady. Besides, I've told you before, you don't know what you might pick up from those people – typhus, malaria, consumption.' She shook her head. 'It's too terrible. I forbid you to go anywhere near those awful establishments. I'd never forgive myself if you caught something.'

She wrung her hands and stared at the window as if expecting the unfortunates to arrive at their door at any minute.

Daphne glared at her mother.

What should I do?

9

FLORA

Corfu, present day

DAPHNE'S EYES CLOSED AND HER head lolled forward so I took off my long cardigan and draped it across her chest. She opened her eyes.

'Would you rather stop now, Granny? I've enough detail to lay down the skin tones and outline.'

'Oh dear, was I snoozing? You carry on, it's not a problem, or we could break for a nice cup of tea and one of your delightful dunkers.'

'Sounds perfect. I'll put the kettle on.'

'No, ask Yánna. She'll be playing poker online if there's any Wi-Fi.'

I smiled. Yánna had to be seventy-plus. Inside, I found my grandmother was correct about the gambling. My first instinct was to grab my phone and check for my results while there was a signal, but I decided to wait until the evening.

'Yánna, can we have some tea and biscuits on the lawn? And you know what? I'll be here all afternoon. If you need to go out for anything, or take a few hours off, just say.'

Yánna's thick, dark eyebrows rose and her plump face broke into a smile.

'Thank you! Thank you! I go to see my friend if Daphne says it's all right. Popi is no so well and I worry. Food is all ready, is in there.' She nodded at the wood-fired oven. The room was bursting with delicious aromas: tomato, oregano, lamb and onions. 'I bring your tea in five minutes. Is OK?'

'Lovely, thanks.'

I returned to Daphne, who seemed alert and was waiting for me.

'If it's all right with you, I'll get a little more done before the sun goes down, then we'll go indoors for supper.'

'Do you have to go back to your hotel, or can you stay longer this evening, child?' Daphne asked. 'I have something important to say.'

'Of course I'll stay, thank you,' I said, although the dark feeling I'd had when I received her letter returned.

* * *

'That was the kindest thing!' Daphne said. 'Her eyes lit up when you said she could have your room and all the hotel facilities until tomorrow evening?' Granny chuckled. 'You know, I don't think Yánna has ever stayed in a hotel, never mind a five-star, bless her. What a wonderful thing to do, Flora. Thank you.'

'The hotel didn't mind. It's all the same to them and, in return, I promised them a first-class write-up on Tripadvisor and Booking.com. Anyway, Yánna has been so thoughtful she deserved it. Did you notice her expression when I told her?'

She had set the table in a bustle of excitement.

'Just to let you know, I've made Corfu chicken pie for later, Flora. I recalled that you and your husband liked it a lot, and lamb *kléftiko* for lunch.' Yánna had stilled for a few seconds. 'It must be very hard to be here without him.'

When Yánna had gone, my heart filled with pathos, remembering how Mark had winked at me before he complimented

Yánna on her delightful cooking. My husband had a knack for sensing what people needed. He'd sense when people were down, and would pick them up with a joke, or a couple of kind words. I laughed to recall his words when she presented her chicken pie: 'Why can't you cook like Yánna, Flora? You must divorce me so that I can marry this wonderful pie maker!' He'd enjoyed making me laugh, too, and this minor incident had become a fun moment between us from that day on. Whenever we disagreed about something, he'd say, 'If you're not careful, I'll run off with the pie maker.' I'd reply in mock anger, 'Can you give me ten minutes to pack your case and make you a sandwich?' Then we'd fall into each other's arms, laughing.

'What are you thinking?' Daphne asked.

'Just remembering. Mark loved coming here, you know. Remember how he clowned around, making Yánna blush when he kissed her hand and begged her to run away with him so he could eat her amazing pies for ever after? He was a such a tease, wasn't he? "Marry me before Flora poisons me with her terrible cooking," he said. I loved him so much, Granny, and he loved me. He never looked at another woman in all our years together.'

Suddenly, tears were tripping down my face. I turned from her and smudged them away.

'He was a wonderful man,' Daphne said, as if she felt my pain. 'We all loved him.'

'He enjoyed coming to Corfu, Granny. Just before the end, he said, "Tell Daphne and Yánna I've had some of the best times of my life with them, and they mustn't be sad." Oh, Granny. I can't imagine ever being as happy as we were when we came on holiday here.'

She patted my hand. 'One day, you'll remember saying that and smile to yourself. I promise you will be as happy in the

future as you have been, on this island of Corfu, in the past –
and Mark would want that for you, too, trust me.'

*   *   *

'So come on, Granny, now that we're on our own.' I raised my
glass. 'It's time to disclose these secrets you've been hinting at.'

She took another sip of wine. 'Are you sure you're up to this,
Flora?'

I stared at my own feet, battling to keep control.

'I wonder if my loss will ever get any easier, Granny.'

'It's difficult to imagine life will ever return to normal, but it
will, dear girl.' It seemed the world was hanging on to her words
as she spoke. 'Let me tell you something, Flora. Many years
ago, I murdered somebody who was precious to me,' she said.
'Somebody I loved.' After a sigh so deep that her whole body
trembled, she drooped with sadness. 'I thought I'd never recover
from that horror. At first, I wanted to join him, to end it all. But
Yánna depended on me, and anyway, the wounds healed. The
pain has never left me, but I know I can go on.' She closed her
eyes for a second. 'Looking back, I realise my love for Aristotle
started with a very simple situation. A workman came to our
apartment to fix the faulty electrics. He should have started the
following month but, because of the situation in Athens, he had
decided to take his family to Cairo in a few days. He hoped to
do the job before he left. Babá had already gone to work at the
town hall, so Mamá wrote a note and instructed me to give it to
the receptionist in the government building and await a reply.'

I wondered where this was leading.

'As I entered the lobby, a rather unusual portrait of our mayor
drew my attention. The eyes followed me as I approached the

desk. There was humour in the mayor's image, as if he was trying not to laugh.'

My grandmother stared into space, her eyes wide, and I guessed she had lost herself in the distant memory.

'Granny?'

'Yes, oh dear, I can see it. Anyway, I went closer and read the brass plate below the picture. The artist was my teacher, Aristotle von Stroop. Imagine . . . It enthralled me that this same person, a genius as far as I could see, was sharing his enormous talent with me, Daphne Abrams. My love for him took root in that moment. But it was also the spawn that led to an appalling tragedy. I killed . . .' She gasped and sobbed. 'It's no good. I can't say it, not yet, even now, in the ninety-ninth year of my life. Will I ever be able to explain, Flora?'

Daphne's eyes glazed over; her ribcage juddered with a sob as she breathed again. Shocked, I peered at her, aware that my mouth hung open, yet I couldn't speak. I reached out and covered her frail fingers with mine.

Was it true? Had she killed somebody?

'This is what you were desperate to tell me, Granny? Somebody died and you blame yourself?' I struggled to get the words out.

She whipped her hand from under mine. 'No, you're not listening to me. If you're going to make light of what I tell you, we may as well stop.' Her voice was brittle with frustration. She bunched her hand into a fist and banged the arm of her chair. 'I took a life – someone I loved – with my bare hands. Can't you understand how terrible that is?'

'I'm so sorry, I didn't mean to sound disrespectful. Please forgive me, Granny. It's just that I don't know what happened . . . I don't understand, that's all. I love you. I'd never make light of what you tell me, honestly.'

She shook her head, wilting with distress as her tears broke free.

'It's my most painful memory – my ghastly punishment. I've suffered for it all these long years. A diabolical monster in my soul, eating me up. I've had to bear this atrocious secret in silence for most of my existence, lugging it around like an inescapable ball and chain.'

'Please, Granny . . .' My trepidation grew. What was this appalling event she had to transfer onto my shoulders in order to rest in peace? 'Let me get you a glass of water.'

She was shifting her load onto me, freeing herself of this burden that weighed her down. My heart went out to her, poor old thing. I suspected she wanted to join my grandfather, but was bound to this earth by her terrible guilt.

After a lengthy silence, in which we both recomposed ourselves, she gave a slight nod.

'I'll begin with the war, when all things changed for us. In 1943, our comfortable family life came to an abrupt end, thanks to Hitler and his hatred of Jews. At that point, I didn't realise the seriousness of my plight. I was so immature, and my art lessons were the highlight of my world. I was in love with my instructor. But he was of German and Austrian ancestry, and I was a young Jewish woman with a strict father. How could we ever find happiness?'

10

DAPHNE

Athens, 1943

'But, Mamá!' Daphne cried. 'You can't forbid me to help. I have to go – the children are starving to death.'

'Don't be so melodramatic. I do forbid it, and if you speak about it again, I'll have to tell your father. Just mind your own business and be grateful you're well fed.'

Daphne knew very well she shouldn't go against her parents. Still, she spent her pocket money on a bag of split peas for the soup kitchen. Although the British had lifted the food blockade on Athens, prices were still unreachable, and her small bag of fava cost twenty times more than before the war. Her parents weren't bad people. They helped their kitchen maid, Tilly, by allowing her to take home any leftover food for her aged parents; she also took the table scraps for their chickens.

Daphne stuffed her pockets with the table scraps – half an apple, a crust of bread; scraps that had been destined for Tilly's father's chickens, but human life was more important now.

'I'm going out to draw city life, Mamá,' Daphne said right after lunch.

She left the house before her face turned red or her mother could protest. Near Aristotle's studio, she noted the shadows and how the light fell just after midday. Her tutor often quizzed her on the light, testing her powers of observation. As she hurried through town, she saw a gigantic German flag hoisted over the golden pillars of the Parthenon. A sudden gust spread the red fabric, which displayed a menacing black swastika over the city. Even the wind made it clear to the Athenians: they were under Nazi rule. Daphne asked herself: could Greece belong to another nation? *No, no, it could not!*

Thanks to her mother, she knew her country's history very well. Others had tried to dominate Greece – the Ottoman Empire had tried for the longest – but in the end, the country had always returned to its rightful owners, the Greeks. The birthplace of democracy was Athens, where all men are equal.

The moment Daphne arrived at the studio, she turned to her tutor.

'It's all too terrible. I'm quite shaken. There's a swastika flying over the Parthenon.'

'To be honest, I'd no idea things were this bad either, Daphne.'

She showed Aristotle her sketches, then told him she'd left scraps at the soup kitchen's back door, on her way to his studio. Her face heated, remembering her father's letter, which remained deep in her pocket.

* * *

That night, Daphne tossed and turned. At three in the morning, she longed for her mind to stop working so that she could sleep, but the faces of starving children returned. She had to help those poor, skinny souls who were crying with hunger.

Food prices were still rising. People were still dying. The Germans had stripped every wheat field and corn harvest to feed their troops. Now, a simple bag of flour was beyond most people's budget. Her stomach rumbled as she headed downstairs for breakfast. Her privileged family were not starving, but they no longer ate chocolate-covered biscuits, and puddings now had the bitter taste of saccharin, which had also replaced sugar in their coffee.

Isaac cut a great wedge from the fresh loaf on the table, slathered it in butter and strawberry *marmeláda*, but only ate half of it.

'Really, Isaac, people are starving out there,' Mamá said, nodding towards the window.

'And if I eat food that I don't want, it will help them?'

'Don't worry, I'll have it,' Daphne said, cutting it in half and placing the two jammed sides together. She had chosen a full skirt with big pockets, intending to collect as many breakfast scraps as possible, and already had her own sandwich squirrelled away. Soon, her pockets were bulging, so she returned to her room and transferred the bread and jam and crusts to her art bag.

'I'm going out to sketch,' she said to her mother. 'If I'm not back in time for lunch, please don't worry. I won't want to stop if I'm working on a masterpiece. You know how it is.'

'Mind you're home by three o'clock, Daphne. The Brandenburgs and their son are paying a visit this afternoon.' She sighed. 'Thanks to the new rules, they have to be home by seven. So, don't be late!'

'I must hurry,' Daphne said, her heart thumping at the disgrace of her own deception. 'I want to capture the morning light in the city. Can I have some of my allowance, in case I need to buy lunch while I'm out, Mamá?'

She glanced at the clock over the fire – 7.30 already! Would the starving boy and his sister be in the soup kitchen?

'What do you know about Kyría Alice, Princess Andrew of Greece and Denmark?' she asked her mother.

'Let's see ... You know I stopped teaching when I married your father in 1922? Still, that was a big year for Alice. Greece, defeated in Asia Minor, was in the throes of a revolution. The Greeks tried her husband, Andrew, for treason in the Greco-Turkish war and his execution seemed likely.'

Mamá thought for a minute, frowning and gazing into the distance.

'The poor woman's deaf as a stone, you know? Comes from a tragic royal family, too. The Russian side were all murdered in a horrible way. Her gigolo husband escaped execution, but there was a strong chance of him being assassinated by a Greek, like his father. The family was saved when King George the Fifth of England sent a ship, the *Calypso*, to ferry them to France. Her baby boy, Fílippos, was about eighteen months old. I believe her husband ran off with a young girl. Alice was put in an asylum and treated quite badly, they say. Her daughters married blue-blooded Germans. Her son was taken in by British aristocracy and got his education in England.' She folded her arms and shuffled her shoulders. 'Although her mother and father were German, Princess Alice regards herself as British because she was born there, in the castle of her grandmother, Queen Victoria, who was at her birth. Why are you asking?'

'She has a very interesting face. I'd like to paint her portrait.'

'Be careful – she's German, don't forget.' Mamá peered at her art bag, then her face. 'Avoid the soldiers at all costs.' She reached up to the dresser cupboard and took an enamelled tea caddy down, then pulled some drachma notes out. 'If you can find a spinach pie, that should be plenty. Take a bottle of water with you.'

* * *

Daphne hurried towards the soup kitchen, uncomfortable to have deceived her mother. She beat on the back door with her fist and ducked inside the moment it opened.

'Good morning, Kyría Alice. I have a little food for you this morning.' Kyría Alice dried her hands on her apron. 'I have an hour before my lesson, Kyría, can I help you?'

'God bless you, that would be wonderful. You can collect the dishes from the table and bring them to the sink.'

'I can wash them, too. Please, let me help.'

'Marvellous!'

Daphne glanced at the front door when a knock sounded. 'What? Is somebody knocking?' Alice asked. Daphne nodded, admiring the Kyría's powers of observation as she excused herself and hurried to answer it. Three children aged between seven and eleven tumbled into the hall.

'Please, miss, do you have anything left to eat?' the oldest one asked.

Their enormous eyes filled with hope and turned towards her.

'There's nothing left, children. You may return at five o'clock.'

Their thin faces fell.

'Wait,' Daphne said, gently tapping her on the shoulder. 'I've brought some bread, Kyría. May I give it to them?'

The boys stared at her again, straightening their slumped bodies while their dark and tired eyes brightened with hope.

'Wash your hands and faces in the cloakroom before you sit at the table.'

Kyría Alice returned to the big room, where twenty children sat in silence at the tables.

'Time to go, everybody. Hands together and repeat after me, "Thank God for a good meal, amen."'

They chorused her, then crossed themselves.

'You may return at five o'clock, no later. Do you hear?' They all nodded. 'Stay out of trouble and stay safe. All together now, what must you do?'

'Stay out of trouble and stay safe, Kyría Alice,' they chanted.

Daphne watched them file on to the street.

'Where do they go?'

'Best not ask. No point in worrying about things we can't change.'

'I brought a few drachmas – not much, but it's all I could manage.' Daphne delved into her pocket and held out her allowance.

Kyría Alice stared at the cash for a moment. 'Thank you. It will buy beans and fill bellies. Place it in the jar on the shelf.'

She nodded at an old ginger jar that Daphne could only just reach. The group of three returned from the smallest room. Kyría Alice sent them to sit at the table, then placed a bowl before each.

The snaps on Daphne's artist's case clicked louder than usual, and everyone's eyes fixed on her as she unfolded a large starched linen napkin. One child gasped when she revealed her ill-gotten gains. She placed the three thick *marmeláda* sandwiches in the chipped enamel bowls as the children sat with their hands in their laps, staring, trembling while they waited for permission to start.

'You may eat,' Kyría Alice said.

Each child hunched over his dish and curled an arm around it, as if to protect his food from robbers. They ate, eyes closed as they chewed. Daphne wanted to weep. From the sad expression on her face, she knew Kyría Alice felt the same. Another knock at the door interrupted their melancholy. Daphne touched the older woman's arm and indicated the front door.

'Oh dear, now we're in trouble,' Kyría Alice said as she stepped into the corridor. When she opened the door, Daphne saw a barefoot boy of about eleven. He had difficulty carrying a small child.

'Please, miss, am I too late? I couldn't get Doris to walk. She just wanted to lie down, so I had to carry her all the way. She's starving, miss.' The little one's dark-rimmed eyes stared.

'God help us. Come in, both of you.' She took the little girl into her arms and turned to Daphne. 'There is a blanket in the chest. Let's settle her down, poor child.' Kyría Alice placed the little girl on a traditional spindle-backed sofa and spread the blanket over her. 'A little water, but not too much, Daphne. You'll find cups under the sink.' The child gulped the liquid down before she closed her eyes. Kyría Alice turned to Daphne again. 'Take that money back and see if you can buy some rice.'

'No, I'll run home and get some. It'll be quicker than standing in a queue at the shops. I'll be back in ten minutes.'

She turned to leave, then her eyes caught the open artist's case and the white napkin containing Noah's crusts. The boy gobbled them down before Alice could tell him to wash his hands and face.

As she fled home, Daphne noticed people staring at the star on her coat. She hurried indoors and straight through towards the kitchen, where she expected to see her mother with their cook. The kitchen was empty, which pleased her. She did not need to explain. She took a paper bag from the drawer, filled it with rice, twisted the top closed and forced it into her coat pocket. A cry sounded from the sitting room, so she hurried to investigate.

'Where've you been?' her father shouted.

She stared at him in his business suit, his face both drawn and angry.

'Answer me, Daphne. Where have you been?' His anger filled the room like static. 'Why didn't you give von Stroop the letter to end your lessons?' She opened her mouth to speak, but her father shouted her down. 'And don't try lying to me!'

'No, Papa. I was hoping I could change your mind. I thought if circumstances altered, you may relent and allow my lessons to continue. They mean such a lot to me . . .' She stared at the floor. 'How did you know?'

'He came here looking for you, worried about your welfare. A German concerned about a Jew – there's a first!'

'I told you, he's Austrian, and a good man, but you don't believe me.'

'How can I believe you when you deceive me? Besides, his cousin is Jürgen Stroop, a major-general in the SS. People have disappeared on a scale that's not explainable. And now the yellow star. Even me, who held a prominent position in the government, until today!'

'I don't understand.'

'Because, like every other Jew, I may not keep my profession, the one that I worked for all my life. Nor can I hold any kind of authority. I may clean toilets, sweep the street, peel potatoes . . . that's all.'

'Please, Papa, Aristotle warned me, too—'

'Aristotle! First-name terms, is it?'

'Papa, he's not like the rest of them. He told me if I work hard, I could be one of the greatest painters of the decade. Please allow me to continue with my art lessons.'

Daphne's father squinted at her. 'And there's another thing. If you weren't with him, and you weren't home, where were you?'

'I went to give a little help in the soup kitchen.'

'Soup kitchen? What is that?'

'Please, Papa, don't be so angry with me. The soup kitchen feeds our starving city children twice a day. It's halfway down Athena Street.'

'I'm not having you going there. It's too dangerous.'

'That's not fair!' she cried. 'Now it's you who's discriminating, Babá. Just because I'm a girl. If Isaac or Noah wanted to help through their own charity, you'd be proud of them.'

He stared at her, shocked that she had answered him back.

'Anyway, my art case is there, so I must go back for it. I'll be home later, when I hope we can discuss this further without raising our voices.'

She spun around and left before he could respond. In the hallway, she recalled the breakfast table set for morning coffee, which they had now finished. A plate of *kourabiethes* – shortbreads dusted with icing sugar – stood next to the coffee pot.

The scullery maid approached with a tray.

'Get me the *kourabiethes*, quick as you can, Tilly,' Daphne ordered.

She could hear raised voices from the sitting room as the maid returned with a loaded tray.

One pocket bulging with biscuits, the other with rice, Daphne hurried back to the soup kitchen, wondering where she had found the nerve to talk to her father with such boldness? Sensing more danger in the air, she kept her head down and walked in the shadows, aware of every sound. Still, her nerves prickled and the urge to run was difficult to resist. She wore her strawberry-pink wool coat with a grey velvet collar, and a burgundy beret, to impress Aristotle. Now feeling all eyes on her, she wished her clothes were less conspicuous. She knocked on the back door, almost shedding tears of relief.

'Sorry I was so long,' she said to Kyría Alice. 'I had a brief altercation at home. I've brought some rice.'

'Put it on the gas to boil. I'm not sure she will last much longer.'

Daphne gasped, then, filled with shame for her privileged life, admitted she didn't know how to boil rice.

'Oh dear. Do I put it in boiling water, or cold water? I've never done this before.' Her cheeks were burning. 'I want to help you so much, but I'm afraid I'm quite useless, Kyría.'

'Never mind, you'll learn. We should wash the rice, then drop it into boiling water, but we need all the starch we can get, so put one cup of rice in four cups of cold water in the pan, and keep stirring until it boils. Her stomach may not be strong enough for solid food.' She turned to the boy. 'What's your name?'

'Petros, Kyría.'

'Petros, take that string bag hanging on the door, then run to the butcher's on October Street. Say – Kyría Alice sent you and does he have any free bones for the children today? Hurry now.'

'Here,' Daphne said, handing him a shortbread as he passed her.

His eyes widened, and he had the biscuit in his mouth before he reached the door. Daphne took a bowl and emptied the rest of the *kourabiethes* into it.

'Oh, lovely. May I have one?' Kyría Alice asked.

'I brought them for you. If you don't mind me saying so, you look half-starved yourself, Kyría Alice.'

Daphne went to the tap to wash the icing sugar off her fingers.

'No!' Alice stopped her. 'Let poor Doris suck the sugar from your fingers. We need to boost her energy one baby step at a time. A little sugar, a little rice starch in an hour, then some soft rice later, and perhaps a little warm milk and one of your biscuits this evening. Tomorrow, a little soup and bread ... if she makes it through the night.'

'I have a lot to learn.' Daphne hooked her arm under the small child's head and lifted it a little. 'I've got some lovely powdered sugar on my finger, Doris. Would you like to taste?'

The toddler's eyelashes fluttered, and her mouth opened a little.

'I'll give you some sweet rice water in a moment. You have a little rest, all right?'

She eased a cushion under the girl's head.

The boy returned with a bag of bones from the butcher.

'Thank you, young man. Take another biscuit, then ask the grocer on the corner if he has any compost.'

Petros nodded, took a biscuit and the string bag, then hurried on his errand.

'Compost?' Daphne asked.

'The outer leaves of cabbage, cauliflower and broccoli, yesterday's lettuce, tops from carrots and sometimes beetroots, pea and bean pods. The soup stock comes from the boiled bones. When he returns, I'll send him to the kitchen door of the Grand Bretagne. They'll give him potato and carrot peelings, meat scraps, and a bucket of plate scrapings.'

'Yuck – sounds disgusting.'

'With salt and herbs, it's not bad, and it puts nourishing food in the bellies of the starving. Most of these little ones have lost their parents to hunger. I've lost count of how many Athenians have died of starvation. Many thousands. We must stop it from happening to the children. They say Churchill is allowing food to come through his blockade at last, but we're not seeing it. We'll manage without fuel and furniture, but if the population doesn't eat, there'll be no one left to save from the Nazis.'

11

FLORA

Corfu, present day

Daphne closed her eyes and leaned into the cushion behind her head. Recalling the soup kitchen story had left her drained. She relaxed, allowing me to absorb the finer details of a face that had known life's extremes. As I studied her, I could see the model in the art gallery painting with all the rigours of life etched in dramatic layers over her beautiful features. Eyes that had cried a thousand tears. Lips, always fixed with the ghost of a smile for Aristotle, as if she continued to share every moment with him. A mouth that had whispered words of endearment, cried for help, and perhaps screamed in terror – and also kissed her lover with passion and her baby with extreme tenderness. A nose that had enjoyed her man's scent, the seasons, and the aroma of foods cooked with love. She took pleasure from the perfume of jasmine and honeysuckle and fresh-baked bread. Her cheeks, although supported by high, aristocratic cheekbones, were soft and pale as a baby's belly, for they'd lain against her newborn's delicate skin and were, too often, drenched by tears of loss. Now, in its final years, her face had settled in soft folds and delicate colours, like abandoned satin.

I analysed the lived-in appearance of my grandmother and transferred the layers of its structure onto the canvas, slowly building an image of this woman who had lived so long and experienced so much. I imagined her hard life as a young Jew in the war, yet I saw no sign of bitterness around her eyes. Although this face had experienced rivers of sadness, the gentle undulations made by smiles, dominated. Granny Daphne was the most precious thing I had.

My heart ached when I heard of the tragedy she had experienced, and I suspected there was more to come. Her situation seemed impossible. How could the world stand by while children starved to death?

I had longed to have a baby with Mark. Longed beyond longing. Yet we were denied that privilege. To hear of Daphne's utter distress when that newborn died in her arms was very hard for me. I returned to my painting determined to stop my anger becoming so intense that it forced its way into my brushstrokes and lurked, like the Ghost of Christmas Past, in bleak shadows on the canvas.

Suddenly, I was full of Mark – his love for me, the precious years we had together. Knowing Daphne had also travelled this awful road of bereavement, and understood my pain, was one vital thing we shared, and her embracing comprehension and sympathy lifted my spirits and set me on a path of healing.

Satisfied with the portrait's foundation, I loaded the palette with fresh acrylics and filled in the shadows by mixing a little dark green and red and laying it on with a flat brush. I wanted heavy brushstrokes to add texture and drama to the portrait's background. Although almost a hundred years old, there was nothing withered about my grandmother's face. Her large, pale eyes, their colour rinsed by a lifetime of tears, remained closed until Yánna arrived with tea and cakes.

'Dearest Granny, you're telling me that when you were only a girl, someone's baby died in your arms?'

She lowered her eyelids and turned her face down and sideways, affirming the truth of her story.

'What an unbearable event for a young girl to live with for the rest of her life.'

'It's not the worst thing that ever happened to me,' she said. 'Let's talk about something else. I find sadness exhausting.'

I considered my own life, but had nothing to say that wouldn't involve Mark and be too painful for our conversation.

'Tell me about Mon Repos. Have there been rumours about its impending demolition?'

A strange sound came from Daphne's throat – part gasp, part cry. Her eyes widened, and she grasped the wheelchair's armrests, trying to pull herself up. She stared across the parkland towards the mansion.

'No,' she gasped. 'They can't do that, Flora!'

Alarmed by Daphne's panic, I eased her back into the chair.

'Granny, take it easy. It's just gossip. I wondered if you knew anything.'

'Where did you hear this?'

'Remember, I told you about the luggage, and how I came to meet the architect, Spyridon? Well, I overheard his conversation with a builder at Mon Repos. I can't quite make sense of him, Granny. He seemed so nice, and even invited me out to lunch, though I didn't accept.'

'You must go,' she said. 'Find out what's happening. I told you, my . . . my husband's . . . canvases are in the cellar. More than that. Oh, if only I could tell you everything!' She thumped herself three times in the chest, muttering a few words of prayer to herself, then I realised she was weeping. 'I can't bear for those pictures, and our secrets, to be buried forever like his poor dead body,' she sobbed. 'You can't imagine how much I loved him, Flora.' She looked up with swimming eyes. 'But then again, you can, can't you? Why is life so cruel to us?' Her chest jerked as her emotions escalated.

'Poor Granny, but why can't you tell me?'

'Because I promised Aristotle I'd never tell. You see . . . terrible things took place. I've never spoken of them because they would put me in prison for murder.'

'Granny, I swear on my life, nobody is going to put you in prison.'

'Say you'll help me? Then I can die in peace. God won't take me until I've told the truth and atoned for my sins.'

'Calm down, darling Granny. Everything will be all right. I give you my word.'

'How can I calm down? I'll go mad. They'll put me in the asylum with the other lunatics. Tie me down and electrocute me. They did it before, after Aristotle died, after they branded me as a collaborator, but I was younger then, and stronger.'

'Please, Granny, take some deep breaths. Where are your pills?' I reached across and took her hand in mine. 'Would you prefer a glass of wine or tea?'

She nodded, smudging her tears away. 'Yes, yes. Forget the pills. Let's finish the *krasí*.'

'That's more like it.' I poured her another glass of red. 'I was thinking about Mark, Granny. Before he died, he begged me to find new love and have the children we wanted so much. We were trying for a child right up to the end. Trying too hard, my doctor said.

I closed my eyes and recalled Mark's voice. 'Just because I couldn't fill your belly with my child, doesn't mean it should remain empty, Flora. I want you to have children, my love.'

'I won't become invisible because the love of my life has died, Granny. I'm determined. Once I'm over the pain, I hope there'll be new love and new life, but only because there has been Mark, first. Does that make sense?'

'Tell me about him,' Granny said. 'I only met him half a dozen times, when you came here on holiday.'

I smiled, as I so often did when I thought about our lives together.

'Few people marry the first person they love and remain happy. Our first holiday together, when we were nineteen, was backpacking around classical Greece. We flew to Athens, stayed in a sweaty, overcrowded hostel and walked the city for four days. Then we bussed it to Corinth, overwhelmed by the archaeological site and the museum.' I laughed, reliving our time together, lost in the adventure.

'Go on,' Granny said.

'We slept in a small two-man tent in an olive grove and woke to the clatter of bells. A herd of curious goats had surrounded us. One stuck its head under the tent flap and nibbled my sleeping bag. The loud voice of a very unkempt shepherd with barking dogs frightened us to death. We scrambled into our clothes. The shaggy-bearded goatherd was only being friendly, though it took us a minute to realise it. He treated us to smelly cheese and raki for breakfast. Then he started playing his goatskin-and-bamboo bagpipes. Oh my God, what a racket.'

Granny grinned, taking in every word.

'Our next destination was the ancient hilltop city of Mycenae, where King Agamemnon ruled. Do you know it?' Granny shook her head. 'The place had been a Bronze Age citadel far above sea level, safe from raiding pirates. The sky seemed to go on forever, blue as can be, Granny. We camped among pine trees that permeated the freshest, sweet-tasting air. We saw Agamemnon's tomb, the remains of his palace, and the Lion Gate.' I smiled, filled with the memory. 'We stood alone, holding hands inside the Treasury of Atreus, which was like one of those old-fashioned beehives made of clay or braided straw ... skeps, I think they're called. However, this building was gigantic.'

My grandmother's eyes widened as her imagination took hold.

I sighed as magical moments came back to me. 'In the treasury, Mark whispered, "One day I'll marry you," and I turned to him and kissed him and said, "Yes, I know." Then I laughed so much when I saw what Mark had written in big letters on the side of our tent – NO GOATS ALLOWED.'

'I'll bet people said you were too young to know what love is.'

I nodded, smiling, remembering. 'In ancient Epidaurus there's a theatre, you can't imagine the size. An enormous semi-circle of seats that got wider as it got higher, and seated fourteen thousand people, can you imagine? The place had perfect acoustics. This meant everyone could enjoy the performance below without microphones or amplifiers.'

'Because of the auditorium's shape?'

'Well, yes, but also because they cut the seats from limestone, which absorbs low-density sounds and amplifies high-frequency sounds. Quite amazing, considering they built it four-hundred years before Christ! Anyway, let me tell you this, Granny – it was mid-August and sweltering hot. Mark stood in the middle of the marble theatre floor while I climbed the blooming seats. Honestly. Shattered and sunburned, I reached the highest row. "Flora!" he shouted from the ground and, though I recognised his voice, he was so far away it took me a moment to pick him out of the other tourists. "I'm here!" I shouted, and stood on the topmost seat, waving back. "Marry me!" he called.'

Granny's smile widened. 'The moment he proposed to you?'

'Everyone heard him – everyone! Tourists turned to see who had asked for my hand, then they peered at me. "Go on, luv! We're all waiting," a British tourist said. "Yes! I'll marry you!"

The acoustics didn't work in the opposite direction, when I shouted back. "Speak up, I can't hear you," he called. The breeze took my voice away at the top of the stadium. Surrounded by clapping, smiling people, they sent my answer back down to ground level. "She said yes!" "She said yes!" "She said yes!" they shouted, passing my reply down the steep semicircle of seats. Blushing, unaccustomed to the attention of strangers, I started down. People patted me on the shoulder and offered their congratulations. People were so happy for us, Granny.'

12

DAPHNE

Athens, 1943

In the studio, Daphne stared at her blank canvas.

'That poor little girl, Aristotle. Have you ever seen such starvation? Arms and legs like matchsticks, and her face shrivelled like an old woman's.' Her heart squeezed with grief. 'It's terrifying to think a person's life could end, just like that. Can we do anything about it?'

'We can do two things as artists. Capture the genuine drama and emotion behind a scene, and also record the truth. Both have their value.'

Daphne swished her brush in a jar of turpentine. 'But how? Her enormous eyes are haunting me, and I'm finding it impossible to focus on anything else. I'll have to end my lesson early. I'm sorry.'

'Because of what happened today, or ...? Well, if it's the money, Daphne, please forget about it. You must keep painting, do you understand? I feel sure there's genius in you and it's my duty to find it.'

'You're too kind, but it's not the money. I have my allowance, so, if my father continues to be difficult, I'll pay you myself.'

'Your father's being difficult?'

'It's nothing. Forget I mentioned it. No, it's the children, you see. They're tearing my heart to pieces, and I can't think of anything but their pale faces and enormous eyes.'

'That's why you can't paint a landscape today. Paint the scenes that move you so much you can't ignore them. That's where you'll find true inspiration.' He smiled. 'That's the very reason I wanted to paint you, dear Daphne. You fill my head with images of great beauty, halting all my other work.' Daphne felt her cheeks heat with a blush. 'Oh dear, there I go embarrassing you again,' he said. 'You must remind me to be more careful with my words. Let me accompany you back to the soup kitchen and set up your easel there. Didn't you say Kyría Alice serves the soup at five o'clock?' Daphne nodded. 'Then you carry your art case and I'll bring the easel. I'm sorry we can't walk together, but I'll not be far behind you.'

* * *

Daphne entered by the back door, guessing Aristotle would enter by the front. Inside, Kyría Alice continued to stir the soup.

'They must wear you out, Kyría,' Daphne said. 'Can't you rest for a while? I can take over from you at the stove.'

She took the spoon and glanced at Aristotle as he set up the easel. He smiled right into her eyes, and although she lowered her head modestly, her heart raced and her soul turned from dust to all-consuming fire, burning in her cheeks and making it difficult to breathe. Would he ever kiss her again?

Kyría Alice dropped into a chair, took a packet of cigarettes from her pocket and lit one.

'Oh my, that's good,' she sighed, blowing smoke towards the ceiling.

Aristotle stared in astonishment, then grabbed Daphne's art case. In moments, he set up the easel and started sketching, eyes alight with a frantic need to record the scene on paper.

The church bell clanged 4.30, making Daphne jump. She remembered the Brandenburgs and the promise to her mother. Distracted by a moan from the little girl on the sofa, she scooped a few spoons of the glutinous rice water into a cup, and added a little icing sugar from her pocket that had held the shortbreads.

'Come on, Doris, get some of this inside you. I know it will make you feel better.'

She slid her arm under the child's head and realised that her life had ended.

'Oh! Oh, Aristotle!' she gasped before clasping a hand over her mouth. 'This poor little girl, I think she's . . . she's gone.'

Kyría Alice let out a huge snore and woke herself up. Aristotle lowered his pencil and came to the sofa. He lifted the edge of the blanket and placed it over the little girl's face.

'I'm sorry, you're right, Daphne. She's gone to a better place.'

'But she made a noise, only a minute ago, just a minute . . .' Daphne fell into her teacher's arms. 'It's not fair! Rich people cut the crusts off their bread, while toddlers starve to death. Oh, what can we do, Aristotle?'

'You did everything you could, Daphne. Try not to get upset.'

He rubbed her back and kissed her forehead, and then an enormous roar made them both jump.

'Take your hands off my daughter! How dare you!' Elijah Abrams yelled.

'Sir, she's had a shock. I suggest—'

'You suggest! Get away from her, I say!' His fists clenched; his eyes bulged from a face puce with anger.

Kyría Alice – frail, middle-aged lady that she was – stepped between them with such bearing and dignity that they all stared at her.

'Let's all take a step back, shall we?' she said.

'How dare you!' Daphne's father yelled again. 'That's my daughter he's manhandling. Get out of my way!'

Kyría Alice stood her ground. 'Who do you think you are?' Elijah blurted.

'As you are asking, my correct title is Her Royal Highness Princess Andrew of Greece and Denmark. My friends call me Kyría Alice, but I am not sure that you fall into that category yet, sir. However, your daughter does. A moment ago, she had a young child die in her arms. She is distraught. Now I will thank you for helping us, or leaving.'

Daphne's sob broke the stony silence.

Elijah stared at Kyría Alice for a moment. 'You're German! He's German, too.' He jerked his head towards Aristotle. 'My daughter and I are not safe here.'

'Sir, I am as Greek as you are, so do not insult me or Daphne's art teacher.'

After a long silence, Elijah's shoulders slumped as he bowed his head.

'I beg your pardon, Your Royal Highness.' He stood to attention. 'Concern brought about my unforgivable outburst. I'm always worried about my daughter.'

'No apologies or formalities needed here. There are starving children outside, and a young boy who is about to be given terrible news. So, if you'll excuse us . . .'

'May I help, madam?' Elijah asked.

'Yes, you can take the poor child and lay her down upstairs.' Kyría Alice turned to Daphne. 'Stack the bowls next to the cauldron before you open the front door.'

Daphne stacked the motley collection of soup dishes, as the back door opened and young Petros came in with his string bag full of stale bread. Who would tell him? The children filed in through the front door and hurried to queue with their dishes held out.

'Manners, everyone!' Kyría Alice cried, trying to dampen a smile that gave praise to God. 'Sit before you sup, children!'

A boy, thin beyond belief, collapsed to the floor – bones in a bag of skin, Daphne thought. Everyone gasped, and the queue stepped around him.

'Daphne!' Kyría Alice called. 'Can you give him some of your sweet rice water?'

She put the same cup to his lips. 'Here we are. Don't let me down, young man. I need you to get stronger and live to fight another day.'

'I'm too tired to fight, miss,' he whispered. 'I want my mother, and she's in Heaven.' He closed his eyes.

Daphne swallowed hard. 'Come on now, you must drink this sweet rice water to relax your stomach. Once you have, I'll give you a nice bowl of soup and bread. What's your name?'

His eyelids lifted. 'I'm Hermes – messenger of the gods, you know.' He closed his eyes and whispered, 'I hope they don't need any errands running today. Know what I mean, miss?'

'You can still make a joke, then? Come on, drink the rest of this rice water before I get you some soup.'

'What flavour's the soup today, miss?'

'Champagne and oyster, served with the crispest white bread that's still warm from the oven.'

'I'll have to get back on my feet.'

'You will, Hermes. Come on, I'll help you.'

Daphne's father appeared. 'What's happening, Daphne?'

'Our Hermes here had a minor problem. I think he's all right now. What do you say, Hermes?'

'Fit as a fiddle.' He forced a smile, thin skin stretching over the bones of his face. 'Now show me this oyster and champagne soup before it's all gone.'

'Can you walk?' The boy nodded. 'Then let's get you to the table before I bring the food over to you.'

'I'll take him,' Elijah said. 'You get the food.'

Daphne felt her anger rise. 'No, Babá. I'll take him. You get the food.'

He stared at her, chewing his lip before he replied. 'Of course.'

She glanced at Aristotle and saw him in a frenzy at the easel, dashing lines and angles, throwing another sheet of sketches over the top of the large pad and continuing on the next sheet. Sweat beaded his brow, and Daphne basked in the light of his genius. Her father came over with the soup and bread for Hermes.

'Are you all right, Papa? You look pale.'

His eyes brimmed with emotion as he stared around the room.

'Her Royal Highness has commanded me to break the bad news to Petros before I take him to see his sister.' Knocked down by recent events, her father couldn't hide behind his rigid shield of authority. Daphne saw him as a caring, sensitive man who did not know how to handle his feelings concerning malnourished children. 'How can our country have abandoned these youngsters?' he muttered.

'She doesn't like to be called Her Royal Highness, Papa. It's Kyría Alice. Petros is the brown-haired boy in the old duffel, at the end of the table. Best wait until he's eaten, and not break the news in front of the others. Many of them have lost brothers and sisters, too.'

Minutes later, the room fell silent as Elijah and Petros left. Every child heard the boy's howl of anguish come from the hallway, followed by the beat of his footsteps as he raced up the bare stairs. The older ones understood. Kyría Alice stood at the head of the table.

'Put your hands together, children.' They did. 'Repeat after me, "Thank God for a good meal, amen." Now let's sit still for a moment and say a quiet prayer for little Doris, who has gone to Heaven.'

Daphne's chest jerked with a sob. She glanced at her tutor, who gave a sharp nod of strength. A hand squeezed hers, and she realised Kyría Alice stood at her side and her father stood in the doorway.

'You are dismissed, children. Stay out of trouble and come back at seven in the morning.'

Kyría Alice opened the front door. As the room emptied, Elijah followed Daphne's lead, and together they gathered the chipped enamel and ceramic bowls and took them to the butler's sink. Daphne felt great comfort from the experience, and as her eyes met her father's, they smiled at each other. That simple moment, she knew, was one that would stay with her for the rest of her life. They had never been close before that day, and later, when she wondered where he was, or what had happened to him, she recalled that one special smile they shared.

Elijah turned to Alice. 'May I ask you something, madam?'

Alice nodded. 'Please, call me Kyría Alice.'

He bowed his head. 'Where do they sleep?' Her eyes widened, and she nodded to encourage him. '. . . Kyría Alice,' he added with a slight gasp.

She smiled. 'There, it wasn't so difficult now, was it? They sleep under hedgerows in the royal park, in doorways, in abandoned cellars, bombed buildings. Anywhere they can find shelter.'

'Can't they sleep here?'

'I'm afraid not. The building is on loan, on condition that we don't use it as a dwelling. Nobody's allowed to sleep here.'

He studied the floor for a moment. 'May I suggest something?'

'You may.'

'I own a derelict property on the Piraeus Road. Most of the windows are in place. It was a hotel. There were still some beds inside, so you can use it if you want, Kyría.'

'You're very kind, sir,' Alice said. 'If there's anything I can do for you, just ask.' She placed her hands together and made a slight nod. 'Now, I suggest you take your daughter home before the curfew.' Her eyes flicked to the yellow star on his lapel.

'Ah, that's another reason I'm here.' He reached inside his jacket. 'Another reason the Brandenburgs came to see us this afternoon was to bring us this.' He handed Daphne a brown envelope. 'You and your sister have new documents, baptism certificates and identity cards. Your family name is now Daphne Papadopoulos.' He gave a sigh so heavy it seemed to come from his boots. 'Always carry the papers with you, and present them to the authorities if you're stopped.'

'Yes, Papa – and I'm sorry I disobeyed you and put you to so much trouble.'

Elijah glanced from Kyría Alice to his daughter. 'No apologies needed. I'm very proud of you, but now I must go. Don't be late home or your mother will worry.' He turned towards the hallway, where the last children were filing out. 'Young man! Petros, isn't it?' The boy nodded. 'Can you polish shoes?'

'Yes, sir. I can polish anything, sir. I'm the best polisher in Athens.'

Daphne's father looked upon the boy's tear-stained face.

'OK, follow me. I've a job for you.'

Kyría Alice and Daphne smiled.

'Excuse me, Mr Papadopoulos,' Kyría Alice said. 'Remember, if ever I can help you . . .'

He blinked at her, digesting his new name, then almost smiled before he left with the boy.

Aristotle closed his sketchbook and joined the two women, helping to dry the last of the bowls.

'Let's have a coffee together before we do anything else,' Kyría Alice said. 'Can you manage it while I talk to Daphne, Aristotle?'

He grinned. 'Of course. It's 'bout time I did something useful.'

Kyría Alice addressed Daphne. 'Come and sit at the trestle. I want to talk to you.' She pulled a packet of Karelia cigarettes from her pocket and was already lighting up when she sat opposite her young helper. 'What's your surname?' she asked with anger in her voice.

Daphne blinked and shrugged. 'Oh dear . . .'

'You see? New identity papers and a baptism certificate won't save you from Hitler's evil,' Kyría Alice said. 'Understand this – the Germans aren't stupid. The opposite, in fact. I'd say they're the most intelligent race in Europe, and way ahead of you in the art of deception.' She shook her head frantically. 'I know it's terrifying, but new papers won't save you from their work camps, or a German bullet. You need to be one hundred per cent convincing.' She drew on her cigarette and aimed a column of smoke at the tobacco-stained ceiling. 'Let's practise. Read through your papers and memorise what you need.' Daphne did as she was instructed. 'Now, put the documents away,' Alice ordered.

Daphne did, but the instant she looked up, Alice slammed her fist on the trestle and yelled, 'Name!'

Daphne flinched and stammered, 'Daphne De-Demopolous.'

'Wrong!' Alice pushed her face up to Daphne's and continued to yell. 'Don't you know your own name, girl? Are you a Jew? Where do you live? Recite the Lord's Prayer!'

'No . . . No, I don't know it . . .'

Before she could stop herself, Daphne was in tears, confused and hurt by Kyría Alice's anger.

Kyría Alice took the girl into her arms. 'It's necessary, dear child. This lesson could save your life. You cannot leave here until you assure me you'll deal with questioning in a convincing manner. Memorise your name, Papadopoulos, which means son of the priest. Learn to cross yourself like a Christian. Thumb, forefinger and middle finger together. Touch your forehead, chest, right shoulder, left shoulder – and three times, one for each of the Trinity. You must be perfectly convincing, Daphne.'

Aristotle brought the coffee.

'I'll help you,' he said. 'Dry your eyes now. We can do this, and although you may not realise it, I think it's true that this wonderful lady is saving your life.' He brushed the tears from her cheeks. 'Also, continue to practise your German, and if they ever stop you, speak German to the soldiers. Tell them you want to learn their language because you admire them and want to live in Germany.'

She longed to see his sketches, but it seemed inappropriate to change the subject when they were all so concerned about her.

'Do you think we should return now?' she asked, hoping he would reveal his work in the studio.

13

FLORA

Corfu, present day

'Kyría Alice sounds like a wonderful woman,' I said, noticing the light turning orange with the sunset. The breeze had died, and leaves overhead stilled. Complete silence surrounded us.

'She was unique, a saint, but she couldn't do anything to prepare us for what happened that evening. My father had taken Petros back with him, and the pair came rushing towards us as we neared our street.'

*   *   *

Daphne closed her eyes and allowed scenes from the past to return. She remembered every detail, every word. The confusion of that moment when her father stopped her from returning home.

'Wait, Daphne!' he said. 'You can't go to the house.'

'But why?' she asked, aware that Aristotle had scooped her arm into his.

'The Nazis 'ave got yer mother an' brothers,' Petros blurted, while Elijah searched for more delicate words. 'They're roundin' up the Jews like they did in Thessaloníki.'

Elijah shoved the boy aside. 'Where does Elizabeth have her English lessons? We must find her.' He spluttered the sentence out, then forced a shaky finger inside his starched collar and tugged, as if the words he wanted to say were stuck in his throat and he needed more room to get them out. A collar stud popped. 'Damnation!' he shouted. 'What will we do?'

Stunned to hear her father swear, Daphne's feet seemed glued to the pavement and she couldn't speak.

'Daphne, listen to me!' her father shouted. 'Where's Elizabeth?' He shook her shoulders.

Snapped into the urgency of the moment, she told him what she knew.

'Her English teacher has a flat above the haberdashery in Platonos Street, Papa. Shall we go there?'

Her father shook his head. 'No, you go back to Kyría Alice. Remind her she offered to help. Ask her to hide you, and keep practising your new identity as you go. You're on their list, they'll be looking for you. I'll find Elizabeth.'

Eager to get them off the street, he stepped into an alley. Aristotle and Daphne followed him.

Aristotle offered to help. 'I can hide you all, sir. I'm much closer, and Kyría Alice has probably left now. I have an attic.'

My father was furious, or perhaps just afraid.

'You're German – how can we trust you?' he growled.

Aristotle's bold reply shocked her. 'With all due respect, you can't judge all Germans as evil. Even Kyría Alice is descended from the house of Hanover. Besides, I wouldn't let anything happen to Daphne. She's a very brave and kind person, and my most talented student. I believe she'll become a great artist one day.'

He turned and stared into Daphne's eyes, and she believed right then, she would spend the rest of her life trying to live up to Aristotle's prediction.

* * *

118

'You must have been terrified, Granny. It's impossible to imagine. God, what did you do?'

'To be honest, I was more afraid of my father. You see, we didn't understand what was happening in Poland.'

As her eyes closed again, a tear trickled from the corner and slid down her cheek.

We sat quietly for a moment as she gathered her strength.

'I suspect your father was very concerned for your safety,' I said.

She nodded. 'It was only then I realised how cherished we were by our parents.'

'How awful. Was it true? I mean, about your brothers and mother? Had the soldiers taken them? What happened to Elizabeth, and how did all this make you feel?'

Her hand slipped from mine and wiped the tears away. 'I don't know how to describe my emotions . . . Well, like all the other Jews who survived, I guess. I wanted an explanation. After the war, when they confirmed the existence of horrific extermination camps, I told myself my missing family was probably living in Italy, where they had made a new life. You peer into the faces of strangers, hoping. Sometimes they stare back, a hysterical need for recognition in their eyes . . . then, in that instant, you understand that they're Jewish, too. Our entire race was lost. Who could bear the facts of what really happened to our families in those hellish places?'

I sat in silence, and tried to imagine how it was for my grandmother to live with such memories, and later, when the facts about Auschwitz had come to light, the knowledge of what had happened to her family – my ancestors. A sharp prick on my calf drew my attention. I slapped it viciously.

'Damn mosquitoes!'

'It's that time of day, *korítsi*. Can you wheel me indoors?'

For a moment, the darkness blinded us after the sunlight outside.

I found the pie Yánna had left, and sliced through the crispy filo pastry to serve it up. The buttery aroma of chicken filled the room and made my mouth water.

'Gosh, I didn't realise how hungry I was, Granny.' I slid a wedge onto her plate.

'There'll be village salad in the fridge,' she said. 'You just need to add the dressing.'

I poured vinegar, olive oil and oregano over chunks of juicy, ripe tomatoes, chopped onion and crunchy cucumber that were topped by a slab of salty feta cheese.

'What did you do?' I asked, once we had made headway into the food and our silence filled the room.

'My father left to find Elizabeth, but the building was empty of people, with no sign of my sister or the teacher. He still had her new identity papers in his pocket. The Nazis had done a house-to-house search down the street. That was the first time – the only time – I ever saw my father cry. Elizabeth was his favourite, you see. They had a special father–daughter bond, adoring each other.'

'How dreadful. Did you stay at Aristotle's that night?'

'Yes, we all slept on the floor in the studio. Throughout the next day, German soldiers rounded up more Jews and force-marched them through the city at sunset. We dared not turn on a light and peered from the upstairs window, trying to recognise family or friends in the murky river of people that flowed down the street. We all held this futile belief . . . hope . . . that if we saw someone we knew, we would find a way to rescue them.' She sighed, her shoulders drooping for a moment. 'The sorry crowd carried bundles and babies. Old people teetered on walking sticks. Toddlers couldn't keep up. Mothers were frantic to gather their young together. When soldiers hammered on the studio door, my heart hammered just as violently. We were petrified they'd break in and storm the place. Aristotle hurried down to speak to them. I could hear him shouting quite violently. He told them his cousin was a high-ranking SS officer, Major-General Jürgen Stroop, serving the SS chief Heinrich Himmler, and if they continued to harass him, he would make sure they were held to account. It worked, and they left.'

'How long did you hide in my grandfather's attic?' I asked.

'We stayed at Aristotle's that night. The next morning, we rushed to the soup kitchen. Kyría Alice hurried us inside. I fell into her open arms, suddenly aware of my rising fear. I knew it was us against the world. "I prayed all night for God to keep you safe," she said. My father wasted no time in asking for her help. "Kyría, I am going to Palestine to organise a home for us. You said you would help if I needed it." Alice nodded, and the relief on Papa's face was clear. "Then please, keep my daughter safe until I return for her," he said. "She is all I have left, but it would be too dangerous for her to travel with me – the Germans will interrogate everyone who tries to leave the city."

'Honestly, Flora, you would not believe the relief on his face when she nodded.'

'So, he left you with the princess?'

Daphne's face softened, then she smiled. 'Papa stayed and helped to feed the children. When it was time for him to go, I flew into his arms and burst into tears. My father shook Aristotle's hand and wished him good luck. Before he hurried out of the front door, Babá handed Kyría Alice my mother's and my sister's false documents. He asked her to keep them in a secret place in case the Gestapo searched her home. A knowing look passed between them, and years passed before I realised he had done that in case he never returned.'

* * *

'*Ela!*' Yánna called, halting our conversation as she opened the cottage door. 'Are you all right in here?'

'Yánna, you're supposed to be at the hotel, having a holiday. Don't you like it there?'

'Is beautiful, Mrs Flora, I just come on the bus to see you is all right, and to get Daphne ready for bed.'

'That's very considerate, thank you.'

'Here, I bring you plenty of Lux shampoo, conditioner, skin cream and two toilet rolls, also, some cookies for Daphne and little packets of coffee and sugar. Is all free gift from hotel. The girl who clean my room tell me it is free, I can have as much as I want. She says I can take more off her trolley if I want, so I do.' She opened the dresser drawer and tipped her handbag upside down. A cascade of coffee, tea, biscuits and toiletries tumbled out. 'The girl, she ask me if I need towels.'

My jaw dropped, and I imagined Yánna's return after clearing the maid's trolley of linen.

'Yánna, I should explain. It's forbidden to take towels or any other linen from the hotel. I think the room-maid misunderstood, or didn't make herself clear.'

'Ah, I understand. OK, is no worries. But is a shame – we need new pillows.'

14

DAPHNE

Athens, 1943

ARISTOTLE GLANCED AT HIS WATCH.

'Come on, Daphne, we must go. The soldiers will check people's papers near curfew. We're not ready to be questioned.' He turned to Kyría Alice. 'I'll try to help you again tomorrow, madam. Meanwhile, may I escort you somewhere?'

She shook her head. 'My chauffeur will be here in half an hour. I assure you Daphne will be fine with me. Go now, and may God keep you safe.'

* * *

The magnificent car smelled of beeswax, like the synagogue. Kyría Alice lived in a splendid house – three floors and a basement – in the centre of Athens, which belonged to her brother-in-law. She took Daphne upstairs to the attic rooms, which were sumptuous.

'It's all rather a waste, with me living here all alone,' she said. 'Now, I'm going to lock you in for two days, Daphne. Learn your documents and new identity until it's as natural as the hair on your head. You'll live on bread, water, fruit and cheese. If I'm satisfied that your responses are natural when I return to interrogate you, I'll let you out. It's vital you accomplish this, and please understand I'm taking this line for your own safety. Do you understand?'

Daphne nodded. 'Yes, Kyría Alice. Thank you, I'm very grateful. I appreciate that you're putting yourself in danger, too.'

'Come, let's say a prayer together.'

She led Daphne to one of the twin beds, which was covered with a blue damask eiderdown. They kneeled together.

'Do the same as me,' the older woman said, crossing herself with a slow hand for Daphne's benefit. Kyría Alice recited the Lord's Prayer and the Hail Mary, line by line.

Daphne repeated them. She gave Daphne a Book of Common Prayer and dog-eared the two pages that she needed to study.

'Learn these off by heart, because one day I fear you might need them. I'll be back soon,' she said, leaving the room.

Ten minutes later, she returned with the chauffeur and together, they brought a bowl of fruit, cheese, a small dish of olives, and two loaves.

'I'm going to lock you in, Daphne,' she said, then nodded at the chauffeur. 'Mikali will drag the cupboard across the door, so you can't come out. There's a water closet, but nothing else. It's a modern contraption that flushes. Pull on the chain above your head. As it makes a terrible gurgling noise right through the building, best only flush late at night, all right?'

Daphne nodded, feeling abandoned and painfully lonely already.

* * *

With no clock in the attic, she lost track of time. Was it two days, or three? What if there was a raid, a fire, a bomb? The sound of the tall cupboard being dragged away from the attic door terrified her. The warning bell had not rung, yet she feared something evil approached. Panicked, she stared around, searching for somewhere to hide. The Jew-haters were coming . . . She crashed to the floor between the two beds, then shuffled in frantic haste under the one that stood against the wall. Her heart beat so hard she feared it would burst while she tugged bed covers down to reach the floor. In her panic, she forgot to be quiet and feared they'd hear her clattering and whimpering. She curled up behind the bed linen and tried to quieten her breathing. When the squeak of stiff hinges caught her attention, she stopped breathing altogether.

A man called out. 'Don't be afraid, it's me, Aristotle!' Her heart exploded with joy. 'The danger's passed,' he said.

She scrambled out of her hiding place and rushed into his arms. Tears almost escaped when he pulled her to his chest and held her tightly.

'Relax, darling Daphne, you're safe for the moment.'

'How can I relax? What if someone informed the Nazis that you helped me, or even that you taught me to paint? They'd shoot you, kill you. I'd never see you again, Aristotle. I would rather die myself than lose you.'

Couldn't he understand? He was everything to her.

Alice, who stood behind him, stepped back and turned her face away, ignoring the emotional outburst.

'If you'll take Daphne downstairs, Aristotle, I'll instruct the maid to deal with the room.'

He led the way. She followed with her hand on his shoulder, as if needing his guidance. On the second landing, he turned and took her in his arms. She tilted her face up and closed her eyes. After an eternity, his lips were soft against hers and they both melted into their vulnerable selves. Her artistic mind, which so often thought in terms of colour, imagined in the first moment of that kiss, the palest pink . . . Then the sweetest passion of love swept through her body and a million romantic thoughts filled her head. Her innocent self surrendered to him, while her heart tumbled with joy. The gentle colour of that first delightful moment soon turned rosy, then intensified and multiplied into the scarlet of hot-blooded passion. The surrounding air exploded and dazzled with every shade and hue. But the greatest thing? In that kiss, they declared their loyalty to each other and made their pledge of eternal love.

'Are you all right? You're trembling,' he said, holding her close.

She nodded, not trusting her voice for a moment.

'Is there any news from my father?' she whispered, panting, gripping the banister for an anchor in case her feet floated up from the stairs as she peered into his eyes. 'I wonder if he made it out of the city.'

'Yes, he paid a stevedore to get a message back to Kyría Alice. As soon as he has something positive to report, he will contact us.'

Her body sagged with relief.

'But I have more news for you, Daphne. Let's get downstairs first.'

He scooped an arm around her waist and swept her around the next balustrade.

Her breath came in little gasps. 'Please, Aristotle, I don't think I can take anything more today. Since that tiny baby died in my arms, then little Doris, and the things that have taken place since . . . it's too much.'

'Come here, into my arms, and trust me.'

They had reached the hall when he took her into his arms. She pressed herself against him.

'This is the only place I feel safe,' she whispered.

'Then have faith, my darling.' He kissed her forehead and guided her towards the salon door. 'Close your eyes.'

He urged her forward, through the doors. Someone gasped. Daphne's eyes flew open and there, Mamá and Elizabeth stood before her. Everything rushed away and, for a second, she knew nothing but the darkness of a faint. Then her heart thrummed with joy. She opened her eyes and found herself on the floor.

'Mamá, Elizabeth . . . Am I dreaming, or is that you?' Weak with emotion and the image of her family swimming before her eyes, Daphne reached out for her mother and sister. 'You're safe! I can't believe my eyes. Where are Noah and Isaac? Are they here, too?'

Her mother and sister fell to their knees at her side but didn't answer her question. The three hugged and shed copious tears.

'I thought they'd got you!' Daphne whispered. 'I feared I'd never see you again.'

Her mother patted her all over, as if ensuring she was real.

'I can't believe it,' Mamá said. 'I thought I'd lost you, and Elizabeth. It's been the most terrible nightmare, but you've given me hope, Daphne.'

'Please, Mamá, tell me what happened. Where are Noah and Isaac?' Daphne asked, getting to her feet and herding her mother and sister towards the sofa.

Mamá chewed her lip and stared at the floor for a minute while she gathered her strength for the emotional account of what had happened.

'The Gestapo soldiers forced us all into cattle trucks at the station. They beat the ones at the rear and yelled at them to hurry. Everyone pushed forward. My poor boys . . . Now, one of them no more because of a murdering Nazi, and the other . . . who knows where?'

She dropped her head in her hands and wailed, the sound so heart-wrenching, everyone stared at the floor trying to block the noise.

Daphne stared at her mother, for a moment filled with horror. Which of her brothers was dead?

'What happened, Mamá? Tell me!' The wait was almost unbearable. She wanted to take her sobbing mother by the arms and shake her. 'Please! I have to know, Mamá.'

Her mother tried to compose herself and, although her chest still jerked with sobs, she told them of the events that had taken place.

'Noah and Isaac said they would make a fuss so that I could escape. I maintained we should just do as we were told, but they insisted.' Mamá pressed her hand over her mouth, stopping her own words, as if saying them aloud made them true. She broke down again. 'Oh, my darling sons!' she howled. Daphne held her mother's hand and waited for her to calm down.

Kyría Alice rushed into the room, placed her arms around Mamá's shoulders, and gave her a hug. 'Your son has gone to God. He's in a better place now, Kyría Lotte, and one day you'll be reunited.'

Mamá nodded and took a deep breath before she continued.

'Noah shouted abuse at the soldiers. "Nazi murderers," he yelled. "Tell us where you are taking us! Tell these old grand-mothers what you're going to do with them, you cowards!"' She wiped her tears away. 'I was so terrified I couldn't breathe. I shoved through the tight crowd, moving away from him, hoping he would stop drawing attention to himself when I was out of the way. I looked over my shoulder and caught a glance of Noah as he threw a punch at a guard.' She drew in a long, juddering breath. 'He was . . . Oh, my son! Why did you do it? The flash of a pistol under his chin . . . There was . . . Oh! They murdered him, Daphne. My beautiful, noble son. People around him in that packed space were spattered with blood. My Noah, my darling firstborn.' She broke down again, sobbing and shaking her head. 'And I can't even collect his body, because I'm Jewish and they will put me on the next train.

Daphne embraced her mother. She and her sister had tears on their faces. Mamá continued.

'Isaac hurried to my side and said Noah had given his life so I could escape. He shook so badly he could hardly speak. "Take Noah's gift and live for him, Mamá. That's what he gave his life for." He pushed me through a doorway. A German soldier saw me. For a terrifying moment, I expected him to raise the alarm or shoot me, but he turned the other way and marched on. I found a little window. I think it was an abandoned ticket office, and I peered through it, searching for Isaac. He was pushed on to the train, his face white with fear as he stared out. The gap in the doorway became narrower and narrower as the guards forced the door shut, but he'd seen me. Our eyes locked until the door closed and the big steel latch dropped into its receiver. There was no escape for him.'

'Oh, Mamá, how terrible for you all, and of course for poor, brave Noah. I can't believe he's dead! He'll always be my hero.'

Kyría Alice stood. 'Everyone must go up to the attic right now. Continue your conversation as quietly as possible, and if the maid's bell rings, it means there's danger. I received word only minutes ago that the troops are doing a house-to-house search for Jews.'

They hurried upstairs. Aristotle held Daphne's arm, keeping her back as her mother and Elizabeth went through the narrow door that led to the attic. Once they started up the stairs, he placed a gentle kiss on her lips. That sweet embrace, filled with promises, held a thousand loving thoughts. She savoured it, clasped it in her heart to be recalled whenever she needed him.

'Stay safe, my precious darling,' he whispered, then closed the door.

On the other side, Daphne touched her lips and wanted to cry with joy, although her heart was still breaking for Noah. Aristotle dragged the wardrobe across the attic door. She took a deep breath with her hand pressing against her heart. When would she feel his arms around her again?

Daphne found her mother trembling as she held Elizabeth. Her lips moved in prayer and Elizabeth wept against her shoulder.

'Calm down now, we're safe,' she said. 'Tell me how you escaped the troops, Elizabeth. I thought I'd lost you both. Come, I'll make coffee. I think we all need something strong to calm our nerves.'

A few essentials remained in the attic from Alice's days of aristocracy, when her kitchen staff lived up there. When war broke out in Athens, there was worry about bombs falling on roofs. Because of this, the staff were accommodated in the basement. Daphne lit the range and put coffee on to boil – appreciating they were lucky to have coffee and sugar when others were starving to death.

Elizabeth screwed her nose with her first sip, making Lotte smile as Daphne guessed she remembered her first taste of the bitter drink.

'Mamá, Elizabeth, listen! Babá left your Greek Orthodox papers with Kyría Alice. You must learn your new names and some Christian prayers and things, like how to cross yourself properly. I'm going to teach you what I know while we're locked in here.'

Mamá nodded; Elizabeth's eyes widened with fear.

Daphne continued. 'Before we start, please, tell me what happened after my precious brother sacrificed his life to save

130

you, Mamá. How did you escape when the place swarmed with enemy soldiers? You were so brave!'

Mamá gulped and dabbed her eyes. 'Nothing heroic, child. I just ripped off my yellow star and hurried through the backstreets towards home. But then I remembered Elizabeth and raced towards Platanos Street, where your sister had her lessons. The troops were coming the opposite way, which terrified me because I thought they'd found her already. There was nothing I could do but turn around and hurry home.'

She ran a hand down her daughter's cheek.

'I was halfway there when her teacher, Kyría Margarita, recognised me. "Kyría Abrams!" she cried, then slapped her hand over her mouth, realising she could have caused my death. "Sorry, sorry," she whispered. I asked where my daughter was, and she said, "At your home, I took her there. She'd finished her lesson but when she saw a column of Hitler's soldiers, and troubled Jews herded into the street, she returned and asked for my help." The brave woman could have been killed for harbouring.'

'So the Germans didn't search her house?' Daphne asked Elizabeth.

'No, they did search. Stormed right through the place looking in every cupboard, under the bed, even in the attic.' The three women considered their situation and glanced at each other. 'Kyría Margarita told me to get in the blanket chest in her bedroom, and said she was going to lock it and put the key in a pot of geraniums on the balcony. The soldiers stomped about the bedroom, opening drawers and cupboards. One soldier demanded she open the blanket chest, but she explained it was only full of her mother's linen and she had lost the key years ago. The sergeant commanded one of his men to put a couple of bullets through the chest as they left. She was sure the soldier caught the dread in her eyes and understood. When they were leaving, and the others had their backs turned, the young man fired two shots at the corner of the mattress.'

The three women sat in silence for a minute, their chests rising and falling as they tried to calm themselves.

'Your father's friends, the Brandenburgs and their son, have also gone,' Mamá whispered. 'I recognised them ahead of us, pushed into the train.'

'Let's say a prayer for Isaac,' Daphne said. 'That he survives, wherever he is, and comes back to us. We must all go to Cairo or Palestine and find Babá – our family must live to honour Noah's great sacrifice.'

15

FLORA

Corfu, present day

YÁNNA DRESSED MY GRANDMOTHER IN her long flannelette nightgown, a loose knitted cardigan, and a pair of towelling socks, then turned down her bed. She explained which pills to administer before the dear old woman slept.

'We'll manage, Yánna,' I cried, exasperated. 'Go, or you'll miss the hotel's wonderful dinner.'

Yánna glanced around. 'I will wash the dishes before I am going, yes?'

'No! Leave now. I can take care of things for one evening, Yánna. Go, have a great time.'

Yánna peered out of the window.

'What is it?' I asked her. 'Something's wrong. Come on, what's worrying you?'

'No, only, the people, they are so nice dressed, Flora. I am afraid. I did not look after myself for so many years. It never mattered what I look like, you see.' She glanced into my eyes. 'I think I embarrass you, Mrs Flora, taking your place in my dusty old dress when you always look very beautiful.'

'How could you ever embarrass me?'

Daphne raised a hand. 'Flora, in the bottom of my wardrobe is a trunk. Bring us the finest dress that will fit my dear Yánna, so she can walk back into the hotel with her head held high. Also, in the second drawer of my dressing table, you'll find a jewellery box with strings of beads, clip earrings, and more. She's looked after me for most of her life. It's time I paid her back, don't you think?'

'You're very kind, Granny. I'll see to it right away.'

* * *

My grandmother had been a slave to fashion in her middle years. We chose a black lace wraparound dress worn with a simple string of pearls, but Yánna's scuffed and trodden-down moccasins were beyond revival and let the outfit down.

'Take my sandals.' I glanced at my feet and the wonderful, outrageously expensive sandals I'd bought three years ago, before Covid, before the tragedy of Mark. ''Tis a far better thing I do now . . .'

I stepped out of the soft, metallic, faux ostrich-skin sandals, adjusted the slingbacks to their furthest eye, and passed them to her.

'Oh, Mrs Flora, I could not.'

'Nonsense. Hurry, or you'll miss the hotel dinner. The taxi will be here any moment.' I dragged my eyes away from her feet, knowing I'd never wear the shoes again. 'Those sandals have been killing me since I got here, so keep them. It gives me an excuse to buy another pair of the right size.'

Daphne tilted her head to one side and patted my knee.

'Very kind,' she muttered.

Yánna peered at herself in the long mirror and, overwhelmed by emotion, sniffed and dabbed at her eyes.

'You're both very wonderful. How will I repay you?'

'Just have a good time,' I told her. 'Now sit here and let me do your hair while we wait for the taxi, Cinderella. And don't

forget, the hotel is all-inclusive, so anything you want is free . . .
Drink Prosecco and eat cream cakes until your heart's content.'

'What is this, Prosecco?'

'It's like champagne, Yánna,'

'Champagne? Oh, Mother of God!' She crossed herself. 'Can
I bathe in champagne like Cleopatra?'

Daphne's shoulders were jigging. 'No, Yánna, just drink it.
Anyway, Cleopatra bathed in asses' milk, and I'm pretty sure,
even though the hotel's all-inclusive, you won't find asses' milk
on the menu. Now have a good time.' She flapped her hand.
'You've earned it.'

* * *

Once we were on our own, I poured my grandmother a glass of
wine. Her smile faded.

'She has a big heart, you know? Yánna, I mean. She saved our
lives, mine and Aristotle's. I believe we would have gone crazy if
it hadn't been for her, and I've always loved her.'

'Granny, I can listen to you all night, so tell me when you
need your bed, all right, promise?'

She nodded. 'Where were we up to?'

'You were with your mother and your sister, hiding in Kyría
Alice's attic.' I turned my phone to record.

The sparkle left Daphne's eyes. 'In the darkness, I tried not to
cry, but my heart was in bits. We were so afraid and upset, sleep
evaded us. We talked in whispers, or lay in the dark thinking
about the enormity of our loss. Dawn broke and with the new
day, I felt the sobs for Noah build again.'

She stopped and sipped her wine, lost in her memories for
a moment.

'That afternoon, other people joined us in the attic – a Jewish jeweller named Solomon Rosenburg and his wife Bella. She had lovely clothes, but I believed she was not beautiful in spirit. It's easy to judge when you're young. She wore gaudy rings on every arthritic finger.'

'It must have been difficult for you, trapped in the attic.'

'Yes, it was. We only stayed for three weeks, but every day we feared capture. Twice a week, to my mother's distress, I went to Aristotle's studio to paint. "Mamá, I'll go mad if I don't have my lessons," I told her. "I'll wear a scarf over my hair and across my face, as many of the Greek women do. Nobody's going to recognise me." In the end, she relented. In Kyría Alice's attic, Mamá and Elizabeth had one bed, and the Rosenburgs had the other. I volunteered to take the eiderdown on the floor, because I couldn't stand to have anyone beside me as I dreamed of my one true love.' She smiled, then continued. 'That evening, young Petros, who'd become everybody's go-between, came with a message for the Rosenburgs. "The chief of police says they're to have their photographs taken tomorrow morning," he told us. "Their new identity documents are ready." We knew this was a risky business. "He says they must pack up their things because they're not coming back here."'

'I find it incredible what the chief of police and the archbishop did, Granny. It just goes to show how we misjudge people.'

'You're right, of course. The following Friday morning, we received a message from my father that Mamá was to withdraw one hundred thousand drachmas from the bank to pay for our tickets to Cairo. It was a huge amount of money. She would have to present her Jewish papers to the bank in order to withdraw. At least, that was what she thought. In those days, married women couldn't have a bank account of their own. We were not even sure she could withdraw money without my father. Still, she had to try.'

'That's ridiculous!' I said. 'Decades after the suffragettes, yet a woman still couldn't have her own bank account?'

Daphne nodded. 'I suggested Mamá telephoned the bank for an appointment with the manager, whom my father knew well. This she did, only to discover that Samuel Kofinas, my father's friend, no longer worked there. We feared they had herded him on to the train with all the other Jews. The new manager knew nothing of him. "May I ask how much is in our account?" my mother said, giving the bank account number and expecting a long wait while he found the file. He answered. "Abrams, you say? We have no accounts in this bank for Abrams. All the Jewish accounts were closed by the authorities." "Can you tell me when they will they open again?" she asked. "Never, is the best answer I can give you. The occupying forces withdrew the funds from Jewish accounts." Devastated, poor Mamá collapsed into a chair. All their money, their life savings, gone! Gasping for breath, she struggled to place the Bakelite receiver back in its cradle.

'We returned to the attic where the Rosenburgs listened to our tale of woe, Bella with her usual rattish expression and Solomon Rosenburg paying great attention. "What shall we do?" Mamá cried. "The Nazis have taken your money?" Bella Rosenburg asked, her fingertips drumming against one another and her scarlet lips pursed. "Do you have anything valuable to sell?" Mamá shook her head. "Only my rings and a gold chain." She touched her neck. Kyría Rosenburg whispered into her husband's ear. He nodded and opened his bloated Gladstone bag. I peered inside and my mouth fell open. The bag contained bundles of money and small, bulging, grey velveteen pouches.'

I gasped. 'What was his job before the war, Granny?'

'One of the largest pawnbrokers in Athens – he had shops all over the city.'

'So, did he help your mother?'

She nodded. 'From the bag, he took a small leather-bound notebook, a beautiful tortoiseshell fountain pen with a gold band and clip, and a jeweller's loupe. He seemed to stretch his face, placed the loupe against his eye, and then allowed his face to return to its usual bulldog appearance, holding the little magnifying glass in place.

'Mamá took off her rings and handed them over one by one. Elizabeth, riveted, watched him study the hallmarks and then asked him about the current price of gold. "Shush!" Mamá said. He put the jewellery to one side, then made notes in his little book. He spent several minutes studying the diamonds in her most valued ring. She took off her gold necklace and laid it before him, then watched as he assembled the various bars and dishes into a small brass scale. Solomon Rosenburg weighed the gold chain, then scribbled numbers in his book. He made us an offer.'

'Was it enough to buy the tickets to Cairo for you all?' I asked.

She shook her head. 'Twenty thousand drachmas.'

'What did you do?'

'He asked if we had anything else to sell. I told him there was a small El Greco at the house. He asked if we had the provenance. I said we did, in the safe at home. But would we dare go there? Mr Rosenburg told us, if we could add the painting to the gold, he would give us the cash we needed to sail away. We had no choice.'

'So, did you go?'

16

DAPHNE

Athens, 1943

DAPHNE HURRIED TOWARDS THE STUDIO. She hadn't seen the soldier standing in a doorway. He grabbed her arm as she passed.

'*Unterlagen!*' he yelled, pressing his other hand down on her shoulder so firmly she couldn't move.

Papers . . .? Yes, that was what he had said. She translated to herself, remembering the plan to be friendly and speak German.

'*Guten Tag, wei kann ich Ihnen helfen.*'

Good day, what can I do for you? She said it with a smile, but a tic jerked the corner of her mouth, and her insides tumbled so violently she was sure he sensed her fear.

'*Ah, du sprichst meine Sprache!*'

Ah, you speak German! He appeared pleasantly surprised.

She stood taller and pushed her shoulders back.

'*Ja, eines Tages hoffe ich, in Deutchland zu arbeiten.*'

Yes, one day, I hope to work in Germany.

So far, so good.

He smiled and relaxed his grip on her. '*Zeigen Sie mir Ihre Papiere, junge Frau.*'

She nodded, passing her documents over.

'*Wohin gehst due so eilig?*'

She struggled to understand for a moment, then realised he was asking where she was going in such a hurry.

'I have an art lesson, and I'm late.'

'Sagen Sie es auf Deutch.'

Say it in German.

She searched to find the right words. *'Ich habe eine ... eine ...* Oh dear, what's the word for "art lesson"? *Kunststunde und k-komme zu spät,'* she stammered.

Satisfied, he handed the papers back and asked the name of her teacher.

'Aristotle von Stroop.'

His eyebrows went up. *'Du darfst gehen,'* he said, dismissing her with a flick of his fingers.

She nodded respectfully, then hurried towards the studio, her feet hardly touching the pavement.

*   *   *

When Aristotle opened the door, she fell into his arms.

'I was stopped!' she cried.

He glanced up and down the street, ducked inside and threw the bolts. She pressed against him, trembling, and followed him up to the loft. From his cabinet, he took a bottle of cognac and poured her a small measure.

'Drink this. It will calm your nerves, Daphne. I think we should forget your lesson today, you're far too shaken.'

'No, today I want to pose for you.'

He stared back, mouth hanging open. 'You have extraordinary determination, given your upsetting encounter. Are you sure you're up to this?'

She slipped her jacket off her shoulders.

'The only thing is, I don't have a lot of time today. I must go to my old home.' She told him about the tickets, the bank, and the El Greco painting.

'You have an El Greco?'

She nodded. 'It's been in my family for generations.' His eyes widened and for a moment he was speechless, so she explained. 'The story goes, one of my ancestors owned a merchant ship and traded between Greece and the Kingdom of Candia, or I should say Crete these days. He became friends with the artist's father, Kýrios Theotokópoulos, who lived in the village of Fodele near Heraklion. When he heard his friend had serious financial problems due to a poor olive harvest and the cost of sending his son abroad to study art, he offered to buy a painting executed by the son, Doménikos, who was working as an artist in Spain at that time. The story goes, the father said his son was doing so well that, one day, the painting would be worth a hundred times more than he had paid. Turns out he was right.'

She could see the shock on Aristotle's face.

'The painting must be worth a fortune – hundreds of millions of drachmas. You can't let it go to the jeweller, Daphne. It belongs in a gallery for the entire world to enjoy. Besides, old Rosenburg will never give you its true value.'

'There's no price too high regarding the safety of my mother and sister, Aristotle. They must get their tickets and leave Europe. Besides, none of us liked the picture.'

'Why? He was a great artist.'

'Firstly, it's a biblical scene from the New Testament. The face of Christ crucified. What a horrible way to torture somebody to death – to nail him to a piece of wood and then jeer at him day and night. Babá said a family home was no place to hang a picture of a dead body. He said art should be uplifting, like Noah's first picture, which I remember so well. Green, lollipop olive trees and a yellow, radiating sun.'

Daphne smiled brightly, her eyes sparkling and heart breaking as she recalled her brother and his great sacrifice to save their mother. To accept that she would never see him again felt like a knife twisting in her heart. She must recover the painting and keep that innocent, vibrant picture by her brother. It held far more value for her than the El Greco.

'And the other reason?' Aristotle asked.

'There's meanness in his work. Pinched noses, pointed beards, sharp ears and fingers. There's nothing warm, or loving, is there?'

Aristotle's mouth curled with pleasure. 'You've learned a lot. Top marks for observation.'

'So, do you think it would be safe for me to go back to my home and get it?'

'No, I do not! You can't go there. You're still on the Axis missing list.'

'But they don't know me, and I've already proved I can carry off my new identity.'

'It only takes one jealous Greek neighbour to point you out, and the Germans will have you. Let me think about it.'

'Well, I'm staying here to finish my art course, and help Kyría Alice. I proved today that I can handle myself if stopped, so I'm no longer afraid of what might happen. Besides, I have other interests here.' She peered into his face and narrowed her eyes. 'Now let's make a start on this painting.'

* * *

Daphne ached all over. This was not how she'd imagined posing would be. She glanced down at her own reclining figure. Her breasts were too small and her belly too round. A dull ache radiated from the elbow she leaned on. Strange twinges that always

142

came before a bout of cramp in her calf warned her she'd soon be writhing if she didn't stand up and stretch that muscle.

'I'm almost finished for today, Daphne. Can you hold the pose for another five minutes?'

'Of course,' she replied, determined to please him.

Aristotle worked, first with pencil, then laying down colour.

'You look very contented there. I feared you'd be embarrassed, or at least too tense.'

She said nothing, so he continued painting.

'All right, you'll be pleased to know I've finished for today.' He brought a sheet and placed it over her naked body. 'You were wonderful, and I've made significant progress for one sitting.'

'May I see?'

He shook his head. 'Not until it's completed.'

He draped a cloth over the canvas.

Daphne wrapped the sheet around herself, shuffled behind the screen and got dressed. The entire episode hadn't been as traumatic as she had feared.

'Are you quite sure you don't mind going to my home?' she asked while they sipped a coffee. 'I admit I'll feel a lot better if you're with me.'

'We'll go together, but there is something I must tell you. I have cousin in Germany. He is . . . Well, I might as well tell you, he's in the SS. We are not close, not at all, as we've always had very different ideals, but if ever I needed help, I would just have to ask him.'

'In the SS?'

Her father had been right. Stunned into silence, she stared at him.

'Don't look so afraid, Daphne. I wouldn't let anything bad happen to you. I am not a supporter of Hitler, or the Nazi regime.

143

Not all Germans are bad people, besides, my mother was Greek, remember. Like you, I was born here, but my father's family were Austrian. You must trust me, Daphne.'

'I do trust you, Aristotle. I trust you with my life.'

'Then we shall go together to your house and see if we can get in.'

'Why shouldn't we get in? I have the key.'

'You haven't heard?'

She shook her head. 'Heard what?'

'The Greeks didn't waste any time. They moved into the Jewish houses as soon as they were empty.'

'What! I don't believe it. You mean they've stolen our home, the things my father worked all his life for? These so-called *Christians* have done that?'

'They don't look at it like that. They're taking care of the property until you return . . .' he muttered, his voice heavy with resignation.

'What do you mean? Where would we go?'

Aristotle glanced into Daphne's face, then turned away.

'I don't know.'

'What are we going to do? I must get the painting.'

'Trust me . . .'

She nodded. 'I do.'

They raced towards Daphne's home. A church bell somewhere rang 6.15, reminding them both that curfew was at seven. Aristotle hurried them through the shadows, alert as a wild animal. They approached the building. Someone came to the window and drew the curtains. Aristotle had been right. People were living in her home. Seething, Daphne wanted to hammer on the door and tell them to get out. Aristotle took hold of her arm and held her back.

'Stay calm. If they recognise you, they may tell the authorities you're still in the area.'

'How dare they just take our home, our belongings, sleep in our beds?'

'Stop it, do as I say!' he retorted. 'You could get us both shot.' He pulled her onwards, past the house, towards the street corner. 'Tell me about the safe. Where is it and what is the combination?'

'The safe is in the big front bedroom, my parents' room, behind a print of van Gogh's *Sunflowers*. The combination is 7315.' She confirmed it in her head: seven dwarves, three little pigs, one golden goose, five gold rings. She said it aloud so that he would know the connection.

'And the El Greco painting?'

'In the hallway. Noah's first painting from school is in the frame, over the painting. My father would not have the painting on show in the house. Its value was the only reason he tolerated its presence.'

'OK, tell me the combination again.'

'Seven dwarves, three little pigs, one golden goose, five gold rings.'

He shook his head with a slight smile. 'Right, here is the key to my studio. Go back now. I'll be there within the hour.'

* * *

Aristotle waited until Daphne was out of sight, then he approached the house and fiercely clattered the knocker.

A young woman came to the door.

'Is the house owner here?' Aristotle asked.

'He is, sir. Do you wish to speak with him?'

'I do. Tell him I am here on behalf of the Gestapo . . .'

Her eyes widened. 'The secret police?'

'Exactly. Quickly, I'm in a hurry!' He loaded his voice with authority.

She glanced up and down the street.

'Please step inside. My employer's upstairs. I won't keep you a moment.'

She closed the door, then ran upstairs to the first floor.

A hallway ran from the front to the back of the house, and both walls supported a row of pictures and photographs on smooth plaster, yellowed by time and cigarette smoke. Aristotle studied the images but saw no El Greco or child's nursery painting. There was, however, a blank square of pale wall where something had hung for a long time.

A few seconds later, the maid returned, scuttling down the stairs with a middle-aged man wearing a pinstriped suit and waistcoat in her wake.

'This is not your house!' Aristotle yelled. 'Unless you are complicit to my demands on behalf of the SS, we will convict you of looting and you'll be shot. Do you understand?'

'Yes, sir.'

'Where is this picture?' He pointed at the blank space.

'Ah, it was only a child's painting, sir,' the man stuttered.

'I didn't ask you what it was. Where is it?'

'Yes, I apologise. It's in the cellar.'

'Bring it, now!'

The man sent the maid.

'Can I offer you a schnapps, sir?'

'No. Take me to the safe.'

'Safe?'

'It's behind the print of van Gogh's *Sunflowers*.'

'Ah, I didn't know. We have only just moved in. Please follow me.'

They went up the stairs, turned on the landing, and entered the front bedroom. There was a large print of the old master's painting over the bed.

'Close the door, then stand in the corner and face the wall.'

Once the old man complied, Aristotle threw the painting onto the bed, then opened the safe. Inside were more contents than he expected: a small pouch of jewellery, a notebook, and several large envelopes. He took everything, slipping the jewellery into his pocket.

'Stay there until I leave. *Heil Hitler!*'

He hurried back downstairs, where the maid stood with the framed child's painting. He took it from her and left, marching to the end of the street. Once around the corner, he broke into a jog. His heart pounded with adrenalin and his whole body trembled.

Have I pulled it off?

Calm down, he told his thudding heart – remembering why he had escaped call-up into the army, and the reason two of his siblings had already met their maker. An inoperable genetic disorder had caused his sister to haemorrhage while giving birth, and die at nineteen. His brother had had an aneurysm while saving a goal in a friendly football match, and bled to death right there on the field. Aristotle knew that any extreme shock or stress could be the end of him, too. Poor Daphne must never know. She adored him, but he could not take the risk of falling in love with her. He should never have kissed her. If ever they had a child . . . he or she could inherit the problem. Besides, Daphne could become a widow long before her time. His heart ached to imagine her with another man, but that was how it had to be. Because of his deep love for her, he would make that sacrifice.

Ten minutes to curfew. Troops would search the streets soon. He strode towards the studio and his darling student.

*   *   *

Daphne's momentary sense of relief vanished when she opened the door and stared into the face of a German soldier. He blinked and said, 'You again! You have many art lessons.'

He banged his heels together and made a stiff little bow, his blond-fringed eyes never leaving hers.

A pang of anger caught in her throat. She had expected to see Aristotle.

'Are you following me?'

He laughed. 'No. Where is von Stroop? I'm here to speak to him?'

'He had to go out.'

'When will he return? Curfew is about to start? And how will you get home, come to that? You're not allowed on the streets after seven. It's forbidden.'

'I was about to leave. Could you come back tomorrow?'

'No, I have to speak to the artist.' They stared at each other. 'I had better come inside and wait for him.'

The soldier had just stepped over the threshold when Aristotle appeared behind him.

'What's happening?' he asked Daphne.

'I don't know. I need to hurry home. Curfew starts in two minutes.' Daphne's stomach churned.

The German faced her. 'Stay here, miss. I'll walk you home.' Horrified, Daphne stared at him. He turned to Aristotle. 'You painted the mayor of Athens' portrait, the one that hangs in the town hall?' Aristotle nodded. The German continued, 'Then I'm here on behalf of my commander-in-chief. You are to paint his portrait.'

Aristotle placed the envelopes and framed picture on a dresser in the narrow hall.

'What is that?' the German asked, picking up the frame and reading the name written across the top of the child's painting. 'Who is Noah Abrams, and why do you have a picture that belongs to a Jew?'

17

FLORA

MY PORTRAIT OF GRANNY DAPHNE came to a halt as I sat, spellbound by her story. What a shock to learn that my grandfather had been so talented and my grandmother so brave. I held immense pride for them both. The devastating impact war had on their lives was worse than I had imagined. These young lovers, in the first exciting embrace of romance, should have had all the joy and anticipation of a new life before them – yet they found themselves on opposite sides of an ugly war.

Daphne's eyelids slid down.

'Come on, Granny, let's feed you these pills.'

She spoke with her eyes closed. 'I'm exhausted. Flora. I hope I'm strong enough to tell you the tough parts of this story.'

I helped her into bed, kissed her forehead, and asked her if there was anything else she needed.

'Leave the light on, please. I am still terrified of the dark, even after all these years.'

'There's nothing to be afraid of here, Granny. If you're a little nervous, would you like me to sit with you?'

'I know I'm quite safe. It's not that – it's the memories in the depths of the night. Images come back to haunt me. Only opening my eyes into a lit room dispels the nightmares.'

I took her hand and patted it, hoping to keep her in the present.

'The past seems to hurt you so much, Granny. Are you sure you want to share it?'

'I have to.' She sobbed. 'I don't remember the worst of my illness. In the hospital, they tied me down, put a leather strap in my mouth to stop me from biting through my tongue, and then gave me electric shocks. Such torture, so terrible, but they made you forget everything, and this was a common treatment for depressives. They did it to my friend Alice, too – that Sigmund Freud. I'll never forgive him.'

'How awful.'

I slipped my arms around her and gave her a gentle hug.

'Poor Aristotle . . . I tried hard to put things right, but you can't give life back once you've taken it.' She grasped my hand and peered into my eyes. 'Will God forgive me, Flora? He shouldn't. What I did was unforgivable.'

'I forgive you, Granny, I forgive you for everything.'

* * *

At 8.30, I glanced around for the TV, then realised Granny didn't have one. It did not bother me until I tried to go online and discovered the Wi-Fi was down. Anyway, my battery appeared to be dead. To make matters worse, I hadn't even brought a book. In my handbag, I found Spiros's business card. Moments later, I was pressing buttons on my grandmother's landline.

'Hello, Spiro. This is Flora, the person who had your suitcase,' I said, remembering the Greek rule and dropping the 's' off his name when addressing him.

'Ah, hello again. What can I do for you? Don't tell me you're taking me up on my offer?'

'Well, not quite, but you gave me your card . . . I wonder if you'd care to share a bottle of wine in the garden of Mon Repos?'

'Have you eaten?' he said with a smile in his voice. 'I could take you somewhere . . .'

'Sorry, no. My grandmother . . . You know how it is. She's sleeping, but I can't leave her alone.'

'How about I bring a couple of *giros* to go with the *krasí*?'

'Sounds amazing, thank you. Hope I'm not interrupting anything?'

'Not at all. I'll be there in thirty minutes.'

* * *

I hurried to the bathroom and tidied myself up. After spraying myself with mosquito repellent, and applying a fresh coat of lipstick, I placed two glasses and a bottle of red on the outside table.

You understand, don't you, Mark? If I don't have an intelligent, adult conversation soon, I'll go mad!

Half an hour later, the sound of an engine, followed by the slam of a car door, echoed through the balmy evening air.

'*Kalispéra!*' he called, looming out of the dark. 'Good evening!'

I echoed his greeting.

He placed a carrier on the table. The smell of roast pork ignited my hunger.

'I'll get some plates and forks,' I said.

'No need, it's eaten out of the paper with your fingers,' he replied. 'You'll find some napkins in the bag.'

We sat opposite each other, delicious, herby aromas enveloping us. A ginger tom appeared, sat next to the table and stared at me. Without thinking, I threw some titbits his way.

'Thanks for this,' I said to Spiros.

We chatted and laughed between mouthfuls of tasty food that would have been better accompanied by a beer, but the wine was fair enough. Without an outside light, our eyes soon adjusted to the dark. We talked about music, then art, and then I brought the conversation round to Mon Repos.

'I heard a rumour that the mansion was about to be demolished.' I nodded towards the trees that hid the majestic building. 'Is it true?'

He paused and turned to face me with a startled look.

'Good God, no! Where did you hear such a thing?'

His voice was so convincing that I thought: either you're an excellent liar, or I'm mistaken.

I took a breath and confessed. 'I was inside, and overheard you saying it should be knocked down as soon as possible.'

'You were eavesdropping?' He frowned.

'Not at all. I was standing right beside you, buying postcards in the lobby.'

'I see. Unfortunately, you only caught half the conversation. We're demolishing the tallest chimney stack. The mortar crumbled, making it unsafe. The pot's an antique, so I want to save it. We must take the stack down before it falls and kills somebody, but we'll rebuild it using the same bricks.'

'I'm so relieved. I'll be able to give Granny some good news in the morning. You can't imagine how concerned she was.'

'Did you find out if your grandmother was the woman in the portrait?'

'I haven't asked her yet. She's almost a hundred, so I have to filter the excitement so she doesn't get too animated.'

'Maybe we should discuss this again over dinner tomorrow evening?'

I hesitated. My heart wouldn't let this virtual stranger step into my darling Mark's shoes just to ease my grief.

'I must be honest, Spiro, I enjoy your company, but I'm not looking for anything romantic. My darling husband has just died and I'm devastated. I'm sorry if I've misled you.'

'I understand. Still, I would like to take you out for the good company and intelligent conversation. We seem to have a lot in common. It's rare for me to find a beautiful woman who can talk about art with some authority. Paintings, architecture and photography are a large part of my life.'

'You're right, we have a lot in common, and you were doing very well until the "beautiful woman" bit.' I looked into his eyes and took a sip of wine.

'Sorry about that, but "say it as you see it" is my motto.'

After a year of Mark's illness, I'd forgotten what flirting was like. With all my heart, I wished it was Mark sitting opposite me at that moment.

We talked until nearly midnight, then I walked down the path that led to the road. There was an awkward moment when we stood there, not knowing what to say. I hoped he would not move in for a kiss, but just as I was about to fill the silence, he lifted my hand towards his mouth and touched the back with his lips.

'Thank you for a very pleasant evening, and goodnight. Call me tomorrow. I want to hear what your grandmother says about the painting.'

*   *   *

After a sound sleep, I stepped out of the cottage to greet a new day that was fresh and full of promise. The yellow sun, like the one I imagined in Noah's childish painting, rose in the deep cerulean sky. A breeze tickled the high treetops, causing a momentary shiver of giggling leaves. The air at ground level became so still it seemed the world had stopped turning. I glanced to the heavens and said 'Good morning' to my husband. A glorious chorus of birdsong struck up, and I took a moment to drink in the beauty of my surroundings.

As Granny wouldn't wake for another hour. I decided on a jog down to the beach. The sun's warmth gathered and touched my bare shoulders. The sea embraced every molecule of sunlight, sparkling with energy, encouraging me to push myself with a longer stride. I raced along the shore past Mon Repos, feeling weightless. The sea lapped the pebbles, and the slight salty scent in the air lifted me even higher. For the first time since Mark's death, I experienced an essence of freedom at being alone.

Back at the cottage, gasping from a final push up the hill to Mon Repos, I collapsed onto a bench outside the door.

'Flora!' Granny called.

* * *

After a breakfast of coffee and toast, Granny gave me a determined nod.

'Let's move outside before I continue. I need sunshine before my mind works.' She poked her head with an arthritic finger. 'I have a solar-powered brain, you know.' She lifted her chin and giggled like a child.

With a grin on my face and love in my heart, I pushed her wheelchair out.

'Now remind me, where was I up to?' she asked.

'The German soldier had picked up the El Greco.'

'Ah, yes. Quite a scary moment.' She placed a hand over her eyes and turned her head away, as if to block the memory. 'Is your recorder turned on, dear girl?'

18

DAPHNE

Athens, 1943

THE SOLDIER STARED AT NOAH'S nursery painting, then at Aristotle.

'Tell me!' he demanded, thrusting the painting at Aristotle.

Daphne almost whimpered, then feared she would attract the soldier's attention. Hurrying to the rudimentary kitchen behind the studio, she stood near the open door, held her breath, and listened.

Aristotle answered the soldier in German. 'Sorry, I don't understand.'

'Noah Abrams is a Jewish name. Who is he, and why do you have his painting?'

'Ah, I see. I hadn't noticed the name.' Aristotle feigned surprise. 'I don't know him. I saw the frame on top of a box of rubbish by the bins. It's a handsome piece of work. Just look at that carving – so well made. I brought it home to clean up. Quality frames are hard to come by these days.' He reached out and took the frame from the soldier. 'Now, what's this about a portrait? Why don't you come in and take some refreshment? Perhaps a brandy?' He turned to the kitchen door and called Daphne. 'Girl, make this fine soldier a coffee, and pour him a cognac to go with it.'

An hour later, the soldier was ready to leave the studio.

'Where's that pretty girl? I'll walk her home.'

His face, flushed from the double cognac, peered towards the kitchen door.

'She's probably asleep in the back,' Aristotle said. 'She can stay until morning, so don't trouble yourself.'

'I see.' The soldier bobbed his eyebrows. 'Does she model for you?' He scratched his lip. 'Without clothes, I mean.'

'No, she cleans and cooks and runs messages for me, to pay for her art lessons. But I hope she'll model for me one day. Why do you ask? Are you an artist, too?'

He laughed. 'No, at least not yet. However, I might take it up as a hobby, and if I do, I'll come to you for the lessons.'

'Good man. I'd be happy to teach you.' He walked the soldier to the door. 'By the way, I didn't catch your name.'

'Klaus Schulze, at your service.' He snapped his heels together and thrust his hand out in a Nazi salute. '*Heil Hitler!*'

* * *

Aristotle took the soldier's cup into the kitchen, where Daphne sat at the table with her head on her arms.

'That was a little scary,' she said. 'I'm so tired. Is it true what you said? Can I sleep here tonight?'

'So, you heard us? Well, I'm not sure that's wise, Daphne. A beautiful young woman spending the night with a man who worships her?'

He worships me?

She blinked at him with adoration shining from her eyes.

'There's nowhere I would rather be.'

'Your mother will be out of her mind with worry.'

'No, I told her I might not be home, not to worry.' She went up close and then, as bold as can be, pressed herself against his body. 'I want to stay the night, Aristotle. You know I'm longing to sleep with you.'

He wrapped his arms around her. 'You are so naughty, darling Daphne. There is nothing I want more, but this is not the time. We must wait a little longer, because you're very young and we must be sure.'

'Is there somebody else?'

He hesitated. 'I can't explain at this moment. You must have faith in me . . . my heart is honourable. Do you trust me, Daphne?' he repeated.

'Yes, of course, I trust you with my life, my honour, and my heart.'

'Then you may sleep in my bed.'

Daphne gasped as that same heart almost leaped out of her chest. He would fall in love with her. They would marry after the war and have many children, a house, perhaps even an automobile. He would open his own gallery and she would teach children languages and art. She saw it all.

'And I will sleep in the studio.'

Her mother would be pleased – she was going to marry a gentleman.

'First, I must study this El Greco.'

He threw a cloth over the bare wooden table, then placed the El Greco face down and removed the backing. He studied the inside, sniffed the back of the canvas, then used a large magnifying glass to peer into the corners of the stretcher.

'Don't you want to see the painting?' Daphne asked. 'What are you doing?'

'I'm checking as best I can that it is real, the genuine article. Was it painted in the sixteenth century? If so, it would smell old, and the back of the canvas and stretcher would be ancient, too.'

159

'But if my ancestors bought the painting from the El Greco family, or whatever they were called, then surely it must be genuine.'

'Perhaps one of his students painted it in his teacher's style. That happened a lot – still does. Look how you paint in my style without realising it.'

'What if he signed El Greco on the painting?'

'If it's signed, El Greco, then I'm certain it's a fake. One thing at a time, Daphne.'

He continued, bent over the work with his magnifying glass, almost absent-mindedly talking about El Greco as he worked. Daphne's heart thumped with anticipation. After an age, he straightened and, by the sparkle in his eyes, she guessed he was satisfied it was genuine so far.

'The Spaniards nicknamed him El Greco, "the Greek", because Doménikos Theotokópoulos was a mouthful for any non-Greek to say. The other thing is, he always signed his paintings with his full name, often followed by the old Greek word for "Cretan", and he inscribed all this using matching paint and in the Greek alphabet.'

Aristotle lifted the canvas out of the frame and turned it over. Noah's picture of lollipop olive trees and a radiant yellow sun seemed stuck in place, so with great caution, millimetre by millimetre, he peeled it back. They both held their breath.

'This is so exciting. I wonder what it looks like.'

'You mean you've never seen it?' He stopped and stared as she shook her head.

'I wasn't even supposed to know about it, but when the war started, Noah took me to one side and said if ever my life was in danger, I could use the painting to get myself out of trouble.' Daphne's emotions rose. 'Poor Noah. He was such a gallant person. If he hadn't fought my father so hard about us getting new documents, where would we be now?' She felt her heart sink. 'I'll never hear him argue with Babá again.'

Aristotle took her in his arms. 'You poor thing. What a terrible thing to happen.'

'Where do you suppose Isaac is, Aristotle? Do you know about these work camps? One of my friends said they were amazing places, with a smart little house for each family and gardens where they could grow vegetables and flowers. She watched a film with her parents that showed these compounds were so much nicer than the other Jewish ghettos. Her family was one of the first volunteers to go when her father lost his job here in Greece.' She remembered the mail. 'They even sent us postcards to say how good it was. They had concerts and everything, and the Red Cross visited them regularly.'

'I don't know, Daphne. It's difficult to know exactly what's happening in this war. Where did your friends go?'

'A camp called Theresienstadt. It sounds German, but I'm not sure where it is. They say it's a spa town, where the old folk can retire in comfort while the younger members of their family work for a living.'

Aristotle stared at her, his mouth turned down and eyes dull with sadness.

'I don't know, Daphne,' he said again. 'We can hope.' He returned his attention to the painting. 'Great, the paper's coming off easily now. Let's see what we have.'

He lifted Noah's work of art to one side.

'Can I keep Noah's picture?' Daphne asked as they both looked down on an oil painting of Christ's face, complete with upturned eyes and a crown of thorns. 'What grief! Whoever painted it liked a bit of misery, didn't they?' she said. 'In my

161

opinion, it has to be an El Greco, with those despairing eyes and that sharp nose, so in tune with his style.'

'Beautiful,' Aristotle breathed, appearing not to hear her. 'Preserved to perfection behind the paper. What amazing colours. It's difficult to accept he probably painted this over three hundred and fifty years ago.'

'What shall we do with it?'

'Let me consider our options overnight. I could contact my cousin and ask him to put me in touch with an art dealer.'

'Your cousin . . .? But you said he was in the SS.'

Daphne felt a chill race down her spine. What if her father had been right about Aristotle? The man she had fallen in love with could have her shot, or taken away, and keep the painting for himself. He'd be a millionaire; he had said as much.

Engrossed by the painting, he seemed to study every brushstroke until he looked up with tears sparkling in his eyes.

'It's so magnificent, I feel quite emotional,' he gasped, then sighed and turned to her. 'Your face is very pale, Daphne. What's worrying you?'

'I'm thinking you could have me killed and keep the painting, and you would become a millionaire in an instant,' she said in one rapid breath.

'You should have thought of that in the first place, don't you think?'

*   *   *

Daphne woke at dawn in Aristotle's bed. She pulled the sheets over her face and inhaled his scent. If only he had joined her, the night could have been perfect. She recalled the German soldier, Klaus Schulze, the painting, and all the excitement and danger

162

of the day before. She was still alive. That was something. Now she had to return home and face her mother's interrogation – more terrifying than anything that had gone before.

'Wake up, dreamer,' Aristotle said, sticking his head inside the small bedroom. 'I have some warm milk and biscuits for breakfast. Then I'm going to telephone my cousin, so I want you out of here in case he sends somebody around.'

'Wouldn't you like ten minutes in your own bed first?' Daphne asked, batting her eyelashes, although she already knew the answer.

'You're a shameless young woman! I should tell your mother.'

Daphne giggled. 'I expect that means no.'

'Yes, you're right. Now come on, out of there!'

She dressed with all haste, kissed him hard on the lips, then left for Kyría Alice's home, only to discover the good woman had already left for the soup kitchen and her starving children.

Daphne found her mother kneading bread.

'Mamá! I hope you didn't worry too much last night,' she said.

Mamá let out a brief scream, then flew at her, yelling and waving her arms.

'Worry? No, of course I didn't worry – I convinced myself you were dead already!' She made hatchet movements with the side of her hand, bits of dough and flour flying into her hair and onto her shoulders. 'They could have murdered you, or stuck you on one of their cattle trains, you stupid child, but you're not dead, so I'll kill you myself!'

She rained blows on her daughter, tears streaming down her face. Daphne buried her face in the side of her mother's neck and clung to her.

'Mamá, stop! Nothing happened to me. Listen to me, I love you, and I've got the painting! Aristotle went to the house and brought it back. There's so much to tell you.'

'I thought you were dead . . . Don't you hear me? I thought I'd never see you again!'

'Oh, Mamá, please dry your eyes. I'm perfectly fine and we're going to be all right. You wait and see.'

'Before you tell me anything, go upstairs and put a uniform on. Your clothes are too crumpled. Did you sleep in them?' Daphne nodded. 'Go and get changed. Kyría Alice says we must dress smartly and play the part of being her staff at all times.'

Elizabeth came hurrying into the kitchen, glanced at her mother's tear-stained eyes, and asked, 'Is something wrong?'

'No, everything's fine. Mamá was worried about me, that's all.'

'My uniform is beautiful, Daphne. Do I look grown-up?' She held the sides of her skirt out and did a twirl. 'The plan is, if there should be a raid on the building, we all behave like live-in domestics for Kyría Alice. Mamá is an assistant cook. I am a scullery maid, and you are part of the general house staff.'

Cook appeared and seemed relieved to see me.

'Let's all take a break and listen to Daphne's news, shall we?' She dropped her bovine behind into a chair and kicked off her shoes. 'Elizabeth, can you make a pot of mountain tea?'

'Yes, Cook, of course. I'm very good at tea, aren't I, Mamá?' She set about the task.

Daphne told them everything that had happened, apart from begging Aristotle to sleep with her. She assured Mamá her art teacher had the painting hidden in a safe place. Her mother, not convinced, continued to harangue her.

'You realise he could disappear with the painting, as he has the provenance as well. We may never see him or the El Greco again.'

'No, Mamá, Aristotle's an honourable man. I know he'll get us the best price for the painting.'

* * *

At first, fourteen-year-old Elizabeth loved her new job. She tied her long ringlets in rags each night and polished her shoes until they shone. Everyone learned their part and put on the uniforms provided by their benefactor: starched white aprons with frilled shoulders worn over simple grey dresses.

Elizabeth had a rude awakening when Cook told her to scour the pans, then get on her knees and scrub the kitchen's stone floor.

'My hands are blistered and cracked and so sore!' she cried later, as tears rolled down her face.

The Rosenburgs were another story. The old couple had to stay in the attic day and night, while everyone fretted about what to say if the couple were found and the staff questioned.

It was three days before Aristotle turned up with news of the painting.

'I have the money for your tickets, and my cousin will put the rest of the money in my bank account as soon as the buyer pays up.'

'But what if he just runs away with our painting?' Mamá asked.

He shook his head. 'Then he won't be able to prove it's a genuine El Greco. I kept the document from El Greco's father that says it's genuine, and told the buyer he can have it when he pays up. Without the provenance, the painting will lose seventy-five per cent of its value.'

'You're so clever, Aristotle,' Daphne said, ignoring Elizabeth's groan while she rolled her eyes.

'Your biggest threat now is the Rosenburgs. We must get their documents and ship them out as soon as possible. I don't want them travelling with you, do you understand? As soon as they've gone, we'll get you on the next ship to Cairo.'

*　*　*

Elizabeth, tired from her domestic chores, had already gone to bed when Alice returned and joined them to eat soup and bread in the kitchen.

'How shall we get them to the photographers?' Daphne asked Aristotle.

Mamá, who was not fond of the elderly couple, said, 'I don't care about this, and I'm exhausted. If you'll excuse me, I'm also off to bed.'

Daphne made excuses for her. 'She was awake all last night, worrying about me. Poor Mamá, I feel so bad.'

'A lesson learned, Daphne,' Kyría Alice said. 'When you're a mother yourself, you'll understand.'

They all watched Mamá close the door behind her, then Aristotle spoke.

'I'm going to tell you something, but first you, Daphne, must promise never to tell anyone – not even your mother, and especially not Elizabeth.'

Daphne nodded. 'I swear, I won't tell a soul.'

She hoped it wasn't something so awful that she felt obliged to share the secret with someone.

He lowered his voice. 'Under the cellars of Athens runs a secret tunnel. We have moved the printing press and the photography equipment down there, and you'll be proud to know this was Noah's idea.'

Daphne's heart was somersaulting at the mention of her brother's name.

'But how will we get the Rosenburgs into this place?' she asked.

He explained that there was an entrance by the kiosk near the front of Kyría Alice's building. The way Kyría Alice nodded, Daphne suspected she knew already.

'The strategy is to move the kiosk over the metal trapdoor in the street. They will go into the kiosk as if to buy something, and not reappear.'

'What a marvellous plan, Aristotle, but is it true?' Daphne asked. 'Are there tunnels under the city?'

Alice placed her hand over Daphne's and smiled.

'Kilometres of them, Daphne. They built most of them towards the end of the Great War, when we all feared the terrible mustard gas.'

'This is wonderful news. The Rosenburgs will go into the tunnels and get their photographs and papers done, but how will they escape?' Daphne asked.

'It's better if you don't know the details,' Kyría Alice said.

* * *

Daphne listened to Kyría Alice. Although her nerves jangled, she would follow the good lady's instructions to the letter.

'Are you sure you understand everything?' Kyría Alice asked, after going over Daphne's part in the procedure. 'Aristotle will walk to the kiosk with you and Kyría Rosenburg. You act as though she's not with you, and that you only have eyes for Aristotle.'

Daphne nodded. 'And when we get to the kiosk, Kyría Rosenburg will slip behind the awning. It seems straightforward, Kyría Alice. What could go wrong?'

'Don't tempt fate, please!' Aristotle muttered. 'What if there's a German in the kiosk? What if the trapdoor won't open? What if the kiosk attendant is a traitor?' He raised his shoulders and lifted his hands in exasperation.

'Sorry, I wasn't thinking. What about Kýrios Rosenburg?'

'One at a time. First, the woman. If all goes well, an hour later, we'll move the man.'

'When?' Daphne asked.

'Four o'clock.'

* * *

Kyría Alice peered out of the window upstairs, checking that the street was clear of troops. She signalled Aristotle and Daphne, who waited in the hall below her, with two loud bangs on the floor, telling them they were clear to go. They instructed Kyría Rosenburg to walk in the direction of the kiosk, not looking left or right. To keep going, no matter what happened to Aristotle or Daphne.

No sooner had they stepped into the street than a door on the opposite side opened. A German soldier marched across the road and shouted 'Halt!'

Kyría Rosenburg kept walking.

The soldier drew his pistol. Daphne almost collapsed, then she realised that once again it was Klaus Schulze.

'My God! You gave me such a fright, sir. I believe you are following me,' she said as cheerfully as she could manage, stepping towards him with her most charming smile and batting her eyelashes. Could she attract his attention away from old Kyría Rosenburg?

'You again!' he said, glancing an inquisitive eye over her uniform. 'What are you doing here?'

As he waved the gun at her chest, the skin tightened over her body and her mouth dried, making it impossible to answer.

'Well?' he yelled, raising the gun to her forehead.

'Sorry ... you're frightening me,' she stammered, peering into his eyes. 'I thought you liked me,' she added in German.

19

FLORA

Corfu, present day

DAPHNE HAD NODDED OFF AGAIN, so I went on with her portrait, pleased as her likeness emerged. I couldn't believe her family – my family – had owned an El Greco painting!

Just imagine, we might have been multi-millionaires. But what had happened to it? Daphne woke and carried on with her memoirs as I continued to paint.

'The thing was, I wasn't sure that he loved me,' she said, squinting into the distance. 'I mean, loved me above all others. He never said so until the end. I longed to hear those words, "I love you, Daphne." But do you know why he never told me?'

I shook my head.

'Because he was sick, and because of his health, he didn't want me to fall in love with him. Wasn't that noble? He knew he'd die young, never reach old age, be a grandfather. Even though he might have children, he wouldn't be around when they grew up, and then where would I be?'

My heart screwed into a knot as I thought about my darling husband. Oh, Mark! I swallowed hard, determined to stay in control of my emotions.

She nodded. 'Is that how he escaped the army, Granny?'

'I was so young, I never even thought about it. His blood vessels . . . His veins were weak, and they grew much weaker as he aged. He bruised with the slightest knock, but that was not

the problem. It was the blood vessels in his head. If one rup-
tured, he would die there and then of a brain haemorrhage, or
live with the disability of a stroke.'

'He didn't encourage you to fall in love with him, but all the
time, he was in love with you. Isn't that so romantic?'

She nodded, staring into the distance. 'I was desperately in
love with him, and I believe he felt the same way about me.' A
tear slid down her face. 'It's sad, isn't it? Now I know he loved
me. And I left no doubt in his mind that I loved him to the ends
of the earth.'

* * *

Yánna phoned to say she would be home that evening. I put the
phone on speaker and set it on the table between me and Daphne.

'Why don't you stay another night?' I asked. 'I'm managing
very well, thank you, and it's lovely to spend some quality time
with my grandmother.'

'But are you sure, Mrs Flora? Don't you want to swim in this
lovely pool and relax on a sunbed? I'm having such a wonderful
time.'

'I'm so glad, Yánna. You deserve it. Besides, I'm enjoying
the extra time with my grandmother. But have you had a
swim, Yánna?'

'Yes, thanks to my friend, the room maid with the trolley,
Chrisoula. I give her a hand to make the beds – it's much quicker
with two. She ask me if I would use the pool, but I told her I
didn't have a costume. Chrisoula was so kind to me. She took me
to the lost property office and found a costume in my size. She
said many people leave them hanging over the balcony to dry
on their last morning, and they get blown away. The gardener

collects the costumes and puts them into lost property. I must tell you how beautiful it is . . . brand new and pure gold, one that glitters in the sunlight. It goes so well with my flashy sandals.' Daphne's eyes met mine, and she grinned. 'To be honest, Flora, it makes me look like a film star. And, the receptionist gave me the most beautiful beach-wrap, also left behind, to drape around myself when I go to eat lunch. They said it's not allowed to go into the restaurant in your swimwear in case you drive the men wild with desire.'

Daphne blew a raspberry and then slapped a hand over her mouth.

'Very wise, Yánna. I'm sure you look stunning in your gold lamé swimwear. Just make sure you use plenty of cream, OK?'

'I asked Chrisoula if she had any larger bottles of moisturiser than the ones she left in the bathroom, because I needed at least ten of them to cover myself for sunbathing. She went and found me four half-full bottles of factor thirty in lost property. Isn't she marvellous?'

After hanging up, I grinned at Daphne.

'Bless her, she's so thrilled with her free holiday and all the perks that go with it.'

My grandmother smiled. 'You're very kind, Flora. I'm proud of you, and very pleased for Yánna. Besides, it's lovely for me to have you all to myself. Can I ask you one thing? Will you make sure she's all right when I've gone? She's taken good care of me for most of her adult life. She'll find it hard.'

'Of course I will. I owe her a lot for looking after you the way she does.'

'Now, tell me how the portrait's coming along. Are you pleased with it? And are you going out with that young man again? You're too young to spend all your time with an old woman.'

I blinked at her. 'Do you think it's all right? I mean, am I a traitor? Now that we know Spiros is trying to conserve Mon Repos, there's no reason to meet him again. Yet I have to admit I enjoy his company.'

'Why should you stop seeing him? It's not as if there's any romance involved, is there? Besides, Mark wouldn't want you to go into deep mourning, would he? It's not part of your culture, and it makes no difference to your sense of loss. There's no doubt you loved Mark.'

'Me and Spiros, we have a lot in common.'

'Good. Now, is that tape recorder of yours turned on?'

20

DAPHNE

DAPHNE TOOK ANOTHER STEP TOWARDS the soldier, holding his stare with her own.

'I am employed by the lady in residence.' She ran a hand over her apron bib in a slightly suggestive way. 'And also by Kýrios von Stroop.'

Schulze stood taller, blinked at her, then turned to Aristotle.

'And you, sir – why are you here?' His eyes narrowed in his pale, smooth-shaven face.

'I'm about to start a portrait for the princess. Why else would I be here, my friend? Which reminds me . . . Your commander's portrait. We never did get around to sorting out the arrangements. Why don't you join me at the studio for a drink? Perhaps try your hand at a little artwork and share a lesson with my student?' He nodded in Daphne's direction and winked.

Schulze lifted his chin, a flicker of confusion in his eyes as he glanced from Aristotle to Daphne and back. After a moment, he accepted the invitation.

'Do I need to bring anything? Brushes, paints, canvas?'

Aristotle shook his head. 'I have everything. Just bring your good self, Sergeant.'

Daphne gasped and slapped her hand over her mouth. Both men looked her way.

'You've reminded me,' she said. 'I left my paintbrushes in the kitchen – I'll have to go back.'

'All right, I'll walk with you,' Aristotle said. 'With Sergeant Schulze's permission.'

The German made a sharp nod before he marched down the street, past the kiosk, and onwards.

Aristotle and Daphne turned back to Alice's home. The door opened as they approached, and they slipped inside. The instant the door was closed, Daphne's knees buckled.

Aristotle caught her. 'Well done. You're a natural actress.'

Daphne pressed her hand against her chest, trying to slow her thudding heart.

'What happened?' Kyría Alice asked nervously, ushering them into the drawing room.

'Daphne saved the day with her quick thinking,' Aristotle replied. 'Kyría Rosenburg completed her journey, but I think we'd be foolish to continue with today's plan. I'll try to get the German drunk this evening. Then we should move Rosenberg immediately after curfew ends tomorrow morning, when we hope Sergeant Schulze has an almighty hangover.'

'Why was he watching the house?' Daphne asked as Kyría Alice rang the maid's bell three times.

'Who knows?' Aristotle said. 'Perhaps it was simply a coincidence.'

Elizabeth appeared in her uniform and curtsied, which amused Daphne.

'Bring tea for my guests, Elizabeth,' Kyría Alice said.

Elizabeth's eyes widened as they met Daphne's. Still, she behaved perfectly. As she turned towards the door, Aristotle said, 'Elizabeth!'

She turned and nodded. 'Yes, sir?'

'What's your name, girl?'

'Elizabeth Papadopoulos, sir.'

175

'Well done.'

She curtsied again, a smile in her eyes.

'Thank you, sir. I'll bring the tea.'

*   *   *

'What's your plan for this evening, Aristotle?' Kyría Alice asked, as he and Daphne were leaving.

'I'll do my best to get Schulze drunk and solidify our acquaintance. It's always useful to have a friend in the opposition's camp.'

Kyría Alice crossed herself. 'Please be careful. He may be very cunning and think he can get the better of you.' She glanced at the window. 'I wonder what he was doing over there.'

'Perhaps I'll find out this evening.'

*   *   *

'Do you think he'll come?' Daphne asked, glancing from the sunset on her canvas to the studio door.

Aristotle shrugged as a knock sounded. 'There's your answer.'

Daphne swished her brush through the water. Magenta and red mingled and swirled as her mouth turned dry as dust.

'Ah, Sergeant Schulze, I'm glad you could make it. Can I get you a coffee or a cognac?'

For the first time, the sergeant's squint of animosity fell away. He appeared almost friendly.

'It's been a difficult day,' he said, turning to Daphne and making a stiff bow.

'Then it's both,' Aristotle said. 'Wise choice. Daphne, put the *briki* on the stove while I pour our sergeant here a large brandy.'

In the kitchen, she took the long-handled copper beaker from a hook and spooned ground coffee into it. 'You'll be pleased to know this is real coffee, Sergeant,' she called through the open door.

Aristotle offered the sergeant a chair. 'Luckily, I had a customer who paid for his portrait with coffee and brandy,' he explained with a smile 'Worth its weight in gold, my friend.'

Daphne delivered the coffee and returned to her easel. In a moment of alarming silence, Schulze watched her intensely, then rose and stood behind her.

'This is fascinating,' the soldier mumbled over Daphne's shoulder, so close she could smell the garlic on his breath. 'Herr von Stroop, can you teach me to paint like this girl?' Walking his fingertips up her arm until his forefinger touched the bare skin of her neck, he said, 'What's your name again, pretty girl?'

She suppressed a shudder. 'I'm Daphne, at your service, sir.'

He turned to Aristotle. 'How long before I can paint her?' He exhaled loudly. 'I want to paint her body, all of it, nude. Can you teach me to do that?'

Bile stung the back of Daphne's throat as she fought against rising nausea.

Aristotle paused, then said, 'I don't think—'

At this point Daphne cut in.

'Oh, sir, you really want to paint me without my clothes on?' She pouted and peered at him from under her long lashes. 'I've never done that before. I can't imagine . . .'

The German's face had become a little puffy and his lips had taken on a deeper hue. Suddenly, Daphne straightened – experiencing a rush of control and power over this man.

I will have you eating out of my hand before the month is past, she thought.

'Despite my inexperience on the dais, I'd be honoured to abandon my clothes in the name of art, just for you, of course. First, give me your word you'd be honourable, sir. I am not experienced at anything like this.'

'But of course!' he blustered.

'And as I'm inexperienced, you'd have to position me, you understand, into a pose you'd find most pleasing.'

She noticed Aristotle's jaw drop, and was glad he was standing behind the soldier.

Sergeant Schulze rubbed his hand over his mouth, and then tried to adjust the front of his trousers inconspicuously.

'Herr von Stroop! How many lessons will I need to be able to paint this young woman with justice?'

'Who can say? Perhaps, as you are so enthusiastic, a hundred hours.'

'So, I'll take fifty double lessons, starting this evening. In two months' time, I will paint the young woman as naked as the day she was born.'

Sensing Aristotle was lost for words, Daphne turned to Schulze.

'Excuse me, Sergeant. I usually work six evenings a week for Herr von Stroop. Will I get paid for the modelling?'

'Of course you will, and very well, too.' Schulze turned towards Aristotle. 'And you, sir, will receive a most valuable painting, worth more than you could earn in five lifetimes. This is on top of the money you will be paid when my major-general confirms he is pleased with his portrait.'

'Thank you, very generous. Let me get you another brandy before we make a start. I have an easel and canvas all ready. Our lesson today is all about composition.'

* * *

178

A car came for Sergeant Schulze at nine o'clock. The moment the door closed behind the soldier, Daphne collapsed into Aristotle's arms.

'That was the hardest thing I've ever done,' she cried.

'You were amazing. He's fallen in love with you, Daphne.'

'Fallen in lust would be a fairer description. Did you get all the information you needed out of him?'

'Not really, but he'll be here tomorrow evening. Perhaps you should not be quite so . . . inviting. You even had me a little hot around the collar this evening.'

'I did?' she said, grinning as she threw her arms around his neck. 'Will you kiss me as hard as you can?'

'No, I won't.' He tried to supress a grin, gently pushing her away then cleaning the brushes. 'You can sleep here tonight if you promise to behave.'

'Oh, Aristotle, how can our love blossom when you keep me at arm's length? I'm going to die of a broken heart.'

'A better end than to die of a German bullet.'

'Will you ever fall in love with me, Aristotle?'

'One day, perhaps, but not now.'

'I was acting a part to get his trust. You don't have to be jealous.'

Aristotle's laugh stabbed her in the heart. 'I think you've set yourself up for more than his trust, Daphne.'

* * *

As dawn broke the next morning, the occupants of Kyría Alice's household were unsettled. The jeweller came down to the ground floor for the first time since he had entered the building weeks earlier with his wife. His eyes were even puffier than usual, and his skin was pale from worry and a lack of sunlight.

179

Aristotle, Daphne and Solomon Rosenburg were about to leave the building when Aristotle told them to wait a moment, count to ten, then proceed to the kiosk as planned, without him. He went out, walked straight across the road, and hammered on the opposite door. Daphne saw a soldier answer, and then he and Aristotle seemed to have a heated conversation.

Daphne turned and walked towards the kiosk, where she stopped to buy a copy of the *Kathimerini* newspaper. Kýrios Rosenburg walked between Daphne and the building, then he disappeared behind the shelves, where Daphne presumed someone was waiting to lead him through the trapdoor and down the ladder.

As she stood holding the newspaper that gave off the pungent odour of printer's ink, she was filled with memories of Noah and felt her tears rise. She wondered where Isaac was at that moment. She tried to imagine him planting flowers in one of the lovely gardens of Theresienstadt, but it didn't seem right and she couldn't say why.

'Will we ever hear from the Rosenburgs again?' she asked Aristotle, when they were waiting for Sergeant Schulze in the studio.

'Probably not, and I'd suggest that everyone forget they ever met them.'

'Are there really kilometres of tunnels under Athens, Aristotle?'

'Yes, more than you would imagine. Many are closed, but a few still exist and will take you from one end of Athens to the other.'

Daphne hoped Kýrios Rosenburg had joined his wife and had been spirited away to safety.

21

FLORA

Corfu, present day

I STARED AT MY GRANDMOTHER. 'Is that true? Do the tunnels really exist?'

'Absolutely. The largest gallery is under Kolonaki and Mount Lycabettus, in the city centre. They've all got a chamber at the entrance to trap gas, and inside there are showers in case of chemical warfare. Everyone remembered and feared the mustard gas used in the Great War. Banned now, thank goodness, but who can be sure they won't use it as a weapon again, in the future?'

'By the way, did I tell you it's only the chimney of Mon Repos that's being knocked down? The old render's crumbled, making it dangerous, but they'll rebuild it to look exactly the same.'

Daphne placed a hand on her chest and took a deep breath. 'That's such a relief! Will you go out with your young man again this evening?'

'Perhaps. It was so good to have a sensible conversation about art. He may even get me some work from the gallery in town, which would be wonderful.' I paused. 'Granny, did you and Aristotle hide valuable paintings in the mansion's basement?'

She made a little whimper and closed her eyes. After a long silence, she raised a hand.

'Wait, I'll get to the cellar of Mon Repos in due course. Don't rush me. It must come at the right time or I'll get muddled.'

'And what about the amorous German, Schulze? What happened to him?'

'He continued to come for his double lessons, and when the time came for me to pose in the nude, I made the excuse that it was the wrong time of the month. I bared my breasts for the picture, and it thrilled him to paint me in a state of half-undress. For weeks he came and continued with that portrait.' She caught my eye. 'I felt so powerful! For the first time in my life, I understood the hold we have over men, and it gave me such confidence.'

'Do you mind me asking, where's the portrait that Schulze did?'

'You can ask me anything you want. I believe the painting's in the basement of the national gallery in Athens, but that's another story. The commissions for portraits came in, and we continued to paint as many as we could, despite everything.'

'We?'

She frowned and glanced around the room. 'Well, I meant to say "he", of course.'

'Is that when you came to Corfu?'

Her face fell and I could see she was struggling again.

'Wait – damn my memory. I must get things in the right order. Let me think for a moment.'

I wheeled her a little further from the cottage for a change of scene. We sat under a magnificent Judas tree in full blossom — vivid purple-pink flowers contrasted with the bare, silver-grey bark.

'Such a beautiful tree,' she said as her eyes became languorous and slowly closed. 'Judas fooled everyone . . . Not who they thought he was. He was a traitor, too. Fooled everybody, just like me.'

182

A traitor, too . . .? What was she saying?

Suddenly, Yánna was beside us.

'Ah, you are here, very good. Is everything OK?'

'We're fine, Yánna, thank you,' I said.

After smoothing a wisp of Daphne's white hair behind her ear, she said, 'We will walk back to the cottage and I make you coffee, Mrs Flora.' She nodded at Daphne. 'Daphne usually has a sleep around this time.'

Yánna pushed the wheelchair while I carried my folding chair.

* * *

'Do you know what she wants to tell me, Yánna?' I asked. 'I'm afraid it might be too emotional for her.'

While Granny slept in her room, Yánna made Greek coffee at the stove. The room filled with the warm, rich aroma of freshly roasted beans. I inhaled deeply, this scent – and also the sweet and yeasty fragrance of freshly baked bread, always took me to my grandmother's home. Whether I found myself standing in a super-market, or at the counter of my local bakery on a rainy Wednesday, a smile would lend itself to my lips as memories of past summers came to mind. I glanced at the empty chair next to me.

Yánna stopped stirring the small copper *briki*.

'Yes, I think I do. She saved my life, you know? My husband was a dangerous man. He nearly killed me, broke my nose and two ribs.'

'Good God! No, I didn't know.'

'There is plenty you don't know. She paid the most high price that any mother can pay, my Daphne, poor woman. It's so tragic. She will tell you. *Ypomoní*, ee-pom-on-nee, you must learn this word. The most important Greek word of all. It means: to be patient.'

'You take such good care of her, Yánna. I'm very grateful.'

She poured the foaming coffee into a little porcelain cup.

'I never dreamed that Daphne had mixed with royalty,' I said.

Yánna nodded towards the mansion. 'Mon Repos was an important place. Many royals came for their summer holiday in the old days. Your Prince Philip was born in there, did you know? He was not much older than my Daphne.' She smiled for a moment. 'Before my time, of course. Your grandmother was a big fan of Queen Elizabeth of England. She wait for Her Majesty to visit Greece – perhaps stay at Mon Repos. I always know, that will not happen because of the past. Now, she hopes King Charles will come one day, to visit his birthplace. Is wrong to let her dream, Mrs Flora?'

'Of course not. Now I remember. I saw the plaque at the garden entrance saying Prince Philip was born here.'

Yánna stuck her chin out. 'I told your grandmother she'd have a long wait to see royalty at Mon Repos again. The Queen stood with her husband, and the Greeks murdered some of his family, so I think she would not come to this country on a royal visit.' She tapped the side of her head knowingly.

'I don't know about any assassinations. I wonder how Granny got from Athens to Corfu. We haven't got that far yet. Were you born in Corfu?'

'Me?' Yánna lifted her chin, bobbed her eyebrows and made a tut – the Greek way to say 'no'.

'Aristotle and Daphne's journey from Athens to Corfu was terrible – very big tragic. They survived the war, yes, but after everything that happened, it changed Daphne. She became a . . . I don't know the English word . . . is so difficult!'

184

'Tell me in Greek, perhaps I will recognise the English word.'

Yánna flapped her hand. 'She fought for the womans, so they is equal to men, like the Kyría Alice, and she became important in a man's world, but nobody ever knew about it because she was hiding what she did.'

'I don't understand.'

'She will tell you. We should give people like Daphne medals because they save us from the Nazis and they saved us from the kitchen. Still, it was Aristotle who held her back in the end. Now, no more questions, please.'

'Granny Daphne sounds like she was a woman ahead of her time, Yánna.'

'She try hard to be strong. But nothing could make her ready for what happened.'

'What are you saying? Daphne had a nervous breakdown?'

Yánna nodded. 'Later, yes, a big one. The shock of Aristotle's death led to screaming and tearing her hair out. She was driven mad, you know. It was a terrible time. Daphne adored him. She had lived for him – gave up her family, her friends, her religion, and even her art for him. She would have died for him in an instant. They put her in the asylum and gave her electric convulsions treatment – do you know it?' I remembered Daphne telling me, yet I sensed Yánna needed to share these terrible things that had happened. 'First, they strapped her down, then they put a leather pad in her mouth to stopped her from hurting herself. They gave her big electric shocks in the head.' She tugged on her lip as if trying to envisage it. 'No anaesthetic, you know. They cooked her brains. My poor Daphne.'

Yánna looked into my eyes, and in that instant, I saw her pain and how much she loved my grandmother.

'The good thing was that it seemed to cure her, although she was a bit ... how shall I say? Slow after.' She poked the side of her head. 'But in a few months, she came back to the way she was before. But not Aristotle, of course. He would never come back.'

22

DAPHNE

Athens, 1943

Daphne lay beside Aristotle under a tree, in the Royal Park, near Syntagma Square. A circle of fallen almond blossom made a pale pink carpet on the spring grass. With each movement, the delicate perfume of sweet marzipan rose around her. She propped herself on her elbows and stared at the delicate flowers covering the silver branches above. A slight breeze loosed another cloud of blossom, which fell like confetti over them both. Soft morning sunlight made a halo around Aristotle's light-brown hair. The powerful ache of love bloomed in her chest so hard she could not speak for a moment. She swallowed hard and said the words she had rehearsed all night.

'I . . . I'm pregnant.'

Aristotle gasped, rolled on to his side, and stared at her.

'Oh no! How did I let this happen?' He dropped his face into his hands and shook his head. 'I'm so sorry – this is too awful . . .'

Daphne waited, heard him gasp and sit up. A long silence followed. Perhaps she had been right. He might love someone else, although she had never seen signs of a girlfriend. Tears gathered as she composed her next sentence.

'You can walk away now, if you want,' she said without drama. 'I won't make a fuss and, I assure you, I will always treasure your child.'

Daphne felt a tear slide down her cheek, heard the scrape of his heels on the lawn as he stood. She trembled, her heart breaking. All the love she had would go to his child, even if he walked out of her life, and who could blame him? From the start, Daphne had thrown herself at Aristotle, the reason clear for anyone to see. She adored him, and could never love another.

His hands took hers. He pulled her to her feet. She felt his breath on her wet face, his arms around her, his voice in her ear.

'Don't cry, my darling. Will you marry me, Daphne?' he said, dropping to one knee.

'Oh!' Her eyes widened, although she could see nothing for tears. 'I was afraid . . .' The lump in her throat was so hard she couldn't say more.

'That I would abandon you and our child? I could never do that.' He pulled her to a park bench. 'Tell me, when is our baby expected?'

'Well, I'm not experienced with these things, but I guess at the end of the year. I believe I'm three months, so I've six months to go.'

'Then we must leave Athens. There's great danger on the horizon, my darling. I've almost finished the major-general's portrait. Yesterday, he confirmed what I feared . . .' He paused, seeming unsure how to proceed, then he took her hand and gazed into her eyes.

'Go on, Aristotle. I need to know the truth.'

'The awful fact is, he thinks the Italian leader's about to surrender – capitulate with the Allies – change sides. This could start a whole new war. Even worse, Mussolini's confirmed the Nazi atrocities we've suspected for some time. Terrible, unspeakable things in the camps. He calls it Hitler's Final Solution.'

Daphne had a sickening feeling. 'What do you mean? The final solution to what?'

'Well ... Basically, he wants to clean up the German race, make it pure, by removing all the Jews and other minorities from Germany. Because the Italians are unreliable and might change sides, the war could come to a sudden end. In one last ditch attempt to remove all the Jews from Europe, Adolf Hitler has intensified his efforts. There's awful news coming from Poland, where he has most of his so-called work camps. People have said the rumours were propaganda to frighten people, but the major-general made proud claims of extermination camps.'

'What do you mean, "extermination camps"? They can't exterminate people, like ...' She gasped, unable to get enough air into her lungs. 'Like rats, no, they can't can they? That's ridiculous – they wouldn't let it happen.'

Aristotle didn't speak.

'Aristotle, tell me this isn't true! My brother Isaac, he's in one of their camps! I have a horrible feeling—' She touched the locket at her neck, remembered the feather inside, Isaac's laughter, the love that shone from his eyes on her birthday.

'Daphne, don't cry, my darling,' he said again, then pulled her back into his arms. 'I had to share what I know with you. Above all things, there has to be complete honesty between us, don't you agree? I'm sure your brother will survive whatever the Nazis are dishing out. After all, he's smart and young and strong. We don't know everything. Perhaps the war will end tomorrow. I'm sharing what I recognise as the truth because I want you to be aware of the danger that you're in as a Jew. More so now.' He placed his hand on her belly. 'We must be extra careful.'

She placed her hands over his and breathed slowly, calming herself.

'Our child is my priority from now on, my darling Aristotle. I'll do everything possible to keep him or her safe. Despite everything, I'm so happy. I'm going to marry you and have your baby.'

'Our baby.' He held her to him. 'At least we know your mother, father, and Elizabeth are safely out of the way, in Cairo. They're probably safer than us. We should leave the city as soon as we can, Daphne. There's a greater chance of heavy bombing now. The war's at a turning point. Let's consider our child, and not take any chances.'

'I got a letter from Kyría Alice,' Daphne said. 'Remember her plans to start a convent of nursing nuns? She's going to train them on the island of Tinos. Her plans are going well. The Red Cross will take over the soup kitchen, and the hostel that Papa offered her, and her convent will be outside Athens. She says we'll always be welcome.'

'I've earned enough from the portraits to keep us going for a while,' he said. 'Even if we're near the end of the war, I suspect we're on the verge of civil war between the Greek Communists and the Royalists. We'll be safer on an island, where people are less political. What do you think?'

Another cloud of blossom showered down. Daphne held out her hand and then inspected the blooms that had landed there, yet her mind was elsewhere.

'Will Kyría Alice be in danger?'

'I believe she'll be safer as a Greek Orthodox nun than a princess,' he assured her.

'What do I know about such things, Aristotle? I've always left politics to Noah and my father. Which island do you suggest we go to? I'd follow you to the ends of the earth, you know that.'

'I think we should go north, as far as we can safely go.'

She stared at him. 'But there's something else worrying you, isn't there?'

He shook his head. 'Nothing.'

'If it was nothing, you wouldn't be jigging your knee like that.'

He sighed. 'I didn't sell the painting.'

'What painting? The one of the major-general?'

'No, the El Greco.'

'What? Where did you get the money for my family's trip to Cairo?'

'There was a bag of jewellery in your father's safe. I took it when I got the provenance for the painting. Rosenburg gave me a fair price for it, to show his appreciation for helping him and his wife escape.'

She stared at him for a minute. 'So, that's great, isn't it? We've still got the El Greco, which is worth a huge amount of money. What's the problem?'

He took a deep breath, his chest expanding, and then the words rushed out.

'My cousin wants the painting. He's sending the Gestapo for it.'

She placed a hand on her belly. 'The Gestapo! We should give it to him. I'm pregnant, remember? The Gestapo kill people for nothing!'

Aristotle shook his head. 'If that was the end, I would. You, and the life of our child, are worth more than any El Greco millions to me, but I'm sorry to say I can no longer trust him. We would be the only people who knew that he had taken it.'

'You don't believe he would have us . . . well . . .?' She gulped. 'For goodness' sake, he's from your own family!' Daphne saw her own horror reflected in his eyes.

191

'If he owned the painting and the provenance, he'd be a multi-millionaire, Daphne. We would be the only people who could say it wasn't his. He was a respectable man once, and I loved him as an older brother. Now, he's poisoned by Hitler's supremacist ideals. Jürgen is convinced he's a member of the master race and that only money will help the Nazis achieve total power. I find his ideology terrifying, to be honest.'

'Then I hope I never meet him. You're right, we have to leave Athens as soon as we can!'

Aristotle slid his arm around her shoulders and held her close. 'You'll never meet him. I'd put my life between you and my cousin.' His mouth turned down, his face a mask of Greek tragedy. 'First, you must marry me and become Daphne von Stroop. Perhaps we'll be able to pass through Europe by train, boat, or plane if we're cautious. If we can cross the English Channel, then head further north, for our child to be born in Great Britain, I think it will be safer for all of us.'

* * *

Two weeks later, a local priest married Daphne Papadopoulos to Aristotle von Stroop. Kyría Alice and the local verger were witnesses. The priest agreed to misplace the documentation for six months, so they would be far from Athens before their wedding went on record and came under the scrutiny of Nazi investigators.

After packing all they needed, Aristotle found transport. Luka, a burly Greek, had a covered wagon and a contract with the German military base in Igoumenitsa to transport flour from the Athenian port of Piraeus. For an extortionate price, he would take Aristotle and Daphne with him on his regular delivery run.

From Igoumenitsa, a short ferry ride would take them to the island of Corfu – where Aristotle hoped his cousin would not consider looking for them.

As Luka took the deposit from Aristotle, his eyes narrowed. He had a face like a sea urchin, puffy and covered in dark, stiff bristles, matching his bushy eyebrows and thick, greasy hair.

'Are you Italian?' he asked Aristotle. 'I hear they've just changed sides – well, most of them. There are still some Blackshirts holding allegiance to Mussolini. What a mess. How do we know who to trust?'

'I'm as Greek as you are,' Aristotle replied. 'We're trying to get to England before our baby is born.'

'I see. I ask because I don't know if you've heard about the massacre? These are dangerous times.'

Aristotle shook his head.

'Five thousand Italians murdered by the Germans on Kefaloniá. Bastards! It happened the moment they surrendered. Poor sods had handed their weapons over already, didn't stand a chance.'

'We need to leave Athens, Luka. Who knows what will happen next in this damned war? I'm going to give you a third of the money now. You'll get the rest when we arrive at our destination, OK?' Aristotle offered his hand.

The driver's eyes narrowed. He was not going to be messed with. He stared at Daphne and Aristotle, weighing them up, then his face relaxed and he shook hands.

'In case of danger, you climb over the seat into the back. You get inside an empty flour sack, you understand?' They nodded. 'You get found, I will kill you myself!'

When they were alone, Daphne clutched Aristotle's arm, horror rising in her chest as she realised more than ever the danger they had put themselves in.

'Do we have to do this?'

He nodded, taking her in his arms. 'I've been told my cousin has instructed the *Abwehrstelle* to find and detain us.'

'What's the *Abwehrstelle*?'

'The German intelligence headquarters in Athens. We're leaving just in time.'

* * *

As the capital city sweltered, Daphne and Aristotle embarked on their escape.

'There's a roadblock two kilometres up the road,' Luka told them. 'Hide in a sack right away.'

They scrambled inside the truck filled with hessian sacks of flour, with Aristotle keeping one arm up, holding the bag closed. The old truck hissed and groaned as it came to a halt. German voices shouted instructions. Light filtered through the hessian as soldiers pulled the tarpaulin back. Daphne trembled and Aristotle hissed, telling her to be quiet. His face pressed to hers, one arm wrapped around her belly, squeezing her tight against him. After what seemed an age, a German voice shouted '*Mach weiter!*' and with great relief, she realised they had instructed their driver to 'Go on!' The old truck started with a shudder that rocked the vehicle before they rumbled on their way.

Five minutes later, Luka yelled, 'You can come out now!'

Once they were back in their seats, he said, 'They're looking for an Austrian guy, a traitor, apparently – von Stroop.'

Daphne's eyes were heavy. She snuggled under Aristotle's protective arm and drifted into sleep. When she woke, they were travelling in the dark with hooded headlights that only allowed a short distance of visibility.

Aristotle spoke to the driver. 'Once my wife's strong enough, after the baby's born, we'll continue to Igoumenitsa and if we can't cross there, we'll go up, into Albania.'

They hit a pothole and almost jolted out of their seats. The driver's eyes widened.

'I forgot, your wife's pregnant. I'll try to avoid the big bumps, OK?' He stood on the brakes.

Aristotle turned to Daphne as he replied. 'Thanks, she's four months. That's why we're trying to escape the war.'

'OK, then we're going to take the safest route available. I'll pull off the road for a few hours, so that you and the young lady can have a sleep on the flour sacks. I'll take a nap in the cab. Do you have any questions?'

Aristotle shook his head.

* * *

Daphne woke to the sound of birdsong. Sunlight flooded in through the windscreen.

'Come on, sleepyhead, we're moving on soon,' Aristotle whispered before kissing her cheek.

She stretched and yawned. 'Where's Luka?' She stared at the empty driver's seat.

'He's gone to get milk for breakfast.' Aristotle nodded at the scene ahead. 'Look.'

Daphne sat up, peered through the windscreen, and saw the truck parked against a drystone wall that surrounded a field of goats. Under the only tree, a shepherdess milked one creature while Luka sat shoulder to shoulder with the woman.

'He appears to know her rather well,' Daphne said, taking in the countryside.

Aristotle grinned. 'I think he knows her very well indeed.'

'You mean she's another girlfriend?'

'Something like that.' He turned her head and kissed her on the lips. 'I can't wait to get you all to myself.'

'Me neither. Where are we?'

'Ten kilometres from the Corinth bridge.'

'It's so beautiful here. You wouldn't know there's a war. I've never been outside Athens, apart from our move from Thessaloníki.' She reached for a map on the dashboard. 'Will it be this quiet all the way? Which road will we take?'

'I'm a little nervous that it's too quiet. Let's hope I'm wrong, Daphne. After the Corinth bridge, we'll drive along the coast to Patras, then take the ferry to Antirrio. We'll be safer there – my cousin can't predict I'd go to such a place. It's quite out of the way.'

Their truck driver returned with a jug of milk.

'We'll eat, then we must turn back. The Germans have blocked the road before the bridge. We can't cross that way. They're searching all vehicles for explosives.'

Aristotle stared at him. 'Why? It's the only way across.'

'They say the British are planning to blow the road and the railway bridges, so they'll fall into the canal and block the shipping lane. A big catastrophe for the Germans if they succeeded! The Germans import most of their oil from Romania, via the Bosphorus, through the Corinth Canal. Imagine if those ships had to go all the way round the Peloponnese. They'd run the gauntlet of British submarines and bombers based in Malta and Egypt. They'd also have hundreds of extra kilometres to travel.'

'So, we can't get across the canal by bridge?' Daphne asked, placing her hands on her belly. 'What will we do?'

Aristotle shook his head, placed his hand over hers, and smiled right into her eyes.

'We'll find a way, Daphne. Luka will help us, won't you?' He turned and peered at their driver.

'We've got choices. We can drive down to Kalamaki at the south end of the Corinth Canal, and try for a ferry to the Peloponnese. Then we can drive up to Patras.'

'Let's do it!' Aristotle said. 'There's no time to lose.'

Daphne sensed his concern. His cousin was more likely to find them if they stayed on the mainland. If someone asked to see their travel papers, they'd be in trouble.

*　*　*

The old truck was always threatening to break down. Travelling the long way, to avoid towns and villages, it took all day before they arrived at the southern entrance of the canal. Outside town, Luka parked in an olive grove. Daphne and Aristotle waited with the truck while their driver went to play *tavli* and gossip with the locals until after midnight.

'Any luck, Luka?' Aristotle asked when he returned.

Luka was crashing around, having imbibed a little too much of the local spirit.

'Yes!' he cried with gusto, slapping his bloated paunch and belching, alarming them both. 'Tomorrow I'll take the car ferry to the Peloponnese. They make a big search for some people, enemies of the Germans, so you can't come with me, but I have good news.' He grinned and scratched his armpit. 'For a few hundred drachmas, the stevedore will hide you on an old ship going up the canal tomorrow morning. It's called the *Saint Barbara*, so we know you'll be safe because she's the patron saint of explosives. Ha, very good! I'll meet you outside the town of Corinth at the other end of the canal and take you to Patras. OK? Now we must sleep – we need our wits about us tomorrow.'

'Luka, you're so good to us. Could I ask you a special favour?' Daphne asked.

He threw her a worried look. 'Go on.'

'I promised my friend I'd write to say we were safe, but I haven't been able to post a letter yet. If I write one, would you deliver it when you're back in Athens?'

23

FLORA

Corfu, present day

I GLANCED AT MY PHONE as the word 'Spiros' flashed across the screen. My heart did a little skip, then the heat of shame flushed my cheeks. I couldn't deny the overwhelming feeling that I'd let my darling husband down. I stared around at the floor, confused and battling against rising tears.

'Hi, Spiro again,' he said. 'Hello, Flora, are you there?'

I gulped, telling myself to grow up. 'Yes, hi, what can I do for you?'

'Thought you might be interested to see the Mon Repos chimney come down in about an hour. Also, the new cafe is open if you'd like a nightcap.'

'That would be lovely. Shall I walk over to the mansion now?'

'Perfect, I'll meet you under the chimney around the back of the building—'

I lost the signal.

After telling Yánna what was happening, I gave my hair a brush and tidied myself up.

'I'll look in before I go back to the hotel, Yánna, unless it's late, OK?'

'Very good! You have a good time, Flora.'

I reminded myself not to drink too much, as I'd eaten very little. Two glasses of wine on an empty stomach and I would be reeling. I remembered my last row with Mark. I was a little drunk after a night out with the girls.

* * *

The leaving do, for my colleague Nicky, had been great. We'd all tumbled into the Pump House on the Royal Albert Dock, eaten, drunk, and told stupid jokes until closing time, then we tumbled out again and returned home. Perfect, except that Mark had waited up for me. Furious. Arms folded across his chest and eyes glaring.

'You cheat on me, just like that, you bitch!' he'd shouted without provocation.

I blinked at him – the man who never raised his voice.

'What are you talking about? I've never cheated on you! I've been out with the girls, a farewell do in the Pump House, you can check.'

'Not like that, not with another man. You betrayed me, Flora. Said you loved me, but lied and cheated on me.'

My stomach tightened as unease kicked in, clawing at my throat. It was true, and I couldn't think of a thing to say. How did he find out? He continued to yell at me.

'Your automatic repeat prescription – birth control pills – you know? Well it came this afternoon.' His words sizzled with sarcasm. He blew down his nose like an angry bull. 'So I went to put them away, and hey . . . guess what? There was more than three-months' supply in the bathroom cabinet already! Planned to surprise me with a baby when I came home from work one day? "Oh, forgot to say, I'm pregnant, honey . . . Now what do you fancy for supper?" Perhaps you thought I would accept it after saying only a couple of months ago that I didn't want to start a family yet.'

'Mark, I'm sorry, I—'

'Of course you're sorry – sorry I found out.'

'Look, be reasonable, Mark. My biological clock's ticking. There are dangers involved when a woman gets older, more chances of problems.'

'Like what? You're being dramatic. Scared of losing your figure, is that it?'

Now he was making me angry.

'Like Down syndrome! Stop it! I want to enjoy my pregnancy, not keep worrying, and it's my right, too, you know. I've a right to have a child. You've put me off for over a decade. You don't even want to discuss it, so that's not fair. Our son or daughter would be almost a teenager by now, if I'd had my way, and you've deprived me of that motherhood. You're the one who's not being fair.'

'Fair? Me, not fair? You've lied to me, you used my body like a sperm bank, you tried to get pregnant behind my back, and now you have the cheek to talk about "not fair". What you've done is despicable. I hope you're ashamed of yourself. I'm leaving you. You'll hear from my solicitors in the next few days.'

'Mark! You're being ridiculous!' I shouted, to no avail.

He pulled a cabin bag from behind the chair and left, just like that.

All the fretting, recriminations, plain ordinary sorrow, screwed up the following seven days. He wasn't answering messages. He'd blocked me on Facebook. Then my period arrived and the bottom fell out of my world. Would he come back sooner if I told him? The truth was, me and my broken heart needed him so badly.

I texted him: I'd have got over you leaving, but now my period is here, and my heart has shattered into a billion pieces. You could at least have left me with a child in my belly, you bastard!

Then he'd feel guilty. The problem – that I was still desperate to get pregnant – hadn't gone away. There would be no 'OK, you win, we won't have children,' because I was going to get pregnant, at least once, with Mark.

His walking-out tantrum was exactly that: a tantrum.

He'll come back. I'll die if he doesn't, and he knows it. We're so alike that we must go way over the top for anything to bear weight. It's been a week; I give him another two days. He'll think: she'll be expecting me back in a week, so I'll give it another two days and scare the shit out of her. When he walks through the door, he'll say, 'We need to talk,' and I'll throw my arms around his neck and weep with joy and perhaps a tiny spark of smugness.

I fell back onto the sofa, my entire body trembling as I thought, what if I'm wrong and he never returns? My world would end because I loved Mark more than life.

He came back two days later, we talked, he told me why he didn't want to start a family. I thought my world had ended.

* * *

'Tests?' I said. 'What do you mean, tests? You mean sperm counts and things? Mark, we need to try for a baby first. After a year or two without success, that's when we need to see if there's a problem.'

Now I understood: he feared he was sterile . . . me, too.

'No, not a sperm count.' He lowered his eyes as he sat down, his shoulders rounded, defeat hanging on to his jawline. 'We need to talk, Flora.'

'What do you mean? Nothing is so serious that we can't deal with it to—'

He leaped up. 'Will you shut the fuck up, you stupid bitch! This is hard enough without you wittering on about having a baby! Why couldn't we just split up like any other normal couple? Get divorced and be done with it? Then I'd be free to deal with my own problems without worrying about you! But no . It's not possible with you, is it?'

He was yelling so loudly I wanted to yell back. Under normal circumstances, I would – stand my ground, give as good as I got – but this time warning bells were ringing and fear turned eve rything leaden-heavy. Something so bad was going on that he wanted us to split up in order to save me from heartache. Bastard!

'What sort of woman are you?' he continued, his face red with anger. 'You couldn't simply tell me to fuck off and change the locks like any normal woman, could you?' His fists bunched. 'I want to thump you, knock you into the back end of next week!'

Fear was balling itself in my belly. Something so bad . . . so bad that I didn't dare try to analyse it. He couldn't tell me. My heart was breaking, because in that instant I knew he had a terrible secret. He couldn't say what was hurting him – hurting us. I went right up to him and glared into his face.

'Hit me! Go on, you hairy, heartless bastard! Hit me if it makes you feel better!'

I stuck my chin out, offering my jaw. Then, so close up, nose to nose, I saw his tears gathering. I gasped, stepped back, then threw myself at him as fear filled my heart. His Adam's apple bobbed and dreadful anticipation overwhelmed me.

'What is it?' I whispered, sliding into his arms and feeling my own tears break free. 'Don't shut me out.'

He swallowed hard and clutched me to him.

'I have leukaemia.'

24

DAPHNE

Athens, 1943

ARISTOTLE TOSSED AND TURNED IN the back of Luka's truck.

'What's bothering you?' Daphne asked. 'Why can't you settle? You're not happy about the canal trip, are you?'

He slid his arm around her. 'I'm afraid we'll be trapped and in danger, and there'll be nothing I can do to protect you. When the ship's in the canal, there'll be no escape, no turning around or climbing out between those ninety-metre cliffs on both sides.'

'But I have false papers and our marriage documents, and I speak German. Who could mean us harm? Besides, why would your cousin look for us outside Athens?'

'Because he understands me as I do him. He'll try to second-guess me, knowing I'll go where he'd least expect – therefore, that's where he'll look for me and the painting. He'll search for you, too, to threaten you against me. He can be very cruel.'

'Why would he look for me? He doesn't even know I'm Jewish. How could he?'

'He knows I wanted to sell the El Greco for as much as possible. He'll ask himself why I didn't keep a masterpiece of such value, which could be worth millions after the war. It must be to help somebody very important to me. He knows I don't share his "master race" ideals. It won't take him long to discover I'm in love with a beautiful Jewish woman.' He stroked her cheek and peered into her eyes. 'Besides, we don't have travel documents. We must be very careful, Daphne.'

They were silent with their thoughts for a while, then Aristotle spoke again.

'At dawn, I'll talk to Luka, to see if he has a connection to the resistance. We need their help. Whatever happens, don't mention the El Greco to him or anyone else. We would be dead before dawn if word got out that we were carrying something so valuable.'

She pushed her body against his chest. He encircled her with his arms.

'I'm afraid,' she said.

'Me, too, but we'll get through this for the sake of our child. He or she is the reason we must survive.' He lowered his voice to a whisper. 'Our baby is the seed of a better world.'

'I love you so much.'

She waited for him to return her words, but as the silence drew out, she drifted off to sleep.

* * *

Woken by birdsong, Daphne reached for Aristotle before opening her eyes. She found the space beside her cold and empty. Scrunching her face against the bright sunlight, she pulled herself on to her elbows and squinted through the windscreen. Luka and Aristotle were deep in conversation.

After a few more minutes, Luka shook Aristotle's hand and marched off towards the town.

'What's happening?' Daphne asked when Aristotle returned.

'Something's going on.'

They sat in glum silence until Luka returned with fresh bread.

205

'The andartes are coming to talk with you. I'd suggest you tell them the truth because if they suspect you're lying, they'll kill you both, but not before they've had their way with your woman.'

'We're on their side,' Aristotle grumbled. 'I can't prove it, but it's a fact. Besides, my wife's pregnant – do you think I'd put her in such danger? Anyway, they're supposed to be freedom fighters, not barbarians.'

Despite what he'd said, he worried his lip.

Luka stared about, rubbing his meaty hand over his mouth.

'Well, they'll be here this afternoon, and to tell the truth, they're not andartes—'

'What are they, to be exact? Bandits? I trusted you, Luka!'

'Special Operations Executive from British Intelligence.'

Aristotle frowned. 'You mean you were lying? Have a heart. My wife's pregnant. A fright like that could jeopardise her and our baby.'

'But I had to be sure you weren't some German spy, didn't I?'

'Well, we're not, but we do both speak German. We're hoping to get to England.'

'Tell only those who need to know. I must drop you at the canal entrance to board the ship at two o'clock. Best take your belongings with you, just in case.'

'In case what?'

'In case I never see you again. Anyway, you'll get to our meeting place before me. It's only an hour to sail up the canal with a good tug. The damn road – in this truck – is another story. Mam's Taverna, six o'clock this evening.'

An hour later, they arrived outside the port of Corinth and unloaded their belongings. Aristotle shook hands with Luka.

'Thanks for getting us this far.' He pulled an envelope from inside his jacket pocket. 'Here's half the money we agreed on, just in case we miss each other at the other end.'

'Appreciated,' Luka said, stuffing the money into his pocket and then slapping Aristotle on the arm. 'This will come in useful. I also have a baby at home. Good luck this afternoon. The British agents will be here soon.' He glanced into an olive grove across the road. 'They might be here already.'

He stroked his bristly jawline and glanced about before hurrying to his vehicle.

* * *

In the corner of the olive grove, they sat on a makeshift bench on the shady side of a small chapel. The dilapidated old truck belched black smoke as it crawled away at full speed. Daphne couldn't imagine how fast a boat would travel down the canal.

'Will we be there by six, Aristotle? It only takes an hour down the canal, but it took us most of the day in the truck. It makes little sense to me.' Her chest tightened with tension; she couldn't breathe.

'"Will he be there by six o'clock?" is more to the point. To complicate things, the Peloponnese side was under Italian rule. Now, the Germans are in control, but it is unfamiliar territory for them. Our side, the east bank, has been under the Germans since they arrived, so no chance of bribing anyone. We'll have to trust our luck. Don't forget to speak German if we're stopped. In fact, from now on, we're only speaking German, all right?'

Daphne nodded. 'We'll run the gauntlet of the enemy, and worse, we can expect a visit from these ... What did you call them? Special Operative Executives?'

He nodded. 'Remember, they're on our side. They'll help the Allies win this cursed war.'

*   *   *

As midday approached, the air had warmed and, without a whisper of wind, they were stifling. The bottle of water they'd brought was tepid and didn't quench their thirst.

'It's cooler in there,' Daphne said, nodding towards the olive grove. 'Can't we sit under a tree?'

'What if they drive past, see nobody here, and just continue along the road? I'll wait here a little longer. You go and find some shade.'

'Are you sure? I'm desperate to pee-pee, too.'

He laughed, and the tension left his face for the first time. 'Go on then. Not too far, though – I need you to hear me if I shout.'

She kissed him, then narrowed her eyes.

'Are you sure you wouldn't like to come into the woods with me, kind sir?' she play-acted. 'I can promise you an interesting interlude.'

'Don't tempt me. Get away with you and give me some peace.'

He laughed again, and joy rose in her heart. She crept into the silent grove and embraced the cool shade. The olives were ready for harvesting. Delicate, pale-leaved branches were weighed down by bunches of glossy black fruit, bending the silver-barked limbs towards earth. A sudden breeze meant the boughs all bobbed gently in unison, like friendly arms reaching to tap her reassuringly on the shoulders as she passed. Daphne sensed that things would work out, then her aching bladder demanded attention. She needed to find a broad tree near the road.

She had just crouched down when a rustling sound to her left made her heart race. She cowered against the tree trunk, making herself as small as possible, her heart thudding. When a tortoise plodded out of the weeds beside her, she almost laughed out loud. While adjusting her clothes, she smiled, thinking how amused Aristotle would be when she told him. Another rustle came from behind her.

'You're not catching me out again,' she muttered.

A hand slapped over her mouth, pulling her backwards. Another hand tugged one arm up behind her back. Pain stabbed her shoulder.

Daphne struggled and kicked, but whoever had hold of her was too strong. She heard a loud whistle; then a motor roared closer. They shoved her towards the road and she saw the same fate had befallen Aristotle. His hands were tied behind his back, and a gag was over his mouth. An army truck roared around the bend and then screeched to a standstill. They were both bundled into the canvas-covered back. The vehicle thundered away. Thrown around so much in the back of the truck, she wondered if they were off the road. All this time, nobody spoke. Would their abductors shoot them and dump their lifeless bodies in a ravine? Would these ruffians torture them for the whereabouts of the El Greco? They could have it if it would keep Aristotle and their baby safe.

Daphne peered up at one man. He appeared more Greek than German. Perhaps a collaborator. A sharp dig on her shin got her attention. She glanced around at Aristotle, who lay on the floor beside her. He stared hard into her eyes, trying to tell her something. His foot moved, slid against her leg, and she realised he was trying to reassure her that everything would be all right.

Darkness fell about them. The truck squealed to a halt. Daphne almost rolled over with the momentum. For the first time, the largest man spoke.

'Listen to me, you two. I'll take the gags off and sit you on the bench. Any noise and they'll go back on and we'll dump you in the canal. Understand?'

Daphne nodded rapidly.

They untied Aristotle first.

'Please . . .' he begged.

'Shut up!' the burly giant yelled, and raised a bunched fist.

'She's pregnant!' Aristotle shouted, screwing his eyes and pulling his head into his shoulders, anticipating a blow.

The big man swung around to Daphne. 'Not a peep, right?'

When she nodded, he ordered one of the other three men to untie her gag. At last, she could breathe.

'Stelio, take the woman inside. I don't want her to hear what he says.'

Daphne threw Aristotle a fearful glance, and the two men manhandled her out of the truck.

'They won't hurt her so long as you're truthful. Now, what's going on?' Daphne heard somebody say to Aristotle.

* * *

The two men kept a firm grip on Daphne's arms as they shoved her towards a stone cottage in the olive grove. Bright sunlight dazzled her and, as her hands were tied behind her back, she couldn't wipe away tears that trickled down her face.

'Don't be afraid – just tell our captain the whole truth.'

He kicked the door open and bundled her inside. The place was basic: a water pump, two chairs and a rough table outside.

Inside, a clay floor littered with olive pips, two simple wooden beds and a fireplace choked with ash and cinders. On the mantel over the fire stood essential paraphernalia: an oil lamp; some cups, jars and plates. In the corner stood two barrels. A coil of rope and a couple of pans hung from nails in the wall. Bunches of dried herbs dangled from the ceiling beams. The dusty room smelled of woodsmoke.

'Can I have some water?' Daphne asked. 'I'm pregnant, which means I get very thirsty, and I'm always needing to pee-pee. Something to do with hormones, you understand?'

One man, the second in command, nodded at the other. He took a jar and went outside. She heard the pump squeaking. Glancing around the room again, she took in more details, and then her skin crawled. The rope looped onto a long nail in the wall was a coiled noose.

25

FLORA

I WALKED OVER TO MON Repos and looked up at the chimney.

Spiros stood at the top of the steps, speaking to the driver of a mechanical lift. I stopped to watch him. His athletic body gave the impression of a soldier in civvies. Dark Mediterranean features, and warm brown eyes, made him so handsome it wasn't fair to other men. He noticed me and waved.

'Hi, Flora, I'm pleased you came.' He kissed my cheek before indicating the guy driving the machinery. 'This is Anton. He'll lift the builder on his platform to dismantle the chimney, brick by brick.'

Anton nodded in my direction.

'Sounds like a delicate operation,' I said.

'That's right. Imagine if a brick fell through the skylight. Not only would it destroy some irreplaceable antique glass, but it might kill a tourist in Mon Repos. Not great publicity.'

My jaw dropped at the callous remark.

He grinned. 'I'm joking!'

I gasped. 'Of course you are. Sorry, my sense of humour seems to be having a vacation, too.'

He smiled and nodded and I knew he understood.

'How familiar are you with the building?' I asked.

He shrugged and lifted the plans. 'Better than most, I guess.'

'Are you sure there's no basement? I know I asked you before and you said not, but my grandmother is quite insistent.'

'I've never seen an entrance to one, and it's not on the topograph.'

'Topograph?'

'The plans. Why do you ask?'

'Granny says she stored some things there in the war.'

'The war?' His eyes narrowed. 'That's interesting. What sort of things?'

'Nothing spectacular. My grandfather's art stuff – some canvases, I guess. She's lived in that cottage since the forties, but I'm afraid her memory's fading fast. As I said, she'll be a hundred in a few months.'

'Yes, a hundred. That's amazing.'

We studied the builder as we spoke. He removed the chimney pot in one piece, holding it to his chest like something precious.

Spiros sighed. 'That's a relief. They cast that pot in 1828. Impossible to find another and, because of its age, I feared it might crumble to dust in his hands.'

He worried his lip as the driver lowered the builder.

'And I thought you were a property speculator who wanted to flatten the building. You really care, don't you? I guess I owe you an apology.'

He smiled. 'Accepted. Now, as the rest of this deconstruction is straightforward, I'm not needed in my capacity as a government building inspector. Shall we make the most of our location with a nightcap?'

We walked in silence towards the cafe bar. The low sunset sliced through the trees, lengthening shadows and giving everything a warm amber glow.

'The light's exceptional at this time of day,' I said. 'But it's rather difficult to capture on canvas because it only lasts a few minutes. By the time I've mixed the right colours, everything's changed.'

213

'I've been thinking about what you asked me. I'm sure there isn't a basement under Mon Repos. The staff quarters are in the attic, as is the original kitchen. However, there are fireplaces in every room, and I suspect they were fuelled by lignite.'

I frowned, my mind racing through science lessons at school. 'Isn't that a type of coal?'

He blinked, surprised. 'Yes, brown coal, terribly unhealthy stuff, most of which is mined in Greece and Germany. We'll close our last mine in two years. Anyway, to get back to your cellar . . . I guess there was a coal hole, because they usually delivered it in sacks and tipped it into a chute that led to a dry storage space under the building.'

'How did the staff get it?'

'That's the point.' He glanced at me with the hint of a smile and, for a second, I saw the mischief of Mark and lost my concentration.

'Sorry, sorry, I was daydreaming. What did you say?'

'How about a gin and tonic? The cafe has an amazing gin selection.'

'That would be perfect,' I said. 'Thank you. My husband's favourite drink. He has a great collection . . . Sorry, I guess I should stop speaking about him, wallowing in the past. I'm afraid it's becoming a habit. Tell me about yourself. I've shared so much about my life, but I know little about you.'

'Don't worry about it. What can I tell you about myself? I'm single, Greek, and an architect. I work as a civil engineer for Corfu's planning office, and in my spare time, I play cricket for the town.'

'Cricket? With your height, I'd have thought basketball.'

He grinned and shook his head. 'Fast bowler. Corfu has the best team in the country. I like to walk, swim, dive, travel . . . and talk to intelligent English women with flaming red hair.' His eyes twinkled. 'What else?'

'Why is a guy like you still single?'

He hesitated and seemed to slump a little. The waiter brought our drinks. He had chosen Eden Mill with tonic and a slice, while I had Michelle's Rhubarb Gin over ice. We chinked glasses.

'To answer your question, for almost the same reason as you.' He folded his arms across his chest and stared into the distance. 'Melody was the love of my life,' he said. 'We should have been married last Saturday.' He pinched the bridge of his nose, silent for a moment. 'Killed in a water sports accident six months ago.' He took a slug of his drink. 'I can't . . .' He took a breath and blew it out hard. 'Sometimes, I can't cope—'

'Yes, I understand.' I swallowed hard. 'It's a bastard, isn't it? Do you want to tell me, share?'

He stared at nothing for a while, and I understood he needed time with his thoughts before he could speak.

'Some inexperienced guys on a speedboat. They'd downed a few beers and were having a good time putting the boat through its paces. At speed, they're supposed to stay a hundred metres from shore. But they hadn't the experience to judge distance.' His fist opened and closed.

'Melody was snorkelling, hunting for octopus with a spear-gun, off the point. Her parents have a taverna. She dived, came up under the blades of the speedboat. She must have heard it, but what could she do? They'd killed her before they even realised she was there. She had a diver's buoy with a flag up, but they hadn't seen it, or didn't understand what it was. They weren't looking for anything but having a good time. They killed her.'

He pulled his feet under his chair, arms resting on his thighs. He leaned forward, peering down between his knees as if looking through the floor, through the water, searching for Melody.

'They say it happened so fast she won't have known a thing. Bullshit. Have you ever been under the water when a speedboat comes near?'

I shook my head.

'The noise is terrific, but it's impossible to get direction, and if you have to come up for air . . .' He lifted his head, his mind reliving Melody's last moments. His eyes snapped shut, and he turned away for a second to recompose. 'So you see, I understand what you're going through.'

My heart ached; poor man.

He ran me back to the hotel and led me to the lift. There, he took my hands and kissed me on the cheek.

'Thank you,' I said.

'Me, too,' he replied.

* * *

Back in my hotel room, I bit down on tears. I understood Spiros's pain, and how alone he felt. He would feel cheated every time he saw a young family enjoying themselves, or a wedding, or even a romantic couple in a restaurant.

For the first time in weeks, sleep came moments after I slipped into bed. I woke at 7.30 with a longing to embrace the day. First, a swim, fifty lengths in the crystal-clear hotel pool, followed by a hearty breakfast on the dining-room terrace. Two hours later, I set out for Granny Daphne's home.

* * *

Granny and Yánna waited on the lawn, in the shade of the towering fir tree. They greeted me with wide smiles, calling, 'Good morning, Flora!'

'You're both exceedingly chirpy this morning,' I said, admiring Daphne's glamorous hairstyle and Yánna's bright red lipstick. 'What's going on?'

'Nothing at all,' Granny said. 'We're taking you out to lunch for your birthday.'

I blinked at them. 'But it's not my birthday.'

'Yes, sorry we missed it. Anyway, you forgot to invite us, so we are having our own celebration today.'

'You're both nuts.'

They grinned at each other.

'There is time to paint before the taxi arrives,' Daphne said. 'Better get on with it.'

'I'll bring your painting stuff out, and make our coffee,' Yánna announced, before scuttling indoors.

'She's amazing, isn't she?' I said to Daphne. 'I'm surprised a good man hasn't snapped her up.'

'She's sweet on the baker's father. He brings the bread sometimes . . . a bit of a Casanova. He's eighty.'

I was grinning, too. 'That's lovely!'

'How do you want me?' Daphne asked, nodding at the canvas.

'I'm putting detail in the eyes right now, so you're fine as you are.'

She lifted her chin and turned her head, knowing it would make life easier for me.

'Did you notice Aristotle's portrait inside?' she asked. 'The one I want to have copied. I painted it when we were in Missolonghi.'

'I guess it's dry, then?' We both laughed. 'Can I ask you something, Granny?'

'You can ask . . .' Her eyes twinkled, and I captured that mischievousness in her likeness.

'I noticed the three beautiful paintings called *Laurel* by Avon Stroop—'

Her hand flew to her mouth. 'You did?' she interrupted. 'Where . . .? Where are they?'

'In the National Gallery of Corfu. Were you the model? They're so beautiful!'

'Oh, yes indeed, I was the model, and my husband the artist. I would love to see them again. After the war, German artists were unpopular, so we changed his signature slightly.'

'All right.' I nodded, but wondered if she had seen me. 'Let's make a deal. I'll take you to see the paintings if you come for an eye examination the day after tomorrow. What do you say?'

She thought about it, then conceded. 'All right, if you insist on being bossy – but only if you allow me to buy lunch.'

'God, you drive a hard bargain. Deal!'

We laughed together, feeling the intense closeness of each other's company.

'Will Yánna come, or would she appreciate a day off?'

'Let's wait and see, shall we? Do I hear the happy whistle of the baker's father?'

Holding a loaf wrapped in a sheet of tissue, a sprightly gentleman wearing light trousers and a check shirt and a tie scuttled towards the cottage, unaware of our presence. He nipped indoors. We heard a squeal and a slap, then the old fellow appeared, minus the loaf. He rubbed his cheek, but wore a wide grin.

'Say nothing when she brings our drinks out,' Daphne said, lifting her chin, posing.

Satisfied with her eyes, I started painting her hair and laid down the darkest of greys for the shadows, then paler hues, followed by silver-white for the highlights. With the paint still wet, I combed through it, revealing strands of darker hair and shadows below the surface. Her tresses were strong and a little wild and wiry and, like her, determined to remain untamed.

26

DAPHNE

Corinth, 1943

THE ANDARTES LIFTED THE CUP to Daphne's mouth, and she drank, feeling the water sweet and cold in her dusty throat. She stared at the coiled rope on the wall. These thugs wouldn't hang them, would they?

'I'm afraid for my baby,' she whispered to the man holding the cup.

What is Aristotle telling the giant? We should have made a plan before . . .

She needed the bathroom. Lately, she couldn't go half an hour before needing privacy behind a bush.

'We volunteered to help,' she said to the giant. 'If we'd known this was how you'd treat us, I'd have kept my mouth shut.'

The door opened. She held her breath, more afraid than ever. Aristotle staggered in, a trickle of blood running from the corner of his mouth. His bruised left eye had already closed.

'Tell them everything, Daphne.'

'Don't speak!' the brute yelled.

She could only gulp for breath, her chest jerking and tears streaming. Her fists clenched and she started shaking. Aristotle saw she was in a state, but couldn't do anything.

'Bring her out, now!' the bully yelled.

The men lifted Daphne and carried her outside. One held her under the arms, the other clutched her feet. Their powerful hands gripped her with bruising violence. She realised the futility of trying to wriggle free. Anyway, she hadn't the energy. She felt sweat trickle down her spine after the cottage door slammed behind her. They sat her on the bench seat in the truck. The bully sat opposite.

'Don't be afraid. I will not hurt you or your husband, so long as you tell me the absolute truth.'

She thought she saw compassion when she looked him in the eyes.

'Who are you working for?' he yelled with a sudden change of mood, slamming his fist into the palm of his other hand.

She quaked so violently she couldn't speak. Then, cowering in her seat, she whispered, 'Please ... I'm not used to this, to violence. I'm not working for anyone. Are you going to kill us? I'm having a baby ... Please, be merciful.'

'Why are you running away?' he yelled even louder. 'Who are you trying to escape from?'

Daphne had no option but to tell him the truth. She took a breath, dared to look into his eyes, and said, 'I'm Jewish.'

He sighed so hard she felt his breath on her face.

'What happened?'

'My father was a minister in the government until the Gestapo made him wash dishes. The bishop and chief of police got us papers so my father, sister and mother could escape to Cairo. The Nazis took my two brothers. One got himself shot so Mamá could escape.' She began sobbing again and had to pause. After hauling in some deep breaths, she continued. 'I wanted to stay with Aristotle. He was my art teacher for many years and I had fallen in love with him. We got married. I'm pregnant. We are trying to get to my cousin's farm on the islet of Aitoliko. My cousin's name is Lola Abad. My family disowned her for marrying a Muslim, not that he's religious at all, neither is she.'

Daphne's older cousin, Lola, was the black sheep of the family. Beautiful Lola with the long, black hair and golden eyes had fallen in love and married an Albanian fisherman. Because of this outrageous and shameful deed, her Greek-Jewish family disowned her. But Daphne and Lola had been great friends when they were young. Daphne knew Lola would help her. She lived on the edge of the sea with their husband, two sons and a daughter.

'Can anyone verify this?'

'Aristotle, of course, and someone called Kyría Alice, but perhaps she has moved on to another island. She hid us in Athens.'

He squinted at her. 'Kyría Alice . . . You know Kyría Alice?'

She nodded.

'Tell me her full title.'

'Princess Andrew of Greece and Denmark.'

He stared hard. 'How did you meet her?'

'I helped her in the soup kitchen in Athens, and she hid me . . .'

Daphne said no more for fear of putting Kyría Alice in danger. After a silent moment, he continued with his questions.

'All right, I believe you. Now tell me about your husband.'

'He is the most brilliant artist. He taught me to paint. I've been having lessons with him for many years, and he also helps me with my German. He's fluent.'

'Tell me about his family.'

'I don't know about them,' she hesitated. 'Except he has an older cousin who joined the Nazi party.'

'When was the last time they met?'

'I don't know – not since the war started, as far as I know. They're not good friends.'

'Whose side are you on?'

'We are trying to get to England because they're our allies. We want our baby to be born there.'

She placed her hands on her belly, feeling a little calmer now.

'Right ... If your husband had told me this, I wouldn't have given him a beating. Don't worry, nothing's broken. He'll have a few bruises tomorrow, but that's about it. How fluent is your German?'

'I'm quite good, but I'd never pass for a native. However, I can translate very well.'

'Would you be prepared to help us?'

'I don't want to put my baby in danger, you understand?'

'All right. We're not heartless bandits, madam, but a young expectant couple who might appear to be on the Axis side, or the Allies' side, could be very useful to us. We'll do all we can to protect you and get you safe passage to England, on the condition you help us with translating the messages we intercept, and do a little information gathering. So, do you agree to help us?'

'Do I have a choice?'

'Yes. We can drop you ten miles from anywhere with no food or water.' He shrugged.

'Is that so? We don't have a choice, then.'

His soft smile unnerved her. He put his fingers to his lips and gave an almighty whistle.

Daphne stared at the ground – the situation was clear. They were trapped.

Two men pushed Aristotle back into the truck.

'My name's Orion,' their interrogator divulged, turning to Aristotle. 'That's all you need to know. Your wife has agreed to help us in return for safe passage to England – which I can't guarantee, but we'll do our best.'

'What do you want us to do?' Aristotle frowned at Daphne while scratching at the blood drying on his cheek. A tic jerked the corner of his mouth, yet he squared his shoulders and lifted his chin with dignity. 'Whatever it is, I want reassurance that they'll keep my wife out of danger.' He took Daphne's hand.

'We'll do everything we can to keep you both safe. I give you my word. We've got you a place on the *Saint Barbara*, she's being tugged through the canal this afternoon.'

'What do you want us to do?'

'Be Greek. The locals will know the Germans are after you, but be discreet, keep your eyes and ears open. We're looking for informers, so make a note of anything unusual.'

'Tugged?' Daphne asked. 'Can't the ship sail through the canal under its own steam?'

'The big ships must be tugged through. Can you imagine the force of water they have to push against, to move forward with only a metre of space each side? Hang on, we're on the move.'

The truck lurched forward.

Aristotle threw an alarmed glance at Daphne's belly and slung his arm around her shoulders.

'Once we get through the canal, that's it?'

'Not exactly. You must take a crate to one of the Peloponnese towns. It's urgent.'

'Can't Luka do it?' Daphne asked.

Orion shook his head. 'The road's too narrow and rough for Luka's truck. Besides, he must deliver his flour. He's a driver and has his own schedule. Also, we don't want any connection between that place and him. There are Germans in the area, that's why you're ideal. Nobody up there speaks German. Luka will take you along the coast towards Patras and then drop you at the train station.'

'Train?' they exclaimed in unison.

'Yes, there's a cog railway that goes up the mountain. It's important that the box looks like part of your belongings. We don't want it to draw attention, otherwise we'd put it on board. Do you understand?' They nodded. 'Good. We'll give you a place to stay and a story to tell. We'll get word to you when it's time to return to the coast road, where Luka will pick you up again. You'll be there for a week or two.'

'And the name of this village?'

'Kalávryta.'

'Right . . . Never heard of it. Any chance of earning some money while we're there?' Aristotle asked.

Orion thought for a moment. 'There might be some manual labour. On the lower slopes, there are olive groves and vineyards. The olive harvest will start soon, and there's been a shortage of fit workers since conscription. There's land to clear and nets to spread under the trees. First, let's get up the canal, yes?'

Aristotle nodded. Daphne glanced at the sun, already on its descent. Luka was meeting them at 6 p.m., so they had time.

* * *

The SS *Saint Barbara* was a rust bucket – clanging and drilling noises below deck made it impossible to hold a conversation. Temperatures rose, and the air became too hot for the time of year. Daphne still suffered from morning sickness. The disorientating noise and the stink of grease, diesel fumes and body odour made her rush to the rail and heave. Aristotle hurried to her side and placed an arm around her shoulders. She sensed he wanted to utter comforting words but, in the racket, there was no chance of hearing him.

'I can't imagine what they're doing down there,' Aristotle said when an abrupt break in the noise allowed. 'It sounds as though they're drilling through the hull!'

'Wouldn't that mean we'd sink?'

He shook his head. 'Not if it's above the waterline.'

'Why would they do that?' She threw her head back and stared at the sheer rock walls that loomed up on both sides. 'We're trapped here. I don't like it. What can they be doing below?'

'If I find out and tell Orion, it might get us safe passage to England.'

'Look!' she nodded ahead. 'Is that the bridge we were supposed to cross with Luka?'

'I think so.'

'I have a horrible feeling. What if the British blow the bridge while we're underneath? We'll sink, and the ship will block the canal.'

'That's what's worrying me. They want to force the German ships to go the long way around to get into the Aegean, an extra two days' sailing. As it is, we're an easy target. I'm going to investigate below. Let's get you under cover – we're too exposed on deck.'

The noise inside was worse, and the air so stale Daphne squinted with each breath. She tugged at Aristotle's sleeve and indicated that they should go back outside.

'That's unbearable!' she said, once they were in the fresh air again.

'Whatever they're doing, it's happening in the stern. Let's go up to the bow. It must be quieter there. Perhaps I can talk to the skipper. You pretend you are interested in sailing.'

They made their way to the wheelhouse and climbed the metal steps.

The Greek captain was a fat man who'd once been much fatter. Slack flesh fell about his body like a half-deflated beach ball. Straight, dark hair stuck to his forehead, and his brown eyes squinted from under lids that glistened with sweat. Jowls hung, quivering, from his stubbled jawline as his voice blasted at them.

'What you want? Get out of here!'

'Sir, I've information you might find useful,' Aristotle said.

'What information?' he roared, making them both flinch. 'Get her out of here! Don't you know it's bad luck to have a female in the wheelhouse?'

With a nod, Aristotle told Daphne she should return to the foredeck. She called 'Sorry!' to the captain. Outside the doorway, she stepped back and listened to what they said.

'Go on!' the captain shouted at Aristotle.

Daphne peeked through the side window and realised the captain's entire concentration was on the tugboat that was pulling them through the narrow passage.

Aristotle spoke above the racket. 'We'd planned to cross by road, but a German blockade stopped us. The Germans said the British were planning to blow the bridge over the canal.' They both squinted ahead at the distant bridge high above the seawater. 'Gossip was, they'd use the falling bridge to sink a ship travelling beneath it.'

The captain's eyes swivelled to stare at Aristotle. A deafening howl of metal against rock poleaxed them all.

'*Gamóti Panagía mou!*' the captain swore in the most blasphemous way possible, swinging around to concentrate on the tug again. 'When did this happen?'

'Day before yesterday.'

'Right. Take the wheel. Keep that centre handle in line with the tug's centre-stern, up ahead. Concentrate, or we'll scrape the sides again. I need a hole in my hull like you need a hole in the head!'

Daphne gasped and her stomach cramped. She took some calming breaths and tried to lower her blood pressure for the sake of their baby. Flattened against the hot metal of the ship's wheelhouse, she remained out of the captain's sight. A strong breeze rushed through the canyon, whipping her hair away from her face and making her eyes water. She strained to hear Aristotle over the noise resonating from the back of the ship. After peeping through the side window again, she saw her husband at the wheel. The captain snatched his binoculars and peered up at the bridge. A distant popping noise snapped the eerie acoustics of sailing along the deep chasm.

'Gunfire!' she muttered, cowering against the wheelhouse.

'*Maláka poutána!*' the foul-mouthed captain blasted.

Daphne held her breath fearing this was the ship they planned to sink with the falling bridge. Even as she stared at the expanse of metal silhouetted against the vivid sky, the news of an impending battle blared out from the captain's radio.

With a flash, an explosion sounded above them. A steel girder came hurtling down right in front of the tug, striking one wall of the canyon with a shower of sparks. The girder bounced across to strike the other wall. With an enormous splash, it hit the water and upended, leaning against the side. Daphne ran into Aristotle's arms.

'Can't we stop?' she cried.

'Get that damned woman out of here, now!' the captain roared.

Their destiny was unavoidable: they had to go on.

The strong little tug continued to pull their ship closer to the bridge. The wail of its foghorn bellowed between the tall, straight sides of the canal, but the battle above continued to rage. Another explosion flashed.

'Come on!' Aristotle cried above the racket. 'We'll be safer at the stern.'

They scrambled aft, trying to outrun the onslaught of falling debris. Feeling the heat from the metal deck rise through her shoes, Daphne was relieved to reach a descending stairway. They hurried down, unable to speak for the din. The work that had caused all the noise stopped, leaving an ominous silence.

'Now! Do it now, before we're hit!' somebody yelled, yet the entire area was empty. A door burst open, and an enormous man loomed over Aristotle and Daphne. 'What the hell are you doing down here? Get up top, or I'll kill you both!'

'We're on your side,' Aristotle said, but to Daphne's horror, the man snatched a handful of his hair, drew a pistol, and held it to her husband's head.

'Prove it!' their aggressor yelled.

'Orion sent us. We're on a mission.' Aristotle's eyes narrowed.

The bully squinted at him. 'What sort of mission?'

'I can't say, but we're both on the same side.' Their aggressor relaxed and lowered his gun. Aristotle continued to explain. 'My wife's pregnant. I was looking for a safer place.' He glanced at what he judged to be incendiary devices. 'Though I suspect this isn't it. Aren't they limpet mines?'

Daphne swung around, her face perplexed. Aristotle reached an arm around her.

'They might be,' the rough guy said, then with a sigh, he elaborated. 'We're trying to lower them into the canal before that lot' – he turned his eyes upwards – 'sink us.' He shook his head. 'They irony is, we're on the same side!'

Aristotle tugged his jacket off. 'You'd better hurry. They're destroying the bridge above, and it's only ten minutes ahead. I'll help. Tell me what to do.'

'Come through!' he shouted, heading for the inside door in the double hull Aristotle guessed was not far above sea level. 'We're dropping the limpet mines on a weight and line to hold them two metres below the surface. That way, any domestic vessels will avoid them, but battleships stand a good chance of attracting them. Once the magnets stick to their metal hull, we can use remote detonation. Come on, we haven't much time.' He turned to Daphne. 'You, miss, had better find some cover up top and wait for your husband.'

She nodded and hurried up top. Was Aristotle involved with the SEO people, or the resistance?

She stared up at the sheer walls hemming them in. If a mine went off in the confined space between the double hull, they'd all die. Fear tingled up her spine. She chewed her lip, glanced about, panic rising.

But if the ship stopped . . . If a girder fell across the tug or the *Saint Barbara's* hull, she might sink between the rock walls and there was no escape. The bridge may well fall on them, anyway. She pressed her hands against her belly. She couldn't swim. How was she supposed to keep her baby safe?

Another explosion clattered from the bridge above. It might fall at any moment. Daphne gulped, pressed her back against hot metal that blistered with rust. At the very least, she needed a flotation aid. She'd seen a white chest bearing a red cross on the deck, and rushed out to investigate. Something raced through the sky overhead, terrifying her to a standstill.

Breathe! Calm down. Think about the baby.

A Spitfire had flown so close to the ground above, it almost entered the gorge. The plane headed for the bridge, guns blazing, then lifted and flew over it. Men rushed up from below decks, punching the air and cheering. Then Aristotle's arms were around her.

'At last, someone has informed the army they shouldn't sink a ship full of British agents trying to do their job.'

All eyes turned upwards. In silence, everyone holding their breath, they passed under the expanse of metal and concrete above, then the tug tootled its foghorn while the men cheered and punched the air.

Aristotle hugged her. 'Are you all right?'

Daphne nodded, pressing against his chest.

'Shaken, but glad it's over. That was enough excitement to last me a lifetime! I'll be glad to climb into Luka's truck.'

27

FLORA

Corfu, present day

DAPHNE HADN'T LEFT HER CHAIR all morning, thanks to their wonderful taxi driver. He lowered a mechanical ramp, wheeled her in, strapped her down, and we set off for town.

'Isn't this marvellous, Flora?' She stretched her neck and did a regal wave at the window. 'I feel like a queen,' she exclaimed.

'And you look very royal, too,' I said. 'I hope Yánna enjoys herself at the cafe. Who will she take for their cream tea – the baker's father or her friend?'

'Who knows? You were very kind to get her the gift voucher.'

'Where are we going, ladies?' the driver called.

I lifted the card from my pocket and called out the name of the street, then turned to Daphne.

'First stop is the optician's, Granny.'

*   *   *

Once inside the place, I sat in the corner behind Daphne, nervous, praying there was hope for her eyesight. Granny forgot I was there and did all the optician asked. Soon, she confirmed my suspicions.

'I can see a little around the edges, but nothing in the middle, young man. So, I can manage all right if I twist my head about like a mad parrot.'

The optician, who was in his early sixties and wore glasses, had a sympathetic face.

'You know what I'm going to tell you, Kyría Stroop. You have age-related macular degeneration. At the moment, there's no cure.'

'Sorry I wasted your time, then. She means well, my grand-daughter.' At this point, I heard a little sob and the optician's eyes met mine. 'But I tried to tell her there was no hope. All the money in the world can't buy something that doesn't exist, can it? It's just, I wished to see her face one last time, you know? She's come all the way from England.' The pride in her voice broke my heart.

'Well, perhaps I can make that one wish come true. Let's see now . . . if you'll pardon the pun. Technology *has* raced ahead in the past decade, Kyría Stroop, and in this case perhaps money *can* buy something that doesn't exist. Let's go back to the eye chart and try something new.' He placed a pair of glasses on Daphne's head, then took a box out of his desk drawer. 'I warn you, there are a lot of adjustments to make, which will take about an hour. Will you be able to cope with that, Kyría?'

'Will you ask my granddaughter? I believe she has lunch planned.'

He looked up at me. I nodded for him to go ahead. His assistant brought us coffee and iced water. At midday, the optician called me over.

'Would you like to share what she sees?' he asked me.

'I would, and also an idea of the cost before we get my grand-mother's hopes up.'

'We're looking at less than ten thousand euros, but I'm not trying to sell them to her. She wants to see you for a few minutes, and I can do that.'

I nodded, the lump in my throat making speech impossible.

'So, if you keep your eyes on the screen, you'll understand what she's seeing.' He turned to Daphne. Are you ready, Kyría?'

'Let's get on with it, young man,' Daphne said. 'I haven't got all day.'

I stared at the screen as he plugged a wire into the arm of what looked like black gaming goggles.

When the eye chart came up, I guessed it to be a test screen.

'All the letters are perfectly clear,' Daphne cried in a tremulous voice. 'All of them! Where's my granddaughter?'

As she turned, I took her hand. The image on the screen turned, too, until it was my head and shoulders. She gasped, then sobbed and squeezed my fingers with surprising strength.

'Oh Flora!' she cried. 'Look at you. You've grown into such a beauty. This is a miracle, an absolute miracle.'

Then I realised she hadn't seen me for many years.

'Dear Granny, I love you so much.'

We sat there, holding each other's hands – unable to hold back the tears.

'I guess you're pleased then,' the optician said, his smile wide and his eyes also a little damp. 'Would you like me to order them for you?'

'You mean I can't keep this pair?' Granny asked, touching the side of the glasses. 'What do I look like, Flora?'

'To be honest, they're like smart, video-gaming goggles.' I turned to the optician. 'Can she keep this pair?'

'Sorry, no. They're just a sample from two years back. Technology has moved on and the latest ones are much thinner and lighter.'

I placed my hand on his arm. 'I understand, but would it be possible to hire them for a few days? It's most important.'

He considered my question for a moment.

'Can you leave a substantial deposit?' I nodded. 'Then, why not?'

* * *

The optician's building was a short distance from the gallery, so I pushed Daphne through the narrow streets. I felt such delight to see her head scanning from left to right – quite unperturbed by the stares of people who'd guessed she was wearing gaming goggles. We stopped at a pavement taverna, the Pergola, and ordered *Sofrito*, a Corfu speciality. Richly flavoured with garlic and herbs, prime beef is slow cooked in a sealed, earthenware pot until meltingly tender. The waiter broke the seal at our table and lifted the lid, surrounding us in an aromatic cloud that woke my tastebuds. He also delivered black olives and a slab of feta sprinkled with fresh oregano and glistening, green olive oil, a dish of glazed tomatoes, a fresh green salad and a basket of the most wholesome multigrain bread encrusted with toasted sesame seeds. A feast! We relished every mouthful.

'It's amazing to have my sight back, Flora. Thank you!' Daphne said, biting her lip and shaking her head. 'I can't wait to see Aristotle's portraits in the gallery. It's so exciting.'

I called for the bill, and ten minutes later, two powerful security guards lifted the wheelchair up the gallery steps. A small crowd had gathered in the entrance. Thanks to my advance phone call, the gallery manager was waiting to introduce himself upon our arrival and a press photographer was also there, snapping everything. Spiros appeared and accompanied us to the gallery with the *Laurel* triptych by Avon Stroop. As we approached the portraits, Daphne gasped with her hand over her mouth. When a tear trickled down her cheek, Spiros appeared and whipped the fresh white handkerchief from his top pocket and gently dabbed it away.

Somebody brought a gallery programme and asked Daphne to sign it, much to the photographer's delight, then she concentrated on the triptych.

'Oh my, they're quite beautiful, aren't they? Aristotle painted the first one in Athens, and the second in Aitoliko.'

What about the third picture?

* * *

Our taxi took us all the way to the small circular road outside Mon Repos mansion. 'Is this all right for you ladies?' the driver asked.

'You've been marvellous, Níko!' I replied, adding a hefty tip to his fare. 'We'll manage from here. And I have your card. Next time I need a cab, expect a call from us, OK?'

Once he'd driven away, we stood for a moment, admiring the regal front of Mon Repos.

'I'd forgotten how beautiful it is,' Daphne whispered with a tremor in her voice. 'I've so many memories of this place. Will you bring me here tomorrow? Oh, Flora, how can I ever thank you for giving me my sight back? It's like a miracle from Heaven.'

I couldn't wait for Granny and Yánna to meet, and for her to see Aristotle's portrait in the cottage. I pushed her along the footpath between towering trees and wild flowers. By the movements of Daphne's head, I knew she was taking it all in. Every now and again, she would gasp at a gorgeous composition of trees and vegetation. I stopped when a pair of yellow and blue swallowtail butterflies fluttered up and down over a patch of wild marigolds.

Daphne said, 'We take things for granted, don't we? Then they're gone . . . sometimes forever.'

We arrived at the cottage, where Yánna came rushing out, eyes fixed on Daphne.

'What on earth . . .?'

I caught her attention and shook my head. She snapped her mouth shut. A loud sob came from my grandmother.

'Oh, Yánna, is that you? It's so good to see you at last. It's been so long.'

Yánna's jaw dropped. 'You can see me, Daphne? Oh!' She started crossing herself like crazy. 'Dear Jesus Christ and all the angels.'

She rushed upon Daphne and started hugging her – within seconds we were all crying.

'The picture of Aristotle – bring it out here, Yánna,' Daphne cried, sobbing and gulping.

Yánna rushed indoors and brought the heavy oil painting out.

'Oh, my beloved husband!' Daphne exclaimed. 'My precious darling.' Her fingertips touched the portrait, feeling the brush-strokes, while tears streamed down her cheeks. 'His face . . . Oh . . . So wonderful, I think I'm steaming up.'

Seeing so much excitement made me a little nervous that any more emotion might be too exhausting for Daphne's heart; she was, after all, ninety-nine years old.

'It's been such a big day, Granny, a nice cup of tea and an early night are called for.'

* * *

'Would you like me to read to you?' I asked, plugging her glasses in to charge.

'Mmmm,' she hummed, sipping her mountain tea. 'That would be nice. There are some letters in a brown envelope in the back of the drawer. Find them for me, would you? I used to read one every day, once dear Aristotle had gone. They calmed me, but since my eyesight let me down, I haven't been able to read anything.'

'Who are they from?'

'They're from Kyría Alice, but now I think about it, they're in Greek. Perhaps with my new glasses, I'll be able to read the letters from my dear friend tomorrow. It's all very exciting.'

'I'm sure you'll be able to read them – and how about doing a little painting? We can get an easel adapted to fit your chair.'

Dear old Daphne turned to stare out of the window. The light was turning golden, that magical hour before sunset.

28

DAPHNE

Peloponnese, 1943

DAPHNE CUPPED HER HAND UNDER her pregnant belly and squinted into the sunset. Many German cars had roared past, yet there was still no sign of Luka. Unease gathered in her chest, weighing on her already expanding frame. What could have happened to him? They had walked along the dusty national road, Poseidon Street, for half an hour. Her ungainly gait was giving her backache. The cobalt sea lapped at rocks to their right, and across the water green mountains rose to meet the sky.

'Please, Aristotle, I need to stop for a minute,' she said, resting her back against a tree. Cicadas sawed all around. She glanced at the turquoise sea and longed to paddle her swollen feet in the shallows. 'Is that where we're heading?' She nodded at another set of distant mountains across the sea. 'I'm desperate to sit down, but fear I'll never get up again.'

'Poor darling.' He took her bundle from her for a few minutes. 'Yes, once we've taken care of this task for the British agents, we'll get the ferry across the Gulf of Corinth.' He followed her gaze to the horizon. 'That's where our baby will be born – over in western Greece. The place where Byron's heart's buried.'

'You're such a romantic,' she said, smiling at him, wiping sweat from her forehead.

'Then, when we're all strong enough, we'll go on to the island of Corfu and everything will be perfect, I promise.'

'Perfect? Is this an island promise, Aristotle, that Corfu will be perfect? And what will you forfeit if you break this magnanimous promise, kind sir?' She shimmied her shoulders while giving him the eye.

'What would you have me give you, mercenary temptress? Gold, jewels?'

'Your brushes! I'll have all your brushes and you shall never paint again.'

'Steady on!' He laughed. 'How can I paint your wonderful naked body if I have no brushes?'

'All right, I'll allow you one last portrait then, when I've had the baby. No, on second thoughts, I want two more. The third one when I'm old and grey. What do you say, Aristotle? Promise me!' Knowing he was not likely to live until she reached old age, they gazed into each other's eyes for a moment. 'Stay with us for that long,' she whispered. 'Please.'

He kissed her tenderly and for a moment their troubles melted away, but then she sensed the pain in his heart.

* * *

'He's not here,' Babis, the taverna owner, said when they came upon his crumbling establishment and hoped to find Luka waiting. Babis brought them a plate of fresh bread drizzled with olive oil, oregano and salt, a plate of anchovies, and a small jug of red wine.

'The best meal!' Daphne exclaimed. 'I'm so hungry.'

Aristotle turned to the taverna owner. 'She's eating for two,' he said with pride in his eyes and a smile on his lips.

Babis nodded at the heavy traffic. 'It's been like this all afternoon. Troops on the move. Puts a bad feeling in my belly.'

They both glanced at his enormous stomach, then ate with their eyes fixed on the bend ahead and their ears straining for the sound of Luka's old truck. An hour passed.

'Now what?' Daphne asked. 'It's almost curfew.' They had watched several truckloads of German soldiers heading towards Patras. 'Even if he turns up in the next few minutes, we can't go along the main road with so many troops about.'

'It's not just that,' Aristotle added. 'We have to get this crate to the andartes at Kalávryta. The freedom fighters are waiting for it.'

He shoved the heavy wooden box, which Daphne suspected was a radio, under the table and then disappeared inside to talk to the taverna owner.

A moment later, a passing truck screeched to a halt and ten German soldiers tumbled out from behind the camouflage canvas back. The sergeant went straight behind the taverna while his men, not one over twenty years of age, took seats around Daphne. One of them sat in Aristotle's place and rested his big army boots on the crate. Daphne's mouth dried. If anyone discovered the contents of the chest, they'd be shot. She tried to ignore it, although her cheeks burned.

They stared at her and made crude and sexist remarks between themselves in German, never thinking she would understand. With eyes sparkling, they stared at her breasts and legs until her anger and embarrassment exploded.

She stood with her hands on her hips, her pregnancy obvious, and spoke to the one nearest to her.

'*Schäm dich!*' she said in his language. Shame on you! What would your mother think if she could hear you now?' she continued in German. 'How would you feel if I was your younger sister, being spoken about in that way? You and your disgusting friends are an embarrassment to your country!'

The young soldier's cheeks flushed. The banter died; some even dropped their heads. One, however, stood up and rubbed his hands together.

'What's in the box?' he demanded, nudging the crate with the toe of his jackboot.

'How should I know? It was here when I arrived,' she said, her mouth now dry as sand, yet she looked him straight in the eye. He reached down and tugged it from under the table.

The taverna owner came rushing out.

'No, don't touch that! It needs to be kept in the shade or they'll die.'

'They?' the soldier asked. 'What's in here – puppy dogs?'

He reached down to untie the knotted rope, but pulled back the instant he heard the taverna owner's one-word reply.

'Snakes!'

'Whaa!'

'Rat snakes to clear my cellar,' Babis said. 'It's the Greek way.'

Chairs scraped back. Babis reached for the crate, lifted it and placed it across the quarrelsome soldier's thighs.

'You want to look? Untie the rope!'

The soldier's face paled with horror. 'I believe you,' he gasped. 'Get them off me.'

'Good. I'm going to take them down and set them free now.' Babis was so convincing that, for a moment, Daphne believed him.

'Bring us some beer and water!' the loud soldier ordered as their group leader reappeared from behind the building.

Aristotle appeared from inside with a tray of bottled beers, a jug of water, and glasses.

'Good evening, gentlemen,' he called in German, placing the tray on the table.

'Were there really snakes in that box?' the leader asked, his eyes narrowing as he spoke.

Aristotle nodded. 'One's a monster, too. Wait, I'll show you.'

He marched inside and returned.

'Here, they left this in the box.'

He dropped a snakeskin onto the soldier's lap

After a second of horrified withdrawal, the young soldiers peered a little more closely at the long tube of tissue-thin snakeskin, transparent scales glinting in the fading sunlight.

'Wow!' somebody whispered. 'How long's that?'

'A metre and a half, I guess.' He held it up so they could compare it with the height of his own body. 'I'd say the snake itself is going on for two metres. They eat small mammals.' He glanced at Daphne and she understood he was enjoying himself. 'Mice, rats, eggs, even kittens and small dogs, they say. They have a little head that fools the prey, but its jaws dislocate to make a massive mouth with backwards-facing fangs. Would get half your neck in one bite.' He pointed at the middle of the snakeskin. 'Huge girth, look – easy to accommodate an unsuspecting pigeon.'

One of the soldiers shuddered. 'They make my skin crawl,' he said, then stared at his comrades.

'Pay up!' the group leader ordered. 'Then back in the truck.'

The Germans drove away. Daphne's shoulders dropped, and Aristotle slid his arm around her trembling body.

'I don't know if I want to vomit or pee-pee,' she said.

'You must have been terrified.'

'I thought I handled it very well, to be honest,' she said, trying to stop the bile rising from the pit of her stomach.

'Look, here's Luka,' Babis said. 'You two should go through to the back. There's a table and chairs out there, and you'll have a bit of privacy while I feed the man. Can you chase the chickens home and shut them in for the night? I've a problem with polecats.'

Behind the higgledy-piggledy stone taverna lay an olive grove; a rusted, tyreless pickup was balanced on breeze blocks and wrapped in wire mesh, converted into a chicken coop. A white cat sat on a swinging seat and challenged them with a blue-eyed stare. The feline watched them for a moment, then lost interest. Aristotle found a pail of corn and threw a handful into the back of the pickup. The chickens heard the clatter and raced, wings outstretched, necks forward, up the extended tailgate and settled in their rusted home to roost for the night.

'Well, that was easy,' he said, evicting the cat and relaxing on the swinging seat.

'I'd like some chickens,' she said, snuggling up to his side.

They sat close, sharing dreams and allowing their tensions to dissipate with the daylight. A gentle breeze whispered through the olive trees, turning leaves silver in the dusk. A nightingale serenaded them, its sharp, musical trilling laced through the treetops, bringing them peace. A buttery moon rose over the orchard. They watched it rise, a beautiful, full sphere that bathed their surroundings in a metallic light. The olive grove was thrown into sharp contrasts, the trees standing guard, making them feel safe. To their right, they caught a glimpse of the sea rolling hypnotically, reflecting the perfect moon from its mercury water like a glittering pathway to heaven. After a difficult day, peace settled over them, enhanced by the perfume of night-scented honeysuckle.

Suddenly, Aristotle put a finger across his lips. He made a slight nod towards the chicken coop. She saw a flash of white fur, then recognised the loose-limbed, panther-like movements of a polecat. It circled the old pickup, then leaped onto the bonnet, and onto the roof of the cab before investigating the chicken-wire covering of the truck. The hens panicked, squawking and flapping. Aristotle made a sharp hissing noise. The polecat froze, then bolted down and disappeared into the trees.

'They're quite beautiful, but it would have ripped the throat out of every chicken.'

Daphne watched the scrawny hens settle.

'Nature can be cruel,' she said.

'Man, too,' he said. 'Can I ask you something?'

She nodded.

'If our baby is a boy . . . Well . . .' He paused, chewed his lip.

'Will I want to have our son circumcised?' she asked.

Aristotle nodded.

'No,' she replied. 'In memory of Noah, I won't.' She was silent for a minute, her mind lost in deep sadness and memories of her brother. Then she felt hot tears run down her cheeks. 'Sorry,' she whispered. 'It's still difficult to accept that he's gone. To do such a brave thing for my mother – for all of us – to save her from the Nazi work camp.' She sighed and smudged away her tears. 'To my father's annoyance, Noah campaigned vigorously against involuntary circumcision. He was the leader of a group of ever-increasing objectors. His group wanted the *brit milah*, the circumcision, replaced by the *brit shalom*, which is a non-violent ceremony where no genital mutilation takes place.'

She used the technical words Noah had used when he explained the reason for her father's terrible anger one night. Voices were raised, and fists were clenched, and Daphne had never seen anything like it in her home before.

'The *brit shalom* serves the same spiritual purpose, but without the blood, pain, trauma and the violation of basic human rights. Noah said that if a man wanted to be circumcised in public, without anaesthetic, then he was free to make that choice once he reached the age of consent.'

Aristotle kept his thoughts to himself, then broke the silence.

'I wish I'd known Noah. He sounds like a brave young man. It takes courage to fight for change . . . to fight for the rights of others . . . to fight for a better world.'

'And to fight with my father,' Daphne said with a sad smile.

Aristotle placed his hand on her belly. 'Boy or girl, I hope our child has such noble morals, dear Daphne. If it's a boy, we should call him Noah. What do you think?'

'If it's a boy, we'll call him Aristotle Noah.'

She smiled to herself, her heart singing with the hopes and dreams experienced by every expectant mother.

He brushed her hair aside and kissed her forehead.

'You look radiant.'

'I've never been so happy.'

'If it's a girl, what do you have in mind?'

She wanted a girl so badly.

'What was your mother's name, Aristotle?'

'She was Austrian and named Angela, but everyone called her Angel.'

'That's so perfect. Angelikí in Greek. Our own little angel.' They smiled together, all worries gone for a second, united in their joy and contentment. The breeze stilled as night fell quickly. An owl hooted somewhere.

Daphne gasped. 'Listen, it's a sign. The owl, symbol of Athena, warrior goddess of wisdom. I believe we shall have a daughter.'

'You are completely crazy, but I love you,' Aristotle said.

Silence fell about them. The distant rumble of traffic had also stopped. Daphne snuggled into his arms, as the moon travelled its arc across the sky.

'Ah, here you are,' Babis said as he barrelled out on his short, bandy legs. 'Luka's asleep in his truck. I'm about to lock up. There's no trade after curfew. The back of that seat opens out flat, and there's a bundle of mosquito net in the kitchen. Throw it over the frame to keep the insects off you. There's a well at the side of the building if you want to wash in the morning. Toilet's in the olive grove, all right? I'll be here at sunrise.' He wished them goodnight. '*Kalinikta!*'

* * *

The day's noise faded. Daphne and Aristotle lay in each other's arms, fitting together like two spoons, contented, silent. All the moist, forest-fruity scents nature could provide enveloped them, while in the distance, the rolling sea played its hypnotic lullaby. Pipistrelle bats danced in the air, catching insects by the light of the moon. As the black of night became unanimous, stars appeared in the dazzling twisting spiral of the Milky Way.

'Do you believe in God?' Daphne whispered.

'No, but it's easy to understand why our forefathers did when you look at those stars.'

'Such breathtaking vastness. I want to paint it, but I can't, of course. It's impossible to capture.' She took his hand and placed it on her belly. 'Your baby wants to play. I suspect he's going to become a footballer.' She felt Aristotle's chest expand against her back while she sensed his wide smile. 'Shall we go for a swim in the dark? I fear that once we're parents, we'll have to forgo all such wild, spontaneous things.'

He brushed her hair aside and kissed the back of her neck.

'That's a wonderful idea! Who knows when we'll have another chance to swim?'

They scurried past the taverna, then across the national highway, and over a low wall. Their eyes adjusted to the night and, although the rocky shore was uneven, they soon managed to remove their clothes and stumble into the warm Mediterranean.

'Oh, this is wonderful, pure bliss!' Daphne cried, dipping her shoulders under and washing a week's sweat away.

'Let me wash your back,' he said, drawing her wet hair to one side and rubbing his hands up and down her spine.

She closed her eyes, enjoying the sensation of his vigorous massage until she caught a splashing sound coming from the shore and heading their way.

'Aristotle, we're not alone!' she whispered urgently. 'I'm naked and my clothes are on the shore.'

They crouched so that only their heads were above water. A dark shape was backlit by a lone taverna light. Seemingly unaware of their presence, it came stumbling and splashing towards them. They cowered lower, so only their up-pointing chins appeared above the water.

Aristotle pulled her to him and whispered, 'On the count of three, we'll leap up and roar and splash like crazy, right?'

She agreed. The intruder grew ever closer.

'One, two, three!'

They leaped up, ignoring the fact that they were both naked, and roared and slammed their hands on the water as they rushed at the intruder, instantly aware they had terrified him.

He hollered, turned tail and raced for the shore. Grabbing his clothes, he hurried across the road, his startling white buttocks wobbling in the moonlight.

* * *

Daphne and Aristotle drank coffee at a table outside the taverna not long after dawn. Luka joined them, and as they were discussing their plans, Daphne noticed Babis across the road at the edge of the sea.

'What's he doing?' she asked.

'He's looking for his shoe. Apparently, he lost it last night He went to bathe in the sea and claims some giant crustacean, a monstrous crab or lobster, he thinks, reared up and terrified the life out of him. Bashing its claws on the water and roaring like a lion. Anyway, when he got back, naked as the day he was born and clutching his balled-up clothes, he discovered one shoe had gone walkabout.'

Daphne and Aristotle bit their lips and avoided looking at each other.

'If you two want to continue to Igoumenitsa,' Luka said, 'just wait for me on the opposite side of the road on any Wednesday afternoon, all right? In the meantime, enjoy Kalávryta – it's a special place.' He gazed up at the mountain peaks.

29

FLORA

Corfu, present day

'THERE'S ONLY ONE WAY TO find out if you'll be able to read these old letters from your friend, Granny.' I removed the glasses from their charger and slipped them on to her head. 'You may have to adjust something, I don't know. Tell me what you see.'

'What is this, Flora?' she asked, picking up the white pebble on the table.

'Ah, I gave it you when I arrived, before I realised you couldn't see too well. An attractive little beach scene painted onto a pebble. I picked it up outside the airport.'

'You won't believe this, but I've been to this place with Aristotle. It's the banks of the lagoon of Aitoliko . . . You'll come to understand why it's so very special to me as you hear more of my story. Thank you.' She wrapped her fingers around it and closed her eyes. After a long silence, she put the pebble down and stared at the brittle, honey-coloured paper. 'Oh, yes. The writing's blurry, but I can make out the letters. They're from my friend, Kyría Alice. She was a real princess, you know,' she whispered, before her voice faded and her chin rested against her chest.

I slipped the contraption off her head and plugged it back into the charger.

While Yánna took care of Daphne, I delved into the packet of papers and correspondence Daphne had long hidden away. It contained thirty or more letters, the envelopes deep yellow with age, crumbling at the corners and as fragile as my grandmother. I eased one out, but as I unfolded it, the paper cracked into four quarters. I nudged them together. The date in the top right corner was November 1943.

Yánna returned. 'She's asleep, poor old girl's exhausted. Too much excitement.'

'Can I trouble you for something, Yánna?'

'Of course, what you like?'

'Could you read this letter to me in English?'

She hesitated. 'I am not sure if I should. There may be private things inside.'

'Don't worry, Daphne asked me to read it to her before she fell asleep. She forgets I don't know the Greek alphabet, so I think you are safe. However, I admire your loyalty.'

'Ah, I understand. OK, I will read and try to translate, one sentence at a time.'

She stumbled through the letter.

My dearest friend, Daphne,

I hope you are safe and well. I received your letter from Luka. It's difficult to know who you can trust these days, but your friend Luka seems like a good man. He agreed to wait so that he could bring my correspondence to you as soon as possible.

I miss you both very much, and I want to tell you, I have a small, two-bedroom apartment, near the Benaki Museum, here in Athens, and you and Aristotle are welcome to it, should you return. I am worried about your safety, but pleased to hear that you made it as far as Corinth.

Here, little has changed. Every day is a struggle for food. Even more children need my help and, by the grace of God, I do all I can.

I must tell you how much you were in my thoughts in October. Please tell this to dear Aristotle. They have posted notices about the Jews all over Athens, by order of the German commander Stroop, concerning restrictive measures for Jews in this zone of occupation. It is quite dreadful.

You got out of here just in time. They are gathering the last Jews and everyone fears they will deport them to work camps, like all the others. They will shoot Greeks who harbour Jews. I wonder if this Stroop is related to your darling Aristotle?

Tomorrow I fly to Sweden to bring back medical supplies. The Hun believe I am visiting my sister, Louise, who is married to the Crown Prince. The Red Cross is most pleased.

I have heard nothing from your family, although they said they would write once they were settled. I will tell you as soon as I get the news.

Write back. Let me know how things are progressing.

All my best wishes, and may God be with you,

Your good friend,

Kyría Alice.

Hit by a sudden longing to connect with home, I took a stroll to the new cafe. It seemed ages since I'd binged on social media. The condolences had upset me too much. However, it calmed me to connect with Mark's parents and a few close Facebook and Twitter friends. They understood. While I had the internet, I looked at flights. If I was going to copy my grandfather's portrait, I'd need another week.

'Hi, what are you doing here?'

I glanced up to see Spiros.

'Hi, I'm looking over a few emails before I go back to the hotel. How did the chimney go?'

'Yes, all good. Just needs pointing and then I'm done here. Is it your last day tomorrow?'

'As it happens, I'm about to book for another week.'

I couldn't bring myself to tell him the truth: that I couldn't face packing up my lovely home in Crosby to move to a squalid little flat in the worst part of the city centre.

He grinned. 'So why are you looking so sad? Let me take you out tomorrow night. Have you ever been to a Greek wedding?' I shook my head. 'I'm invited to one tomorrow evening. The groom is a Cretan mountain-man, so there'll be some high jinks. Most of the time, I don't go to these things. It's still painful, you know, but he's a cricket teammate so I can't get out of it. Will you come with me? Oh, and there'll be around a thousand guests, so if you want to invite your grandmother and her carer for a couple of hours, feel free. There'll be more than enough food and drink. As soon as they need to leave, I'll make sure there's a taxi for them.'

I smiled, unable to think of a reason not to go.

'It sounds wonderful, thanks. Though I'm not sure I have anything suitable to wear.'

'Great. Look, it's a Greek wedding. Over the top will be par for the course. Be as outrageous as you like.'

'Outrageous, you say.'

He lifted his arm to call the waiter. 'Let's examine the gin list, shall we? How's your grandmother's portrait going?'

'Yes, OK. Now she wants me to paint a replica of my grand-father's portrait.'

'What – you mean von Stroop? You have a self-portrait of von Stroop?' He sat up straight and stared at me.

'Yes ... at least, I think it is. I can't figure out why she would want two, both the same. Anyway, I'll start it tomorrow.

Meanwhile, I need to collect some ashtrays full of dog-ends to taint my canvas.'

His mouth fell open. 'Are you telling me you're going to produce a forgery?'

'Well, no, not an exact forgery, just one that looks, smells and feels the same. Under the eye of an expert, it wouldn't stand a chance of being mistaken for the real thing. I don't have any lead to mix with oil paint, to start with.' His face was a picture, so the mischievous side of me decided not to tell him I was using acrylics. 'Now, can you tell me where I'll find the best art supply shop on the island?'

'Near my office. If you make a list, I'll get what you need when I'm at work tomorrow morning. Then I'll drop them in when I pick you up for the wedding.'

'What time do I have to be ready?'

'About six o'clock.'

'That would work well, because I have something to ask you.' I drew in a breath. 'I'm unveiling my grandmother's portrait tomorrow afternoon. Will you come?'

* * *

We had taken Granny for a stroll in her chair around Mon Repos park. Her head moved from left to right, scanning her surroundings. She pointed out a blackbird here, a butterfly there, a white fluffy cloud that looked like a sheep, all with great enthusiasm. It was then that I suspected her eyesight had been failing for almost as long as I have lived.

We'd had a busy day so far. First, I completed her portrait. She didn't know it was finished because I wanted to surprise her. I'd studied my grandfather's portrait in great detail. Aristotle's portrait would have fooled any layman, so good was the antique finish it appeared to have come from the sixteenth century or thereabouts. I tapped the back with my fingernail. It even sounded hundreds of years old – and I was an expert, after all. The cracked glaze and dirty canvas even smelled of old wood ash and cigarette smoke. I could see Daphne was excited. She glanced around as if expecting someone, licked her lips and drummed her fingers.

'Are you all right, Granny? You seem a little agitated.'

'Yes, yes! It's the portrait. I'm so excited about having another. I should explain.' She stopped, rolled her shoulders, opened her mouth, then shut it again.

'You don't have to tell me anything, Granny.'

'But I do, you see.' She sighed and started again. 'This image of Aristotle has held me in its power ever since I painted it in Missolonghi in 1944.'

'So, Granny had painted Aristotle's portrait. I'd wondered if it was a self-portrait by Aristotle.'

'Every day I've looked at it and thought about destroying it . . . Even after I lost my sight, I could see it in my mind. Every day he's looked down on me, hiding his big secret that only I know. I didn't even tell Kyría Alice, and it's almost driven me mad. You can see it in his eyes – the deceit. I'll be so pleased to have another to hang in its place.' She scratched her lip, eyes sparkling, face twitchy.

I wondered if she had overdosed on her medication.

'I want you to paint such a copy, so perfect that even I can't tell the difference, Flora. Can you do that, dearest girl?'

This didn't make sense, but I thought it best to humour her.

'I promise I'll do my best, Granny. But what will you do with two identical portraits?'

'I'll destroy the first one. I can't bear to lay eyes on it any longer. Every day, it reminds me of what happened and what that painting cost me . . . cost us both.' She smiled, but I saw terrible sadness in her eyes. 'Now, the secret of my eternal youth and incredible intelligence is a lot of naps, so I'm going to lie down and leave you in peace for an hour while my eyes recharge.'

* * *

As soon as Daphne was asleep, Yánna and I came together to organise our surprise. I telephoned the local florist and requested delivery of the bouquet I had ordered. We gathered chairs and arranged small tables under the fir tree for a little party to celebrate the completion of my grandmother's portrait, which stood on its easel, covered with a tablecloth. I still had to varnish it, but I could do that the next time I came on holiday.

At four o'clock, Yánna woke my grandmother.

'Come on, Daphne,' she said, helping Granny into her wheelchair. 'Let's change your blouse and brush your hair before we go outside. We want you at your best for Flora, don't we? Your fancy eyeglasses are charged and your granddaughter's waiting for you.'

'Are you wearing lipstick?' Daphne asked once her cyberglasses were in place. 'And are those the posh gold sandals from Flora on your feet?'

'I often wear lipstick,' Yánna said, nodding like a liar. 'What's wrong with that?'

She wheeled Daphne out and parked her next to me before Granny noticed her blush.

Spiros came marching towards us. He carried a huge supermarket bag and wore a grin.

Daphne turned to me. 'And here comes your young man, I believe. I say, he is a handsome devil, isn't he?'

'Behave, Granny, or I'll confiscate your goggles.' I turned to greet him. 'Hi, Spiro, how's the chimney going? Sorry I haven't had time for a walk over to the big house. It's been a crazy day.'

I could see he was trying not to stare at Daphne.

'Special glasses,' I whispered. 'Quite amazing.'

'I'm blind, not deaf,' Daphne said. 'Aren't you going to introduce me properly, although we did see each other for a moment in the gallery.'

'Daphne von Stroop, meet Spyridon Faliraki.'

'A pleasure to meet you again, Kyría von Stroop,' he said, making a little bow.

Daphne lifted her hand like a duchess and, as he stooped to kiss it, she grinned at me, mischief radiating from her face.

Right behind Spiros, Constantinos, the baker's father, appeared with a box of cheese and spinach pies tied up with a red foil ribbon. Yánna glanced my way, introduced him to us all as her friend, then blushed as she thanked him for the savouries. He tugged at his tie and made a little bow. They were like teenagers on their first date, glancing at each other. Seeing them together sent a frisson of happiness through me.

Spiros produced six champagne flutes, a bag of ice, and a bottle of Moët.

'Do you have a big casserole, Yánna?' he asked.

She brought one from the house, along with a plate for the snacks.

He stood the champagne in the pan and then emptied the sack of ice cubes over the bottle.

'We'll just give it five minutes to chill,' he said. 'Shall we sit down?' He turned to Granny. 'How are the new eyeglasses, Kyría Daphne?'

'They are splendiferous, young man. A major achievement in medical science, and they have brought me more delight in two days than you can ever imagine.' She glanced around. 'Will somebody tell me what this is all about? Is it somebody's birthday?'

Everyone smiled, uplifted by her pleasure.

Spiros glanced my way and raised his eyebrows in a silent question. I made a nod.

'Right, let me deal with this cork,' he said, whipping the foil off and easing the stopper out of the champagne bottle. 'Pop!' He poured everyone a drink and in an official voice, said, 'Ladies and gentlemen, please raise your glasses to the latest portrait of our beautiful host Daphne von Stroop, painted by artist extraordinaire, Flora Champion!'

He whipped the tablecloth off the easel, and they all raised their glasses to the painting, then sipped, their eyes never leaving the canvas.

'You made me look beautiful . . .' Daphne whispered, reciting Aristotle's words when she had finished his portrait many moons ago.

30

DAPHNE

Peloponnese, 1943

THE SINKING SUN BLAZED THROUGH Luka's windscreen, lighting Aristotle's face, turning his fair hair into strands of gold as the truck trundled along the national road towards Patras' ferry-port. Looking at him, Daphne decided on her vision for his portrait. A modern work of colour and light, because that was what he brought into her world.

'I wish we could stay with you, Luka!' Aristotle shouted over the engine noise. 'But we have to deliver this box to the village of Kalávryta.'

'I know!' Luka yelled in reply. 'I'd take you, but Kalávryta's about a thousand metres above sea level, and my old truck would never make it. Besides, I need to keep to my schedule or I'll lose my delivery contract with the Axis.'

'It's OK, Luka,' Daphne said. 'You've been really good about everything. Someone will pick us up from the train, so you just drop us by the station at Diakopto and don't worry.'

Luka glanced at Aristotle, then stared ahead while changing gear. He shouted above the din. 'You're a lucky man, Aristotle. Take good care of her.'

A few kilometres further along, he ground to a halt and helped drag the crate and their belongings out of the back.

'I'll be coming past here, on the main road, around three in the afternoon every Wednesday. I'll look out for you, right? Just be here if you want a lift to Patras or Igoumenitsa.'

The men shook hands and slapped each other's shoulders. Luka bowed at Daphne.

'You make sure you take care of yourself, Kyría, and if I don't see you, good luck with the baby.'

Aristotle and Daphne watched the old truck disappear in a plume of black smoke, then they took a rope handle each and carried the crate a short way up the side street to the narrow-gauge railway. Aristotle bought their tickets and some bread and cheese. The steam train would leave Diakopto at nine the next morning, so with the help of the stationmaster, they got a room for the night.

* * *

After lugging the box back to the station the next morning, along with their meagre possessions, they settled opposite each other at a window. The black steam engine billowed and chuffed at surprising speed up the mountain. Daphne looked out over the amazing scenery as they rattled along precarious ledges and through narrow tunnels, tootling blasts on the whistle to warn goats of their imminent presence. They startled a pair of vultures feeding on a sheep or goat carcass, and they both ducked instinctively when the enormous birds flew clumsily up and over their carriage.

The train raced through pine forests to the Vouraikos gorge, then continued uphill on what seemed little more than a ledge cut into the side of a cliff, until they pulled into the station at Kato Zachlorou. The air grew cooler and Aristotle wound the window up. Between the tall trees, they fell into gloomy shade, and a feeling of foreboding settled on Daphne as they climbed ever higher.

Despite the closed window, she shivered and moved next to Aristotle. As she snuggled against his arm, she watched half the passengers disembark at the next station. Two Germans entered their carriage and sat opposite them. She recognised one immediately and let her head fall forward as if asleep, hoping he wouldn't remember her.

'Salutations!' the taller man in a grey coat and peaked cap called out. 'Von Stroop, isn't it? We meet again.' He spoke German, thrusting his leather-gloved hand towards Aristotle.

Aristotle hesitated, then shook the man's hand.

'Sorry, but where did we meet?'

'Klaus Schulze, late last year, over Christmas and New Year. I drove my commander-in-chief to your studio in Athens several time a week to have his portrait painted. You gave me lessons, remember? I seem to think I drank most of your best brandy.'

'Ah, yes. Sorry, so much has happened since – work, you understand. I struggle to stay on top of it. I hope you're well and continuing with your painting. You have talent, if I remember rightly.' He laughed casually, but Daphne sensed his tension.

'My commander was delighted with his portrait, as I was with mine. The one I did of your lovely student. Some associates have been looking for you. They also want to take advantage of your talent.' He turned to his companion. 'I recommend this man if you want to learn to paint – and this is his beautiful model, Daphne. Her likeness hangs on my bedroom wall.'

Daphne continued to feign sleep, although her skin crawled.

Turning back to Aristotle, Schulze continued. 'You'll be hearing from my associates once I've informed them of your location. Also, your cousin is looking for you. What's your final destination?'

'Ah . . . I'll be returning to Athens soon, hopefully.'

'What are you doing here, on the train to Kalávryta?'

'Another portrait commission,' Aristotle replied. 'All very top secret, I'm afraid. Someone flying in for a single sitting. Even I don't know who it is.'

Daphne felt a bolt of alarm in her chest. The last thing they wanted was for Aristotle's cousin to hear where they were. She clutched her belly that bit tighter.

'I see congratulations are in order,' Schulze continued. 'When's the baby due?'

'Soon, the end of December or January – we're not too sure,' Daphne replied, looking up and blinking at him.

Up and up they went, through the most rugged scenery. Olive groves gave way to pine forests. Overwhelmed by the scenery, too soon they arrived at the surprisingly modern town of Kalávryta.

'Oh goodness, that was an amazing journey!' Daphne exclaimed, her legs a little wobbly after sitting in the shaky carriage for so long.

'Let's sit for a while, Daphne. There's no rush. You're shivering. Let me get you a shawl. It's quite cold at this altitude, isn't it?'

Aristotle rummaged in their bundle and tugged a crocheted triangle out, then draped it over her shoulders.

The two Germans stuck their arms out and cried '*Heil Hitler!*', then left hurriedly.

Daphne sighed. 'Thank goodness they've gone. What happens now?'

Before Aristotle could speak, a man of about thirty years old approached them.

'You must be Aristotle and Daphne?'

Aristotle nodded. 'We are, who wants to know?'

He grinned, his wide face honest and friendly.

'I'm Krístos. Orion sent me,' he said quietly, shaking Aristotle's hand and making a slight bow towards Daphne.

The small town of stone houses surrounded by green vegetation stood before a backdrop of snow-covered mountain peaks. Children played in the street; old women sat together crocheting under an enormous plane tree in the centre of the square. The men drank coffee at rickety tables outside a *kafenio*. Cats sat tall, tails wrapped around their base, still and upright as china bookends, observing everything. Crystal-clear water gurgled from a small fountain; the gentle sound broken by two men playing *tavli*. They threw dice onto a backgammon board, then victoriously slammed their round tiles onto the black or white triangles. Outside the *kafenio*, old men tossed their amber *kom-* *bolloi* over arthritic knuckles, the glassy beads clacking rhythmically. They drank raki and smoked the local tobacco, which left a sickly-sweet scent of burning hemp on the air. A couple of feral cats drooling deliriously at the aroma of anchovies, circled the square table. More smells were carried in on the breeze; pine resin, fresh bread, and sweat – each with a story to tell.

Aristotle and Daphne gazed around, then looked knowingly at each other. At last, they had found a town bypassed by war. Here, they could settle and bring up their family. Kalávryta appeared to be a small pocket of peace and tranquillity, where time stood still and the war passed by unnoticed. A place of families and neighbourliness, where nothing bad could happen.

Except, Schulze had just arrived.

Krístos led them to a neat stone house with a wooden roof, on the outskirts of the community. A third of the one-room dwelling was taken up by a carved olive-wood bed that could accommodate an entire family. A straw mattress, woven blankets and several sheepskins topped their sleeping accommodation. Daphne's eyes narrowed with her longing to lie down. An elbow or knee slid across her belly, and she lost herself in the glory of the moment.

Their baby felt at home, too. She placed a hand on her baby-bump and glanced across at Aristotle, who was talking to Krístos. He caught her glance, understood immediately, and smiled.

She sat on the edge of the bed and peered across the room. The cooking and eating area had a stone sink and tap, a fireplace with a pot stand, a cauldron hanging in the hearth, and a rough wooden table with four chairs.

Aristotle's eyes sparkled as he turned to Daphne.

'It's all we need.'

'Not quite all. Come around the back,' Krístos said.

Attached to the rear of the house, an L-shaped wall with a curtain strung across the open end formed a roofless rectangular room.

'Your bathroom,' Krístos said.

They peered inside. A white porcelain square in the floor had a hole in the centre and above it, just over head height, hung a tin watering can.

'It's very good, isn't it? We've all got one. Saves a lot of time trekking out to find another bush in the winter,' Krístos said, grinning proudly. 'You'll stay here for a week or two. It's too dangerous to be on the move after the Kefaloniá massacre.'

They stared at the ground for a moment, out of respect for the thousands of Italian boys, slaughtered by the Germans after they surrendered their Italian army weapons. They should have been taken prisoners of war.

'Orion mentioned you're looking for work,' Krístos said after the dutiful silence.

'I am,' Aristotle replied. 'I'm not very strong, that's . . . a bit of a medical problem, you know. That's why I couldn't get into the army or navy. Still, I can work long hours, I'm always careful in what I do, and I'm trustworthy.'

'OK. The olive harvest is only halfway through, so there are nets to be laid. It's urgent now, because the snow will be here in a couple of weeks and then any remaining fruit will be ruined.' He glanced up at white peaks in the distance. 'We always get snow in January. Also, the British agents are busy with something a few kilometres from here. The andartes need extra hands, so you can come along and help.'

'It seems far from strife here in these peaceful villages,' Aristotle said. 'I mean, have you ever even seen a tank?' He gazed down at the lower elevations that consisted of cultivated, winter-bare foothills. 'What are they growing down there?'

'They're vineyards. Some grapes for wine, and others for eating, but they grow most of them for raisins. Also, we grow tiny black grapes from Corinth . . . currants. The vines are dormant twigs now, but they'll be vivid green through spring and summer, an amazing sight. There are olive groves lower down. The big, black Kalamata olives do well here. You're a city boy, yes?' Aristotle nodded. 'Every part of the olive trees are used for something. Oil for cooking, cleaning, lamps and medication. Olives for food. The leaves go for rabbit fodder, the wood for furniture and building – even the pips are stored for smokeless fuel in the winter. Olive blossom feeds the bees before the spring flowers arrive, improving the early honey yield. Pine trees grow above the cultivated land. From these we harvest building materials and resin to flavour retsina; and we collect pine nuts from the cones. They're a valuable food when we're snowed in and the hens stop laying.' He turned to stare up the mountain. 'Above us are fir trees, providing heat for cooking and the home.'

Aristotle stood with his hands on his hips and took it all in.

'Isn't it rather remote for the andartes to operate from here?'

'It is – that's why we're so successful. We've only been operating for a year, but now we have the support of the British, who supply us with guns and ammunition when they can. The roads are unsuitable for tanks, or heavy vehicles, and the area's not well mapped. Our knowledge of the terrain is integral to our survival, making this the perfect place for the andartes network to operate from – with the Allies, of course.'

'Couldn't you protect yourselves from the enemy by sabotaging the train? After all, you know your way around the cliffs and ravines of these mountains, and they don't.'

'Yes, we thought of that, but you know what they do, the Germans? They make a *kloúva,* a cage containing a dozen of our villagers, women and young boys, and they put it in an open wagon covered in barbed wire. Then they pack explosives under the carriage and connect it with a wire to the guard's car. The train driver can explode the *kloúva* and blow the hostages to pieces at any time, so we make sure the train is protected from sabotage.'

Aristotle shuddered, then turned to Daphne.

'It's night work. Will you be all right?'

'Yes, of course,' she said, glancing back at the sturdy pine roof-beams crossed by olive branches and then topped by half a metre of compact, waterproof, clay.

Before she could say more, an attractive woman with a baby over her shoulder sashayed her wide hips towards Krístos. She pouted and fluttered her lashes. He grinned back, sweeping his arm around her waist and pulling her against his hip.

'You got some food ready, woman?' he said with a smile in his voice. 'These people are starving.' He turned to Aristotle. 'This is Georgia, Orion's sister, and the little imp on her shoulder is my daughter. We'll name Yánna as soon as the priest has a moment to bless her.' He glared at Georgia. 'She's just a week old, and supposed to be kept indoors for thirty days, of course, but Georgia has her own ideas. You're invited to the baptism, if you're still here.'

Aristotle and Daphne grinned at each other, imagining how Krístos must feel to have a child, and knowing their turn would come.

'You must eat with us this evening,' Krístos added.

Georgia never took her eyes from his face. 'Fresh bread, cheese, olives, winter greens with pomegranate, and a great dish of my delicious home-made macaroni with wild mushrooms and oregano. Will that satisfy your greedy belly, you ugly caveman?' Her teasing eyes sparkled with love for him.

'Sounds like I'll have to make an honest woman of you one of these days. How's Yánna behaving?'

'She's being very good, considering you men make so much noise.' She turned to the infant. 'Aren't you just perfect, my little darling?' Two young teenagers, a girl and a boy, came rushing up, then stood behind Georgia. They peered at Aristotle with wide brown eyes.

'And who are these two beautiful children?' Daphne asked.

'Ah, they're Orion's. Lydia's ten and Pavlo's fourteen.'

'I'm fifteen, Uncle. Fifteen!'

Krístos laughed and bumped his fist against the boy's shoulder.

'Fifteen? My mistake. A man, then.' He turned back to Daphne. 'Their mother works in the bakery.'

'Beautiful children,' Daphne said, admiring their olive skin and thick, curly hair. She slipped her hand over her belly and smiled, catching Aristotle's eye again and realising the triumphant moments motherhood would bring. Strangers would admire their children, too.

As the sun went down, Daphne and Aristotle stored their belongings under the bed in their house, contented smiles etched on their faces.

'Let's go out for a moment and watch the sunset,' Aristotle said when they'd finished.

Against the front of the cottage, two upended lengths of pine supported a rough plank. They sat close, arms around each other and a blanket over their shoulders to protect them from December's evening chill. A great orange sun slipped down, behind distant mountains. The sky permeated into a soft kaleidoscope of pigments, constantly changing.

'The clouds look like coloured feathers floating across the sky,' Daphne whispered.

Then, overwhelmed by sadness, she turned her face into Aristotle's chest and sobbed.

'Darling, what is it? What's making you so sad?'

She sniffed hard, smudged the tears from her face and told him about Isaac and the pillow fight. 'When we were young, Isaac and I had a pillow fight. One pillow burst, which meant trouble from Mamá. Anyway, Noah gave me this locket for my seventeenth birthday.' She touched the chain around her neck. 'Isaac didn't have money, so he gave me a tiny feather to remind me of our crazy day. It's in here now.' She stared at the deep red sky, now as fierce as a furnace, but continuing to darken. 'I wonder where he is at this moment, and if he ever thinks of me . . . I miss him so much, Aristotle.'

Dying embers of the sun threw a rim of light around every solid object and fizzed from clumps of dried grass and old sandstone.

'Do you think Isaac's all right, Aristotle? I've prayed for him every night, but do you think God might punish me for giving up my religion to save myself? I'm afraid if anything happens to Isaac, it will be my fault.' Her tears welled up again.

'Oh, my poor darling. Of course, it's not your fault. God wouldn't be so cruel, would He? You can be sure that Isaac will remember those feathers, too. That moment will come back, to give him hope and strength when he needs it most.'

Daphne sighed and rested her head against Aristotle's shoulder.

'You're so wise and kind. Isn't it beautiful here? I don't believe I'll ever be able to live in a city again.'

'Aristotle, Daphne!' a man's voice called.

When Orion appear out of the gloom, Daphne glanced at the magnificent night sky and once again wondered which was his constellation. After exchanging greetings, the SOE agent led them down the hill to the next cottage, where they joined Georgia and Krístos at a long table.

'Can I take her?' Daphne asked, holding her hands out for Georgia's baby.

'Sure, any time you want. When did you say yours is due?'

'Not too sure.' The baby curved herself around Daphne's breast and snuggled against her body. For a moment, Daphne lost herself in a bubble of love and contentment, then she realised Georgia was talking to her. 'Sorry, what was that? She's so delightful I forgot what I was saying.'

'When's the baby due?'

'Ah, in the next few weeks, between now and mid-January, I guess. We can't wait, but I wish this war was over.'

Georgia nodded. 'Orion seems to think it won't last much longer, now the Italians have changed sides and the Americans are being more active. Still, it was horrendous, what happened to them in Kefaloniá. I had nothing against the Italians. Well, apart from the Blackshirts – those *maláka* Mussolini supporters behaved like Nazis. Still do, in fact. They refused to surrender with the rest of the Italians and moved over to join Hitler's mob. The Italians were all right. They didn't want a war any more than we did.' She crossed herself three times. 'Poor devils . . . slaughtered like that, every one a mother's son.'

*   *   *

After supper, Daphne cradled baby Yánna in her arms. All her motherly instincts rose and filled her heart with contentment when the infant fell asleep. They returned to the house and, soon after, a gang of men called for Aristotle. She grabbed his hand and squeezed it hard as he passed her at the doorway.

'Come back without a scratch,' she said.

'Don't worry,' he whispered, then kissed her hard.

She watched them tramp off, over the hill and out of sight. Restless all night, Daphne dreamed she had given birth, the dream so real she looked under the covers, expecting to find her baby when she woke. Although it had all been in her imagination, the experience comforted her. All her uncertainties faded as she knew she could cope with childbirth.

*   *   *

Aristotle, exhausted yet elated, returned with the first light of dawn.

'Tell me everything!' Daphne demanded, throwing her arms around his neck, wanting to share his victorious mood.

He pulled her back into the bed and curled his tired, cold body around hers.

'We cleared a runway. They'd been working on it for some time because it was flat, about a kilometre long, and ended at a deep ravine. We could hear the plane droning towards us, but we couldn't be sure it was one of ours. That was a scary moment, and for a second, I wished I was back in Athens. Each of us lit a small fire we'd prepared on opposite sides of the landing strip, to mark out the airfield. The plane flew straight towards us, so low, frightening, then it dropped about fifty packages. We thought they might be bombs and most of us dropped to the ground. Anyway, without touching down, the plane lifted and flew into the night. We doused the fires and disguised the area by dragging tree trunks and branches so it didn't look obvious from the air.'

'What was in the parcels?'

He shook his head. 'Some sacks of supplies, equipment for the local militia, medicines or ammunition, perhaps.'

Daphne lay on her back and felt him draw heat from her body and relax. She told him about her dream, how real it was, but when she turned, expecting to see his elation and receive a kiss, he was fast asleep.

* * *

Three nights later, Daphne lay awake, tossing and turning while Aristotle was out working again. She wondered if this was one of the main supply points for the Peloponnese and Athens.

* * *

Under the largest church in Kalávryta, thirty roughly-bearded partisans, wearing an odd selection of uniforms and ammunition belts across their chests, had gathered. Orion informed the men of the night's mission, then cornered Aristotle and gave him special instructions.

31

FLORA

Corfu, present day

'KALAVRYTA? I'VE NEVER HEARD OF the place,' I said when Daphne came to the end of her monologue.

Yánna's and Daphne's heads snapped up. They stared at me, then at each other. Neither spoke. I realised this place, Kalávryta, meant a lot to them both. However, they decided to change the subject and suggested a walk in the grounds.

* * *

At six o'clock, I found Spiros, dressed in a pale cream linen suit and sky-blue shirt, waiting in the hotel lobby. I'd chosen a retro, pale blue brocade dress with a Bardot neckline, silver jewellery, killer heels and a cream pashmina. My retro clothing might be stylish, but the heavy fabric made me hotter with each step.

'You look stunning,' he said, spreading his arms and flashing a dazzling smile.

'You, too – wow!' I replied.

Deciding to ignore our freaky colour co-ordination, I threw my shoulders back and walked the walk.

He scooped my arm into his, and we sauntered out to a waiting taxi.

'I have some good news for you,' he said as we headed into town. 'I may have found your cellar.'

'What? How amazing! I wonder what's in there.'

'No idea. I haven't checked it out yet, but it seems we were right. There was a coal chute around the back of the building. Apparently, the Germans occupied Mon Repos after the Italians capitulated. Rumour says they used the place as a storeroom, but for what, I don't know. There may be munitions down there, which would be dangerous, so we're obliged to investigate.'

'Perhaps there's a way we can discover what's below ground? Thermal vision technology?'

He grinned. 'Watch much TV, do you?'

I laughed. 'No, but I'm interested in archaeology, and they often use such technology to find ancient burial sites.'

'Leave it with me. I'll let you know what we find.'

A little twitch of uncertainty wriggled about in the pit of my stomach, although I couldn't say why I felt uneasy. The taxi dropped us near the beautiful, marble-tiled square before the town hall where the wedding would take place. Side by side, we headed for the entrance, but suddenly I realised something was going on with my right shoe.

'Can we stop a moment?' I said. 'Something's wrong.'

I looked down and realised my stiletto had speared a white plastic cup and, despite my effort to dislodge it with the other shoe, it was firmly stuck.

'Damn!'

Teetering on one leg, I grabbed Spiros's shoulder to steady myself, and at that moment my pashmina slid to the floor, caught a breeze and skittered into the road.

Spiros laughed. 'Sit at a table and don't move,' he said. 'I'll get your wrap before a car runs over it, then sort your shoe out.'

He rescued my pashmina from passing traffic, removed the white plastic from my heel, then slipped the shoe back on to my foot in a Prince Charming moment.

Minutes later, we were off again, but this time I took the man's arm, to navigate slippery, uneven, marble under my stilettos. People crowded in as the boisterous sound of car horns announced the bride and groom's arrival.

'Wow, this building's a work of art!' I exclaimed, peering up at the arched windows and doors, and the ornately carved stone façade.

'It has a glorious history, too, which I'll tell you about another time. Listen, here comes the wedding party.'

The noise intensified, then a bouzouki player, along with two guitar players, stepped towards the far side of the square and waited for the bride's car to appear. The bridal couple held hands and walked between the serenading musicians, across the square. The onlookers did a lot of pretend spitting, between shouts of 'Long life!'

'They're spitting at the Devil to send him away,' Spiros explained. 'This wedding's a good mix of modern and traditional. It should be fun.'

Six bridesmaids followed, all dressed in very tight, very low-necked, shocking pink satin gowns. A photographer ran around popping shots at the wedding party, then an elderly gentleman appeared with the bride's flowers.

'Her father,' Spiros said.

The square filled with guests, all dressed for the red carpet. They crowded together in tight groups, some of whom entered the town hall. Above us, as dusk descended, a chorus of shrieking birds with sickle-shaped wings whirled across the sky like the lights from a disco ball.

'They're swifts, on a feeding frenzy for the flying insects that descend as the temperature drops.'

'There must be thousands.'

274

I stared at them, fascinated, remembering a murmuration of starlings over the Mersey that had blown me away and thrilled my birdwatching Mark.

Spiros nodded. 'They mate for life, did you know? And they do everything on the wing, never putting a foot down.' He bobbed his eyebrows. 'Eat, sleep, mate . . .'

'But not quite everything,' I said.

He glanced sideways at me. I paused for him to think about it, aware that his eyes never left my face.

'Lay their eggs? Would be an omelette, I think.'

He laughed.

I remembered Mark: how we would sit in the dunes at Blundellsands with a picnic and our binoculars when the birds were migrating. Suddenly, in this crowd of happy people, I wanted to cry, and had to pinch the bridge of my nose to stop tears from gathering.

'Don't be sad,' Spiros whispered. 'What's the matter?'

'Sorry, silly of me. I just remembered my own wedding day. It was nothing so grand, but still, the most precious day of my life.'

His smile fell, and he stared at the ground, then his hand took mine and squeezed.

'Yes,' he said. 'It's hard, isn't it?'

Our eyes met for a heartbreaking moment.

* * *

At three o'clock in the morning, we arrived back at my hotel.

'I should offer you a last drink,' he said, 'but I must leave for Paleokastritsa at nine. I don't blame you if you'd rather sleep in.'

'No, honestly, if it's not too much trouble, I'd love to explore another part of the island.'

He grinned with open pleasure.

'Then I'll pick you up at 8.45. Bring a towel and swim things.'

He put his hand under my chin and kissed me firmly on the mouth, pulling away before I could react. Quite speechless, I blinked at him.

'Sorry, couldn't resist,' he said. 'You're so lovely. Thanks for a great evening. It's been so long since I had fun.'

'It was nice,' I said, realising how ridiculous that sounded.

Back in my room, I removed my make-up, hung up the blue brocade and folded my pashmina. With my alarm set for eight, I slid into bed and, for the first time in a year, fell asleep without talking to Mark.

* * *

The damn alarm! On and on.

I woke with a start and realised my phone was about to die. I plugged the charger in. It was 8.30, and Spiros would arrive in a few minutes. I dived into the shower, gasping at the first gush of cold water, then dressed in my white swimming costume under a shapeless white linen dress. I shoved a set of underwear, make-up bag, brush, towel, phone and Kindle into my beach bag. Clipped my flaming hair under a wide-brimmed red hat, slipped a huge pair of fake Gucci glasses on, and hurried to the hotel foyer.

We entered the lobby from opposite ends of the hotel.

'We made it!' Spiros laughed, kissed my cheek and led me to his waiting car.

'How long's the drive to Paliokas—? Sorry, it's a bit of a mouthful.'

'OK, *Paleo* means old, *Kastri*, castle. Half an hour or more, depending on the traffic. I'll take the old road so you can enjoy more of the island.'

We stopped at Gouvia marina for strong coffee and a plate of delicious home-made *koulouria* – plaited shortbread biscuits dusted with icing sugar. The beautiful waitress flirted with Spiros, and, clearly, he enjoyed the attention.

'She likes me a lot,' he said, grinning.

'Aren't you tempted?'

He shook his head. 'She's very beautiful. What man wouldn't be tempted? But even a child tires of dolls. I need challenging conversation – fine art, sports and politics. What do you search for when you want good company?'

'All those things, I guess, and I run, and cook.'

'Perfect,' he said, looking into my eyes.

I reminded myself not to get involved. I was leaving in six days.

We passed through the verdant landscape, sometimes catching sight of blue-green waters and white sand that shimmered in the fresh morning light. I longed to swim and explore peninsulas of soft, pale cream rock, wind-worn into slabs of deserted lunar landscape, stacked in layers like fresh filo pastry. Sometimes, giant fingers of this limestone reached up from the palest turquoise sea as if Poseidon himself were asking for a helping hand.

'All the times I've visited Corfu, I had no idea the coast was so spectacular,' I whispered in awe.

We turned away from the beach and headed across country, through vineyards, olive groves and small villages. I caught glimpses of bent old ladies in their widow's weeds, ancient priests with grey beards that sometimes reached to their waist, and donkeys loaded with fresh vegetation. Outside one village, a woman in an embroidered apron sold honey in glass jars, from a table at the side of the road. Outside another village, bags of oranges hung from a mulberry tree, and a young man stood at the edge of the highway selling the fruit to passing drivers. We came to a halt as an enormous herd of goats with long, shaggy white coats and oddly twisted horns crossed the road. Their clanging bells and constant bleating made a terrific din. We passed a distillery, leather workshop, olive oil refinery and a ceramics factory – places I promised myself I would explore on my next trip to Corfu. Soon we descended through an undulating landscape towards the coast.

'Here we are.' He glanced at his Rolex. 'I'm going to drop you here at the beach bar and leave you to swim and catch up on your sleep. Anything you want will go on my tab, so don't worry about it, just enjoy yourself. I'll be back before 12.30 and we'll have lunch together, OK?'

'You're too kind,' I said, hearing the happiness in my own voice. 'Thank you.'

He carried my bag to the beach and placed it on a sunlounger. 'I'll be back later.'

I pretended not to notice him tuck a tip into the bartender's top pocket.

* * *

I'd forgotten suntan oil, so I spent the morning sleeping under the brolly, or in the water. As I woke up from a short nap, I wasn't sure if I was awake or dreaming when I realised Spiros was lying beside me in his swim shorts. I peered at him through my sunglasses.

'Hello there. Was it a good day?' I asked.

'Quite good, yes. I'm working on that half-built hotel, on the cliff top. You can just catch a glimpse of it through the trees.' He pointed at a clump of Cyprus trees. 'The owner died without a will and owed lots of taxes, but the grandson wants to sort it out and the local government is being sympathetic. It's my job to organise the building plan, and make sure what's there is still good to go.'

'Interesting. Will you have a say in the design, too?'

'A Venetian façade, in keeping with the island's history and style, is what I'll suggest, at least for the frontage. Inside will be modern and eco-friendly. Now, how about some food?'

The day was delightful – everything a holiday brochure would promise.

'Can I take you for dinner?' Spiros asked, catching my hand as we walked back to the car.

I hesitated, feeling a little overwhelmed.

'I'd love to, but I should spend a little time with Granny. I have less than a week left, and my grandfather's portrait is most important to her.'

He smiled, although his eyes dulled, and he sucked his lip.

'Perhaps tomorrow evening?'

'Perhaps.'

He kissed me hard on the mouth again, more than platonic, but not quite romantic. Then, he gave me a beaming smile.

'Tomorrow evening, then?'

'Spiro, thank you. It's been a lovely day.'

'For me, too. I'll make some enquiries about the cellar and get back to you, tomorrow.'

He dropped me outside the mansion of Mon Repos, and I walked through the parkland to the cottage, ready for the big interrogation.

The place was in darkness, and silent. I scratched about in my bag, searching for my phone, which was flat. Something didn't feel right. Then, I realised the table and chairs were under the tree, and my heartbeat accelerated. Yánna always brought them in before dark. I went over and noticed a scrap of paper under a stone on the table. I snatched it up.

Flora Dafnee is sick in ospitals. I come backs soonas.

My stomach tied itself in knots, torn in every direction, but my feet still felt like cement boots. How long had they been in the hospital? What could be wrong? In my mind, I had a horrible image of Yánna on her knees in the hospital chapel. Daphne couldn't die – she mustn't! I dragged my heavy legs and broke into a run. The cafe would call me a cab.

32

ARISTOTLE

Kalávryta, 1943

SINCE THE WAR OF INDEPENDENCE from the Turks, the church of Agía Lavra in Kalávryta had represented freedom and solidarity. The andartes huddled there, waiting until they were all assembled and clear about the task ahead. With axes and ropes balanced over shoulders, they marched towards the distant mountaintop where the next drop would be. Heavy cloud blotted the moon. In the pitch dark, men trod with the stealth of wild animals. They didn't speak, but communicated by a tap on the arm, a quick mime, or the simple point of a finger. The usual night rustling of badgers and polecats kept them alert, but they all pulled to a sudden halt when Orion raised his hand and hissed. An owl hooted. Orion headed for the sound, then disappeared into a wooded area. When he returned minutes later, Aristotle's muscles relaxed. Everything would be all right. With a stirring motion over his head, Orion signalled for his men to gather.

'The place is swarming with Nazis, perhaps a hundred of Schober's troops. They know about tonight's drop.'

'*Maláka Hun!*' Krístos cursed, receiving glares from everyone for unnecessary noise.

'Retreat, regroup. Go to to the next village, find the other andartes. There're too many of Schober's troops for us. Absolute silence now.'

They hurried back, staying in the shadows. At the rear, Aristotle was unsure of his footing in the dark. Startled by a sudden noise behind him, he turned. An enemy soldier, a glint of steel. A knife gripped in a white fist lunged at his throat. He stuck out a hand to ward off the blade, but felt the sting of a cut across his palm. He was an artist, and didn't stand a chance against a trained soldier.

In the silence of the mountainside, a human shape dived at him. Aristotle sensed his attacker's strength – fear exploded in his chest. Too stunned to shout, images of his life, Daphne and the baby flooded his mind. What would she do without him?

In an instant, as the knife swiped centimetres from his throat, fate or fury made him lash out, causing the blade to whirl into the air. It caught his ear as the soldier spun in the opposite direction. Unbalanced, Aristotle found himself on the edge of an abyss, on the brink between life and death. So unreal was the entire experience, he wondered if he was dead already, reliving his last moments, over and over again. A gut reaction made him grab at the soldier as he hurtled over the edge. A fierce tug on his leg dragged him down onto the solid ground beneath his feet. From the chasm, only half a metre from his boots, came a thud, the sound of smashing shrubbery, then nothing.

Wild-eyed and panting, Aristotle lay glued to the ground. He twisted his head around to see Krístos' hand on his ankle.

'That was close. You were going over, *Maláka!*'

A sob jerked Aristotle's chest. His thoughts went to Daphne – what would happen to her if . . .?

'You need to stop that bleeding,' Krístos muttered, taking a rag from his pocket and rolling it into a pad. 'Close your fist around this and keep it pressed against the wound. We'll look at it when we get home.'

Trembling, Aristotle felt warm blood from his missing ear-lobe trickle down his neck. Fearing he was about to faint, he turned to Krístos. 'I'm not a soldier – not a fighter. You saved my life. Thank you. One day I'll repay you, I swear.'

'Part of the job, my friend. He was a lookout.' He nodded towards the canyon, slapped Aristotle on the arm, then walked towards the other men.

* * *

They arrived in the next village, two kilometres away. Local partisans were informed of the situation.

'We'll surround them, then close in,' Orion said. 'Arm your-selves with knives and clubs, but don't use firearms. Surprise is our best tactic, so it's absolute silence at all times.'

The andartes crept around the base of the mountain, then ascended. They captured the lookouts, killing four on the spot, with three more knocked unconscious. Having no spare men, Orion ordered the senseless soldiers to be bound and gagged, ready to be moved to the hospital in Kalávryta, in compliance with military law. The drone of an approaching plane distracted both sides. Orion recognised an opportunity to attack the Axis troops. One shrill whistle and his men pounced on the unsus-pecting soldiers.

'Surrender, and we'll treat you as prisoners of war!' Aristotle yelled in German, as instructed. 'You're surrounded and out-numbered.'

For a moment, the full moon showed herself in a cloudy sky, throwing silver light over the scene. A breeze made distant shad-ows dance and convinced the Germans that a greater number of Greeks occupied the area. They believed themselves encircled and outnumbered by local militias armed with rifles and pistols. They dropped their weapons and raised their hands, as the Italians had in Kefaloniá two months before, probably convinced the same fate would not befall them.

Aristotle guessed they held about eighty enemy soldiers. One group of partisans hurried around collecting arms that lay at the feet of the German soldiers. His stomach churned with the premonition of a catastrophe. A pulse thudded in his neck. It would only take one German to realise they outnumbered the Greeks, and carnage would follow. He watched as the men lined up the captured soldiers on the ridge and checked for concealed weapons.

'What will happen to them?' he asked Orion.

'They're prisoners of war. Problem is, we've no prison large enough to hold them.' He stroked his chin. 'We'll lock them in the school and guard them until the army arrives. This is a disaster! We haven't enough food for ourselves. What are we supposed to do with another eighty mouths to feed?'

Low cloud fell over them like blanket fog, dulling words and hiding the moon and the footpaths. The sudden rattle of machine guns shattered the night. Both Orion and Aristotle swung around and ran through the mist screaming 'Stop! Stop!' In the mist of low cloud, swirling about them, horror-stricken German soldiers performed an obscene dance of death. Bullets decimated their bodies and blood sprayed everywhere, then ran in rivers. Knocked back by bullets, the German soldiers plunged over the cliff and into the ravine.

Horrified, Orion and Aristotle ran at the executioners yelling 'Stop!', but it was too late. The Greek men had murdered the surrendering Germans. Overwhelmed by blood and gore, shattered bones and bodies, and terrified expressions on the young soldiers' faces, Aristotle tasted bile in his throat. He pressed his hand against a sturdy tree and vomited. The faces of those pale Aryan boys, sprayed with their comrades' blood and wearing the terrified grimace of death would stay with him for the rest of his life.

Shaking violently, Aristotle placed his bloodied hand on Orion's shoulder.

'What in the name of Jesus Christ happened? They were kids! Young boys, conscripts obeying orders. You monsters! They'd have spent the rest of the war in prison, then gone home to their mothers. There are rules, Orion!'

Orion shook his head. 'Some were high-ranking officers, for sure. Still, it shouldn't have happened. The leader of another andartes group used his initiative. He insists we couldn't hold them prisoner, and they wouldn't have hesitated to kill us. They've already massacred the men in the next village. We don't have a facility to lock them up, or the food to keep them, so he claims it's better if we say we killed them in a fair fight.'

'You know what that does – murdering them, then lying about it? It makes us no better than the Nazis. The andartes will be judged for this.'

Aristotle heard pent-up anger in Orion's reply. 'Understand this – three days ago, a German battalion killed all the men in Dimitris's small village, including that andartes' old grandfather and his daughter's little boy. First, they called all the villagers to the square, put a noose around his teenage son's neck, sat him on a donkey under the plane tree, then gave the beast a kick. Hanging is the worst death of all! And his own boy! Now, his wife has lost her mind and has to be tied to her bed day and night. So don't judge these people for wanting revenge.'

'But *we* are not bandits! I won't be a part of this. What if someone discovers the truth? These men murdered those soldiers in cold blood after they'd surrendered.'

'God knows, but we can't undo what's happened. No good standing around talking about it. We have to clean up, deal with it as best we can. For now, our men need sleep, then they'll return to bury the dead.'

They stumbled back towards Kalávryta, losing the path and falling into sharp branches that snagged their faces and clothes. The dank air and the blackness of the forest forced a slick of sweat over Aristotle's freezing body. He stumbled on with the horror of what he'd witnessed, now understanding the true meaning of the word *nightmare*.

* * *

Daphne half woke from a restless sleep when Aristotle returned. He abandoned his clothes in the dark, left them in a heap on the floor, then slid into bed beside her. She felt the tremble in his body as she took him into her arms.

'What terrible thing has happened?' she murmured, stroking his hair and pressing her warm body against his. Then, as she kissed him, she felt the stickiness of blood in his hair, and the metallic taste of fear filled her senses.

She scrambled to her knees.

'You're hurt . . . There's blood, Aristotle. What happened?'

He mumbled, only just coherent, and she feared it was because of the loss of blood.

'Daphne, bad news travels fast and we're in danger. We must leave in a few hours. First, I have to sleep.'

He told her everything, sometimes stopping to gulp air or shed tears. They pressed their bodies together like one being.

'We must leave here,' he repeated. 'There'll be reprisals. Hitler made it clear, for every dead German he'll murder ten Greeks. They murdered . . . I don't know, perhaps eighty soldiers.'

Daphne gasped. How could Hitler justify such a threat? People now whispered that the Nazi leader was killing Jews by the thousands in his awful work camps? How could the Greek andartes break all the rules and still wallow in self-righteousness? She held Aristotle's shivering body and realised she no longer feared Hitler for her own safety as a Jew. She would fight him, too, if she could. However, she longed to know what was happening to Isaac. Where was he? When would she see him again?

When he woke four hours later, Aristotle said, 'I'll go back up the mountain to help bury the dead.'

'You can't do anything with a slashed hand and half your ear missing. Do you want gangrene?'

'All right, I'm too tired to argue. Start packing, Daphne, We should leave, soon as we can. How far can you walk?'

She could hear the tension in his voice.

'Well, it's awkward now, but the midwife told me the baby's head will go down soon, then I'll be more comfortable. She's pressing against my ribs, which can get painful.'

'She? It's going to be a girl?' he asked, tears welling in his tired eyes. They were both struggling to swallow their fear.

'I suspect. Would that disappoint you?'

'Of course not. Who wants to bring a boy into this world?'

Daphne kissed him hard. 'I love you. Now get some more sleep before we go out again.'

Once Aristotle's body relaxed against her, Daphne slipped out of bed. She bundled their few belongings: a change of clothes, art supplies, and a few baby essentials the villagers had passed on.

Aristotle slept until Orion and Krístos called.

'Some of the town's council have already fled to Patras, or relations on the coast. They're terrified of retaliations once word gets out about the butchering.'

'We're leaving as soon as we can, Orion. I can't risk the danger with my wife about to give birth. Besides, if my SS cousin hears I'm here, he'll come after me.'

Krístos frowned and stared at Aristotle's boots.

'That's not good. Where will you go?'

'Western Greece. Daphne has family on the little island of Aitoliko, in the lagoon. We'll stay there until after the baby's born and Daphne can travel again. We're hoping to get passage to England.'

'I know Aitoliko,' Krístos said. 'My family is there. I'll give you their location and if you need anything, call on them.' He extended his hand. 'Good luck with the baby, my friend.'

Orion walked outside with them. 'I'll get one of my men to accompany you down the mountain. The Germans have blown the bridge over an old riverbed. He'll help get you across, then you're on your own.' He kissed Daphne's cheeks and shook Aristotle's hand. 'And a word of advice. Don't tell people where you're headed.'

Aristotle glanced over at Krístos.

'You don't think . . .? But he saved my life last night.'

'No, not at all, but somebody informed the Germans about last night's drop. Until we find out who it was, everyone's under suspicion.'

Aristotle and Daphne said goodbye to their new friends, then decided on a last coffee in the little house they loved. Georgia came to wish them a safe journey and Daphne held baby Yánna for a minute.

'Why don't you come with us, Georgia?' Daphne asked. 'Why put this little one in danger?'

'Krístos would never leave this place. Believe me, he'll die here.'

'We should make a move, Daphne,' Aristotle said. 'The train won't leave for an hour, but I want to make sure you get a seat.

I see several families are planning to leave today.' He glanced around and chewed his lip.

* * *

Daphne had just taken the coffee cups into the house when a yell startled her. She dropped a cup as Orion burst into the house.

'My friends, get out of here now! Right now! The Nazis are storming the town. They're locking the women and children in the school and herding the men and boys on to the hillside.'

'Why? God forbid, you don't think they'll ... ?' Aristotle stammered.

Orion shook his head. 'They claim the men must witness the town being burned to the ground as a warning to anyone trying to ambush German troops in the future.'

'But the women and children ... They built the school with wood – it will burn.'

'I don't know what to do! But you must leave. Go now! Before they find you.'

Daphne and Aristotle grabbed their bundles and rushed towards the little station. A group of German soldiers barred their way.

'Where are you going?'

Aristotle snatched Daphne's hand and squeezed it hard as he turned to the soldier.

'To the train,' he replied in German. 'We're leaving.'

'Papers!'

Aristotle showed him, and was told to step to one side. Daphne felt his hand give an extra squeeze of courage before letting go. They examined Daphne's documents. She quaked as they scrutinised the forger's artwork.

'You're both from Athens. Where are your travel documents, and what business do you have in Kalávryta?' the leader of the group demanded.

'I am an artist, here to paint one of your official's portraits. My wife is close to confinement, so I wouldn't leave her in Athens. Ask your commander, Schulze, for confirmation,' he bluffed, hoping Schulze would back him.

The leader stared at his severed ear and bandaged hand.

'You've been fighting.' He turned to his corporal. 'Take the woman to the school and put him in the field with the other men.'

They dragged Daphne away.

'But you can't take him!' she cried as they shoved her into the school. 'His cousin is in the SS. He's Himmler's right-hand man!'

They slammed the door closed, and as Daphne turned to face a room full of terrified women and children, every eye was on her. She cowered under their scrutiny and found herself overwhelmed by stares of hatred and loathing.

'No,' she said. 'It's not true. I was just trying to get them to let him go.'

'Traitor!' somebody yelled, and then others joined in the chanting. 'Traitor, traitor!'

She was spat on and shoved against the door. Fearing for the life of her baby, she tried to protect her belly as the first fist cracked a blinding blow against her nose. The next punch crashed against her mouth and in seconds she tasted blood.

'No, no!' she cried. 'You've got it wrong!'

Young Pavlo rushed to the door and hammered with both fists.

'I'm fifteen – I should be with my father! Don't leave me with the women!'

The door opened. Schulze appeared and glared at Daphne.

'Get her out of here!' he ordered the guard.

'Traitor,' someone hissed behind her.

'Nazi whore!'

'It's her fault this has happened!'

'We'll get you for this, Nazi *poutána!*'

The soldier hauled Daphne outside, and Pavlo escaped beside her.

'Catch him!' Schulze ordered. 'Put him with the men. Where's von Stroop?' he demanded, turning to Daphne.

'In the field with the men.'

Horrified, she saw young Pavlo race past several soldiers assembling machine guns near the field.

'Papa!' he yelled. 'Papa! I'm coming.'

Schulze shouted at a German, 'Get von Stroop out of that field!'

Before a minute passed, Aristotle stood, ashen-faced, beside Daphne. Schulze pulled his pistol from a leather holster on his belt, and pressed it against Aristotle's temple. He turned to the soldier at his side and nodded at Daphne.

'Bring her along.'

Her knees folded, but the soldier caught her and marched her along behind Schulze. Too terrified to speak, Aristotle couldn't protest. He allowed himself to be marched back towards the station.

'You owe me a portrait when this war is over, von Stroop,' Schulze said in German. 'Now get the hell out of here on that train.'

The two soldiers swung around and returned to the school.

Daphne scooped her hands under her distended belly, and they bolted for the train. Their belongings still lay on the platform. Aristotle pulled her towards the last carriage, picked up their belongings and hurled them in.

'Thank the stars we're leaving,' Daphne whispered. 'But look at that smoke. There's a fire in the town. They locked the women and children in the school, Aristotle. It's a wooden building, we must go back and help!'

'Get on the train! We must think of our unborn child and get you to safety.'

'What about Georgia and little Yánna! Oh, Aristotle, can you believe Pavlo demanded to be with his father? Why did he insist on telling the Nazis he was fifteen?' She sobbed.

Aristotle shook his head. 'Pride. I heard tears in his father's voice. He yelled again and again that his boy was only fourteen, begging that he be allowed to go back to the women.'

'What will happen to them all?'

'Don't think about it. We can't help them, Daphne. We owe it to them to escape and tell the world what's happened.'

A rattle of gunfire ripped through the air. Daphne shrieked, her legs folding and her heart thumping as she stumbled against the carriage. Aristotle caught her and tried to lift her on to the train.

Behind them, screaming filled the air and chilled Daphne's blood. She couldn't breathe, couldn't stand.

Aristotle slapped her face.

'Get on the train and stay down!' he yelled, pushing her from behind. 'Do you want us all killed?!'

Shocked by his aggression, she dragged herself onto the carriage and scrambled towards the corner. Her head exploded with a cacophony of gunfire and the terrified voices of their friends. She crawled across the carriage floor on her hands and knees, protecting her belly. The horror built up in her chest and hysteria threatened to take over. Rocking back and forth, she recalled the calming voice of Kyría Alice.

Learn this prayer. One day, you might need it for reasons you can't imagine.

Daphne whispered the words as tears raced down her face. 'Pray for us sinners now and at the hour of our death, amen . . .'

The door flew open as the train lurched forward with the first chug of its pistons. Daphne feared they were about to be dragged out by soldiers, but a bundle of bedding, hurled into the compartment, landed next to her on the floor. She stared at the door. A man clung to the frame, trying to pull himself on to the moving train. Fresh blood disguised his face for a moment, then she recognised the contorted features of Kristos, his eyes begging for help.

'Orion's dead . . . and Georgia. They're all dead! Save our—' was all he managed before a shot rang out and cut him off.

Aristotle reached for his friend's arm when blood spurted from Kristos' neck, and in the same instant, the window on the opposite side of the carriage shattered. The freedom fighter's mouth opened wide in a silent scream. He let go and fell away before Aristotle could get a grip on him. They never saw him again. Aristotle flung his arm around Daphne, helped her up onto the seat, and held her to him, his chest jerking against her ribs in horror.

'God help us all,' he whispered.

33

FLORA

Corfu, present day

PLEASE, MARK, PLEASE! DON'T LET *Granny die. This is all my fault. I shouldn't have left them.*

At the hospital, I shoved a note into the taxi driver's hand.

'Keep the change,' I said, then raced to reception. Three people waited in a queue, but I barged to the front.

'Please, Kyría Daphne von Stroop – where is she?'

'Wait in the queue, madam,' the receptionist said.

Tears raced down my face. 'No!'

I faced the queue.

'She's all I've got left. Please!'

One of the women crossed herself and nodded to the receptionist, who glared at me.

'Name!' she honked.

'Daphne von Stroop.'

She hammered her keyboard with ridiculous, fluorescent orange acrylic nails.

'Ward 16, third floor. Next!'

After a quick nod at the woman who had let me go before her, I raced to the lift. It had stopped on the second floor. I hopped from one foot to the other, then decided on the stairs. Just as I turned away, I heard it descending again. At last, the window lit and the doors opened. I rushed in as passengers stepped out. At the same time, a voice called 'Flora!' I turned and stuck my arm between the closing doors. They flung back open, revealing tear-stained Yánna.

'Oh, Flora, I am very sorry,' she said. 'I don't know what to do. Is like—'

I took her by the shoulders. 'Yánna, is she alive?'

The longest seconds of my life stretched out while Yánna crossed herself. Then she nodded.

'Oh, thank God! Let's go back up to the ward. I need to talk to the doctor.'

I spotted Granny as soon as we walked into the ward where I approached the desk and explained the situation.

'The doctor is still about, so if you can wait in the corridor for five minutes, he'll come and speak to you. Meanwhile, do you have a mask?'

I shook my head, and she gave me one, then stared at Yánna.

'Sorry, yes, is in my pocket.'

* * *

'Angina attack,' the doctor said, her eyes full of concern. 'Her heart's strong for her age. We'll do a few tests tomorrow morning and, if all goes to plan, you can take her home around noon.'

'Can I see her, please?' Adrenalin surged through me and palpitations thudded in my chest.

'If the ward sister says so; give me a moment.' After talking to the woman behind the desk, she nodded and said, 'Five minutes only. She's had some sedation, so your grandmother might slur her words a little but don't be alarmed. She's doing fine, considering her age.'

That was twice in five minutes they had mentioned her age, were they trying to tell me something?

At Daphne's bedside, I took her pale old hand. Her eyes flickered open.

'It's me, Granny.'

'Flora . . .' She smiled and closed her eyes again. 'Did you have fun with your young man? Did he kiss you?'

'Granny . . . you're incorrigible!'

She giggled to herself. 'Go now, I'm exhausted. I love you.'

'Sleep well, Granny. I'm taking you home tomorrow.'

* * *

The following afternoon, we were back to normal in the garden outside the cottage. Daphne had new medication, which she claimed made her feel much better. By mid-afternoon, she embarked on her usual nap.

Exhausted, Yánna and I nibbled on a cheese and spinach pie which Yánna's friend had brought to the hospital. I called Spiros, told him what had happened, and gave him a list of art supplies to buy for my grandfather's portrait. He turned up later with everything, so I made a start while the light held.

'Would you like a drink, Flora?' Yánna asked.

'A glass of iced water would be nice. Keep me company if you're not too busy.'

Her face lit up, and a few minutes later, she sat beside me with her embroidery hoop and a ball of silken thread.

'I was shocked by what Daphne told me, Yánna, and I can't help wondering if recalling it all, caused her to have the angina attack.'

'Where was she up to?'

'On the train, escaping from Kalávryta. Aristotle's friend, who saved his life on the mountain, was murdered right in front of her. How horrific!'

Yánna stopped sewing and took a shaky breath. 'It's a terrible story, so sad.'

'It must be tough for those who lost family in the massacre,' I exclaimed, finding it difficult to imagine.

'Yes.' After a moment of poignant silence, Yánna changed the subject.

'Constantinos was very pleased to be invited to your portrait unveiling, Flora, thank you.'

'You know what, Yánna, I'll bet Daphne wouldn't mind if he came around some evenings and kept you company.'

'Do you think so?' She smiled and once again, I thought she might be very lonely. 'There's a diary at the bottom of my sewing basket. Daphne wrote everything down just after it happened, but I believe she has forgotten about it. Would you like to read it?'

'I would indeed.'

* * *

The next morning, Daphne and I decided we could manage without Yánna, so she set off to see her friend.

'I tried to read your diary last night, Granny, but it's written in Greek.'

'Ah, yes, my diary,' she said. 'You found it.'

'No wonder you didn't want to recall this huge story. It must be very difficult to tell.'

'It is, Flora.' She closed her eyes for a moment. 'What you don't know is, inside the bundle of bedding that Krístos threw into the train, I discovered baby Yánna, almost suffocated, overheated, and yelling her head off. I lifted the infant against my heart and wept for them all. Aristotle held me close, as if

297

afraid I would fall from the train, too. The carriage chugged down the mountain with us as its only passengers. I found the ride uncomfortable. The execution of Krístos, and fear that the Nazis would pounce at any moment, had us both on the brink of hysteria. Yet the presence of baby Yánna calmed us.'

'I can't imagine what you were feeling.'

She nodded, a distant look in her eye as she recalled the following events. 'Ten minutes later, the train came to a halt in the middle of nowhere. The driver came along the carriage and pulled the door closed. Despite the cold, neither of us had thought to close it. I guess we were both in shock. He stared at the blood spattered across the floor and the broken window. "Are you all right? Do you need anything?" he asked, glancing at the baby in my arms.'

Daphne sighed and stared into the past again.

'I told him we did. "Can we get a baby's bottle, some boiled water, and a little milk from somewhere?" I asked. "I'm afraid . . . this little newborn. She's not ours, but you see . . . You see . . ." I bit my lip. Choking back tears and verging on hysteria, I couldn't say more.

'Aristotle came to my rescue. "It's all right, Daphne. We don't have to explain. It's enough that we've saved her life." He turned to the train driver and asked for his help. The driver looked at my red eyes, then at Aristotle's ashen face. "I'll try when we get down to Diakopton." His soot-streaked cheeks softened as he peered at the baby. Moments after he left, the train shuddered into motion and resumed its journey down the mountain. We caught glimpses of the sea and, with the sight of it, found a kind of rigid calmness. Most of the journey is lost to my memory, apart from when we got off the train with the baby and our bundles and struggled over a dried-up river, and then up a bank on

298

the other side. The driver helped us. We both saw the remains of the smashed bridge scattered over the waterway's slippery-smooth boulders, and wondered which of the belligerents had destroyed the crossing. Faint with hunger and thirst, we climbed aboard a waiting train on the other side.'

Daphne closed her eyes and sat still.

'It's hard to imagine how difficult this must have been, Granny.'

'Aristotle was worried, too. "We'll find a taverna, someone to help us," he said. The sound of continued gunfire filled my head every time I closed my eyes.'

I had brought Aristotle's portrait outside to study in natural light, but I could hardly take my eyes off Daphne's face. She stared at it, her face full of revulsion, although I doubted she could see much without her special glasses.

'His fault, how I hate his picture, reminding me every day . . .' she mumbled.

What?!

'Sorry, Granny, I didn't quite catch what you said.'

She frowned. 'Just talking to myself again, take no notice. Now where was I up to? Oh, yes, escaping from Kalávryta. On top of all this horror, our unborn baby reminded me of its presence by jabbing my belly with an elbow or knee at every opportunity. Yet my heart melted. I longed to hold our child. Still, I knew the safest place for our baby was inside me.'

'Did you know where you were going?'

'We were headed to my cousin Lola on the island of Aitoliko. We'd be much safer there. I wanted to keep a record, before details faded from my memory.' She frowned, then smiled. 'You say you found my notebooks in the sewing stool?'

'I did, but as I said, they're in Greek. It's difficult to imagine how alone and frightened you must have been, Granny.'

'People who could help us did so. The train driver wished us good luck and insisted we wait while he fetched a baby bottle of boiled water and goat's milk. "Thanks for everything!" I said. "What would we have done without you?" The wiry little man seemed quite flustered and stumbled for words. "Stay safe, and, umm . . . I'll pray to the Virgin for you," he said.'

I smiled to think how much faith the Greeks had in their old religion.

'Then we walked away from the little Kalávryta railway, putting it, and those terrible goings-on, behind us.' She tugged the shawl over her shoulders.

'Shall we go inside, Granny, have a glass of that red wine? The doctor said only one small glass a day, because of your medication, so let's make the most of it.'

She nodded and smiled. 'Let's change the subject for a while. I find the past quite exhausting. I'd like to hear about you, and your life in England.'

'Oh, yes, some good news. I passed my exams with merit, so I'm now qualified to restore sixteenth-century art. And while we're talking about art, can I ask why you want me to forge a painting that you did? I've tried and tried to figure it out, but you've got me.'

'We'll see. If it's good enough, I'll tell you when you've finished.'

She gave me a devilish smile, eyes narrow, lips wide, and in that moment, I knew she was well on the mend.

34

DAPHNE

Western Greece, 1943

ON THE CORNER OF THE national highway, where Luka had first dropped them, Aristotle and Daphne peered up the road. They carried their chattels and baby Yánna into a neighbouring olive grove. They were relieved to find, although it was December, it was much warmer at sea level, and the olive trees protected them from a fresh sea breeze.

'Luka will be here this afternoon. How are you, my darling?'

Daphne wiped the sweat from her brow. 'I'm all right, just driven mad by the backache. I'll be relieved to lie down, if I'm honest.'

'Once we get on the ferry, we'll be safer.' He nodded towards the mountain region of the Peloponnese. 'I never want to go back there. Soon, we'll be on the island of Aitoliko and you'll be able to relax with your cousin.'

'Where can we sleep, I'm so tired?'

She rested a hand on her belly while rocking baby Yánna.

'I'm about to build you your own private castle, my lady. A place where you can lie down and relax for a few hours.' He forced a grin, his even white teeth flashing more brightly in his unshaven face. He had no idea how gruesome he looked with half an ear and blood encrusted hair. 'As your devoted servant, I'll be at your beck and call for the rest of my life.' They shared a loving glance, then dropped the pretence.

'I don't know what I would have done if anything had happened to you,' Aristotle said, placing his hand on her belly. He gave her a tender kiss on the mouth. 'Now relax and I'll set about building your fabulous residence.'

Daphne watched him untie their bedding bundle, knot the fringes of two blankets together, and then sling them over a low horizontal branch.

'The roof's on,' he called, then spread another blanket on the ground under the apex. 'Now the floor's laid,' he announced, before stacking the remains of their bundle against the tree trunk. 'You may retire, madam.' He forced a laugh and made a deep Shakespearean bow.

'This baby needs food and water,' Daphne said. 'Thank goodness for the train driver.' She rubbed her back. 'On top of everything, my back pain is so bad now I could scream.' She lay flat in the makeshift tent. 'That's better.' She sighed. 'Could you roll something up and stuff it under my knees?' As her spine relaxed against the flat earth, the pain eased. 'Oh, that's such a help.'

Aristotle spread his hand over her bump.

'Is our baby asleep?' he asked. 'I don't feel any movement.'

'I guess it's getting cramped in there,' Daphne reassured him.

'You poor darling.' He held her hand for a moment. 'You'll be glad when it's all over.' He nodded towards the sound of a passing convoy. 'I'm just going to the corner to see whose trucks they are.'

'Please don't leave me alone when I could go into labour at any moment.'

* * *

For the next few hours, the rumble of heavy traffic drew their attention. Was it heading up towards Kalávryta? She thought about their new friends. If any had survived, they would have to deal with the unimaginable mayhem alone. However, Daphne had more pressing responsibilities. With every moment that she held little Yánna, a stronger bond grew between them.

Aristotle's body slumped with tiredness as he went to the roadside. Daphne's resilience left her. She pressed a hand over her mouth to muffle her crying. Aristotle was safe, but how many bodies had bled into the soil of Kalávryta? Good will and friendship had abounded in the short time they had lived on the mountain. Tears ran down her face and dripped on to the tiny orphaned baby in her arms.

* * *

While Aristotle stood at the roadside looking for Luka, Yánna fell asleep, and Daphne's backache eased a little. The bright winter sun provided a shadow theatre of olive branches dancing over her blanket tent. The spear-shaped leaves quivered and skipped, soothing her stress. Whenever the rumble of traffic paused, she heard the gentle swoosh of the sea rolling small pebbles on the shoreline. The hypnotic sound made her drowsy. She needed sleep. Her eyelids slid down, and she succumbed to the luxury of uninterrupted slumber.

'Daphne,' Aristotle said. 'Daphne, wake up.' In an instant, she was alert and cursing him.

'What is it?'

'Luka's here, and he's offered to take us straight to Aitoliko. Isn't that amazing?' he said, dismantling the surrounding tent.

She stretched, enjoying the looseness of her rejuvenated spine, wondering if she would ever get back on her feet.

Luka, grinning like a madman, nodded at her then picked up one of their bundles.

'Can you big strong men help me up? I'm finding it difficult to stand with a baby beside me and a baby inside me?'

Aristotle and Luka chortled at each other, then lifted Daphne to her feet.

'Thank you! It is good to be standing again. I'm much better after the rest.'

Aristotle picked Yánna up and smiled, showing her to Luka.

'Look at her. She's trying to get her fist into her mouth.'

'She's hungry, again!' Daphne said. 'That baby's a little feeding, pooping machine.'

'They are all the same,' Luka said, stepping back as if the child were contagious. 'I have two of my own.'

Daphne saw Luka in a new light.

'I didn't realise you were married, Luka.'

'You're right, I'm not, but the woman in Thessaloníki thinks I'm married to the woman in Athens, and the woman in Athens thinks I'm married to the woman in Thessaloníki. I've a boy in Athens and a girl in Thessaloníki.' He turned to Aristotle. 'So let me give you some advice, my friend. Make sure your wife keeps that baby on the breast for as long as possible.'

'Because it will make her a healthier child?' Aristotle asked.

'No, because once they come off the breast, they eat money, and you will never have a penny for yourself!' he roared, turning to stare at his battered old truck.

Daphne put a hand over her mouth to hide a giggle. Then, ashamed of her mirth after all that had happened in Kalávryta, tears sprang to her eyes. She wondered if the hysterical feeling that unbalanced her would ever go away.

Luka caught her expression. 'It will get easier,' he whispered. 'I stopped for coffee with Babis this morning. Word's already spreading about the massacre. Shocking.'

Daphne swallowed hard. 'So, they did murder them all? I was hoping . . .'

He nodded. 'Every man and boy aged fifteen and over. They killed a woman, too, but I don't have details.'

'That must have been Georgia.' Aristotle rocked the baby in his arms. 'Look, she's gone to sleep,' he whispered. 'I'm getting good at this.'

Daphne sidled up to him for comfort. 'Poor Pavlo, so proud to be fifteen. How awful for his father when the boy joined him. He must have understood what was about to happen to his child.'

She shook her head and tears rolled down her cheeks again.

*   *   *

They got out of Luka's truck to stretch their legs on the Antirrio ferry. Both of them felt a spark of relief to be leaving the Peloponnese and its nightmares behind. When Daphne peered over her shoulder, Aristotle placed his hand on her cheek and turned her head.

'Don't look back,' he whispered as they crossed the Gulf of Patras. 'We must let it go, or it will cast its gloom over us for the rest of our lives. Turn your sad eyes to the sun and let your shadows fall behind you.'

With a heavy heart, she smiled at him.

'That's very poetic.'

They returned to the truck and disembarked from the ferry. The old vehicle trundled along, following the provincial road along the coastline of western Greece. They stopped for a nappy change when Luka insisted, and because Daphne's backache was picking up again. They would never understand her immense relief to stand and stretch after hours in the cab.

'This is where we go our separate ways,' Luka said, slowing the truck to a halt at dusk.

He jumped down and unloaded their few possessions on to the side of the road. Then he shook Aristotle's hand with vigour.

'Good luck to you both, my friends – and the baby, of course!' he yelled. 'You know where to find me. I'll always have an eye out for you.'

'Here's what we owe you, Luka, and a little extra. Thanks for everything,' Aristotle said, passing him an envelope.

The lorry driver stuffed it inside his vest, then they shook hands again and slapped each other with affection, but avoided eye contact.

'I have a stone in my throat,' Daphne said, stroking her neck. She wrapped her arms around their driver and laid her head against his chest. 'Give us both a big hug, Luka! You've been wonderful. Come and see us when the baby's born.'

'I will! I will!' he said, repeating himself, as he always did when stuck for words.

They stood at the side of the road and waved as he drove away. Turning, they gazed at the long bridge of many stone arches spanning a lagoon so flat it mirrored the vivid sky.

'It's not as far as it looks,' Aristotle murmured, staring at the crossing that stretched into the distance. 'We'll be there before dark.'

Daphne had Yánna in a shawl on her back, and a bundle in each hand. Aristotle had a bundle on his back and two in his hands.

'It seems like we're not moving,' Daphne said after walking for half an hour. 'I need to stop for five minutes.'

The endless bridge reached across the lagoon to the small island in the distance. Daphne heard the gathering hum of flying insects as the December sun slid below the horizon.

'I'll bet these are vampire mosquitoes waiting for their supper,' she muttered.

Aristotle laughed. 'Come on, my darling, we can do it. We've got about ten minutes of light left.'

'Promise me something?'

'Anything.'

He put down his bundles and took her in his arms.

'Tomorrow evening, we'll paint the sunset.'

He kissed her with such tenderness that she dropped her bundles.

'Yes! Tomorrow evening, we'll paint the sunset. That's a certainty.'

'We'd better walk on, then,' she said, picking up her baggage. 'Curfew's in twenty minutes, so we need to be there.'

* * *

After the sun set, the sky and the lagoon turned blood-red. Daphne said a silent prayer for the souls of their friends. Arriving in Aitoliko, they headed for the first taverna they saw. Before long they were eating beef *stiffádo*, Greek salad, and crusty fresh bread. They drank ice-cold water that tasted as sweet as champagne on their lips.

The taverna owner sent a message to Daphne's cousin Lola, and also to the local midwife. Daphne felt her body relax. She glanced at the bundles that included the paints and canvases, and longed to unpack.

'I'm thrilled that we're going to paint the sunset tomorrow evening, my darling. You know if I don't transfer some of my emotions on to canvas soon, I'll go mad,' she whispered, feeding Yánna a bottle of milk the cook had fixed for her.

'How are you now, my darling?'

'I'm having a baby, not a heart attack. Don't start treating me like a sick person!'

'Can't help it.' Aristotle grinned and ran his hand down her cheek.

'I'm desperate to sleep in a proper bed again. This has been the longest two days of my life! How's your hand?'

'Hot. I'll soak it in some salt water, then see if I can find a doctor.' He kissed her cheek and whispered, 'I can't wait to make love to you again, you know? You look so sexy, so womanly, with your swollen belly and large breasts. I want to paint you naked and pregnant. The goddess of fertility.'

Daphne blushed. 'Behave!'

Yet his words uplifted her because she didn't feel sexy. She felt frumpy and tired.

'Right, once you're settled with Lola, I'll search for some work. They're not too strict about the curfew on the islet, just the black-out. I'll be back in an hour or two, all right?'

She didn't want him out of her sight, but forced a smile.

'Of course. You go and make new friends, find work and a pharmacy. That hand needs treating.'

Aristotle hesitated, sensing her worry, remembering the men of Kalávryta divided from their loved ones in the last moments of their lives. They would never talk about it, but that day in the Peloponnese mountains would always be with them.

'*Ela*, Daphne!' a woman cried as she approached the taverna. 'Wow! The little girl grew into a woman . . . and more. When is the baby due?'

Lola's wide face beamed as she rushed towards Daphne, her muscular arms outstretched.

Daphne got to her feet, happy to be reunited with her favourite cousin. They embraced, and in a moment, tears of joy overwhelmed her.

'It's good to see you, Lola!'

'Let's have some coffee. Akis!' Lola called to the taverna owner, then winked at him.

He turned away, blushing, trying to control a grin.

'He loves me,' she whispered.

'You're as mischievous as ever, I see,' Daphne said.

Lola nodded 'I try. When are you expecting this little one?' She patted Daphne's belly.

'Any day now.'

'And who's this little beauty?'

She picked up Yánna, who was lying on Daphne's folded shawl, in an orange crate that the taverna owner had provided.

'Are you the father of them both?' Lola placed a hand on her hip and wagged a finger at Aristotle. 'Because if so, you need to slow down a bit, my friend. This is a small island. At this rate, you'll have us overrun in a year.'

Aristotle leaped to his feet and shook his head.

'No . . . at least, not that one. Only the one in her belly.'

Daphne was laughing hard. 'She's joking!'

Life would be fun with Lola at her side.

Aristotle glanced at his wife, and then at Lola.

'I can see you're in expert hands, Daphne.' A tic tugged at the corner of his mouth as he attempted a smile.

Daphne and Lola chuckled as he scurried away.

'Handsome man,' Lola said. 'Do you have anywhere to stay?'

'No, haven't had a moment.'

'Right . . . Old Toppo's just died and as he had no family, his house is free. It needs a bit of cleaning out, but I reckon we could have it ready in a couple of days. I'll ask the priest; he runs the island. When he knows you're fostering a little orphan, I'm sure it will be fine. Meanwhile, you can camp at mine.'

'That's wonderful, thank you, Lola.'

* * *

Three days later, the event they had waited for was imminent.

'The baby's crowned,' Magdalena, the midwife, said, a cigarette hanging from her mouth. 'Almost there.'

Just before her next contraction, a bolt of anger ran through Daphne. With her foot pressed against the midwife's shoulder, she squinted at the older woman.

The midwife took a drag on her cigarette, dropped it in the ashtray and patted Daphne's knee as if she'd read her mind.

'Save your energy for the next push, girl.'

Almost immediately, the flesh over her belly gathered with the tense and tingling preliminaries of another contraction.

'Here comes baby,' the midwife announced. 'Give it everything you've got now.'

Daphne pressed her chin to her chest, held her breath, and pushed every abdominal muscle against the stubborn foetus that only inched its way towards the outside world. Exhausted before the end of a terrific cramp that gripped her insides from armpits to anus, she stopped to breathe.

'Come on, Daphne! Big breath and push again. Your baby's tired and stressed. Move it forward while the contraction is with you!'

Daphne gulped, refilled her lungs, and gave it everything. Just as she thought her child was unmovable, there came a sudden relief.

'Bravo! Holy Mother of God!' Magdalena hollered, as if she'd done the job herself. 'The worst is over, look.'

She came up to Daphne, slid an arm under her shoulders and lifted her off the pillow. As she did, Daphne realised the bump of her belly had gone down.

'Say hello to your child, Daphne,' Magdalena said.

There, between her thighs, was the crumpled, angry face of her baby, eyes scrunched closed, and dark, wet hair plastered to its head.

'Two more contractions. Come on. Soon it'll be a separate life joined to you only by love. The greatest miracle on earth. Your own child.'

Daphne couldn't speak. Filled with sudden, overwhelming emotion, she wanted to cry. The little face. Her baby. Girl or boy, she didn't know. The child would be loved beyond all others. Minutes later, the midwife lifted the infant and its trembling cry brought tears of joy to Daphne.

35

FLORA

Corfu, present day

STILL TRYING TO TAKE IN all the things Daphne had spoken
about, I turned off the recorder and watched my dear grandmother sleep. I wondered if her carer, Yánna, was the newborn
from Kalávryta? Although it was possible, I knew Yánna was
one of the most common names in Greece, so I shouldn't jump
to conclusions.

Was the scene my granny had just described the birth of my
mother? All I knew for certain was that my grandmother was a
special person. Perhaps all grandmothers were. The tower of
strength and understanding that came from a lifetime of expe-
riences and regrets, hidden under the fluffy blanket of old age.
Unfortunately, that special knowledge of life often dissolved into
frailty and dementia before those precious lessons were passed on.

* * *

Spiros telephoned.

'Did you find any more information about the cellar, Flora?
There's nothing on the plans, so I checked the archives, but once
again, nothing. Could there have been an air-raid shelter under
the house?'

'I don't understand why it's so important to her, Spiro. She
says there are some canvases from her and Aristotle down there.
But she might be confused.'

'Canvases from Aristotle von Stroop?'

He paused and, in the silence, I remembered he invested in art – and, judging by the Rolex, he must be a very successful dealer. His voice broke my thoughts.

'If I had more to go on, I could order an investigation into the foundations of the building. If there was a cellar, we'd find it.'

'Best wait until she's moved on with her story. We're not even up to Corfu yet. All I understand for sure is that there's an El Greco involved.'

'An El Greco?' I heard him gulp. 'I see,' he said with a slight tremble.

Another silence stretched out.

'Spiro?' I said, wondering if we had lost the connection.

'Yes, sorry . . . Too much on my mind. I'm calling because I have a job to do at the other end of the island – a beautiful spot, Sidari, as north as you can go. Have you been up there?'

'No, we always stayed close to Mon Repos because of Granny.'

'It's the most beautiful place on the island. There are ruins – medieval fortifications and ancient towers lying in the shrubbery or clinging to the sides of the cliff. Also, you'll love the quaint villages, the true atmosphere of old Corfu. The people are friendly, and those communities are alive with original music and traditional food. Besides all that, you can't come to Corfu without swimming in the Canal d'Amour.'

'Excuse me? My French isn't brilliant, but did you say, the Canal of Love?'

Now he was laughing. 'Yes, a beautiful place. Have you seen it?'

'The only canal I know is the Manchester Ship Canal. Doesn't quite have the same ring to it.'

He laughed again. 'Sidari's a special place. Say you'll come.'

I was afraid of projecting qualities on to Spiros that answered my secret needs: the ache of wanting to love, the need to be loved – not only the thrill of romance tugging on my heart, but also a physical need that had increased with my longing for a child. Spiros was very like Mark. The same age, same good looks, they shared the same interests. Yet, I wasn't ready to trust Spiros. Nor was I ready to let Mark go. Also, the expensive watch unnerved me. His intense interest in what might be in the cellar of Mon Repos . . . and there was something else – although I couldn't quite place it.

'Flora, it's not for me to say, but perhaps you need a break,' he said. 'A day for yourself. My job will take most of the morning, so I could deposit you on the beach, and meet you for lunch later. Perhaps we'll have time to swim in the Canal d'Amour. What do you think?'

I searched for Mark's permission, telling myself it would make a change – a platonic afternoon away from the tragedy of my grandmother's story. Perhaps Granny would like a rest, too. Visitors every day can be tiring. However, the last time I was self-indulgent, I returned to find Daphne in hospital.

'Why don't you think about it and I'll buy you a drink at your hotel this evening? Eight o'clock in the cocktail bar?'

'Oh! Except that I've moved out. I've booked myself into a rent-rooms nearer to Mon Repos.'

'OK, that sounds nice. Shall I meet you at the café again?'

* * *

Yánna came out with a tray of coffee and glanced at Daphne.

'She's sleeping again?' She shook her head and sighed, her peppermint breath clouding around me. 'It's all she does these days.'

314

She lit a spiral under the table, the thin line of blue smoke warding off early evening mosquitoes.

'Why don't you join us, Yánna? Granny's out of it – you may as well drink her coffee.'

Yánna smiled and sat. 'You will stay for dinner, Flora? We have beautiful bourdeto.' When I frowned, she explained. 'Is shark, we cook in spicy red sauce, and serve with much lemon juice. Plenty of fresh bread, too, for the sauce, and a village salad. Very delicious.'

'Shark? There are sharks in these waters?'

'Is no a real shark. Is no dangerous, but the taste is delicious.' She laughed behind her hand.

'Sounds wonderful, and I'll be sorry to miss it, but I am meeting Spiros this evening.'

'No problems, we'll have it tomorrow, too. Is the Greek way, to make the big casserole and eat it for two or three days. You English spend too much time cooking the different food every day, Virgin Mary! Why you do that?'

I smiled. 'You're right, Yánna.'

'How is the painting? You make very good at this job, Mrs Flora.'

'I studied art at uni, Yánna, and I have a small studio in the spare bedroom at home. I often paint.'

Gloom fell over me like a dark blanket, and my heart plummeted. That bedroom had been my sanctuary from the moment we moved in. The only place where I could lose myself against the inevitability of Mark's illness. It seemed obscene that my studio would become somebody else's spare room – or, more heartbreakingly, a nursery. Where was my baby – my chance to play happy families? This was all I had wanted from life: Mark and my precious dream child. The small fantasy that meant so much to me had crumbled with Mark's death.

Why did you have to go, Mark? Why did it happen to us?

'You is sad now?'

'Ah, sorry, yes. I was thinking about my studio back home. It's full of canvases propped up against the gable end. What will I do with them all when I move out?'

'You will leave?'

'I have to. The bank is taking the house.'

She gasped. 'This is not good. Where will you live?'

I told her about the little flat in the city centre, and she seemed satisfied once she understood I would not be homeless.

'Anyway,' I explained, 'it will be more convenient living nearer the gallery.'

Mark and I had spent many happy hours in the art galleries of the north-west, peering into faces from the past.

'When I was young, I wanted to be a great artist, Yánna,' I said. 'Young people have such big ideas, but life tends to get in the way.'

'Yes, so did Daphne. Very much she wants to paint her own things. I try to remember what she tell me, but I am not sure of the correct English. She say, "I must capture the fury and the tender-ness of life." She would say this when her memories give her bad suffering in the heart. I try to say that correct, but she had the big passion . . . *passion*, for these things. Her life, it was not normal. It was too big for one person. Too full with the happy, and the sad.'

I blinked at her. 'Why didn't she paint more?'

Yánna nodded, staring blankly – not quite compos mentis for a moment. She shook her head.

'Yes, she painted a lot, more than Aristotle. When he died . . . Well, Daphne will tell you. I have said too much now.'

'Spiros is taking me to Sidari tomorrow. He's working there, so he'll drop me at the beach and pick me up when he's finished.

He said I should see the place, so it makes sense for me to go while I have the chance.'

'Is a beautiful place! Is good you go out. You want I make you a sandwich?'

* * *

We spent most of the journey in silence, apart from Spiros answering a couple of calls on his hands-free.

'I'm running late, so I'll drop you at the car park if that's OK with you?' he asked as we pulled to a halt.

'That's fine. I'll see you later.'

Filled with the urge to run, I found a sunbed with a large blue and white striped beach umbrella, and paid a ticket collector five euros before dumping my belongings on it. Although there didn't appear to be any shady-looking characters about, I put my phone, money, passport and cards in a runner's pouch and clipped it around my waist. The sand was solid near the water-line, so I set off with the ambitious target of five kilometres.

As I jogged along the edge of the sea, the distant cries of two excited children throwing a ball to each other reached me. Each gentle wave drew back into the endless expanse, and the rhythm of my footfalls soothed my mind. The mesmerising water drew my attention as I jogged along the shoreline, but stopped in the nick of time.

'Sorry! Sorry!'

I'd almost run into an elderly couple taking a stroll.

I must look ahead, I told myself.

There it was – the answer to my problems hit me in a blinding flash. Of course, I must look ahead! Because I was self-employed, I couldn't get a second mortgage . . . so why didn't I go to my employers and tell them the situation? I picked up the pace as everything fell into place. I excelled at my job. I'd been loyal to them for fifteen years, and now I had extra qualifications. Why shouldn't they help me with an employment contract, so I could approach the bank again? I was in a much better place now, and felt a spark of hope when it came to saving my home.

I returned to the sunbed, but found the sparkling sea irresistible. Iridescent turquoise water tingled against my sweat-dried skin. I sat in the shallows and tugged on my fins and mask, before sliding under the surface. Mesmerised by the patterns of refracted light on the pale, undulating seabed, I watched a shoal of delicate fish, flat and angular with large fins, swirl like a flock of birds gathering for an autumn migration.

A flick of my fins propelled me into deeper water where the sea was slightly cooler against my skin. A distant buzzing quickly grew horribly loud and gave me a sick feeling of panic. I stuck my head up through the surface and peered around, ready to wave my arms above my head. A sleek, white, speedboat cut its engines and dropped anchor. Only then did I notice the row of yellow floats connected by an orange rope to mark off the swimming area. I could have snorkelled right under it. How quickly everything might have changed. One minute you're safe, the next in mortal danger. This made me think of Spiros and his great loss. After checking there was nothing else heading my way, I turned my face towards the seabed once again.

A cluster of synchronised shadows, torpedo-shaped, slid over the sand beneath me. The silver fish, so well disguised, were almost impossible to see. Could they be sardines? A rock formation drew my attention. An orange starfish and several sea anemones decorated this undersea world of peace and tranquillity.

The morning passed. Slathered in bergamot suntan oil, I dozed on the sunbed until after noon, then went for another swim. I returned to find Spiros on my sunbed with my phone in his hand.

'Hello!' I said, making him jump.

'Hi. Your phone was ringing.'

'I see. Who was it?'

'Ah . . . It had stopped by the time I found it. Time for lunch. Are you hungry?'

I nodded, aware of an odd feeling in the pit of my stomach.

'How did you find my sunbed?'

'I phoned you from the car park, ten minutes ago, but when you didn't answer I asked the ticket collector if he'd seen a beautiful woman with flaming red hair. When he pointed this way, I recognised your *Mona Lisa* beach-towel, from last time.'

I laughed. 'OK, Sherlock, well done.'

36

DAPHNE

Aitoliko, Greece, 1944

'It's a fine boy,' the midwife announced, cutting the cord and wrapping the child in a towel. 'Aristotle! You can come in.'

The door flew open before she had finished the sentence.

'You have a strong, healthy boy. Congratulations!' Magdalena passed the swaddled baby over. 'Hold him while I finish dealing with Daphne.'

'Wait!' Aristotle said. 'My wife – how is she?'

'She's perfect. You're a lucky young man.'

In an instant, Aristotle was at Daphne's side.

'Where did you find the strength for fourteen hours of labour?' He kissed her hard on the mouth. 'You're a precious wife and mother . . . To give me a perfect son – how will I ever thank you?'

Daphne studied her husband's face, pleased she had a boy for him. There was time for daughters. His face was creased with worry, but it was love that she saw shining from his eyes.

He turned to the midwife.

'Is he healthy, Magdalena?'

'He's perfect. Strong as you, but far more beautiful.'

'Don't say such things, Magdalena, tempting fate and inviting the Devil. It's enough to say he's strong.'

Daphne knew their exquisite child would make him happier than he could imagine. She recalled how Noah had been the love of her father's heart. Babá had worshipped his first-born son.

Though they'd seemed at loggerheads from dawn till dusk, her father could never disguise the pride Noah had brought him.

'Do you have a name for this little mite?' the midwife asked.

'Yes, we'll call him Aris Noah von Stroop, after my husband and my brother,' Daphne replied, gazing down at the infant. 'He will be a leader, and a great sailor, like Noah, and a good, honest man like my husband.'

Aristotle lifted his head and smiled at Daphne, his eyes sparkling with unshed tears.

'Thank you,' he whispered. 'You've made me the happiest man.'

Daphne relaxed. 'Did you want a boy, Aristotle?'

'I will never lie to you, my darling Daphne. I wanted a boy because I hoped he would look after you and keep you safe in your old age.'

'But why say such a thing? I know you'll take care of us all, Aristotle.'

He blinked at her, confused for a moment. 'Yes, of course I will. Of course, I will.'

Magdalena cleared her throat. 'Are you going to take this baby or what? I need to get on, mister. There's another birthing mother on the next farm.'

Aristotle's face shone with love as he held out his arms for baby Aris.

'Give that precious child to his father.' He took Aris and gazed in awe at his little cherub face. To his wife, he said, 'Thank you, my darling. You've given me the greatest gift I shall ever have.'

The moment Aristotle stroked his son's cheek, the baby grabbed hold of his finger, pulling it towards his mouth.

'Oh, my, he's so strong, this child of ours. I'm sure he'll do well in life. This is no ordinary baby we have here, Daphne.'

The midwife straightened.

'If I had a hundred drachmas for every time I heard that said, I'd be a rich woman. Now hand him back to your wife. He needs to be put to the breast.'

* * *

The next day, Aristotle rocked Aris in his arms while Daphne gave Yánna a bottle.

'We must talk about what we should do with baby Yánna,' she said. 'I've grown so attached to her, I don't think I ever want to let her go.'

Yánna stopped suckling for a moment and gazed into Daphne's eyes, as if waiting for an answer.

Aristotle sighed. 'I know what you mean. She's delightful, isn't she?'

'Poor Krístos and Georgia. To think they will never see her grow up. It's so sad.'

'Krístos saved my life, if not for him, I'd be dead now.'

Their eyes met; Daphne's wide with horror.

'Don't remind me.' She swallowed hard, remembering when they'd dragged her husband off towards Kappis field in Kalávryta. 'And me locked in the school.'

'Not then. I mean up on the mountain.' He stared at the scar across the palm of his hand. 'It would have been me with my throat cut, plummeting into that bottomless gully. I owe Krístos my life. You'd be a widow with a baby, no income, and no home. I want to do my best for their daughter.'

Daphne nodded. 'You want them to grow up together – Yánna and Aris?'

She placed Yánna in the drawer that was balanced on two wooden crates and served as a crib for them both.

'Would it be double the work?'

'It doesn't seem so if you help when you can.'

'I will, I swear. You won't believe how happy I am.' He gazed at Aris in his arms. 'Look, Daphne, he's going to sleep. There is something I must tell you before we make a decision. It's only fair.' He hesitated, laid his son in the drawer, then continued. 'I have to emphasize, I'm not a healthy man, Daphne. I tried to tell you before, but you didn't want to listen. My heart, well, my veins to be correct, are not good. I will grow weaker as I age. You will outlive me, of this I am sure.'

Daphne's eyes widened. She couldn't speak.

'Now you understand why I tried so hard not to fall in love with you. I could not stand the thought of you being alone, or having to look after me in my old age.'

Daphne struggled to take in what he'd said.

'So, what will ...? I mean, how ...? Oh, no! I can't bear to think of these things, Aristotle. What will happen?'

'What will happen?' he repeated. 'A heart attack or a stroke, most probably. Sorry, darling. I know I should have made you listen at the start, but it was never the right time somehow. Can you forgive me?'

'I don't know. I'm in shock. But, Aristotle, medicine is improving all the time. There might be a cure long before you need it.'

He shook his head. 'Perhaps I would need a new heart, and no matter how medicine improves, we know that is too far-fetched to hope for. Science will never advance to such extremes.' He brought her hand to his lips and kissed it. 'Sorry, my darling. The best I can do is make sure there is enough money to keep you and my children comfortable for the rest of your lives.'

She stared at him. 'That's why you kept the El Greco?'

He nodded. 'Best not sell it until after the war. It's rightfully yours anyway, so you could say I'm just taking care of your interests, as your father would want.'

They sat in silence for a while.

'What do you think has happened to my parents and Elizabeth? Aristotle? I'm longing to share this day with them. My parents have a grandson – isn't that amazing? And what about poor Isaac? He's an uncle. I hope he's staying strong, wherever he is.' She raised a smile. 'I'm longing to tell Kyría Alice.'

'Perhaps they've settled somewhere in North Africa. Although I wonder why they didn't contact Kyría Alice to say they were safe.'

'I hope Isaac is bearing up in the work camp. I think about him every day.'

Aristotle lowered his eyes. 'We must hope. He was a sturdy boy when he left Athens, so there's a good chance.'

* * *

Lola's husband, Adam, earned his living as a wood merchant. He rowed over to the mainland, cut down a tree, cut it into firewood, then rowed his loaded caïque back to Aitoliko, where he sold the wood. Most evenings, Aristotle waited for him at the end of a long floating jetty on the opposite side of the island. The pier stuck out fifty metres from the colourful huts on stilts that covered the island's shoreline. On each side of the jetty, long narrow fishing boats, painted in an array of primary colours, were tied to mooring posts.

When Adam returned, he would throw the logs for Aristotle to catch and stack in his barrow. Aristotle took a rest while Adam took the wood to his yard. Then the whole procedure started again, until the caïque was empty. A black tarpaulin was secured over the empty boat, snugly as a drum-skin, then Adam would take Aristotle to the *kafenio* and buy him a drink. Leading members of the community would also gather there to discuss politics over a *carafaki* of raki and a few cigarettes. They talked about the atrocities of war and how many lives had been lost locally.

'They say thousands were killed on an Ionian island not long ago,' the doctor said.

'No, no, I heard it was in the Peloponnese mountains,' another said.

Aristotle interrupted. 'I think you're confusing the Kefaloniá massacre of the Italians, with the holocaust of all the Greek men in Kalávryta.'

'Kalávryta? I don't know about that one,' the headmaster replied. 'When did it happen?'

'A month ago. I was there with my wife. We were lucky to escape with our lives.'

'And you witnessed the whole thing?'

'Most of it, yes. They killed our friends, that's why we're bringing up their baby daughter. Why do you ask?'

'You're not concerned that the Nazis might not want any witnesses left standing?' he asked. 'You're not afraid they might come here looking for you?'

Aristotle shrugged. 'I've never thought about it, but now that I do, I've come to a different conclusion. I guess they'd want everyone to know, as a warning to deter anyone from believing they can ambush the Nazis without reprisals.'

'Our biggest problem here is EAM,' Adam grumbled. 'So far, more people have been killed in Aitoliko by the partisans than by the Germans. Sometimes it's hard to know who's your friend and who's a traitor.'

* * *

Daphne watched Aristotle more than usual. He had taken to sketching her, especially when she fed Aris. He didn't appear ill or weak at all. In fact, now that he helped Adam every evening, he seemed healthier than ever. Aristotle's pale skin had taken on a golden tan. She caught the light in his grey eyes, the line of his jaw, the way the sun bounced off his sandy-coloured hair, the slope of his shoulders, the bulge of his biceps. He filled her artistic requirement for a David, a Romeo, a Hermes. The need to paint his portrait built up in her like a secret seeking freedom.

As the days slipped by, they both settled into parenthood. The priest asked Aristotle to paint his portrait for a generous fee. Before he'd finished, the mayor wanted one, too. The portraits fascinated Daphne. She had missed painting so much that now, she *longed* to paint Aristotle's likeness. She practised her craft whenever she had time, and was embarrassed, yet flattered, when he lavished praise on her.

'I've told you, over and over, you have the makings of a great artist, Daphne. It's such a pity you're a woman.'

'Cheeky! You seem happy that I'm a woman when we're between the sheets.'

'You know what I mean. Even in 1944, women artists are not taken seriously.'

* * *

Word spread, and soon, thanks to Aristotle's portraits, they were financially viable. They even saved a little towards the next leg of their journey, which would take them to Corfu.

Daphne gazed down at Aris as she fed him. Yánna lay at her side with a bottle propped up by a rolled towel. The setting sun streamed honeyed light through the window, sparking off dust motes like flecks of gold as they rose in the warm air. The room smelled of honeysuckle, which arched over the half-open barn door. Aristotle had gone to help Adam after a day of portrait painting. Daphne had made bread and a pot of fish soup with rice and lemon for supper.

She smiled, contented with her life; then she jumped when Aristotle barged through the door. The babies, startled, started howling together, as they always did.

'Sorry, sorry,' he called, his arm outstretched, thrusting a note at Daphne.

'What's happened?' She covered her breast, put Aris over her shoulder and rubbed his back. 'There, there, silly Daddy, no need to fuss now,' she crooned as she rocked.

Aristotle picked up Yánna and jigged her about against his chest.

'Look here, Daphne. A truck driver told the ferryman, who told the headmaster, that the Germans were marching towards our little island. I didn't believe it. I mean, why would they? But I received this letter just now. Luka sent a young man to find us and deliver it.'

She took the letter from his hand and read it.

Dear Aristotle and Daphne and the little one. Forgive me for not coming to deliver this myself. I heard there is a plan to invade the island of Aitoliko. The Germans are searching for somebody, an Austrian artist who I suspect is you, Aristotle. Get out of there now. They're about to comb every centimetre of the place! I'm afraid. You have no time to spare. I can pick you up at Missolonghi, the gate into the Garden of Heroes, at four o'clock any Wednesday, and then take you up to Igoumenitsa.

Your loyal friend,

Luka.

327

'What shall we do? It's not just us now. We're responsible for these two lives as well.'

'I'm going to organise a boat – they'll be watching the bridge. You pack our absolute essentials quickly. We're leaving in less than an hour! Wear dark clothes.'

He shoved the letter back in his pocket, put Yánna down on the cushion next to Daphne, and then rushed out.

Daphne shoved nappies, a bottle and a blanket into a duffel bag, then wrapped each of the babies in a shawl. She folded another blanket onto the bottom of a fisherman's wicker basket, large enough for the two infants. Where had Aristotle hidden the El Greco? He had hardly talked about it since they'd first left Athens. She added a bottle of water and a loaf of fresh bread. Where was her husband? She went to the door and looked out. The air was much cooler now. She strained to listen for him, then her skin shrank over her body. The stamp of marching feet on the cobbled bridge!

Tramp. Tramp. Tramp.

A drop of sweat trickled past her eye, despite the chill in the air. Her mouth dried. What if they had Aristotle already? She could not escape with two babies. More marching boots, louder now. Her belly knotted. She closed the curtains and the front door, then dropped the big metal latch into the receiver. Nobody could get through that door. She remembered Kalávryta. What if they set the house on fire? Her heart thumped so hard she feared it would stop. She might end up trapped in a burning building with the babies! The wooden roof would collapse onto them. Where was Aristotle?!

A thud against the front door startled her. Shaking with terror, she snatched Aris and held him against her body.

'It's me, Daphne!'

Aristotle's voice. She threw back the hasp, but before she could speak, he gave her orders.

'Come on, it's my cousin's men,' he hissed. 'They'll kill us all for the painting. Adam has given us the use of his boat.'

'Where is it?' she hissed.

'Safe, don't worry about that now.'

They each grabbed a bag with one hand, Aristotle taking the bigger bundle, their possessions, while she snatched their painting paraphernalia. Each gripped a handle of the wicker basket with the babies, then they hurried towards the jetty. The moon was not yet up, and the water appeared black and oily. The jetty seemed narrower than usual as they struggled to board the boat with their precious passengers. Every small noise seemed like an explosion. A gunshot rang out from the town. Distant noises became louder. Aristotle untied one of the cover's ropes.

'Can you slide in there, and I'll pass the babies in?'

She slithered under the tarpaulin, feet first, most ungraciously wriggling through the narrow gap. Aristotle slipped the babies' basket in, but Daphne couldn't see anything and didn't know the anatomy of the vessel. She rested the basket on something, then felt around with her free hand. There was a plank bench wide enough to hold the basket. While she took care of the infants, Aristotle's body slid in beside her. He fumbled with the tarpaulin, and she saw the slit of the night sky disappear as he tied it down.

'Stay still,' he whispered, 'so the boat doesn't rock and give the game away.'

'Here, take Yánna and her bottle. It's the only thing guaranteed to keep her quiet. I'll put Aris on my breast.'

They hardly dared to breathe. The sound of soldiers on the move increased: stamping, shouting, people crying out; the occasional gunshot. All the horror of Kalávryta came back as the boat started bobbing up and down. Soldiers were marching along the jetty. Daphne remembered Elizabeth's ordeal when they ordered the soldier to shoot at the linen chest.

What if they shoot at all the boats?

As if she had tempted fate, a shot rang out, making Aris jump. Daphne pressed the baby's face to her breast, holding him snugly. There, there, she thought, not daring to speak.

'Stop!' a voice ordered, so close it seemed he was in the boat with them.

Aris's arms and legs bolted out stiffly. Daphne's skin crawled over her body. It seemed even the air in the boat buzzed with terror.

37

DAPHNE

Aitoliko, Greece, 1944

DAPHNE CLUTCHED ARIS TO HER breast. He wriggled and struggled, but she held him firm, desperate to keep him quiet. Their lives depended on it. She knew he couldn't keep up such a fight for long; he would soon tire and relax. Despite their terrifying situation, her heart filled with pride. Aris was so strong, so determined, a real warrior. It took all her strength to keep him still and quiet. Their baby would grow into a fine man with a big heart, and have many children. He had an amazing life ahead of him, but one tiny sound now, and he would disclose their hiding place. And once Jürgen Stroop had the El Greco, she knew they'd all be killed.

'I don't want von Stroop harmed!' a German voice barked. 'He has vital information, so I'm offering a quarter of a million Reichsmarks to the man who brings him to me.'

Somewhere above them, on the pier, two soldiers spoke in German.

'We'll do a systematic search of the island at first light. Block the bridges to ensure there's no way off. I want this man found at all costs.'

Daphne kept Aris's head pressed against her breast. One whimper from either of the babies would put them in mortal danger. Yánna wriggled. Wind, Daphne suspected. A faint plop told her Aristotle had pulled the teat from her mouth.

They both froze when baby Yánna made the loudest belch. Immediately, the boat bobbed as soldiers stomped towards them along the floating pier. She continued to hug Aris against her, and prayed he wouldn't make a sound.

'*Frösche,*' one of the soldiers said: Frogs.

Daphne felt Aris relax, as if he knew a great danger had just passed. Asleep at last, she thought. Exhausted from holding the little wriggler so tightly against her tender breast, she feared she had bruises, and hoped they wouldn't affect her milk flow. In the pitch dark, she sensed her son had gone to sleep. For now, they were safe. Again, she thought of her days helping Kyría Alice in the soup kitchen. *Pray for us sinners now and at the hour of our death, amen.* Her arms ached. She longed to put her son in the basket. However, she must keep him against her breast in case he woke and hollered.

Around midnight, the town became quiet as death. Aristotle dared to undo one of the tarpaulin ties and peer out.

'There's no sign of life,' he whispered. 'I'll see if I can move us across to the mainland while it's dark. Once the moon is up, we'll be seen.'

'How are you going to move us?'

'I'll get in the water and swim.'

'But it's so dark, Aristotle, and what about eels and sea snakes and who knows what . . .? Leeches?' She shuddered.

'Don't think about it. I reckon I can do it in an hour. Let me get that big coil of rope from under the bench. I'll tie it on to the boat and swim as far away from you as the line will allow, then I'll pull you.'

'Sounds like a ridiculous idea.'

'We're upstream of the old wooden bridge, so if anything goes wrong, you will drift to the bridge, and you can stay there until somebody comes to rescue you.'

332

Horrified at the thought of being left alone in a moving boat with two babies and a drift tide that was heading for the open sea, Daphne took a deep breath.

'If that's all we've got, let's get on with it before the moon comes up.'

'Right, settle both babies in the basket while they're still asleep, and let's get going.'

They both lay flat under the tarpaulin. Aristotle struggled out of his clothes, undid some fastenings, and lifted a corner of the tarpaulin. Daphne welcomed the rush of cool, sweet air in their stuffy hiding place. Aristotle slid over the side without a sound.

'When an owl hoots, untie the mooring rope, Daphne.'

He took a big breath, then slipped away like a phantom in the night. Aris had finally relaxed and, sensing he was sound asleep, she placed him in the basket, next to Yánna. With great tenderness, she covered both with a blanket to protect them from the night's chill and rogue mosquitoes. The gentle motion of the boat seemed to relax and quieten the babies. Daphne smiled at the idea that she was rather a good mother.

She listened for noises coming from the water. Night insects buzzed and hummed. Apart from the mild slip-slop from the gentle movement of other boats, everything was still. Her heavy eyelids slid down, and she felt herself sinking close to sleep. How wonderful it would be to forget about everything and relax. To be free of the horrors of war and the obligations of parenthood. Lying still in the dark boat, the night's chill seeped into her bones. She thought about Aristotle in the water. How cold he must be. What if he never came back? What if he also had moments when he wished to be free of all responsibility? This situation had given him the perfect opportunity to escape alone.

Daphne, a city girl, had never learned to swim. She wondered how it felt to be out there in the dark water. Because of the curfew, there was no beacon to aim for. He might easily have swum straight out to sea and been swept away. Aristotle's medical condition came to mind. She wondered if, for all his good intentions, he was strong enough to complete the task he'd set for himself. Perhaps he had succumbed to the cold, dark water, and his lifeless body lay on the lagoon's watery floor.

Still weak after childbirth, now fear exhausted her.

The minutes ticked by. His warning haunted her. A heart attack or a stroke, he'd said. Convincing herself she would never see him again, Daphne's distress built. Cold and afraid, she cried in silence for all the things they hadn't done together, for the portrait she had never painted, and for Aris, who would never know his father.

She would stay in the bottom of the boat until morning light and pray the German soldiers would give up and leave the little island. She also prayed the babies would sleep until dawn, but even if they did, what could she do without Aristotle by her side?

The sharp tug on the little boat woke Daphne and Yánna with a start.

Oh, Aristotle! How could I fall asleep and miss your owl call?

She crawled to the stern and untied the mooring rope. The boat slid away from the pier. Yánna snuffled and whimpered and, afraid the baby would draw the attention of a soldier, Daphne took the restless baby from the basket and nursed her.

Now the boat was moving. She eased the tarpaulin up and glimpsed a half-moon on the rise. They seemed to head straight for the wooden bridge, but they must get there before the moon found another break in the clouds. If they were seen . . . But how was it possible that they were moving so quickly with no means of propulsion.

Terrified that, at any moment, a soldier might see the boat shifting across the lagoon, she considered the consequences. If they shot at the boat, they might kill her, or the boat might sink. She couldn't swim and there were two babies on board. Even if she could swim, after spending hours almost horizontal over the sharp wooden ribs of the vessel, she was too stiff to move much, let alone save two helpless infants. How deep was the lagoon, she wondered – two metres, or a hundred metres?

Daphne peered out again. The dark water reflected the moon again. She guessed it was around three in the morning. They hurtled towards the old broken bridge, but stopped before crashing into one of the upright poles. Aristotle leaped up from the water, making Daphne whimper.

'Shhh, it's me. Are you all right?'

'You frightened me. Everything frightens me. I can't swim.'

He hung on to the side of the boat. 'What? Why didn't you tell me?'

'I didn't want to worry you,' she said, remembering that she had told him when they were in the Corinth canal.

'How have the babies been?'

'Aris is oblivious. Yánna woke, so I nursed her and she's gone back to sleep. How did we move so fast?'

'The rope's longer than I thought, so I pulled it around one of the bridge supports and hauled as quickly as I could. It appears we weren't seen, and it's not much further to the land, so I'm going to do the same again. I noticed a young tamarisk tree on the shore. I'll use that as a post if the rope reaches.' Off he went again, then turned back. 'By the way, I'm standing on the bottom. It's not too deep, and the basket will float ... so you know. I don't want you afraid. Sleep if you can.'

Wasn't he the most wonderful man in the world?

He struck out for the shore and soon disappeared into the night.

* * *

The moon slipped towards the western horizon. Daphne and Aristotle had beached the boat and unloaded most of their things while the babies slept.

'Let's move away from the water's edge so we're not as noticeable. I'll secure the boat for Adam. Someone will bring him over for it.'

The sky in the east took on a mauve hue, lightening to peach as dawn approached. Insects woke and sang like an orchestra tuning its string section. The birds joined in with a magnificent chorus. Flamingos, pink and ungainly with their back-to-front legs and upside-down beaks, rose in a great, flapping, rose-coloured mass. Against the lilac sky, they circled once before returning to the shallow water, trowelling the mud for a shrimp breakfast.

Aristotle peeled back the tarpaulin, and each took a handle of the wicker basket.

'We should leave the blanket over them while they sleep, to keep the insects away,' Daphne said. 'I can't believe Aris slept all night. What a perfect little baby. Mind you, he did put up a terrific fight. Wore himself out, I guess.' She smiled at the temporary crib. 'I'd better change and feed him while Yánna's sleeping.'

'I'll bring the rest of our stuff from the boat, then we can decide what to do next.'

A sense of excitement rose with the new day. Soon they would be in Corfu – far from the war in Greece. Aristotle turned back towards the shore, eager to finish with the boat and relieved he could now move his family to safety. He glanced back at Daphne and mouthed; I love you! Everything would work out.

He was lifting their bale of meagre belongings when Daphne's scream poleaxed him. He dropped the blanket-bundle in the boat and ran to her side. On her knees, she rocked back and forth with Aris clutched to her breast.

'Daphne! Daphne! What is it?'

His first thought was: she had been shot.

Her high-pitched keening persisted. He dropped to his knees and eased his son away from his wife's body.

'Let me take a look, my darling. Are you hurt? Let me see . . .'

38

DAPHNE

Western Greece, 1944

WITH A LEADEN HEART, ARISTOTLE realised his son's life had ended many hours before. His perfect little face was translucent, ghostly white. His limbs as stiff as a papier-mâché doll. Large, baby-blue eyes were open but sightless, staring back at his father. How could this nightmare happen? He released a low moan that came from deep within. He placed his arms around his wife and child and rocked them both, unashamed of the tears that poured down his face.

Aristotle was not a religious man, but at that moment he needed to believe in an afterlife. Still on his knees, he begged God to take the soul of his first-born son into Heaven, and to forgive him for any transgression that had earned him this terrible punishment. Then he held Daphne and Aris until their tears ran dry.

*   *   *

Daphne couldn't explain what had happened to the day. It passed in a timeless fug. At some point, Aristotle lifted Aris from her arms and placed Yánna on her bosom. Daphne's tears fell onto the child's cheek. When she saw the bruises on her breast, she recalled the terrible threat of being discovered by the German soldiers. How tightly she had held baby Aris to her body, to keep him quiet, to protect them all. Now, with terrible horror rising inside her, she realised she had suffocated her own baby – an agony she would live with for the rest of her life. Darling Aris had died in her arms in the pitch dark of the boat, while Daphne believed he slept. The very part of her body that should give comfort and nurture had taken her precious son's life.

Aristotle dug a small grave. As he closed his son's eyes, a tear splashed onto the boy's cheek and trickled to the corner of his mouth. From the depths of Aristotle's soul rose his debilitating sadness. He swallowed hard and swiped his tears away, hoping he could utter a few words as he buried his boy.

'Our son sleeps in the arms of angels, Daphne, and we shall always love him, our beautiful baby, Aris.'

Daphne sang a lullaby through her tears while rocking the tiny, lifeless body one last time. Aristotle found a myrtle bush and covered their child in a blanket of the sweet, scented leaves. Together, they cried, and laid soft earth over their baby boy, on the banks of the Missolonghi lagoon.

*   *   *

They slept in each other's arms, with Yánna in the fishing basket beside them. After consuming the last of the bread and water, each succumbed to a bout of sobbing when they believed the other was asleep.

Woken by the sound of shooting that came from across the flat lagoon. Daphne whimpered. Aristotle pulled her to him. Yánna woke hungry, boxing an invisible foe with her little fists.

'Please tell me it's not happening here, too!' Daphne cried as she lifted the baby. 'I couldn't stand any more killing after Kalávryta!'

Her breasts were heavy with milk meant for Aris. 'What will happen to us, Aristotle?' she asked as she nursed Yánna.

He sat behind her, massaging her shoulders and rubbing her back. She rested against his chest as she looked out over the peaceful lagoon. The water, flat as a mirror, reflected everything, thus giving her the sensation of floating above reality.

Aristotle's deep sigh breezed over her shoulder and, after a moment, he answered her question.

'We'll recover from this, survive the war, and I know it's hard to believe, but we *will* live in contentment for ever after, my darling.' He tried to smile reassuringly through his tears.

Daphne turned her face to the side, accepting his kisses on her cheek. She wanted to believe him.

'Can we go back, across the island and over the other lagoon bridge, to the main road and find Luka? He said he would take us up to Igoumenitsa, remember? What day is it today?'

'It's Saturday. We have until Wednesday to decide. I don't know what to suggest now, but we'll find a way, Daphne. We'll find a way *together*.'

He wrapped his arms around her, as if the very act of protecting her, gave him strength.

Silently, in each other's arms, they watched the dawn sky turn golden, then a piercing blue. A strip of white cloud drifted over the horizon, bringing a V-shaped flock of honking geese. All this was reflected in the magical lagoon.

'It's so beautiful.' She made a sigh so deep, it seemed to come from underground. 'Who would think anything so tragic could ever happen here, Aristotle?' she mumbled, tonelessly, her turned down mouth so slackened by sadness she barely formed the words.

'I don't know, my darling,' he said, his heart breaking into a thousand pieces for his wife, for his child.

The beautiful reflections dissolved into ripples as one of the gondola-shaped fishing boats floated towards them.

'*Yia sou! Ela!*' the silhouetted oarsman called. 'My friends, are you there? It's me, Adam. I've come for my boat.' As he drew nearer, rowing the Greek way, facing forward, he lowered his voice. 'I bring you some food and water, but if you want to come back with me, it is safe now. The Hun have gone.'

Daphne placed Yánna back in the basket and then stared at Aristotle, her chest still heaving and her eyes bloodshot and burned red by endless, salty, tears.

'I'll feel safer once we're on Corfu,' she whispered. 'When we all stayed at her apartment in Athens, Kyría Alice gave me the address of her friend in Corfu who will help us if we need.'

They both watched Adam pull the boat half out of the water and tie the mooring line around the same young tamarisk tree that anchored his own boat. He wore an old shirt cut off at the elbows and black trousers that were patched at his knees. Times were hard for everyone, yet this Albanian had found the generosity to bring them bread and water, and his voice resonated with concern for their safety.

'Are you all right?' He could see by their faces; something was very wrong.

Daphne peered into his eyes as she spoke.

'We're so grateful for all you and Lola have done for us, but now we are at a loss as to what to do, you see . . .' Her chest jerked with a sob. 'Our baby . . . Our beautiful Aris that Lola helped to deliver, he . . . Oh, Adam, our baby . . .' Daphne couldn't continue, as if saying it aloud made it real.

Adam looked at Aristotle for an explanation, but he couldn't speak and simply shook his head. He turned his eyes towards the small mound covered in white stones on the bank of the lagoon.

'Oh no,' Adam said, staring at the two devastated parents. 'I am very sorry for you. May God and his angels welcome your child into Heaven.'

This was too much for Daphne. Her face crumpled again. She curled her body into Aristotle's lap and cried into his chest. Adam's voice reached her.

'Don't worry, I'll come back this evening. The Germans have gone, but there's EAM, the Greek communist party. You have all day to decide, but I must tell you, the Germans have left the reward in place and there are a lot of starving people with children on the island.'

He stepped back, glanced at the little grave, then spun around. He tied a lead from his boat to the one he'd arrived in.

'I'll be back around five o'clock,' he called over his shoulder, pushing the boats into the water.

'*Ta léme,*' Aristotle replied: See you.

He turned his attention to Daphne. 'Come on darling, I know it's difficult, but we've got an uninterrupted day to make our plans. Let's concentrate on the future.'

Daphne dried her eyes and uncurled from his lap. Yánna, now asleep in the basket, looked so peaceful.

'She's so sweet, isn't she? Poor baby. What are we going to do, Aristotle? It seems your cousin is always one step behind us.'

'That's what we should talk about today, here, with no distractions.'

'No distractions . . . apart from the ever-hungry pooping machine there.' She nodded at the fishing basket and forced a faint smile.

Aristotle smiled, too, a little of the sadness leaving his face.

'I'm inclined to suggest we sell him the El Greco,' she mumbled. 'For a decent amount, to be rid of him.'

'When I offered him the painting, in Athens, I thought I knew him, but after the offer of such a big reward for our capture, I believe he is firmly in the grip of Nazi power now. He'll kill us for the painting – I'm sure of it.'

'Why don't we play him at his own game? What if we forge the painting and give him the forgery? Claim we didn't know it was a fake.' She considered this sudden idea for a moment. 'Where is it, anyway?'

He shook his head. 'Better if you don't know.'

'Well, I guess it's with us, in with your art supplies.' He pulled in his chin, eyes wide. 'And if I got it right the first time, so will your cousin. We have a choice. To protect it and bury it somewhere, but if he kills us both, it will be lost, forever. Or we can take it with us, but disguise it.' She gasped. 'Aristotle! I've got the perfect hiding place – so perfect!'

He blinked at her, confused. 'Go on, tell me.'

'We have some blank canvas, yes?'

'We do, but not mounted.'

'Do we have any mounts?'

'We have the struts, so I can soon put a mount together and stretch a canvas on to it. Why, what's your plan?'

'We're going to paint an El Greco – mostly you, of course. An El Greco so good, it could fool him.'

Aristotle shook his head. 'You'd never get away with it. My cousin has experts.'

'That's the idea. We don't have to get away with it, in fact we don't want to deceive his art experts. All we need to do is convince him *we* believe it's genuine. To make myself clear, the painting must be good enough to fool you, an artist, and him, a collector, but not his art experts. You told me, your cousin's experts always travel with him when you first called him in Athens, and that he wouldn't consider buying the El Greco until his specialists verified it was the genuine article. There's a fine line we must walk.'

Aristotle stared at her, considering the suggestion.

'You might be right. Except he'll search every inch of our belongings before he accepts we were duped in the first place. Let me chew it over. You might have something.'

'No, listen to me, there's more. The best place to hide something is right under the seeker's nose, yes?' Aristotle nodded. 'In that case, we'll paint two layers of varnish over the El Greco and paint the forgery right over the original. That way, if they X-ray the painting, they won't see the original underneath.'

Aristotle's eyes widened. 'You might have something there.' He frowned, his eyes staring as he mulled over her proposal. 'That's quite ingenious, you clever darling!'

Yánna drew their attention. She made a little squealing noise as she wriggled and punched in her basket.

'Look, even the baby approves.'

Daphne's eyes turned towards the small mound on the edge of the lagoon. The heavy weight of mourning returned. It was because of that cursed work of art the soldiers had come after them. If not for the El Greco, Aris would be alive, in her arms. How she hated that painting, and always would, until the day they sold it and could start a real life together after the war. She wondered if Aris could hear her thoughts up in Heaven? They would overcome this. Determination strengthened her, along with the promise to herself that she would care for Yánna, as long as the child needed her.

'Right, no time to waste,' she said. 'Please show me the El Greco and while I study it, get to work and stretch me a canvas, Aristotle.'

He blinked at her, shocked, as if trying to understand a stranger – she was a different person now.

'Don't look at me as though I'm heartless. From now on, I will live for Aris. I'm going to embrace all the successes and triumphs and everything that we wanted our son to enjoy. As for the El Greco, I will try my very best to help, but most of the work must come from you, of course. The experts will realise the painting is a fake, but a fake so good that it fooled you.'

'There are problems with your painting idea, darling Daphne. We have no access to the correct, heavy, paint of El Greco's time. In the sixteenth century, they mixed their lead-based pigment with oil, it took an age to dry. Nor can we buy the same thick linen canvas. Those two things alone will prove the picture a forgery. It took about fifty years for the oil paints to harden . . . and another fifty before the varnish cracked. We have several weeks, three months at the most.'

39

FLORA

Corfu, present day

'So, do you believe in fate, Flora?'

I made a non-committal shrug.

'Then let me tell you why this pebble is so important to me. This is the place where my Aris is buried. Of all the painted pebbles in the world, you chose this one to bring me. Look, there is the wooden bridge, and there is the tamarisk tree. My heart weeps when I look at it.'

'What? Wow, that is quite a coincidence, Granny.'

She curled her fingers around the stone again.

'Perhaps the girl with the stones was an angel.'

I shook my head. 'Don't tell me you believe in angels.'

'I believe in everything and nothing.'

She clutched the pebble against her heart.

Aristotle's portrait fascinated me, not just as the grandfather I'd never met, but also because his portrait and his works were reminiscent of Rembrandt. I'd blocked in all the dominant colours of background, hair and skin. Now, I mixed a little burnt umber to mark out his features. As he revealed himself, I sensed a perceptive, handsome man with discerning eyes. By adding more detail, the person my grandmother had talked about came to life, brushstroke by brushstroke. Lost in my work, in the garden of perfume and birdsong, I felt a weight lift from me.

Daphne sighed and closed her eyes and, once again, I wondered if she had nodded off. Her new medication seemed to make her sleepy.

I used a wide brush and worked hard to capture the highlights and shadows of Aristotle's face before we had to retire indoors.

Daphne woke with a start. She glanced at my painting, nodded, then continued with vigour, as if it had all just come back to her.

'The next morning, Aristotle started work on the El Greco while I prepared for my portrait of him. He continued to teach me – and I hung on to every word, doing my best, hoping to please him. My first task was to prepare the canvas. I copied his every step for my own portrait. That day re-ignited my artistic skills. It also stopped me thinking about how much the El Greco had cost us.'

She reached out and touched the pebble, a trembling smile on her lips. 'Although we shared a palette, I would never paint my husband's face in the style of El Greco. I found no joy in the artist's work, especially now. His drooping eyes and miserable mouth . . . He might have been a genius, but I also believe the artist was an unhappy, conflicted man.'

'I understand where you're coming from, Granny. That was the very reason I wanted to paint you. I needed to do something that would totally absorb me, lift me away from Mark and my grief. You have a beautiful face, you know that?'

She smiled. 'Aristotle would often say so. You know, twice I allowed him to paint me naked.'

I frowned. *There were three nudes in the Laurel triptych.*

She studied my face for a moment.

'Did you paint your husband's portrait, Flora? He was a good-looking man.'

'I never did. Isn't that sad? I wish I had, and I've tried since he died, but I can't. Sometimes I see him so clearly, but I can't fix his likeness to the canvas. It seems irreverent somehow.' I gulped and clutched my throat for a second. 'There's so much pain in my heart, Granny. I can't put paint on such an emotive subject, or even depict his features. I can't explain why. Does that make any sense?'

She nodded. 'It will come back, your ability to paint, like a gift from him. Trust me.'

'So, tell me what happened. Did you really forge an El Greco?' I studied my grandfather's likeness on the canvas. 'This looks rather good, Granny. Certainly, a lot older than eighty years. Don't forget, I'm a professional, and I've uncovered several fakes in my time. Tell me how you prepared the canvas?'

'Let me think now . . . I have to get things in the right order. Aristotle did most of the artwork, but as he explained each procedure, I practised on my portrait of him.' She nodded at the picture I was copying. 'That's why he's in the style of an old master. I could have made a profession out of forging.' She giggled, making me smile.

'You're so naughty!'

'I know.' She beamed at me. 'We painted diluted bleach on the back of the canvas to make it feel old and brittle. After soaking cigarette ends in turpentine for a couple of days, we strained it, added a little burnt umber, and drenched the entire canvas and stretcher. That was before the primer, of course.'

She nodded slowly, the mischievous sparkle fading from her eyes. She stared into the past and allowed old ghosts to gather around her. In the garden, everything took on a rosy hue as the late afternoon sun threw longer shadows. The perfume of night-scented jasmine drifted over from the cottage, warning me that the special light wouldn't last much longer.

'Come on, darling Granny. If you're up to it, tell me what happened next.'

'Aristotle photographed the El Greco with his prized Zeiss, so he had a reference before he fixed the masterpiece to the prepared canvas. He applied a couple of layers of varnish to protect the old painting. When that was dry, we started again with two layers of oil ground lead primer which needed a month to dry. By this time, Aristotle was working on another portrait, which boosted our funds. We both knew it was time to move on. The reward on Aristotle's head became a constant threat. I spent my days taking care of Yánna and packing up our belongings. We left Aitoliko by rowing boat in the dead of night. After, we walked to the main road and slept in an olive grove until Luka picked us up.'

'How big was the El Greco, Granny?'

'Not so big, thank goodness. About thirty by forty. Don't forget, it was only Noah's nursery painting that hid the El Greco at home.' She frowned. 'But I'm ahead of myself. A lot happened before we started on the actual painting.'

The stark blue of the sky mellowed into mauve with distant pinks, gathering strength. The sun, dazzling white, morphed into a dramatic red ball as it neared the horizon and slid through a bank of cloud. In silence, we watched the sunset. I remembered my last walk with Mark, along Crosby shore. The warm light faded, silhouetting Gormley's statues in the most glorious way. We sat on a dune as darkness fell. He slipped his arm around my shoulders and whispered, 'You'll be all right.'

'Granny, I'm going to push you indoors before I pack up my paraphernalia, all right?'

* * *

Yánna bustled in, all rosy cheeks and sparkling eyes.

'There's fresh bread, tzatziki, fava and hummus. The moussaka will be ready in thirty minutes. Is all right?'

Daphne and I exchanged a glance and laughed.

'Fabulous, Yánna, thank you.'

I poured three glasses of red wine before Daphne continued with her story.

'After a lunch of bread and water, Aristotle waited for Luka by the road. "Good to see you," Luka greeted us with his wide smile. "There's an ouzeria in Kefaloryisi. It's near here. Let's go eat." He paused, stared at Yánna, then glanced around. "Only the one baby?" Aristotle turned his mouth down and nodded. "I'm sorry, my friend. One day you must tell me about it, but I see now's not the time," Luka said.'

Yánna put small plates of food on the table. Granny took a sip of wine before she continued.

'The old truck pulled to a squealing halt outside a ramshackle ouzeria with half oil barrels for tables and hefty logs for chairs. The owner came rushing out, took one look at Aristotle's fair hair and decided to speak English. He shouted "*Ela! Ela*, my friends! Sit. Sit!" He stared at me and the baby, and said, "Wait. Wait!" He dashed inside and came out with a real chair. "For the lady. For the lady!" He grinned at me, smoothing his hand-knitted sweater, which was full of holes and ladders. It was difficult not to laugh. He peeked at Yánna. "Aww, beautiful! Beautiful. You want food? I have the best chickpea soup and fresh bread on the island. On any island. Is my grandmother's recipe. She make herself." "We're on an island?" I asked Aristotle, quietly. He shook his head. "Your English is good," I said to the owner. "I am Bacchus. I learn English in the Great war when I is in Africa. You like soup?"

'They exchanged a glance, then replied, "Yes. Yes!"'

*   *   *

'"There's a steady build-up of German troops in Igoumenitsa," Luka said. "It seems they're looking for somebody, even offering a big reward." He squinted at us both. "You have any idea who they want?" We shook our heads. When Luka disappeared behind the ouzeria, to relieve himself, I turned to Aristotle. "What should we do? The painting has to be ready before your cousin catches up with us. How long will it take?" "In truth, I'd say three years, but we hardly have three months. We'll just have to do our best." "But can we trust Luka? He's bound to put two and two together." I glanced at the ramshackle building. "First chance, he could phone someone. We know he needs the money." Aristotle replied, "As you say, it's a lot of money and he's desperate for a new truck. His engine could give up at any moment, and clearly his brakes are down to the metal. Let's tell him we're returning to Athens on the bus."'

'But I suspect you didn't actually return to Athens, Granny?'

'That's right, and a good job, too. The next day we learned they were gathering the last of the Jews in Athens and deporting them to Auschwitz. The war was on the turn and the Germans were frantic. Luka helped us on to the Athens bus with all our possessions, but we got off a few stops later at the Garden of Heroes, in Missolonghi.'

She sighed and placed a hand over her eyes. I wondered what she was trying to block.

'Are you tired, Granny?'

She nodded. 'Just talking about it's so exhausting. I need a rest now. Will you see that young man again today?'

'Do you think it's wrong of me? I miss Mark, but talking about art and history with somebody who has the same interests helps steady me a little.'

'But it makes you feel disloyal.' I nodded and Daphne smiled. 'It's not me you should ask, child, it's Mark. If he'd been here, would he mind?'

'Well, no, of course not. He would be with us.' I struggled to speak. 'Will it ever go away, this awful pain?'

'It will visit less often as time goes by. Your husband loved you. He wouldn't want you to isolate yourself like some nineteenth-century widow woman. Go, relax, talk about art and architecture. Enjoy yourself.'

40

DAPHNE

Western Greece, 1944

'CHANGE OF PLAN, LUKA. We're going home. We'll get the bus across the road and return to Athens. It's too difficult, all this running and hiding with the baby.'

Their host arrived with three bowls of *revíthia soupá* and a small loaf hacked into eight slices.

'Enjoy! Enjoy!' he shouted.

Two hours later, they waved at Luka from the back window of their bus.

* * *

Worry travelled with Daphne and Aristotle. Yánna sensed their disquiet and grizzled until she fell asleep.

'What are we going to do, Aristotle?' Daphne whispered. 'I have a bad feeling and it won't go away.'

'Me, too. I'm going to talk to the conductor.'

Daphne watched an elderly man sidle down the aisle with his ticket machine hanging from a strap around his neck.

'Where to?'

'Igoumenitsa,' Aristotle said.

'Igoumenitsa? You're on the wrong bus. We're heading in the opposite direction, towards Athens.'

Several passengers turned around to stare at them.

Daphne wailed, 'Oh, Yianni, what are we going to do? My father's waiting for us in Igoumenitsa, and Mama's so sick. What if we're too late?'

She started crying and crossing herself and calling on the Blessed Virgin's help.

The ticket collector appeared alarmed.

'Madam, Madam, we'll stop opposite the correct bus stop for Igoumenitsa. You'll be fine, I promise.'

Daphne continued with the dramatics, drawing attention away from Aristotle until the bus stopped outside the Garden of the Heroes.

'Cross the road for the Igoumenitsa bus,' the ticket collector said. 'Come, I'll help with your things.'

Aristotle knew her performance was to distract people from him. He kept his head down and his collar up.

When the ticket collector had unloaded the last bundle, Daphne slipped some coins into his hand and kissed his cheek.

'Thank you!' she cried.

Aristotle struggled to contain his smile when the man blushed and hurried back onto the bus. They watched the vehicle disappear into the distance before they took refuge in the Garden of the Heroes.

She nodded. 'Now what will we do?' They sat on a bench near Lord Byron's epitaph while Daphne fed Yánna. 'I think you're too recognisable. Can't you grow a beard and dye your hair black?'

He nodded. 'That's an idea. I'm thinking of changing our names, too. What do you think? Evert was pleased with his portrait. He said if I ever needed something, to tell him.'

'You think he'd organise documents for you?' Daphne thought for a moment. 'I've still got my papers for Daphne Papadopoulos, from before we were married. You could be Adonis

354

Papadopoulos, an older brother taking care of his widowed sister.' She smiled. 'We could disappear into the nearest town. Contact the chief of police in Athens, or find the local British liaison and ask them to organise fresh papers.'

'After Kalávryta, I hope I never meet another British agent as long as I live,' Aristotle said. 'No, I'll phone Evert, then get a job while we complete the painting and wait for it to dry.'

Daphne closed her eyes, pinched the bridge of her nose.

Alarmed to see her distressed, Aristotle slipped his arm around her shoulders.

'Come on, Daphne, don't be afraid. We've come through so much – we'll get around this somehow.'

'I know. It's just . . . Noah would have taken care of all this. He was so good at organising everyone's safety . . .' She sniffed again. 'Sorry.'

* * *

They walked into town and sat at a cafe in the square. When the pharmacy door flew open, a strip of golden light leaped across the flagstones like a welcome mat thrown towards them.

'Now's the time for a hair dye,' she said. 'I'll be back in five minutes.'

Daphne took Yánna into the shop and bought a dye.

'So, it's no wonder I have grey hairs already,' she said, ending her tale of woe to the chemist. 'Without my brother to help me, I don't know where I'd be.'

'You have somewhere to stay?' the man asked, 'My cousin has rooms to rent, just outside town, spotless and very cheap. You want? You just telephone her.'

He scribbled a number on the paper bag.

Aristotle glanced around, but saw no sign of soldiers checking papers. The sun hit the horizon and as it did, the temperature dropped, too. Daphne tugged Yánna's blanket over her head, but she boxed it away.

'Naughty girl,' Daphne said, smiling. 'She's such a determined little monkey, this one. Now behave yourself or I'm going to tell your daddy!' Hit by her own words, she glanced up into Aristotle's eyes. 'I don't know where that came from,' she explained, her eyes filling. 'I guess I say it in my dreams, and it just broke into real life.'

He kissed her forehead. 'I think it means you are accepting her as our child,' he said. 'Let me get your shawl.'

Aristotle rummaged in their bundle. She sat on a bench under a plane tree, shoulders hunched, wishing she had gloves.

Aristotle pulled the crocheted wrap free and draped it over her shoulders, tying it loosely over Yánna. He stepped back and stared at them, his eyes soft with love.

'What a beautiful composition. I wish I could paint you right now.'

* * *

By nightfall they had settled in a fisherman's cottage outside town, just off the Tourlida road. A few eucalyptus trees stood behind them, and a shallow bay with primitive fish farms and multicoloured fishing boats stretched out before them. Elegant boats were perfectly mirrored in the flat water. They had more of a large canoe shape than the traditional, chunky Greek caïque. The stone cottage they were renting was simple. Four distempered walls, a clay floor, a wood burner, and a bed. Two small windows and a blue door. The flat roof was bamboo layered over with half a metre of clay. Outside, a water pump stood at an old marble sink. The location was idyllic, surrounded by utter peace and tranquillity.

Their priority was the painting.

'Humidity will be a problem,' Aristotle told her. 'We must work at the side of the house with the greatest draught of air to dry the oil. Also, if we lay it in the sun each day, we can work on it more often.'

'So let's not waste an opportunity. You unpack the oils and canvas while I figure what we'll have to eat.' She remembered the pump out the back. 'There's a gas ring. If there's any gas, I'll make some coffee as soon as I find the *briki* in this bundle.'

She tugged at their balled-up belongings, pulling out blankets and clothes.

'Shouldn't I dye my hair first?'

'You'll have another day's growth by tomorrow morning, so do it then.'

She found the long-handled copper jug and pulled it from their possessions.

'You have a lot of intelligence for a woman.'

She swung around and smacked him firmly over the head with the coffee pot.

'You're right,' she said.

*   *   *

As spring blossomed into summer, they completed their portraits. Yánna had grown into a healthy infant and was a joy to them both. Somebody gave them an old coach pram, which they cleaned up. Each evening, as the sun turned towards the horizon, they promenaded with 'their' baby along the edge of the sea. The sky turned every shade of red, orange and yellow, and the sea, flat as black glass, reflected everything and silhouetted them as the perfect family. As the weeks passed, they were happier than ever. The vista of Missolonghi was an artist's dream, which they both absorbed. With great joy, they painted the sunrises and enjoyed the sunsets. In that magical light, it was impossible to see where reality ended and reflections began.

On one of these surreal evenings, Aristotle slipped his arm around Daphne's waist as they returned to the cottage.

'I guess it's time we made a move. I'll be sorry to leave this place.'

'Then why don't we stay until we have to leave? Please. Who knows, perhaps the war will end tomorrow.'

'Because it's better if we're on top of the situation, rather than always running and hiding. We've been lucky to be left in peace for so long, but the Axis might march in tomorrow. We're surrounded on three sides by a vast spread of water, so we'd have no escape.' He took her hands and lifted them to his mouth. 'I worry about you and Yánna every single day, my darling. The painting's ready. My papers have arrived from Athens, and I've earned a little money. Now, I have an urgent feeling – a premonition. It's time for Corfu.'

'But we've had only just recovered from all the heartbreak of Kalávryta and Aitoliko. I long to put down roots, now the painting's complete.'

'We have to age the portrait, dry it, and then move on. I know you'll want to leave this place spotless, so I can age the painting while you clean and pack . . . but only if you like.'

He lifted his hands defensively, glanced at the coffee pot and stepped back.

She laughed, and the tension between them lifted.

'We'd better get started, then. How will you age the painting? Can I age my portrait of you so that I learn the process?'

He grinned and kissed her on the cheek.

'Of course you can. It's the best way to learn.'

Aristotle lifted his paint-spattered cloth off the painting and they both stared at the new El Greco in revered silence.

'A picture of Christ at his death. Quite beautiful, isn't it?' He sighed. 'It's expressive, typical of his work. Death and immortality fascinated El Greco. Jesus is dead, but is he? His eyes are turned up, but is it that he's simply gazing at his father in Heaven?'

'I'd never have thought, but . . .'

'And although there's always an element of gloom in El Greco's work, there are also vibrant colours and intricate detail that won't allow us to wallow in misery.'

'You're changing my views. It's quite amazing, isn't it? Difficult to imagine that we painted it, my darling.'

'But now we must age it. It takes half a century for cracks to appear on a painting's surface. We have to make my cousin believe he's looking at something more than three hundred years old. The back of the canvas looks authentic, so let's get this last step started today.'

He placed the El Greco on his easel, and Daphne placed her portrait of Aristotle on her easel beside him. She watched him mix a varnish and add a pinch of burnt umber and then a little water.

'Oil-and water-based liquids applied to a painting together will crack as they dry,' he said, applying the mixture in long sweeping strokes with a wide brush. 'Here, you try it.'

He handed her the brush, which she loaded and used to spread the pale tea-coloured concoction over her portrait.

'Now we'll leave them to dry. Tomorrow, we'll apply a thin coat of umber to fill in the cracks, then wipe it off again. This will look like dirt, which is what we want. The following day, we'll finish with a final coat of varnish to protect everything.' He stood back and nodded. 'I'm pleased with it.'

Convincing his cousin that they themselves had been fooled was their ticket to freedom. Their lives depended on it.

'I'm pleased with my portrait of you,' Daphne said with a smile in her voice.

He turned away from his masterpiece to study her work.

'To be honest, it's not bad, Daphne.' He moved to her side and gave the painting his full attention for the first time. 'Now that I look at it properly, it's rather good. In my style, of course. But that's because you haven't painted many portraits and developed your own style.' He stroked his black dyed beard. 'OK, as your teacher, I'll award you nine-point-five for the painting.'

Her lip curled. 'What did I lose half a mark for?'

'Ha! Sleeping with the teacher to gain favour, and also sleeping with the model because he's a very handsome devil. Both are not allowed. You're lucky I don't disqualify you!'

'Oh, please, sir, please! Give me another chance to prove how artistic I can be.'

She shimmied her shoulders, her eyes half-closed and a pout on her lips.

He grinned. 'I'll need more persuading than that.'

41

DAPHNE

Corfu, 1944

ON THE FIRST OF JUNE, the von Stroop family caught the bus from Missolonghi to Igoumenitsa, then stood on the top deck of the Corfu ferry as it sailed past the city fort and into the castellated port.

'Let the rush go before we disembark,' Aristotle said.

They watched the bedlam below, knowing the ship wouldn't depart for another three hours. People tried to board with their boxes and bundles and crates of live chickens before everyone had disembarked. Handshaking and hugging took place on the gangway, halting traffic. The air hung heavy with the fumes of diesel and stink of sweat, and the unmistakable scent of the sea. Horns honked. Stevedores yelled '*Ela! Ela!*', twirling a hand in the air to guide truck drivers. Everyone shouted in the happy, frantic chaos, and it seemed every policeman on duty had swallowed his whistle.

'We made it, Aristotle!' Daphne said as they set foot on the quayside, swaying on their sea legs. 'We got here, and no sign of you-know-who.'

'Don't push fate, my darling. Now, let's sit on that bench while I read through the letter from Kyría Alice, telling us where to go.'

Daphne pulled the envelope from her pocket and glanced over the correspondence before she handed it to Aristotle.

My dearest friend, Daphne,

I rejoiced to get your last letter. I am also delighted that the three of you are safe and well.

I can imagine how you suffered when Aris joined the angels in Heaven. My heart was breaking for you. God has sent Yánna to ease your burden, but I imagine you are overwhelmed by the injustice.

I pray for you all.

On a lighter note, Corfu is a beautiful place, and I am sure you will find happiness. The island is special to me because I lived there for a long time, and it is the place I gave birth to my own son. My only boy, Philip, came into this world on the dining room table of Mon Repos, twenty-three years ago. Quite an entrance into this crazy world of ours. It is a beautiful house, but I fear it is used by the Axis now. However, in the grounds you'll find a small cottage hidden in the trees. It belongs to the municipality, but after a few telephone calls, I have secured it for you and Aristotle, in return for a portrait of the mayor of the island. Be aware that Mayor Kollas is a known collaborator. Be warned, he has many followers in Corfu. Do not trust even the friendliest people.

Here in Athens, little has changed. My trip to Sweden, to bring back medical supplies, was a great success.

I am sorry to say there is still no news from your family.

Write back and let me know how things are progressing.

All my best wishes, and may God be with you,

Your good friend,

Kyría Alice.

Aristotle took the letter from Daphne and read it for himself, then picked up their bundle.

'Come on, Daphne, let's get ourselves a coffee and see if we can find some help.'

Daphne followed him to a quayside cafe, wishing they still had the pram. Yánna was growing, and any day now Daphne would try her with a little solid food. She sipped her drink, enjoying the strong bitter coffee while Aristotle talked to the owner. Soon, he returned to her pavement table.

'If we can wait half an hour, the baker's van goes that way. He'll give us a lift to the gates.'

* * *

They squeezed into the bread van which, twenty minutes later, drove through wide gates and entered the tranquil parkland surrounding Mon Repos

'*Maláka!* I'll never get out of here now!'

'Ladies present!' Aristotle reprimanded.

'Sorry Kyría, sorry, all these trucks, I didn't have time to stop.'

Swept along a driveway between German army lorries, they soon found themselves outside the magnificent building that was once a royal residence and the home of Princess Alice. Tall marble columns, balconies and balustrades, curved steps and wide doors gave the property a sense of magnificence.

'This is Mon Repos, the residence,' the driver said.

Daphne gasped.

The driver continued. 'You want Mon Repos, the cottage, which is in the woods. Just follow that path through the trees for about two hundred metres.'

A hammering on the driver's door made them all jump.

'*Was willst du*?' A German soldier demanded.

'Leave this to me, I speak German,' Aristotle said, before turning to the guard.

'Good morning, sergeant. We head for the cottage of Mon Repos, which I believe is in the grounds, just down there.' He pointed down the path.

'By whose order?' The soldier waved a clipboard.

'Princess Alice of Greece and Denmark, and Major-General Jürgen Stroop of the SS. Unfortunately, our vehicle has broken down and this kind gentleman came to our help. He'll be out of your way the moment he's dropped us off. The kind man has bread to deliver.'

Daphne stared at the magnificent building, trying to imagine Kyría Alice, who always seemed so humble, living there as a royal princess.

The truck behind honked.

'Go, get out of our way!' the guard yelled. 'You're holding everything up.'

The delivery man crunched his gears and then bunny-hopped them onto a verge so the trucks could get past.

'Terrifying people,' he muttered. 'They shake me up. Here, out you get. Don't forget your bundles in the back. Bang on the door when you're done.'

Daphne had the strangest feeling as she approached the house, as if she'd arrived home. This odd emotion resonated through her, along with a great sense of relief. Standing in the dappled sunlight between the tall trees, she watched the goings-on at the palace while Aristotle took their belongings halfway down the path.

'Come on, I'll feel better away from this pandemonium. I wonder what's happening.'

'I've been watching them. All the trucks are delivering wooden crates that are taken through the front doors. I hope it's not bombs or ammunition.'

She waited under an ancient oak tree with their chattels while he continued to shift the bundles one by one, closer to the cottage. Recent rain had washed nature's dust away, and the wooded area had a fragrance of moss and compost and traces of spring wild flowers.

'Nearly there. You're going to love it!' he said when he returned wearing a wide smile.

They walked together, Daphne carrying the baby and Aristotle with the last bundles. Mature trees arched over the path, letting dappled light into the tunnel of foliage. Their cool, fresh surroundings were very welcome. Colourful wild flowers clustered in the abandoned parkland, and the air trilled with birdsong.

'It's a dream,' Daphne whispered, staring up at the tallest trees she had ever seen. 'Such a sense of peace.'

The path turned. As they walked around the bend, she gasped.

'Stop for a moment, please,' she said, staring at the abandoned building. 'I want to take it in and remember this moment for the rest of my life.'

Aristotle sighed and grinned. 'You're such a romantic fool, my darling. You'll probably be painting it before the week's out.'

She grinned at him, her heart brimming. 'Isn't this bliss, Aristotle?'

The peeling, whitewashed house had an unusual covered entrance with a pointed finial on its slate roof.

'It's so charming,' she whispered. 'As if it's come out of a fairy tale.' She had Yánna over her shoulder, and patted the restless child's back. 'All right, I'll feed you just now, baby girl.'

Aristotle disappeared inside and returned with a chair, which he placed under a fir tree that stood opposite the house.

'Feed the baby while I take our stuff inside.'

Once Yánna had settled, Daphne turned to the house. A four-metre square block to the left appeared to be two storeys high. An ornate, bright green gloss-painted front door completed the scene. To the right of this structure, a single-storey extension displayed two fancy louvre-shuttered windows divided by a tall chimney. At the very end of the extension, a small lean-to might be a bathroom.

Aristotle came out of the front door, a great smile across his face.

'Come on, then, let's get you inside.'

* * *

The following week passed in peace. Their only misgiving was that the Germans had taken over Mon Repos, only two hundred metres away from the cottage.

'Look, the back is almost surrounded by vegetation. We'll make a nice place to sit outside and keep ourselves to ourselves, all right?' Aristotle offered. 'Just one thing, I need to dye my hair again. I have a light stripe. For the moment, I can tie a *mandili* around my head, like a Cretan, or wear a cap.'

'I'll get a dye tomorrow. Also, I thought we should get Yánna baptised, you know – it would be safer for us all if she had a baptismal certificate.'

'Good plan. I'll talk to the priest.'

The next morning, Aristotle went down to the village to drink coffee. Daphne worried when he wasn't home for lunch, but when he still hadn't returned by six o'clock, she was out of her mind.

'Where've you been?' She peered into his face to see if he was drunk.

'Sorry.' He wrapped his arms around her. 'There's new information – been coming in all day.'

She pushed him away, anxious.

'Come on, then, let's hear it.' She peered into his eyes, fearing the worst.

He reached inside his jacket, pulled out a bottle of wine, and thrust it at her.

'It's a peace offering. Sorry it's not flowers and chocolates, but it's the best I could do.' He dropped onto a chair, gave her bottom a friendly slap, and said, 'Bring us a couple of glasses, beautiful.'

'Cheeky!' she warned, relief in her voice now.

He pulled the cork from the bottle with his teeth, then poured them both a tumbler of the local plonk.

She put some olives in a bowl, then peeled a couple of boiled eggs.

'Come on, then, tell me everything.'

She glanced at Yánna, hoping she'd sleep a little longer. The fire had been lit all day, heating water and cooking food, so now they all felt a little drowsy in the warm room.

'First, the good news. I have a job – a portrait of the bishop. I hope this will bring in more work, and also bring my cousin to Corfu for the El Greco.'

'I'm dreading that part.' She cut the eggs into quarters, sprinkled them with salt, oregano and black pepper, then drizzled a little olive oil over the top. 'Eat, eat!' she said, and they exchanged a smile, remembering Bacchus and his ramshackle ouzeria. She lifted a fresh baked loaf out of a nook in the chimney. 'That's perfect,' she said, knocking the crust with her knuckle to hear a hollow sound that told her it was done.

'I learned that the Germans have shut down the Jewish school and put restrictive measures into effect. A few weeks ago, Oberst Emil Jäger said—'

'Stop! Who's that? Who are you talking about now?'

'Sorry . . . he's the German in charge of Corfu. Jäger's a member of Hitler's Nazi Party, who became Territorial Commander of the island earlier this year. I can't quite make him out. The gossip is, he told his high command that expelling the Jews from Corfu to the Polish work camps wasn't possible.'

'Polish work camps?'

Aristotle nodded. 'He says it's because the Red Cross are stationed here. Come to think of it, that's right. There was a Red Cross ship in the harbour when we arrived, remember?'

'How would I know?'

'Big red cross on the side – doh!' He crossed his eyes.

'No need to be rude.' She wagged a finger at him.

He grinned and pulled her onto his lap.

'Anyway, this Jäger, who's from Austria like my ancestors, claimed the locals might object if they rounded the Jews up like sheep.'

'Did anyone object before?' she said. 'In Thessaloníki, or Athens?'

'No, true. Don't let them fool you, this is a divided island. They say more than half the Greek officials running the island are Nazi collaborators, as Kyría Alice warned us in her letter. On the other hand, they say many locals are hiding Jews.'

Yánna woke and made it clear she was hungry. Daphne nursed her and then gave her a little mashed, boiled rice.

'She's always hungry, aren't you, my little babushka?' Yánna gurgled, grabbed a handful of Daphne's hair and tugged. 'Ouch! You little piggy. She's got two teeth now, Daddy, so she'll eat us out of house and home.'

Yánna gurgled, displaying her new teeth.

Aristotle laughed and filled Daphne's glass again.

'Come to bed,' he whispered, nuzzling her neck.

*   *   *

Three days later, Aristotle left home to work on his painting in the mayor's office. Yánna lay in yet another borrowed pram in a shady space behind the house. Daphne fed laundry through a mangle while she hummed a song her mother used to sing to Elizabeth. She stopped suddenly, realising she must learn some nursery songs that weren't Jewish, for everyone's sake. The washing seemed whiter than usual, the sky bluer, and the birds more vocal. A feeling of contentment settled over her, broken when a bomber skimmed the treetops, taking the air from Daphne's lungs.

The air vibrated when the plane's payload of bombs and malice fell to the ground. In a moment, the earth exploded around her. She snatched Yánna from the pram, dived indoors, and holding the baby against her body, she used her hips to drive the heavy olive-wood dining table against the walls. She scrambled underneath, then tried to pacify her screaming child.

'It's all right, we'll be OK,' she soothed, while ratcheting herself and Yánna into the corner.

Another low grumble grew unbearably loud as a second bomber roared overhead. What was happening? She closed her eyes and had a flashback to the moment she had looked up, outside. Yes . . . it was a British plane!

What was going on. Why were the Allies bombing them? Was Aristotle safe? She wished she could go outside and see what was happening, but she couldn't leave Yánna, who had screamed herself to sleep in Daphne's arms.

After an hour of peace, Daphne shuffled from her corner and ventured outside. She lowered her sleeping baby into the Silver Cross and eased the hood up to shade her face. Oh, the relief! Only now did she allow herself to inspect the place for damage. The bomb sounded as though it had exploded right outside, but it hadn't. She got on with the laundry, her ears alert for the sound of another plane, and her eyes roaming the sky every few minutes.

An hour later, Aristotle returned home, calling her name, racing around the house when she wasn't to be found inside.

'Are you all right? When they said a bomb had dropped near Mon Repos I was out of my mind with worry.'

'We're fine, just had a fright. What happened? I can't believe it was a British plane.'

'There's a lot of talk going on. The Germans have been on alert all afternoon. It's rumoured that the British are about to invade Greece.'

'You mean we'll be liberated?' She choked on the words, hysterical tears of joy rising. 'My family, reunited? Isaac would come home? Oh, Aristotle!'

She fell against his chest and clutched the little locket that hung from her neck. He held her against his heart and kissed the top of her head.

'We hope so, Daphne. We hope so.'

* * *

Twenty-four hours later, their hopes were dashed.

'They just can't help it,' Aristotle said. 'It's as if I'm not there at all. While I'm painting, they talk, and talk, and talk. Sometimes they apologise. I say, "Do whatever relaxes you, because every tense muscle will show in your face. After all, you only have to see a woman's face to know her shoes are killing her, isn't that so?" Anyway, I tell them I'm oblivious to anything they say when I'm concentrating on a portrait.'

'So, what did you hear today?' Daphne asked, dishing up a small portion of stewed lamb with little onions swimming in spicy tomato sauce.

Aristotle put down his fork and spoon and stared into space.

'They're rounding up the Jews tomorrow . . . and the Maltese Catholics, and anyone suspected of being homosexual, and anyone deformed or mentally retarded, regardless of age or gender.'

Daphne's eyes widened as her hand slid over her mouth.

'We have to warn people!' she cried after a moment of shocked silence.

'We can't do anything. I'm not risking your life, or Yánna's life, to save a stranger. I love you both too much for that.' He stared at his food. 'They've been warned by the underground, Daphne, and some have gone up into the mountains. But like your father and the people of Kalávryta, many refuse to believe anything bad will happen to them because they've done nothing wrong. To be exact, they believe in justice but there's no justice in war.'

42

FLORA

Corfu, present day

'IT'S HARD BEING BLIND AGAIN, Flora, but the optician was so generous, lending us those splendiferous glasses for the weekend.' She slid her hand along the table until it rested on the pebble. 'I lost my sight gradually, over the span of half a century, hour by hour, day by day, so I hardly noticed. But to be given the glorious gift of sight, and have it taken away three days later, feels very harsh.'

'You remind me not to take the marvellous gifts of sight for granted, Granny.'

I patted the back of her hand, wondering if her condition was hereditary. Would I go blind? I stared at my palette of acrylic colours, took a little brown and darkened it with black.

'I'm adding detail to Aristotle's eyebrows. They're a good shape for a man, aren't they? Big and strong, but still well defined.'

'It was his eyes that got me, dear girl. I could barely look into them when I first started my art lessons as a child. I didn't realise it was because I would fall so completely in love with him. However, not being able to see helps me concentrate on my story, and when I get my new glasses, I'll appreciate them all the more.' She sighed, then uttered a little whimper.

'Are you all right, Granny?'

'It's an odd thing, but when I was blind, I accepted my family had gone, that I would never see them again. But now, I'm peering in everyone's face, hoping to recognise somebody from the past. Anybody. Isn't that crazy? I'm ninety-nine – of course they're all dead and gone.' She sighed again. 'It's been so long to be alone. Yet still I have this secret dream of coming across Isaac, or Elizabeth. I lost touch with them all, you understand. Who knows if they even made it to Australia? But I like to think they did.'

'I'm going to turn my phone on to record, Granny, then we can crack on.'

'Crack on? I like it.' She grinned at the new expression. Her grasp of English was excellent, but she loved using new words and expressions, especially when she hadn't heard them before. 'I was very naive, Flora. When Aristotle said they were rounding up the Corfu Jews the next day, you can't imagine what I asked him.' She put her hand over her mouth and shook her head.

Silence stretched out as Daphne sank into her memories.

'No. What did you ask him, Granny?'

She bit down on her lip and pinched the bridge of her nose for a moment before she spoke again.

'I peered right into my husband's eyes, searching for the truth. He understood my heart was both breaking and bursting with hope. "Oh, Aristotle, could I write a letter to Isaac and give it to somebody? Would they be able to find my brother in the work camp?" I asked.' She drew in a shaky breath.

'That's so sad, Granny.'

'I didn't realise how bad things were. There were hints that the Jews wouldn't be coming back, but like most of my race, I put it down to hurtful gossip and refused to accept it. By this time, many of the Germans knew of the Holocaust, and lots of the Greeks suspected, too. I believe the Allies knew, but they all had their own problems, so, for whatever reasons, they kept quiet about the Nazi death camps, and allowed many millions of people to be murdered. I guess all the resources they had were being used to fight the war – to free Europe from the Axis.'

'It's difficult to imagine how a world war could happen, isn't it? What did Aristotle say about the letter?'

'Well, he loved me, and I guess my question broke his heart, so he tried to protect me from further hurt. "Write the letter and I'll take it to work with me tomorrow morning and give it to somebody," he promised.'

Daphne lifted the little gold locket from her neck and kissed it.

'I can still remember what I wrote . . . "Dear Isaac, I hope you are well. I kiss the locket that contains that special feather and think about you every day . . ."' Her chest jerked with a sob. 'When I first glimpsed pictures from Auschwitz in the papers, those starved, naked men, with their ribs sticking out and their heads shaved for . . . what? I searched their faces . . . Is that Isaac . . .? No, is that one Isaac . . .? But they were so emaciated that I couldn't tell. I couldn't identify my brother, and that made me ashamed . . . Still, I convince myself I was mistaken. If I caught sight of Isaac, surely I would recognise him instantly . . . so I keep looking into the faces of strangers, like every other Jewish survivor of the Holocaust.'

She'd told me this before – about looking into the faces of strangers – but I hadn't the heart to remind her. Tears tripped down her face.

'Please, Granny, it's all right. You don't have to say more. Whether Isaac got the letter or not, he'd have known you held him in your thoughts every day. I'll bet he had lots of imaginary conversations with you when times were hard. You will have been a great comfort to him, I'm certain.'

'Oh, I hope so, Flora. You can't imagine . . . but let's move on. Aristotle told me he'd heard his cousin was on the island.

I remember my heart racing. "We need to be organised," I said. "We should do what Papa did. Hang the painting with another picture over the top.'"

'Good plan,' I said.

'Aristotle glanced at my portrait of him. "Don't even consider it!" I said. "It's my best work. Cut one of my sunsets from Missolonghi down to size and slide it over the top." He did. "We need to get our story straight. He's going to ask why you were trying to sell the painting?" In the end, we decided to say we wanted to set up an art school for the underprivileged in Athens.'

'What about the bombing?' I asked. 'Did you find out what was going on?'

'Well, not immediately. It was all rather confusing because nobody seemed to have the facts. But a few months later, we discovered it was a diversion to keep the German planes on the tarmac in Greece, where they were. The Allies launched the Normandy Landings the very next day, which led to the end of the war in Europe a year later. Still, it was too late to save almost two thousand Corfiot Jews who were rounded up the following morning.'

'What an awful time, Granny.'

She looked up into the branches of the fir tree and stopped talking for a moment.

'They say you never forget the things you're doing when catastrophe strikes,' she said, 'and I'm sure it's true. I was mending some baby clothes given to me for Yánna. A bucket of fresh water stood by the fireplace, ready for me to wash them. The clothes horse was full of washing in front of the fire. It was a windy day, and I didn't want the washing to get dusty.'

She smiled to herself. 'All those nappies to wash! At about five o'clock, Vangelis, a Mon Repos gardener we'd become friends with, came tearing into the house. "There's a gang of Nazis heading this way! They look like trouble. Thought you should be warned." He disappeared out the back door. My instinct was to grab Yánna and run. Get as far away from the park as possible. But we couldn't run forever. I knew the time had come to face Jürgen Stroop.'

'You must have been terrified, all alone.'

'You can't imagine. I realised, unlike every Greek house I had ever been in, there was nothing religious on display. No crucifix, no icons, no flickering oil lamp before a religious statue. What a stupid mistake! There'd been a crucifix over the bed when we moved in. Please understand, I respect that this image means a lot to many people. But seeing that barbaric effigy of a human corpse nailed to a piece of wood always made me feel ill, so I'd taken it down. Now I wondered where I'd put it.

'As if sensing my distress, Yánna started yelling, and at seven months, she had quite a voice. "Hush your squealing, little piglet!" I called down the stairs. "Crucifix, crucifix, where are you?" I muttered. "Chest of drawers, bottom drawer." I yanked it open. "Yes!" Downstairs, I peered around the room. One empty nail over the fireplace beckoned me. That would have to do. Yánna continued to yell, so I picked her up. Someone hammered on the door. This was it! I snatched a chunk of stale bread from the kitchen and offered it to my baby girl. Thankfully, she decided it tasted better than her own fist. The hammering continued. "I'm coming!" I shouted, and opened the door. "Sorry, I was feeding the baby," I said, fumbling with the top button of my dress. The three German soldiers glanced at my rather full breasts.'

Daphne laid a hand on her flat chest and stared into the distance.

'My goodness, it was difficult to hide my fear, and now I feel quite exhausted, Flora. Would you mind if we continued with this tomorrow?'

I turned my phone off. 'Whenever you want, darling Granny. Let me take you inside for a nap.'

* * *

'I'm not looking for a relationship, and I believe you're not either,' Spiros said when I met him in the café-bar that evening. 'But I must tell you, I'm delighted to hear you're staying another week.'

I smiled. 'Unfinished business, Spiro. I have Grandfather Aristotle's portrait to finish, my first commission as a forger of art.'

He laughed.

'Besides,' I continued, 'I'm curious to find out what's in the basement of Mon Repos. What's the plan with that?'

He took a deep breath and nodded. 'I'm curious, too. We have our most experienced civil engineer coming from Athens tomorrow, so I'll pick his brains.'

'Sorry, I forgot to quiz Daphne. She seems a little confused about it all. She's been talking about the Holocaust – such tragedy.'

'A terrible time. Have you eaten? We could go somewhere.'

'To be honest, I'm quite happy with a gin and tonic and a packet of crisps,' I said, noticing a small band setting up in the corner.

He grinned like a mischievous boy. 'Cheap date, I guess.'

* * *

At two in the morning, giggling like teenagers, we arrived at my hotel room.

'I had such a good evening, thank you,' I said, three large gins and a bit of a dance later. 'I can't remember the last time—'

Spiros leaned in and kissed me gently on the lips.

'I thank you. I haven't enjoyed myself so much since . . .' He stared at the carpet. 'It's great to have your company, yet not feel unfaithful to the memory of Melody.'

'It still hurts?' I asked. He nodded. 'So, you'll understand why I can't ask you in?'

'Of course. I wouldn't expect you to. You have your own demons. So, I'll bid you goodnight and hope we can meet tomorrow with more news about the cellar.'

He leaned in and kissed me just a fraction harder, just a moment longer.

'Goodnight, and thank you.'

I swiped my card and closed the door behind me without looking back.

* * *

'You're late this morning, Flora. Is everything all right?' Yánna asked.

'Yes, everything's fine. I overslept and missed breakfast, so I picked up some doughnuts on the way here. Is Granny having a nap?'

'I'm sure she'll wake any minute now. Give me those. I'll put them on a plate and make coffee while you sort your painting things out.'

'Do you have any idea why she wants two identical pictures of my grandfather, Yánna?'

'None at all. I can't imagine, but I'm sure she will tell us in the end. Perhaps she wants to gift one to you.'

'Or to you? That would be nice. How well did you know Aristotle?'

'He was my father, and I loved him dearly. She has told you how they saved me, yes?' I nodded. 'I was fifteen years old when they explain me the story of Kalávryta.' She stared at the sky and shook her head. 'I went crazy. All my life had been a lie. My parents, who I never knew, were murdered . . . dead and buried on some mountain in the Peloponnese. Aristotle and Daphne were imposters.' She exhaled. 'I felt so alone, so angry. I went a little crazy, stole Daphne's savings, and ran away.'

43

DAPHNE

Corfu, 1944

ALL THREE SOLDIERS WORE GREY uniforms and highly polished knee-length jackboots. Two stood slightly behind the central figure, whose uniform, adorned with braid, stripes and pips, made his authority clear: Jürgen Stroop, the major-general of their worst nightmares. Behind the three soldiers stood two men in smart civilian dress; each one carried an attaché case.

'You know who I am?' the central figure said coldly.

Daphne lifted Yánna over her shoulder and patted her back. She shook her head and spoke to him in German.

'Sorry, no, but if you want your portrait painted, I must warn you there's a queue. Besides, my husband is in town at this moment, painting Mayor Kollas' picture. He'll be home in the next hour, if you'd like to come back.' She peered over their shoulders, looking worried. 'Shall I make you an appointment for you to see him tomorrow morning?'

Aristotle's voice came from behind.

'No need to make an appointment. What's going on?'

Everyone turned to look his way.

'Jürgen! What a surprise.' He marched through them and stood at Daphne's side. 'Daphne, meet my cousin, Jürgen. Jürgen, this is my wife, Daphne Papadopoulos, and my daughter, Yánna. Come on in.'

'A pleasure to meet you at last. My husband talks about you often,' Daphne said, hoping her smile wasn't too icy. 'I'm afraid you caught me in the middle of my laundry.'

Jürgen shook his head. 'This isn't a social visit. I've come for the El Greco. I'll give you a fair price once it's authenticated.'

'I don't want to sell it, Aristotle,' Daphne cried, turning to Jürgen. 'It's been in my family for generations. It belonged to my ancestors and I know it's very old, a family treasure that I would like to hand down to our first-born son.' She turned to Jürgen. 'I'm sure you understand. You can't have the painting, it's not for sale.'

Jürgen glared at her, clearly not used to being refused anything. He was almost as frightening when he burst out laughing.

'Kyría, nobody says "No" to me!' he yelled.

His companions joined in the guffaws.

Startled, Yánna whimpered so Daphne held the baby on her hip and continued with her performance, crossing herself three times, as Kyría Alice had taught her so long ago.

'I'm sorry, but there's a first time for everything. I would really like to help you, but my grandfather would turn in his grave.'

'And where is that grave?' Jürgen demanded.

'S-s . . .' She nearly said 'Spain', where most of the Athenian Jews had originated from, but then he would have guessed her true nationality. 'Smyrna,' she said. 'They killed him when he fought for Greece in '22.'

'Where's the El Greco?'

As Daphne opened her mouth, Aristotle cut in.

'We have to give it to him, darling. He'll give us a fair price, and we can still use the money to set up the school.' He turned to his cousin. 'We want to set up an art school for the poor in Athens. It's Daphne's dream.'

381

Daphne stared at him. 'But I don't want to,' she said, seating Yánna in her pram before she folded the laundry on the clothes-maiden.

'We don't have a choice, Daphne!' Aristotle was angry now. He turned to his cousin again. 'She can be stubborn!'

Jürgen addressed his men.

He turned to Daphne's husband. 'Aristotle, you're my cousin. We've never been close, but I don't want you harmed. Still, one way or another, we will find the El Greco.' He turned to stare at Daphne, then at Yánna, his eyes, glittering ice, darkened with malevolence. 'We have methods, they're not "nice". Could you bear to see your wife and your daughter tortured and disfigured in the most horrible way, screaming for the release that death would bring?' He snatched Daphne's chin in his leather glove and turned her face left and right. 'Such a pity to destroy this beauty.' He squeezed hard, knowing he hurt her, his eyes narrowing with pleasure. 'And what about the baby?'

Daphne gasped with pain. He applied even more pressure to her jaw, and she feared it would dislocate. Hatred sparked in his eyes. Did he sense she was Jewish? Again, he turned her head this way and that, his face intense with scrutiny.

'You have the appearance of . . .' He pushed back slightly and let go of her. She had never felt such fear or sensed such unbridled evil. 'Check her papers,' he said to one soldier. 'If she's a Jew, kill her.' He held her gaze, lifted his right hand with thumb raised and index finger pointing at Daphne's temple. 'Boom!' he said.

'I'm not Jewish!' Daphne cried.

Jürgen smiled slowly. His small, white teeth appeared too sharp for a human, more suited to a fast predator that fed on others. A piranha.

Aristotle slipped his arm around her shoulders and held her protectively.

Jürgen smirked.

'Leave her alone, cousin!' Aristotle said. 'She's not a Jew.' He turned to Daphne. 'I can't let him hurt you,' he whispered, stroking the side of her face, which was already starting to bruise. He turned back to Jürgen. 'You bastard! You couldn't leave us alone, could you? It's behind the sunset.'

He nodded at the painting of Missolonghi opposite the window.

Jürgen didn't move, didn't break eye contact with Daphne. He continued to stare into her face as his lips curled. 'Very good.'

Her stomach clenched and her chest tightened as he unhurriedly lifted a tendril of hair away from her face and pushed it over her shoulder. His hand slid down her back, out of Aristotle's view, and slid over the curve of her buttocks and then between her thighs. It took all her strength not to shudder. She stretched her neck arrogantly.

'I'm not Jewish, but I am married to your cousin, which makes us family, sir. Now if you'll excuse me, a nappy change is required here.' She jigged Yánna on her hip then took her over to the pram and set about changing her nappy.

'Spunky woman, Aristotle, well done!' Jürgen's smile widened. 'I like her!' He called two names, and the men with the brown leather bags came inside. Aristotle's cousin lifted the sunset down and told his experts to check its authenticity. They detached the painting from its frame and removed the sunset. They all stared in silence at the painting.

'Magnificent,' Jürgen muttered. 'It had better be the real thing, because if you're trying to cheat me, I'll kill you both – and the child.'

One man took a magnifying glass to El Greco's long signature that ran the width of the painting: Δομήνικος Θεοτοκόπουλος, the artist's real name, followed by the word Κρής, which they both knew meant 'Cretan'.

'The signature seems genuine,' the man with the magnifying glass said.

'Of course it's genuine. My ancestor bought it from El Greco's father in the village of Fodele. That's where they lived, in Crete.'

Aristotle and Daphne shared a thought: *What if the men claimed the painting was genuine?*

One man tipped the canvas over and tapped the back with his nail.

'It sounds genuine. I'll test a varnish sample.'

He withdrew a fine scalpel from his bag and scraped a little varnish from an area that would be under the frame. Major-General Jürgen Stroop squared his shoulders and nodded.

Aristotle's cousin was not a big man, but he exuded an aura of evil. Daphne's nerves jangled. She had heard of Jürgen Stroop's unpredictable disposition – that he could explode at any moment.

'I'm going to put the baby outside for some fresh air,' she said, clipping Yánna's baby-harness into loops inside the coach-pram. 'These fumes are no good for a baby.'

The child had become so active, she gave her another chunk of bread, praying she wouldn't choke on it.

When she returned, both scientists were examining minute varnish samples. One of them huffed and shook his head.

Aristotle's cousin took a step forward.

'What?'

The two men muttered at each other. Both took a sample of the paint.

'Soft,' one of them said, peering through his magnifying glass at the craquelure again. The other took a white rag, tipped turpentine onto it, and dabbed at the signature.

'Look,' he said to his colleague, showing the patch of burnt umber he had rubbed off the painting.

'Well?' Jürgen asked his experts.

They shook their heads.

'Nearly fooled us,' one said. 'I'd say they've painted this in the last fifty years. It's very good – a copy of an original, I'd say.'

'No, you're wrong!' Daphne cried. 'My father kept this painting hidden in his safe. He claimed it would make us millionaires one day. Would he do that for a fake? I know it's genuine.'

The two scientists shook their heads. One spoke.

'Definitely a modern work.' He scraped his fingernail down the face of Christ and stared at the wedge of paint under his nail. 'Clearly, this is nowhere near a four-hundred-year-old painting. In fact, I doubt it's a forty-year-old painting.'

Jürgen roared and glared at Aristotle. 'After all that, you tried to cheat me!'

'No, I'm a hundred per cent sure it's genuine!' Aristotle replied.

'Well, we'll see.'

Jürgen's fury exploded. He picked up the painting and hurled it into the fire.

Aristotle gagged. 'No! The El Greco!' he screamed, pushing one scientist so fiercely that he dropped the bottle of turpentine on the table. The highly-flammable liquid splashed over Aristotle's sleeves.

'No!' Aristotle cried again, reaching into the fire for the blazing picture.

The soft oil paint, where swabs of turpentine had soaked into the canvas, exploded into flames. Oil paint melted on Aristotle's skin, where it continued to burn like tar on his flesh. Helped by the turpentine, his sleeves caught alight and blazed towards his elbows. His beard and hair caught next.

Daphne screamed, 'My husband's on fire!' She tried to lift the metal bucket of laundry water, but it was too heavy. Screaming, 'Help me!' she hauled a soaking baby blanket out of the washing and threw it over him.

Aristotle felt nothing. All he could think was that the priceless El Greco lay under the fake. His beard and hair had shrivelled back. The skin on his hands and arms blistered, but his real agony was to see a great masterpiece burn before his eyes.

Major-General Jürgen Stroop watched his cousin crouching in the hearth, inflamed.

'Clearly, he genuinely believed he had an El Greco there. Look at him. Punishment enough.' He laughed. 'Let's go.'

The men turned and walked away.

'Aristotle!' Daphne cried. 'Aristotle!' She pulled on his shoulders, causing him to lose his balance and fall back. She dragged the bucket of water next to him and plunged his hands into it. 'Oh, Aristotle, you're so badly burned!'

The gardener burst into the room.

'Are you all right?' he cried. 'I saw them go. My God! What's going on?'

They tried to pull Aristotle onto the sofa, but he seemed strangely unbalanced, his face oddly contorted, and his arm and leg not working at all.

'He's having a stroke,' the gardener said. 'My father had one. He was exactly the same when it happened. We need a doctor right away! You stay with him. I'll run to the mansion and call an ambulance.'

* * *

For the first month, Daphne struggled to take care of Aristotle and Yánna. Some burns on Aristotle's hands were very severe, and the paralysis of his left arm and leg made it impossible to walk, never mind paint. His recovery was slow, and it was doubtful he would ever have full use of his left side again. The irony was that, although they were running out of money, Aristotle's fame as a portrait painter had spread through Greece.

Yánna grew into a healthy toddler and gave them a great deal of pleasure. Daphne continued to paint with Aristotle's guidance, until one day, she came rushing out of the house and fell at his feet under the fir tree, where he sat in his wheelchair.

'I have a marvellous idea!' she cried.

'That can only mean trouble,' Aristotle slurred, one side of his mouth turning up with a smile while he tried to squeeze a rubber ball in his left hand for exercise.

'I received another letter from the mayor. When can you finish his portrait?'

'Daphne, it's never going to happen,' Aristotle said. 'I can't even hold a paintbrush.'

'No, you can't, my darling, but I can.'

'You know that, unlike me, they have no reverence for female painters in Greece.'

'I know – we're only good for housekeeping and laying under our men.' She inspected his chin. 'These burns have almost completely healed now. I'll be able to give you a shave in a week or two. By the way, I wrote to Kyría Alice and told her everything.'

Aristotle's eyes widened. 'Everything?'

'Almost everything. I left out the details about painting a copy of our Cretan friend. You know?' Neither of them mentioned the El Greco by name. It was gone, and that was the end of it. 'She's sending a nurse to help me take care of you.'

I'm pregnant, I'm pregnant, I'm pregnant, Daphne sang in her head. She didn't say anything because this could not have happened at a worse time.

'We don't have the money to feed another mouth, Daphne, let alone pay a nurse.'

'No, don't worry, my darling. I told you, I have an amazing idea.'

'Oh God, why do I always feel afraid when you say those words?'

'I've been studying the light in the big room, so here's my plan. We take the shutters off to let maximum light inside and build a low dais for our model. The model must keep his head turned to the right. We set your easel and paints in the middle of the room, with a comfortable chair for you, of course.'

'I can't hold a paintbrush, Daphne,' he said impatiently.

'Wait! Listen. Trust me.'

'All right, go on.'

'Behind you, we hang a big, heavy white curtain to reflect the light back towards the windows, all right?' He nodded. 'You pretend to paint with your right hand.'

'Oh no! I think I know where this is going.'

She ignored him and continued. 'The model may not see the portrait until it's finished, but here's the genius. Behind the big white curtain, I sit with my easel and canvas and paint the portrait. When the sitter has gone, you can instruct me on how I can improve it.'

He sat there, staring at her as if she were mad, but after a moment, he started laughing.

'Where do you get these crazy ideas? I love you . . . but it's crazy!'

'Don't you think it's a good idea?'

Yánna sat on her hip, so Daphne jigged her about, keeping her quiet.

'Daphne, it would never work!'

Certain that it would, she felt a little indignant.

'Why not?'

'Da-da!' Yánna said, before blowing a raspberry into her palm and giving Daphne a hefty slap on her cheek.

'Ow! Little piglet! Did our daughter just say "Daddy" or "Daphne"?'

'I think she said "Daddy". In fact, I'm pretty sure.' He gave a lopsided grin. 'To get back to your plan . . . where will we get white curtains that size, and how much will they cost?'

'Ha – I've got them already.' She couldn't keep the triumph out of her voice. 'I think they're from the big house, but anyway, I found them under the mattress. There's a few rusty bedspring marks, but they'll do the job.'

Aristotle sighed noisily. 'Who's going to fit them to the ceiling? I can't.'

Perplexed, she scratched her head, then brightened.

'I know – the gardener, in return for a portrait. If he doesn't suspect what we're doing, we know we can go ahead with the mayor – and future clients.'

'You are completely bonkers, but if it will make you happy, I'll give it a go.'

* * *

It took them a week to set the studio up, followed by another week in which to paint the gardener's portrait. At first, the man kept turning towards Aristotle when he spoke, but they got around this problem by hanging a mirror on the adjacent wall, so he talked to his own reflection. The exercise went well, so they contacted the mayor.

Daphne greeted Mayor Kollas, offered him coffee, and told him she would be right behind the curtain getting on with the painting exercise her husband had set her, because she wanted to be an artist, too.

'If you need anything, sir, just call out,' she told him.

Daphne used the same technique as Aristotle. She painted an accurate likeness, but used the light to flatter her model's features, producing a most pleasing portrait. Once again, they succeeded in their deception and, under Aristotle's guidance, Daphne's skills improved with each painting.

Soon, they could afford a few luxuries like a new mattress, and a babysitter. The gardener's wife took Yánna for a long walk and kept her for the afternoons when Daphne painted. Aristotle's health continued to improve, and, for a time, they were happy.

44

FLORA

Corfu, present day

'You're saying that all the paintings after 1944, by Avon Stroop, are in fact by you, Granny?'

'Yes, that's what I'm telling you. What you do with the information is up to you. My darling Aristotle would never paint again, although he was still a genius. I became his hands. It's as simple as that. He showed me how to improve every painting I did on his behalf, and everyone was delighted with their portrait.'

My phone pinged as my new travel details and confirmation came through.

'Right, I hope you'll be pleased when I tell you I have another week, Granny. Are you up to it?'

She nodded, gave me a gentle smile, then patted my hand.

'Thank you. You being here a little longer takes the pressure off me. I'm finding all these emotional moments quite draining. I buried them so long ago, and I still have a lot to tell you, so we'd better *crack on*, Flora.'

She smiled, pleased to have expanded her English with a colloquialism, but then she half-closed her eyes and rolled her head a little.

'Are you getting tired, Granny? We can stop for a break if you like. Don't forget, we've a big day tomorrow. Your marvellous new glasses will be ready, so we'll have a pleasant lunch while we're out. Also, I've moved into a smaller place for the rest of my time in Corfu. I've got a simple room just up the road. Silly to be in an all-inclusive when I'm only there to sleep most days. I only had the grand hotel because we booked it before the pandemic, three years ago now, so it just got carried over.' I thought back. 'So much has changed. Money wasn't a problem back then. Mark and I worked hard and played hard. At least we had that wonderful time together.'

'And now? You're struggling a bit, Flora?'

I shrugged and blurted out the facts.

'Just a bit, to be honest. The bank repossessed the house. Mark's illness wiped out our reserves, and there was little work for me through the pandemic, with the galleries being closed. I'm not sure what I'm going to do, Granny.' I took a deep breath and sniffed back tears. 'Sorry, I didn't mean to burden you with my problems. Of course I'll manage. I'm going to ask the gallery for a contract, then I can get a mortgage and keep my house. Everything will sort itself out. If it doesn't, I'm moving into a little flat in town. I'll soon be on my feet. I will. Besides, with my extra art qualifications, the work will roll in and I'll have more money than I can spend.'

I forced another smile. Mark would always live in my heart. Wherever I stayed, the time I'd had with him would remain the same. I sniffed again. 'Sorry, I don't know what's the matter with me today, emotions all over the place, and I'm a bit tired myself to be honest.'

'How many weeks is it since Mark died, Flora?'

'Almost five, Granny.'

She sat there, smiling at me, a strange, almost saintly look on her face as if waiting for something. Then she said, 'The house is not a big thing to worry about at the moment. As for children, millions of people live long and happy lives without children.'

What was she saying? I'd never mentioned children, or our big fight because I'd come off the Pill. She was still talking.

'Besides, they're not children forever. They grow up and become complicated adults themselves ... like me, like you. Anyway, who knows what's in the future? In your future '

Something inside me stirred, a flutter in my stomach. Daphne's knowing smile set me off, but how could she know anything when I didn't? I went over it again in my head, conscious I was blinking at her while I did the maths. Five weeks since Mark died; we'd made love two weeks before, in the middle of my monthly cycle ... seven weeks ago. Could it be possible? My body trembled. Dare I think it ... that I might be pregnant with Mark's child? If I allowed my hopes to soar, only to have them dashed once again, I would go crazy. I had to ask myself again ... Could I be pregnant?

I forgot to breathe, then gasped as I went dizzy. My skin tingled with excitement and I flapped my hand about in front of my mouth with no idea why. I was going to cry.

Don't cry! Dear God, yes, I might be pregnant!

A little voice in my head said, 'Don't hope – don't dream. If you fall into the pit of disappointment again, you might not be able to claw your way out.'

Granny's saintly smile remained in place, even as she drifted off to sleep.

* * *

Stunned by this latest development, I worked on my grandfather's portrait while Granny snoozed. My mind was everywhere but on Aristotle's face. Could I be holding a tiny life in my womb? A life that was a part of my darling Mark? It seemed impossible, miraculous, and awesome all at the same time.

I'm probably wrong – forget it.

Still, I had to put down the paintbrush when tears of joy sprang to my eyes. I was gripped in deep regret that my dearest darling was gone and could never see his child. And yet, still, I might be wrong. Yes, I was probably wrong – clutching at straws – unable to let go.

An hour had passed before my thoughts were broken by Yánna.

'How is Aristotle's portrait going?' Her voice made me jump. With a bright smile stuck in place, I answered.

'I'm just about finished. The acrylic looks a little brighter, but the colours will settle as they dry out, and I doubt you'll be able to tell the difference. The varnish will have to wait until my next visit. I'm pleased with it, but more important, I hope Granny is, too.'

'Is she still asleep?' Yánna asked as she came across the lawn with two cups of coffee and a plate of biscuits on a tray. 'Here, I thought you might need a pick-me-up. I know it can be exhausting listening to the horrors of her past.'

'You must have your own story to tell, Yánna. What's your earliest memory of all this?'

'My first recollections are from after the World War, of course, but I'm sure Daphne wants to give you the facts herself. Besides, there are some events so awful that she may not want to you to learn of them.'

'She had a dramatic life, I hadn't realised. I knew so little about her past, Yánna. It's terrible that I don't even know how or when my grandfather died.'

'I wish I could help you, Flora.' She smiled. 'But my first loyalty is to Daphne.'

'But you do know? I mean, if anything should happen, God forbid, you would be able to fill in the gaps?'

She thought for a moment, then nodded.

'That's a relief. Will you come into town with us tomorrow? We're going to get Granny's new glasses.'

'I'd love to, but I get so little time for myself. Would you mind if I stayed behind?'

'Not at all. It's just that I wanted to buy you lunch.'

She grinned. 'I think I'll be all right for lunch.'

Half an hour later, Daphne was wide awake and as chirpy as a canary.

'So it's all right if I stay another few days, Granny?'

'More than all right. When do you think you'll be back for another holiday?'

'I'll be back for your big birthday, of course. Wild horses couldn't keep me away from that. A hundred years, wow!'

We grinned at each other. My phone pinged. I glanced down and saw Spiros on the screen, but I couldn't face seeing him until I knew the result of a pregnancy test. I'd intended to ignore the call, but Granny caught my eye.

'Don't close doors,' she said. 'Go, share your glorious news.'

How could she possibly know what I was thinking?

'But I don't know anything yet, Granny.'

She smiled at me. 'Maybe *you* don't . . .'

* * *

The next morning, we called our special taxi driver, who took us to the optician's. By eleven o'clock, we were grinning at each other in the town. Daphne wore her slick, ultra-light glasses. We headed for the older part of town, because I wanted to show her the synagogue. She'd never seen it, and it was, after all, part of her heritage. Besides, I'd reserved a table at the nearby taverna we'd visited before, reminding them I needed space for the wheelchair. Daphne scanned pedestrians and the buildings as I pushed her along. Suddenly, she started screeching, terrifying the life out of me. I feared she was in pain. She clutched her throat while her other hand pointed at a group of boys.

'Isaac! Isaac!' she shrieked, trembling, crying, seeming near to collapse.

The youths noticed her pointing their way and used bravado to hide their embarrassment.

'Hey, what's happening, *Yiayá*? Chill out, old lady, nobody's going to hurt you.'

I was quite afraid that my grandmother was about to suffer some kind of aneurysm, and wondered where the nearest hospital was.

A youth came over.

'Sorry, Kyría, we did nothing, honestly.'

'Isaac! Isaac!' Daphne continued to screech.

Trembling, she grasped the boy's hand and held it to her cheek.

'Calm down, Granny, it's not Isaac. It can't be Isaac, can it? He'd be too old now, wouldn't he?'

I turned to the puzzled youth.

'They took her brother to Auschwitz when he was your age. It seems you look like him.'

'*Ela maláka*, that's awful.' Then, realising he'd sworn, he added, 'Sorry Kyría.'

He lowered his gaze, then flapped his hand at his friends, telling them to be quiet.

He bent down and took Granny's hand.

'What's happening ...?' He glanced up at me. 'What's her name?'

'Daphne,' I said with an encouraging smile.

'What's happening, Daphne?' the youth asked, crouching at the side of her chair.

'I've missed you so much, Isaac!' she said. 'Why didn't you visit me or write?'

I sensed the boy was struggling for an answer, so I cut in.

'I don't think Isaac had any idea where you'd gone after Athens, Granny.'

'That's right,' the boy said. 'But I never forgot you, Daphne.'

'My glasses have steamed up now,' Daphne complained, pulling her new goggles off.

I whispered to the youth, 'Thank you,' and gave him a sharp sideways nod, suggesting he should leave in haste. He didn't waste time.

'Let's go the taverna, and treat ourselves to a nice lunch,' I said to Daphne as I dried her glasses and slipped them back on.

She glanced around.

'Where's Isaac?'

'I think you were dreaming, Granny. Anyway, Isaac would be well over a hundred by now. How would you recognise him?'

'You're right, I must have nodded off.' She dried her eyes. 'Have you seen his picture? It's in my locket. There's a photo of us all together. Papa had it taken in 1941. Elizabeth has one, too. A locket with a photo, I mean,'

'Then you must show it to me when we get home, dear Granny.'

45

DAPHNE

Corfu, 1944

Daphne unfolded Kyría Alice's letter and raced through it. Aristotle saw her blush with excitement and then noticed the sparkle of tears in her eyes.

'Good news from Athens?'

'How wonderful!' she said with a gasp. 'Mamá, Babá, and Elizabeth appear to be safe and well. They came to Athens for one day, then returned to Cairo. Oh, if only we had news from Isaac, then life would be perfect.'

She gulped, desperate to tell him her other news. Yet, for a reason she couldn't explain, she was afraid to do so. Daphne took a breath, closed her eyes, and said the words she had rehearsed so many times.

'This is a big day in my life, Aristotle. I have some incredible news to tell you, too.'

An unreasonable flourish of nerves made her heart patter. She tangled her fingers, too shy to look him in the face.

He, in a frisky mood, took her hand and pulled her onto his lap.

'Go on, let's hear it,' he said, while stroking her long, glossy hair and giving her a lopsided grin. 'No, let me guess. Churchill wants his portrait painted?'

Daphne's eyes sparkled with emotion. 'No, something far more wonderful.' She recalled the first time she'd told him of her pregnancy, on the lawn of the Royal Gardens in Athens. So much had happened to them since then. She thought of baby Aris, his lonely little grave on the banks of Missolonghi lagoon. One day she would go back there.

'Here it is, my darling. Well, the thing is . . . I'm having our baby, Aristotle.'

He stared at her, then at Yánna, who lay on her back, playing with her toes.

'Another baby? Holy Virgin! I didn't realise.' He blinked several times, absorbing the information, then cupped her face and kissed her on the lips. 'How wonderful! How absolutely perfect!' He laid his hand on her belly.

Relief flooded through her. She reached down and covered his hand with hers.

'You're pleased, then?' Her tears broke free, and joy filled her heart.

'You need to ask, Daphne? Please don't cry, I'm delighted!' He pulled out his handkerchief and lovingly dabbed at her face.

'Shall I read you the letter from Kyría Alice?'

'You can do anything you want, my beautiful darling.'

My Dearest Friend, Daphne,

I have the most wonderful news for you. This morning, your father came to the soup kitchen. Your family are living in Cairo for the moment, although they are planning to get the next available boat to Australia, where they hope you and Aristotle will join them. They came into Athens for one day only. Something to do with your father's finances. Your mother refused to be separated from him, and they could not leave Elizabeth behind, so they all came together. They send you their love, and hope one day soon you will join them on the other side of the world.

I'm sorry, there is no information about your brother Isaac.

I am thrilled to hear your wonderful news about the baby, and it is easy to imagine how delighted you must be.

The Red Cross needs my help now and again, and I am still running the soup kitchen twice daily. Starting my convent requires more funds than I have, but I continue to move forward.

I am very sorry to hear about Aristotle's stroke, and have sent one of my nursing sisters to help you. If you need anything, let me know.

My prayers go with you, and all my love,
Kyría Alice

At the height of a glorious spring, when wild flowers littered the ground and the sky was as blue as a cornflower, Sister Judith arrived and became one of the family. Her wide smile and powerful arms took care of everything and, for the first time, Aristotle and Daphne felt some relief from the rigours of war and Aristotle's poor health. Daphne blossomed with pregnancy. Yánna thrived on all the love and attention, and took her first steps.

After the Normandy landing, the war in Europe changed direction. The Germans lost ground and pushed to rid Greece of the last remaining Jews. On the island of Corfu, they made a newspaper announcement and, in town, pasted posters onto the walls.

* * *

Attention! All Jews of Corfu. Assemble tomorrow morning, 10th June, at the Royal Palace Gardens.

* * *

Sister Judith gasped and stared at the words as if they were burning into her eyeballs. Aristotle and Daphne exchanged a questioning glance: Was Sister Judith a Jew in disguise? Hadn't Kyría Alice saved Daphne by teaching her Christian ways?

'Are your papers in order, Sister Judith?' Daphne asked.

'Yes, they are – thanks to Kyría Alice. Would you like to see them?'

She reached into the deep pocket of her habit and pulled out a Christian Orthodox baptismal certificate, and a Greek identity card that displayed Sister Judith's photograph.

The next two days were terrifying for the von Stroop family. Although they said nothing, Daphne kept Sister Judith out of sight whenever a Nazi portrait was in progress. Daphne couldn't sleep for fear of being raided.

In the middle of June, Oberst Emil Jäger, Commander of Corfu, demanded their presence in Mon Repos. He had admired the mayor's portrait and wanted to commission one of his own. He invited them over to the mansion to discuss the procedure.

'Don't forget to speak German once we're inside,' Aristotle said.

* * *

After his meeting with the German Commander of Corfu, two soldiers lifted Aristotle's chair down the steps of Mon Repos. Daphne's nerves were still jangling when she took over and pushed Aristotle towards the path home. Just before they disappeared into the parkland, a German truck packed with crates drove up to the building. They stopped, watched for a few minutes, then they continued along the path to the cottage. Neither spoke until they were safely inside with the door locked.

'I was nervous when he insisted you paint his portrait on the mansion premises, Aristotle.'

'Me, too. Still, he came around when you explained it was all about the light. A stroke of genius, telling him we're set up to produce the most flattering likeness. Did you notice all the pale squares on the walls where paintings have been removed?'

'I found it difficult not to stare. I remember some interesting portraits in Mon Repos, and, if I remember correctly, there was a small landscape by Constable too.'

'Did you see those crates on the truck? We can only guess what's happening.'

'You think they're raiding the Jewish homes, removing works of art and storing them in Mon Repos?' she asked. 'What do you think we should we do, Aristotle?'

'Nothing,' he replied. 'When this war's over, we'll speak out. Until then, we know nothing, we see nothing, and we do nothing. Our priority is to protect our children and survive.' He took her hand. 'Now I have a task for you.' With his lopsided smile, he reached out and ran his hand over her belly. 'Before our child grows any bigger, I want to paint the third picture of the triptych. Although we both know that's impossible, I have the answer.'

Daphne's curiosity rose. He had painted the first study, *Laurel in Spring*, in the Athens studio, and the second, *Laurel in Summer*, after Aris was born on the islet of Aitoliko. How they loved that painting, especially now Aris was in Heaven. Although Daphne could paint in his style, she found it impossible to do a portrait of herself naked.

'What are you thinking?' she asked.

'You'll paint it, of course. You've become my hands, Daphne, but I'll choose the colours and composition and so on. I need a photo of you, nude. Then I'll have something to work with.

402

Do it for me, my darling. It's my one request – to see the triptych of my beloved family completed.'

How could she refuse him? Together, they set about the project. The gardener made a wooden tripod to hold Aristotle's Zeiss, and Daphne bought a new film in town for an absolute fortune. After a lesson in finding the focus and pressing the shutter button, Sister Judith, her face as red as a boiled beetroot, took several photographs of Daphne naked on the dais, with Aristotle's loaded palette and a jar of brushes arranged at her feet. Yánna, disgruntled by the lack of attention, and having found her feet, toddled over to the dais and knocked the jar of water and paintbrushes over.

'Leave it!' Aristotle cried. 'It's fate that she has contributed something to the painting.'

As Daphne's waistline grew, so did Aristotle's obsession with the third painting. He had a clear vision, and sometimes frustration drove him crazy. Unable to paint the portrait himself, he would explode with fury, throwing a jar of water at the dais, or yelling obscenities at the canvas. Christmas came and went, and at the end of January, when Daphne was eight months pregnant, Aristotle finished the third painting of the *Laurel* triptych. An unveiling ceremony followed, although they had all seen it.

On Valentine's Day, 1945, Rachelle Stroop, named after her great-grandmother, came into the world. Daphne wept for Aris as she held the newborn to her breast for the first time. Aristotle cradled the baby in his good arm and promised her all the love in the world.

46

FLORA

Corfu, present day

'WHAT A POWERFUL STORY, GRANNY,' I said. 'I can't imagine how you felt holding my mother for the first time. I feel like crying myself, just thinking about it.' I sniffed hard and took a sip of my morning coffee.

'She was the most beautiful baby – the double of Aris, and you, too.'

Yánna appeared. 'Flora, I'm going into town to buy a few bits. Do you need anything for your journey home?'

I shook my head. 'Thanks, I'm fine.'

'Wait,' Daphne said. 'There's one last thing I'd like you to do, Flora. Can you clean a painting for me if Yánna brings the right things from the shops? It's your line of work, isn't it?'

I nodded. 'Yes, it's what I do for a living, cleaning and restoring old masters for the gallery, and sometimes for private individuals, too.'

'Good. In the war we were very short of artists' supplies, so we often painted over pictures we weren't keen on. I had an old oil painting from my family, which I painted the portrait of Aristotle over, so long ago.' She touched the locket at her throat. 'Now, it would be marvellous if I could have the original back. Could you clean my darling Aristotle away?'

'Ah . . . now I understand! That's why you wanted me to copy the picture of my grandfather?'

'Yes, exactly. Could you remove my oil painting and leave the original portrait undamaged?'

'If the original was protected before you painted over it, yes, of course.'

'Yes, it was well protected, several coats of varnish if I remember correctly. I'd be very pleased if you could do that one last job for me.'

I made a list of solvents and swabs needed to complete my grandmother's request. This had been an eventful holiday. With my hand on my belly, I added one more thing to the list before handing it to Yánna.

'Would you be kind enough to pick these things up for me?'

She scanned down the page, then looked at me, her eyes widening.

'Pregnancy test kit? Oh, Flora!'

* * *

Yánna had just left when the baker's father arrived.

'Good afternoon, ladies,' he said with a bow and a smile. 'Would you mind if I had a quick word with Yánna?'

Before I could stop her, my incorrigible grandmother almost killed poor Constantinos with shock.

'You've just missed her, Costa. She's gone into town for a pregnancy test.'

His jaw dropped. He staggered to the nearest chair, dropped into it, and stared at his knees.

'Granny! You are so naughty,' I cried. 'You could give the poor man a heart attack.' I turned to the baker's father. 'The test is for me, Costa. Granny's pulling your leg!'

'Pulling my leg?' His eyes widened. Granny was still giggling.

'Joking, Costa. Now, what can we do for you?' I asked.

He stared at me. 'I forget what I came for. Please ask Yánna to call me.'

Then he scuttled away.

*   *   *

Two hours later, Daphne and Yánna were waiting outside the bathroom door. I'd left it open a few inches so that I could keep them informed. I guess they heard me flush the loo.

Daphne's voice came through the door.

'How long do you have to wait for the result?'

Yánna answered on my behalf. 'Another six minutes, I think. I'll just check my watch.'

After two minutes of silence, Daphne asked, 'How long now?' I heard a nervous tremor in her voice.

'Four minutes to go,' I called through the door.

'Hello!' a man's voice called. 'Anyone here?'

'It sounds like Spiros,' Yánna said. 'He's been phoning. Shall I let him in?'

'Yes,' Daphne said impatiently. 'How much longer?'

'Two minutes,' I called.

Yánna opened the front door.

'Flora's busy. Do you want to wait, Spiro?'

'Yes, thank you,' he answered. 'I wanted to see her before she left.'

Yánna called to Daphne, 'One minute to go!' She turned back to Spiros with an explanation. 'We're doing a pregnancy test.'

'Daphne ...? A pregnancy test ...?' he said with a frisson of alarm.

Yánna realised his confusion, so she explained. 'It's Flora – she's in the bathroom.'

'Flora? I think this is a private moment for family members,' he said, sounding panicky, and I guessed he was already heading for the door. 'I'll be back later.'

Seconds after I'd heard the front door close, I checked the test strip, then came out of the bathroom, unable to speak. Unable to even look at Daphne or Yánna, I dropped into an armchair and hugged myself. All I wanted was to feel the arms of Mark around me.

Nobody spoke until I broke the silence with a sob and a nod.

My grandmother's hand went over her mouth, and Yánna threw her arms around me in a bear hug.

'Ladies, we're going to have a baby,' I whispered before allowing my own tears to fall.

We all sniffed and hugged and congratulated one another. Exhausted from the emotion, I said I'd try to deal with Aristotle's painting before Spiros returned, and then set about organising my solvents, scrapers and swabs.

Yánna served us a colourful plate of stuffed tomatoes, peppers and onions, while the solvents went to work at softening eighty years of oil paint.

After eating, I went to work, scraping away the portrait of Aristotle, which my grandmother had painted at such a traumatic time in her life. I had just finished for the day, worn out from the emotion and the work, when my phone pinged, and Spiros's name came up on the screen. I hesitated. Even though our friendship had been platonic, I didn't know what to say. I tried to answer, but the signal was so bad, the call crashed moments after saying 'hello'. The landline rang.

'Hi, it's me. I wanted to see you this evening. Could I take you for dinner?'

'That would be great, Spiro, but I should spend my last night with Granny. Why don't you come around here for a drink with us all? You'll be very welcome.'

After a brief pause, he replied. 'Yes, thanks. Eight o'clock?'

I continued to work on the oil painting, only stopping to take a shower and get changed. Daphne talked about my mother, baby Rachelle, and her early years – little insights that I enjoyed very much – and how Aristotle had adored his daughter. She also talked about the end of war celebrations, and finally, she described how her world ended with the sad demise of Aristotle, who died in his sleep of a brain aneurysm, twelve years after the war.

'Kyría Alice came to Corfu for his funeral,' she said. 'It was so good to see her again, and while she was here, she persuaded me to paint her portrait. She was such a good woman; she knew it would help me. She stayed for a month, then left for Buckingham Palace. I never saw her again. My dearest friend, Princess Alice, died in London in December 1969, aged 84. I believe her son, Prince Philip, was with his mother at the time. I'll never forget her, Flora, or the limitless kindness she showed to everyone she came into contact with. The world was a better place because Kyría Alice lived in it.'

At eleven o'clock, Yánna settled Daphne in bed for her regular mid-morning nap, then, with her ubiquitous tray of coffee, came to watch me deal with the Aristotle oil painting.

'What a life my grandmother's had, Theía Yánna,' I said, noticing her eyes light up when I addressed her as 'auntie'. 'I loved hearing her talk about my mother. Especially now.'

Our eyes met.

'You'll make a wonderful mother,' she said. 'Me and Rachelle were best friends, really, like sisters. I remember she was a very beautiful child. I wanted to be just like her, but of course I never could. I was never beautiful, but I was strong and very good for hard work.'

Her shoulders slumped as she hugged her tiny coffee cup.

I tried to imagine what it had been like for Yánna, poor woman. No wonder she'd gone off the rails a bit as a teenager, though I hadn't heard the full story of her stealing Granny's money and running away.

'Well, I think you're absolutely amazing, Theía. What would have happened to Daphne if you hadn't taken such good care of her for all these years?'

'What else could I do? She saved my life. After Aristotle died, Daphne was overwhelmed by grief, and swore she'd never love another man. She didn't eat and became very thin. Everyone feared she would die to be with her husband, you understand? However, she recovered with the help of me and Rachelle. The bond between the three of us grew even stronger. But Rachelle had been born early, and although she was very beautiful, she was never strong. Daphne saw her happily married, and then celebrated your birth. Oh my, she was so pleased to be a *yiayá*. I remember how she showed your baby photo to everyone! But then the cancer took your mother away from us all.'

* * *

Spiros arrived on the dot of eight o'clock, with a bunch of mixed roses and a bottle of champagne. The baker's father, Constantinos, arrived next. Yánna, in a new floral-print dress and her gold sandals, simply glowed with happiness. An air of celebration filled the cottage as we sipped fizz and chatted with one another. Eager to finish cleaning Granny's picture, I continued to work away, and was down to the white primer when I stopped for a drink. Her family's portrait lay under it, she had said, and after hearing Daphne's story, I was eager to see them all.

'You've stopped,' Daphne said. 'Is there a problem?'

'No, no, just having a sip of my farewell drink, Granny.' Everyone laughed. 'I'll get back on it right now.'

I continued to dab away the layer of white, lead-based primer. However, we were all startled by the slow revelation of ancient, cracked varnish that hinted at a hidden masterpiece.

'What have we here, Granny? I'm proceeding with caution because the painting I'm uncovering appears to be very old, but you said it was a family portrait.'

'No, I said it was a portrait *from* my family. It belonged to them, but was not of them. Best if you turn on your recorder, Flora.'

I did. 'How exciting! What is it? Do you know?'

After a long pause, she uttered, 'It's the El Greco.'

There was a unified intake of breath. For a moment, nobody spoke.

'What?' I whispered. 'But you told me that the El Greco went up in flames, and that Aristotle burned his hands trying to rescue it.'

'No, I didn't. Listen to your tape recording.' Daphne closed her eyes and shook her head. 'When we both laid down the primer for our individual paintings, I swapped the canvases. Aristotle was not a good liar, and I was sure his cousin knew that, too. I felt certain that for Aristotle to be utterly convincing, he had to believe the fake El Greco hid the real one when his cousin turned up. It seemed I was right. His instinctive reaction, to rescue what he thought was a great masterpiece, clearly saved his life.' Her face, as serene as ever, stared ahead as tears ran down her cheeks. 'However, my actions may have caused his stroke. Can I ever forgive myself?'

I continued to dab at the primer, now with Spiros at my side.

Daphne continued. 'How I hate that painting for what it did to my darling Aristotle, but now it's yours, Flora. I suggest you sell it as soon as possible. It will make you an extremely rich woman – your money worries will be over – so I'm very pleased for that one thing. There's a double layer of varnish under the primer so you can safely – to use one of your own terms – crack on!'

We were all shocked into silence, and stared at the painting as more of the masterpiece became exposed.

'The provenance papers are all dated, signed and stamped. You'll find them in the bottom of my sewing basket, with my diaries, Flora. You'll have no problem proving you own it. Everything else that I have, including my jewellery and everything that's in my bank account, will go to my darling Yánna when I leave. She has looked after me so well, all my life.' She turned to her carer. 'I will love her forever.'

'Daphne, stop it! You're not going anywhere. Now drink your champagne before I do,' Yánna blustered.

Spiros opened a second bottle and charged every glass, which we raised for a united toast.

'To Granny Daphne!'

47

FLORA

Corfu, present day

THIS WAS IT – THE DAY before Granny's hundredth birthday, and I was so excited! I stepped outside Corfu airport to see the bluest sky and not a cloud in sight. The late summer sun seeped through my linen shirt and warmed me through. It was such a special moment to arrive. I twisted my long red hair into a knot and pulled on a wide-brimmed hat. With my fair skin, I had to be careful. All the pleasant memories of past holidays, and the present thrill of expectancy, pulled together. This would be a great week. I glanced around for Spiros, who had offered to meet me.

He had visited me twice in England, since my spring holiday, and returned with Granny's ginger snaps and my love. We had become very close, and his interest in my pregnancy was a wonderful bonus to our relationship. I knew I was falling in love again, and he, too. To see him standing in the sunshine outside 'Arrivals' was a joy, but I quickly realised something was wrong.

'Darling, it's lovely to see you,' he said, kissing my cheeks and knocking my hat off in the process.

'Is everything all right?' I asked as he swooped down to pick it up, then grabbed my cases.

'I'll tell you in the car. Come on, let's get out of this heat.' He hurried me to the car, then laughed as he lifted my cases in the boot. 'Glad to see you have luggage straps around your cases,' he quipped. 'We can't have you running off with other people's luggage again, can we?'

I forced a laugh, but wasn't fooled.

'Something's wrong, isn't it?'

He opened the car door for me, then got in the driver's side, but before he started the engine, he took my hand.

'Don't get upset,' he said, 'but I'm sorry to tell you, Daphne had a heart attack just before breakfast this morning. Poor Yánna's devastated. She called an ambulance, and she's been with her at the hospital ever since.'

I gasped, afraid, hardly able to put my thoughts into words.

'Oh no. Is she . . .?'

'I've just spoken to Yánna on the phone, Daphne's conscious and asking for you. I'll take you straight to the hospital, but I must warn you, she's fading. The doctor has told us there's not much hope, Flora.'

Outside her hospital room, Spiros held me.

'Come on, dry those tears, my darling. You can do this. You know how much she loves you, and how pleased she is that you came back for her special birthday. Find a smile and be very brave.'

I took a big breath and entered the private room. She appeared to be sleeping, so I sat on the bedside chair, coming to terms with the situation as best I could. Eventually, she opened her eyes.

'Hello, my lovely Granny.'

She smiled. 'You're here.'

'Of course. And I have an early birthday card for you, from someone very special.'

I slipped the beautiful embossed card from its heavy manila envelope and opened it before her. A gold cord and tassel hung down the centre, and the royal shield, complete with unicorn, lion and crown, emblazoned the right flyleaf in gold, blue and red foil.'

Daphne gasped.

'He really sent me a birthday card? How extraordinary! Oh, my darling, I think I'm going to cry! Please pass my splendiferous glasses so I can see you properly, then read it for me, Flora.'

I slipped her glasses on.

'It says, "I am pleased to know that you are celebrating your one hundredth birthday on 31st October 2023. I send my congratulations and best wishes to you on such a special occasion." And there's his personal handwritten signature: Charles R. Then your name is printed, all official, Mrs Daphne Stroop, under our king's signed name.'

'Can you believe it? My best friend, Kyría Alice, was very proud of her daughter-in-law, Her Majesty Queen Elizabeth. I wanted the birthday card from her son so badly, in memory of my dear friend, because darling Alice was King Charles the Third's grandmother, and she never, ever, wanted anything for herself. Her only desire in life was to ease the suffering of others, especially children.' Her voice became faint.

I placed the royal card on her bedside locker.

'I don't want to tire you, but I've brought another surprise, Granny.' I stood up and placed her hand on my seven-month bump. 'Granny Daphne, I'm pleased to introduce you to your great-granddaughter, Daphne Elizabeth Mark Champion. And also, Spiros and I would like to invite you to our wedding, here in Corfu, at Mon Repos, next year as our guest of honour.'

'Oh . . .' She made a little whimper of joy. 'You've made my glasses steam up! I'm so pleased for you, Flora.' Her voice was barely a whisper. 'You and Spiros were made for each other – you didn't need to wait years to know that. I'll be there at your

414

wedding, my darling girl, along with my beloved Aristotle, Rachelle, Aris, Kyría Alice, your cherished Mark and all my family. Raise your champagne glass to us on the day, we'll be having our own private party.'

She smiled softly, patted my belly again, and then closed her eyes for the last time.

EPILOGUE

GRANNY DAPHNE WAS BURIED THE day after her hundredth birthday. She had a plot in the cemetery where the marble tomb of Aristotle waited for her. Before the funeral, it was the duty of the next of kin to wash and dress the deceased. When I heard this, I was quite shocked, and a little horrified. However, on reflection, I didn't want some stranger handling my dear grandmother's body. Filled with utter sadness, and moved by Yánna's terrible grief, I said I wanted to help her.

'I loved her,' she sobbed. 'I could not have wished for a more good mother, Flora. She gave her life to me.'

'She loved you, Yánna. You were always a daughter to her, and I think you should have her locket.'

'That is a wonderful idea you tell me, Flora, but this is a family thing and Daphne would say it should go to your child one day, you take it.' She unfastened the chain from Daphne's neck and placed it in the palm of my hand. 'Besides, I have the other one, that belonged to Elizabeth. It is exactly the same, with a miniature family portrait inside, but not the little feather which was from Isaac.'

'But how did you get the locket, Yánna?'

'Ah, Daphne never knew the whole truth. When her family is back for the one day to Athens, it is to collect the family jewels from the safe in their old house. They did not know Aristotle had taken them, and use the money to buy their tickets. They believe they are safe with the new documents, but the people in the house told Mr Abrams an SS officer with name, Stroop, had been and opened the safe. He knew the combination. Mr Abrams believed Daphne had been forced to give the safe numbers to Aristotle, and he think she is now dead, or sent to a camp thanks to her art teacher. He went crazy, he tell the people, "This is my house! Get out! Get out!" The noise, it got the attention of neighbours. They betray them as Jews to passing soldiers. It was a day after the big round-up, so they were shot dead.'

'Oh my God, how terrible! And Daphne never knew? She went on believing they were happily living in Australia?'

'That is true. Kyría Alice heard about it and managed to get hold of Elizabeth's locket, but I don't know how. She brought it when she came to Aristotle's funeral, but then decided Daphne could not stand any more loss. She gave the locket to me. I could not tell her, Flora. I think she would go too crazy.'

We used special, sweet-scented soap and a sponge to wash her tired skin.

'You don't have to help me,' Yánna said. 'I know this is not your way in England.'

'I want to help you, Auntie,' I said. 'You have been so amazing.' I realised she was crying and felt so sorry for her. 'Do you want to talk about how you feel? It might help.'

She shook her head. 'But I must say you something. Daphne did not tell one of the worst things in her big life. What you will to see now . . . I am sorry, it will make you more sad.'

I stepped away, suddenly afraid.

'Perhaps you'd better explain first.'

'I was five years when it happen, so I remember very well how cruel people can be. How they can believe somebody's lies, or mistakes, and say wrong things about others.' She shook her head and stared at Daphne, then laid a hand on her cheek. 'The worst thing I ever saw, Flora . . . It was so terrible that I didn't speak for a year after. The school said I was dumb mute . . . but I wasn't. It was the shock to my young brains, you see. Like my voice was trapped inside my broken heart.' She thumped herself in the chest. 'Still, Daphne rise above it and she say it would give some tormented people a sense of justice.'

'Go on.'

'Someone trapped in that school in Kalávryta recognised her later, in Corfu. This woman, who had lost all her menfolk – grandfather, father, brothers and sons – was sure that Aristotle was a German spy, and Daphne, his Greek lover. After all, she herself had shouted that Aristotle's cousin was the infamous Jürgen Stroop of the SS. They all saw the Nazi, Schulze, pull her out of the school and set her free.'

Yánna took a brush and ran it through Daphne's white hair.

'I am sorry, my Daphne, she was punished like all Greek womans that was going with German mans. They stood her in the town *platía* and takes off her clothes, then shaves off all her beautiful, long hair. They painted a Nazi sign on her head in hot tar. Then, they bend her over a wine barrel, and . . .'

Sobbing, Yánna suddenly swung around and pushed herself into the corner of the room, facing the wall like a naughty child. Her plump hands, that had spent a lifetime caring for others, pushed into her short curly hair and tugged it left and right as she howled with all the heartache imaginable. Her crying was loud and hysterical.

I slid my hand around her shoulders and took her into my arms. There, I held her as she wailed for long minutes. I hardly dared to imagine what was coming.

Once she had exhausted herself, Yánna took a deep breath and continued. 'They bend her over a barrel and burn the swastika on each of her behinds with the iron the farmers use on the cows. I try to stop them. I punch the man on his legs and scream, "Stop! Stop!" but I was five, he just kick me away. The burn is so deep, is not possible to take the terrible pain. My Daphne, she lose conscious. The tragedy is, she save my life. But you understands, I was too young to help her when she need me. I see that day, again and again, of when they burn her in so bad way, her flesh it was smoke and sizzle under the iron, and all her terrible screams of pain, I will remember me all my life. So, now we turn her over and you will see. Sorry, but you should know what really make her crazy for a while.'

*   *   *

After dear Daphne's funeral, I hung back. Broken-hearted, I wanted a minute alone at her graveside. She had meant so much to me, and now I carried her great-granddaughter, who would have her name and would one day learn about the bravery of Granny Daphne. I pushed my hands deep into my pockets as I turned to leave, but then stopped. My left hand had touched something, and when I lifted it out, I recognised the pebble with the painting of the Aitoliko shore. I wished I'd buried it with her, but then remembered a Jewish custom and placed it gently on her gravestone.

'Sleep well, Granny Daphne,' I whispered.

We went back to Mon Repos cottage for an hour, then walked to the big house, where the stolen art treasures of World War II, most of them paintings, were being removed from the basement.

'What will happen to them?' I asked Spiros.

'They'll be returned to their rightful owners, but if that's not possible, I promise they'll be exhibited in one of the island's museums for future generations to enjoy.'

I placed my hand on my belly and smiled, knowing my Granny Daphne would approve.

ACKNOWLEDGEMENTS

MANY THANKS TO FRANK WILSON for inviting me to Corfu many years ago and instigating my passion for the Greek islands. Also, to Tony Wilson for telling me about Princess Alice, who will forever be my hero. My gratitude also to the staff and caretakers of Mon Repos, who were informative and inspiring when I arrived to investigate the possibilities of a novel. The British Vice Consulate of Corfu pointed me in the right direction when I arrived in their beautiful city and saved me many hours of wandering aimlessly about – thank you! Also, Athenian singer Rania Dizikiriki for her hospitality in Athens and her great-aunt's war-time stories from the little island of Aitoliko.

As always, I owe a great debt of gratitude to my editor, Sarah Bauer, for her incredible patience correcting and guiding this terribly dyslexic author. Also, Katie Meegan and the entire team at Bonnier Books UK who have supported me since my first novel, *Island of Secrets*, seven years ago.

To write a bestselling novel every year would be impossible without the help of my husband, Berty, who makes sure life runs smoothly around me, so that I can continue at the keyboard.

However, my greatest debt of gratitude goes to my readers. To those who have reviewed my novels, boosted my trembling confidence over the years and encouraged me to go on writing: thank you so much! Whether you borrow my novel from the library, buy the paperbacks, or download the ebook or audiobook: thank you! You are the ones who make my world go around. It is for you, my dear readers, that I go to my keyboard at five a.m. every morning and do my best to make you laugh or cry, and entice you away from your everyday to the beauty of a Greek island with tales that are inspired by history.

THE STORY BEHIND
THE STORY

AN ISLAND PROMISE IS A work of fiction inspired by several events in Greek history. Many places featured are real, although the cottage in the grounds of Mon Repos is now derelict. The people – ah, now there is a tricky one. When I read about amazing real people while researching for my novels, the charisma that I imagine they have seeps into my characters. Strong women, charming men, an insoluble problem, and an appealing Greek island setting make, for me, the perfect recipe for an irresistible novel!

Her Royal Highness Princess Andrew of Greece and Denmark (Princess Alice)

When my brother Tony asked, 'What's the next book about?' I told him I wasn't sure at that point, but that I rather liked Corfu for a location. 'Then you must read the life story of Princess Alice,' he said.

Princess Alice, a great-granddaughter of Queen Victoria, was born in 1885 at Windsor Castle, UK. She was born deaf; her mother insisted that she learn to lipread, which she did, mastering four languages fluently.

In 1903, aged eighteen and completely in love, she wedded the good-looking but dreadfully inconsiderate Prince Andrew of Greece, achieving the official title of Her Royal Highness Princess Andrew of Greece and Denmark.

Her life was a tumultuous one. In 1913, her father-in-law, George I of Greece, was assassinated, shot in the back while out for a walk. During the Balkan Wars, Princess Alice served as a nurse, set up field hospitals, and assisted with surgeries on wounded soldiers. In 1922, her husband was accused of, and court-martialled for, causing the decimation of the Greek army at Smyrna. Alice and her family fled Greece when King George V of Great Britain sent the warship Calypso to rescue them.

In 1930, Princess Alice had a nervous breakdown and was taken by force to a sanatorium, first in Berlin, then in Switzerland. While held against her will for almost three years, she was given severe electric shock treatment and her ovaries were subjected to massive doses of X-rays, a barbaric treatment that caused her difficulties right up to the end of her life. Meanwhile, her four daughters married into German families who were great supporters of the Nazis. Her son, Prince Philip, was sent to relatives in England, and her husband moved to Monte Carlo to be with his mistress.

In 1938, after her release, Princess Alice returned to Athens. Despite the hardships she had suffered, all she wanted to do was help the poor and underprivileged. She facilitated the Red Cross by smuggling medical supplies into Greece from Sweden. She ran a soup kitchen for the starving children of Athens, and in 1943 she hid a Jewish family in her own attic, standing up fearlessly to the Gestapo. When questioned, she said she didn't understand what they wanted because she was deaf. Many years after her death, she was honoured as 'Righteous Among the Nations' by the Yad Vashem Holocaust Memorial for this act of kindness.

After World War II, Princess Alice founded the Christian Sisterhood of Martha and Mary, a nursing order of nuns dedicated to healing the sick and helping the poor. She continued to assist the needy until 1967. With Greece under dictatorship, it became unsafe for her to remain in the country, so her son, Prince Philip, now married to Queen Elizabeth II of Great Britain, summoned Alice to live in Buckingham Palace, where she died peacefully in 1969. She owned nothing, having given everything she had to the poor.

It is impossible not to admire this quiet woman with her strong sense of duty, devotion to others, and unremitting courage.

Athens Chief of Police, Angelos Evart

During the Holocaust, many Athenian Jews were saved from deportation to Auschwitz by the actions of Angelos Evart, the chief of Athens police. Although he hung the Nazi flag in his office and had a picture of 'Mein Fuhrer' on the wall, this was all a ploy to fool the Germans. In fact, Angelos Evart ordered thousands of fake identity documents for the local Jewish population. He too was honoured as 'Righteous Among the Nations' by the Yad Vashem Holocaust Memorial.

Mon Repos, Corfu

Mon Repos is a beautiful villa set in the Palaeopolis forest and parkland, just south of Corfu Town. It was originally built in 1831 for the British Lord High Commissioner of the Ionian Islands, Frederick Adam, who married a local Corfiot woman. However, only a year later, he was posted

423

to India. Another year passed before the villa was turned into a school for fine arts.

In 1864, Mon Repos became the summer residence of George I of Greece, and the royal family used it until 1967. Princess Alice gave birth to Prince Philip in the villa, and Princesses Sophie and Alexia of Greece and Denmark were also born there.

The Massacre of Kalávryta

The massacres in and around Kalávryta in 1943 were some of the worst atrocities in World War II. For anyone who wants to learn more, I recommend *The Cursed Day: Eyewitness Accounts of the Nazi Massacres during Operation Kalavryta* by Antonis Kakoyannis.

By mid-December 1943, many skirmishes between German troops, andartes (Greek freedom fighters) and the local village population had taken place in the area, and resulted in casualties and deaths. The tension escalated when the andartes captured eighty-one German soldiers. Most were held for some days as prisoners of war, but then they were lined up and executed by the Greek andartes.

A few days later, the Germans took reprisals. Approximately 1,300 women and children were locked into the schoolhouse of Kalávryta. Almost 700 men and boys were herded to a field above the village and machine-gunned down. The village was burned to the ground.

Major Ebersberger, responsible for the destruction of Kalávryta, and Captain Dohnert, who led the firing party against the Greek men and boys, were never brought to justice for these crimes.

Jürgen Stroop

Jürgen Stroop was an SS commander and police leader in Poland and Greece, and was responsible for the liquidation of the Warsaw Ghetto. For crimes against humanity, and for other war crimes, Stroop was executed by hanging in Mokotów Prison, Warsaw on 6th March 1952. Stroop did have a cyanide capsule in case of capture but chose not to take it.

Aristotle von Stroop, Daphne von Stroop, Yánna and the rest of the cast are figments of my imagination.

El Greco

Born in 1541 in the beautiful village of Fodele, outside Heraklion, Crete, Greece, El Greco's real name was Doménikos Theotokópoulos. This great artist died in Toledo, Spain, in 1614, but his paintings can still be seen in galleries all over the world.